C. J. CHERRYH

EXPLORER

DAW BOOKS, INC.

DONALD A. WOLLHEIM, FOUNDER

375 Hudson Street, New York, NY 10014

ELIZABETH R. WOLLHEIM
SHEILA E. GILBERT
PUBLISHERS

http://www.dawbooks.com

First Paperback Printing, November 2003
4 5 6 7 8 9 10

DAW TRADEMARK REGISTERED
U.S. PAT. OFF. AND FOREIGN COUNTRIES
—MARCA REGISTRADA
HECHO EN U.S.A.

PRINTED IN THE U.S.A.

For my father

1

Steam went up as the shower needled Bren's back—a moment of blissful content in a voyage neither that blissful nor content.

And considering the call he'd just gotten in the middle of his night, he stayed, head against the wall, longer than his habit, eyes shut, letting the steam make a warm, blind cocoon around him, letting the shower run on recycle for uncounted warm minutes. Complex input was suspended, output temporarily unnecessary.

But a brain habituated to adrenaline could stand tranquility only so long before worry tunneled its way back.

What's Jase want?—followed closely by—*We're not that far from moving*—and:

This could be the big move. Natural, wouldn't it be, if that's what the navigators are doing up there, setting up the final move, that Jase would want to talk now?

It's my night. He knew he'd wake me up. Jase could come here.

Couldn't be any ship-problem, could it? Nothing mechanical. Mechanical problems surely couldn't be at issue.

That was it. Now he'd done it. He'd thought about the ship itself . . . about the frail bubble of metal and ceramics around his cabin, beyond the shower, beyond the diplomatic enclave of passengers on five-deck.

Said ship had already endured, be it centuries ago, one spectacular and notorious navigational failure, stranding the original colonial mission in the great uncharted nowhere of the universe—after which everything else had happened: escaping a nearly lethal star, reaching an inhabited planet. The survivors had built Alpha Station, in orbit about that planet—and developed a bitter rift between those who wanted to stay in space and serve the ship, and those who wanted to go down to the green planet, take their fortunes and their lives in their hands and cast their lot with the steam-age locals.

A whole *world* of things had happened after that. The Alpha colonists, taking that dive into atmosphere, forever changed themselves, their culture *and* the native people in a direction no one had predicted.

Meanwhile that faction of humans who'd stayed in space had taken the ship and gone searching for their misplaced homeworld. But the fervor for that mission had come aground a second time. They'd ended up building another station in a fuel-rich system. Reunion was its name. And things had gone not so badly for them—until a hundred-odd years into that station's existence, an unknown species had taken exception to their poking into other solar neighborhoods and attacked Reunion to make the point.

So the ship had come running frantically back to Alpha looking for fuel and help.

Which was at least the beginning of reasons why this ship now, with a sizeable delegation of concerned parties from the former Alpha colony and the indigenous government, was headed back out to that remote station—ten years late, because things at Alpha hadn't been quite in order to jump to the ship's commands. The captain who'd ordered the mission was dead, Alpha Station was in the hands of the atevi, the native, once steam-age species, who'd taken command of their own destiny—and the aiji, the atevi ruler, had sent his grandmother and his heir, among others, to see for themselves what sort of mess the ship-folk had made of their affairs at Reunion.

That was the quick version of ship history: a breakdown, a stranding, and local wars wherever they went. Given the ship's run of luck at important moments, and given a "see-me-in-my-office" from a friend who also happened to be one of the ship's two captains, well, yes, a dedicated planet-dweller, descendant of the Alpha colonists, could feel just a little bit of anxiety about this after-midnight summons.

Maybe he shouldn't have stopped to shower. Maybe he should have pulled on a pair of pants and a sweater and gotten straight up there.

But there'd been a sense of "when-you-can" when he'd gotten the summons. It was Jase's watch, so anything Jase wanted to say really was logically said in the middle of the night, granted the breakfast hour would have been far more convenient. "Time to dress?" he'd asked. "Yes," Jase had said. So he'd blundered into the shower half-asleep.

And the black-skinned, pastel-clad figures that moved calmly about duties outside the steamed-over shower glass—they were fresh from their beds, too, his atevi staff, his protectors, getting his clothes ready. Hence the shower—a blast of warm water to elevate his fallen body temperature and call said brain online.

He toggled off *recycle*. The shower circulation, formerly parked on endless loop, sucked up the damp from the air until what blew past was dry and warm as any desert. It stopped, preset, while his past-the-shoulder hair, that dignity of an atevi lord, still retained a residual, workable damp.

His servants would have heard the shower enter final cycle. He stepped out into comparatively cold air, and immediately Bindanda—to whose stature he was about the size of a ten-year-old—flung an appropriately child-sized robe about him. Bindanda, broad as well as tall, black-skinned, golden-eyed—atevi, in short, and a somewhat plump fellow, very fond of food—lapped the belt about him with hands that could break human arms and tied it with a delicacy that required no adjustment.

Perfect. The dressing-bench awaited. Bren sat down and let Asicho, the sole female among the servant staff, comb and braid his hair in its requisite pigtail.

Lord of the province of the heavens, Tabini-aiji had named him, sending him up from the planet to manage the space program—oh so casually claiming in that action all the power that a newly named lord of the heavens could possibly lay at the aiji's feet, a small fact which Bren wasn't sure any of the ship's captains had ever quite grasped. It had taken *him* a little time to figure it—and he'd been Tabini's chief translator.

But it was perfectly reasonable, in the atevi view of things, to believe that where the aiji's representative went, so went the aiji's sphere of influence. Therefore sending the lord of the heavens to the limits of explored space expanded the aiji's claim of power, absent some strongly dissenting power in his path. There was a space station. So of *course* there was now a province of the heavens. Had not the aiji sent him there and appointed a lord to rule it? Second point—had anyone contested that appointment? Had anyone else attempted to exert authority over the station? The Mospheirans, that island nation of former human colonists, couldn't make up their minds without a committee decision and the ship-folk certainly weren't interested in administering an orbiting province. The ship-folk as well as the Mospheirans had actually seemed glad to have some competent individual, atevi or human, handle it and see that the vending machines stayed full and the air stayed pure.

So that claim stuck. There *was* a province of the heavens.

And now that the ship-folk took their starship back to Reunion to deal with matters the ship had left unfinished—dangerous ones at that—the aiji in Shejidan sent out his emissaries to deal with deep space. Tabini-aiji sent his own grandmother, the aiji-dowager, and he sent his heir—a minor child—both constituting representation of the aiji's house itself, to show the flag, so to speak—but to make that claim of a more permanent nature, he sent out his lord of the heavens to claim whatever territory seemed available. A man who'd originally hoped to add a few words to the atevi-human lexicon as the sole monument to his life, Bren Cameron had certainly gotten farther than he intended.

By various small steps accelerating to a headlong downhill rush, his life hadn't gone as planned. Bren found himself here, wherever here was. He found himself assigned to assert a claim the aiji-dowager would . . . well, *witness* or *bless* or otherwise legitimize . . . establishing an atevi claim to presence in the universe at large. Most pointedly, he would assert the atevi right to have a major say in the diplomatic outcome of whatever they met, and the dowager would look it all over and nod politely. And he wasn't sure the ship-folk, except Jase, remotely understood what he was doing here.

Maybe, Bren said to himself, he ought to be honest

about his mission—not go on wearing the white ribbon of the neutral paidhiin, the translators. Maybe he should adopt a plain one, black, for a province of empty space—

Black, for the Assassins who watched over him. Black, for the lawyers of atevi society, the mediators of last resort. White of the paidhiin was, well, what he hoped to go on doing: translate, mediate, straighten out messes. Lord's title and assignment to the heavens be damned, he planned to come home and ask for his old job back: more extravagantly, someday next year or so he hoped, at lordly leisure, to sit on his porch and watch the sea for three days straight. . . . granted Jase wasn't calling him up there at the moment to give him advance warning that the ship had broken down and stranded the lot of them forever in deep space.

Asicho finished the ribbon-arranging. He stood up from the bench. Narani, his white-haired and grandfatherly head of staff, had already laid out the appropriate clothing on the bed, and Jeladi, the man of all work, assistant to everyone on staff, waited quietly to help him on with the starched, lace-cuffed shirt. The stockings and the trousers, he managed for himself. And the glove-leather, knee-high boots.

"Nadi," he said then to Jeladi, inviting the assistance. Narani had pressed the lace to knife-edged perfection, and Jeladi moved carefully, so the all-grasping lace failed to snag his pigtail. Asicho, in turn, helped him on with his knee-length day-coat while Jeladi held the pigtail safely aside from its high collar, and Bindanda helped arrange the shirttail.

Not so much froth on the shirt sleeves as to make it necessary to put both coat and shirt on together— but not quite a one-person operation, as styles had gotten to be. His increased rank had increased the

amount of lace—which had turned up in baggage: trust
Narani. The lord of this household would go out the
door, onto executive levels, as if he walked the halls
of the Bu-javid in Shejidan.

The shirttail went in immaculately. The pigtail survived the collar. His two servants gently tugged the
starched lace from under the cuffs, adjusted the
prickly fichu, and pronounced him fit to face outsiders.

In no sense was a man of rank alone . . . not for a
breath, not an instant. The servants, including Narani,
including Bindanda, lined his doorway. The sort of
subterranean signals that had permeated the tradi-
tional arrangements of his onworld apartments, that
they had translated to the space station, had likewise
established themselves very efficiently on the ship, in
human-built rooms, rooms with a linear arrangement
in—that abomination to atevi sensibilities—pairs. In
their section of five-deck, in loose combination with
the aiji-dowager's staff in the rooms considerably
down the hall, the staff still managed to pass their
signals and work their domestic miracles outside the
ship's communications and outside his own understanding.

So it was no surprise to him at all that Banichi and
Jago likewise turned up ready to go with him; his security, uniformed in black leather and silver metal, and
carrying a fairly discreet array of electronics and armament for this peaceful occasion: a lord didn't leave his
quarters without his bodyguards, not on earth, not on
the station, and not here in the sealed steel world of
the ship, and his bodyguards never gave up their
weapons, not even at their lord's table or in his bedroom.

"Asicho will take the security station," Jago said,
pro forma. Jago and Banichi were now off that station.
Of course Asicho would. In this place with only a

handful of staff, they all did double and triple duty, and even Asicho managed, somehow, despite the language barrier, to know a great deal that went on in ship's business.

But not everything. Not middle-of-the-night summonses from the second captain.

Guards they passed in the corridor marked Ilisidi's residency—her security office, her kitchen, her personal rooms. No more than polite acknowledgment from that quarter attended their passage: but that they were awake and about, the dowager's staff now knew. Ilisidi's security, perhaps Cenedi himself, given the unusual nature of this call, would be in constant touch with Asicho—not the dowager's idle curiosity. It was Cenedi's job, at whatever hour.

Two more of Ilisidi's young men guarded the section door. Beyond that, at a three-way intersection of the curving corridors, on the Mospheirans' collective doorstep (meaning Ginny Kroger and her aides and technicians, their robotics and refueling operations specialists) was the short alcove of the so-named personnel lift. They walked in and Banichi immediately pushed the requisite buttons.

The lift this time lifted fairly well straight up, where it stopped and opened its doors onto the bridge with a pressurized wheeze. They exited in that short transverse walkway at the aft end of the bridge. Beyond it, banks of consoles and near a hundred techs and seniors stayed at work by shifts—half a hundred tightly arranged consoles, the real running of the ship. The walkway aimed at the short corridor on the far side of the bridge, where the executive offices, as well as the captains' private cabins—and Jase's security guards on duty in that corridor—were found.

If those two were there, Jase was there. On Jase's watch, the senior captain, Sabin, was likely snug abed at the moment—a favorable circumstance, since Sabin had a curious, suspicious nature and wasn't wholly reconciled to atevi wandering through her operations. She was bound to have an opinion on the matter—but at the moment it was all Jase's show.

So they walked straight through, keeping to that designated passage-zone where they weren't in the way of the techs—not even a couple of towering dark atevi or a human in atevi court dress rated notice from navigators trying to figure where they were. Business proceeded. And the two men, Kaplan and Polano, on a let-down bench at Jase's office door, stood up calmly, men as wired-in as Jago and Banichi. No question Jase had known the moment the lift moved. No question Jase, like his bodyguards, was waiting for him. No question Jase had expected Banichi and Jago to come up here with him when he called, and no question Jase knew they'd be armed and wired.

"Sir." Kaplan opened the office door for him.

Jase looked up from his desk and waved him toward a seat, there being no formality between them. And since it was a meeting of intimates, Banichi and Jago automatically lagged to talk to Kaplan and Polano outside, such as they could. Atevi security regularly socialized during their lords' personal meetings, if they were of compatible allegiances—as Kaplan and Polano indisputably were; so Bren discreetly touched the on-button of his pocket com as he went in, being sure by that means that Asicho, on five-deck, would have a record for staff review.

The door shut. Bren dragged one of the interview chairs around on its track. Sat.

Unlike Sabin's office, which had a lifetime accumulation of storage cabinets, Jase's office was new and barren: a desk, two interview chairs—no books, in all those bookcases and cabinets—and only one framed photo, a slightly tilted picture of Jase holding up a spiny, striped fish. It was his most predatory moment on the planet.

What would you do with it? shipmates might ask; and if Jase wanted to unsettle them, he might say, truthfully, horrifying most of them, that they had had it for supper that night—a rather fine supper, too.

They shared that memory. They shared a great many things, not least of which was joint experience in the aiji's court, with all that entailed, before Jase had gotten an unwanted captaincy.

"Good you came," Jase said. "Sorry about the midnight hour. But I've got something for you."

"Got something." He had niggling second thoughts about the pocket-com, and confessed it. "I'm wired."

"I'm always sure you are." Jase two-sided the console at a keystroke and gave him a confusing semi-transparent view of a split screen.

Bren leaned forward in the chair, arm on the desk edge. With a better light angle, he figured it out for a view through a helmet-cam on one side and, on the other, a diagram of the walking route among rooms and corridors.

His heart went thump. He knew what it was, then. And he'd expected *this* revelation eight moves and eleven months ago.

Now they had it? Close to the end of their journey, this showed up?

"Sabin knows?" he asked, regarding the extraction of this particular segment out of the log records.

"Not exactly," Jase said.

There was the timing. There was the non-cooperation of the senior captain. That Jase called him up here to see it, instead of bringing it down to five-deck . . . he wasn't sure what that meant. Relations between the two on-board captains had been uneasily cordial since—well, since the unfortunate incident at undock, Sabin having insulted the dowager within the first few hours and the dowager having poisoned the captain in retaliation. The two women had gotten along since, wary as fighting fish in a tank. The two captains had gotten along because they had to: the ship regularly had four, and ran now on part of its crew, part of its population, and two of the three surviving captains.

And despite his conviction this tape existed and despite the dowager's demands and Jase's requests for the senior captain to locate it in log and produce it— Sabin hadn't acknowledged it existed, hadn't cooperated, hadn't acknowledged the situation they suspected lay behind the tape. In short, no, Sabin hadn't helped find it in the last number of months, and now that it had turned up, didn't know Jase had it. And what was the object of their long search? The mission-tape from the ship's last visit, the record none of the crew had seen, the record that Ramirez, the late senior captain, had deliberately held secret from the crew. A man named Jenrette, chief of Ramirez's personal bodyguard, had entered that station and met survivors—and those survivors had allegedly refused to be taken off the station.

Those survivors included, one suspected, the hierarchy of the old Pilots' Guild, an organization whose management had caused the original schism between colonists and crew—and managed the contact with aliens who'd already taken offense and launched an attack. Not a sterling record. Not a record that inspired confidence. Or love.

Captain Ramirez, during that strange port-call, had told his own crew that Reunion was dead . . . destroyed by the alien attack. He'd refueled off the supposedly dead station, and run back to Alpha, where that lie about Reunion's condition had held firm and credible for nearly a decade—until Ramirez' deathbed confession had blown matters wide.

But secrecy hadn't ended with one deathbed revelation. His suspicion of other facts withheld had made this particular tape an item of contention between Sabin, who'd been one of the captains nine years ago, and Jase, Ramirez's appointee, whose assignment to a captaincy had nothing to do with knowledge of ship's operations. Jase had been aboard that day they'd found Reunion in ruins, but he hadn't been on the bridge—he'd been twenty-odd, junior, and not consulted, far from it. Sabin wouldn't talk about that time at dock; no member of the bridge crews had talked to anyone they could access. Every member of Ramirez' personal security team except Jenrette was dead— killed in a mutiny against Ramirez—and Sabin had snatched Jenrette into her security team immediately after Ramirez' death, the very day, in fact, that Jase had wanted to ask him questions about this tape.

That was the state of relations between the ship's captains—Sabin, very senior, and Jase, appointed by the late senior captain, very junior—and a lot of data not shared between them.

"Anything entirely astonishing about the tape?" Bren asked. "I trust you've reviewed it to the end."

"The match-up with station plans is my work," Jase muttered, keying while the tape proceeded. The screen afforded them a helmet-cam view of airless, ravaged halls picked out in portable lights as Jase skipped through the venues, freezing key scenes. "For a long stretch, things go pretty much as you'd expect to see. Fire damage. Explosion damage. Outwardly, the kind of thing you'd expect of a station in ruins. But the boarding team doesn't wander around much. No exploring. Straight on."

"As if they knew where they were going?"

"Exactly." Jase skipped ahead through the record, and now, in motion, the exploration reached a section that looked far less ravaged. "Their entry into the station, which is a long, tedious sequence, was through the hole in the mast; but after they got in, the lift worked on emergency power, which saved them quite a bit of effort. Piece of luck, eh? Emergency generators back up a lot of functions. Fuel port. Critical accesses. No questions there. Now we're in the C corridor, section. . . . about 10. Notice anything really odd here?"

The matching map had the numbers. If one could assume the station architecture as similar to the atevi earth station's structure, the investigating crew was on second level near the cargo offices at the moment. Lights were out. Power was down. Helmet lights still picked out walls and closed doors. Intact doors.

"It's not that badly damaged here," Bren observed.

"No, it's not." A small pause. "But we did see part of the station survived. What else do you notice? For God's sake, Bren . . ."

He was entirely puzzled. After a silence, Jase had to prompt him:

"They're *walking*."

God. *God*. Of course. They were walking. Walking was so ordinary. But he'd helped revive a space station. He knew better. Walking, in space, was a carefully managed miracle . . . and on a station with an altered center of mass? Not easy, was it?

He felt like a fool. "The station's rotating."

"As good as put out a neon sign," Jase said. "To anyone born in space."

A sign to tell more than the investigating ship. A sign to advise any alien enemies that this station wasn't utterly destroyed. That much beyond any small pocket of light or heat where a handful of surviving tenants might cling to life, as they'd assumed all through this voyage was the case—this huge structure was rotating and managing its damage in ways very suggestive of life, intact systems, and sufficient internal energy to hold itself in trim.

"Computer couldn't manage this on auto," he said to Jase, "could it?"

"Less than likely. A dumb system—possible, I suppose, but I don't believe it. I don't think crew will."

"But you can see rotation from outside," Bren said, confused. "The ship docked, didn't they? How can crew not have seen it?"

Jase gave him a dark look. "We've never left home. We're still sitting at dock at Alpha. The atevi world's below us. Can you prove differently? Can you prove we've ever traveled at all?"

Once he thought of it, no, he couldn't. There was no view of outside . . . except what the cameras provided the viewing screens. They underwent periods of inconvenience and strangeness that made it credible they moved, but there was no visual proof that didn't come through the cameras.

And had Ramirez somehow ordered a lie fed to those cameras? A simple still image, that crew would take for the station's lifeless hulk, when the truth was moving, lively, self-adjusting?

From when? God, from how early in the ship's approach had Ramirez faked that output?

"If Ramirez faked the camera images," he asked Jase, "how early did he? Did he come into Reunion system expecting disaster in the first place?"

"I'll tell you that niggling suspicion did occur to me. But long-range optics might have seen there was a problem, way far off. Down below, I assure you, we didn't get an image . . . we don't, routinely until bridge has time to key it to belowdecks. It's not often important. It's protocols. And if bridge is busy, if a captain's too busy, or off-shift, or in a meeting, we sometimes don't get image for a while. For a long while, in this case. We saw the still image. We saw the team entering the mast."

"Where it's always null-gee."

"No feed from helmet cam beyond that. This section went straight into the log's black box and nobody belowdecks *ever* saw it."

Anger. No *wonder* this particular tape had stayed buried for nine years. No wonder the current senior captain had silenced the last living member of the group that had made that tape and challenged the technically untrained junior captain to find the log record—if he could.

"But the captains all knew," Bren surmised. "Sabin was there. She had to know the station wasn't dead. Anybody on the bridge, any of the techs, they had to know, all along, didn't they?" *That* had been a question before they launched on this mission. It loomed darker and darker now, damning all chance of honesty between executive and crew.

"It's all numbers readout on those screens," Jase said. "You get what the station transmits. Or doesn't transmit. Or if *it* feeds you a lie—you'd have that on your screen, wouldn't you? I'm not sure that all the ops techs on the bridge knew. Some had to. But it's possible some didn't."

More and more sinister, Bren thought, wishing that at some time, at any convenient time, the late captain Ramirez had leveled with his atevi allies . . . and his own crew.

"I'll imagine, too," Jase went on, "that the minute we got into the solar system and got any initial visual inkling there was trouble, bridge showed a succession of still images from then on out—in space, you can't always tell live from still. I'll imagine, for charity's sake, that Ramirez ran the whole thing off some archive tape and a still shot and nobody else knew. He might have been the only captain on the bridge during the investigation: you just don't budge from quarters until you get the all-clear, and it didn't come for us belowdecks for hours. Maybe he didn't tell anybody but his own techs. Maybe the other captains got his still image and *they* didn't leave their executive meeting to find out. I can construct a dozen scenarios that might have applied. But I'll tell you I'm not happy with anything I can imagine. The more I think about it, I'm sure Sabin had to know."

"You docked at the station, for God's sake."

"Tethered. Simple guides for fueling. We're not the space shuttle."

Not the space shuttle. Not providing passenger video on the approach. Not providing a cushy pressurized and heated tube link.

Entry through the null-g mast, where even a trained eye couldn't easily detect a lie.

"There's another tape," Bren said, on that surmise. "There's got to be some log record where the station contacted *Phoenix* and gave Ramirez the order not to let the crew know there was anybody alive."

"You know, I'd like to think that was where the orders originated," Jase said calmly. "And I earnestly tried to find a record to prove that theory. But I couldn't. My level of skill, I'm afraid. Took me eleven months to break this much out. I know a lot more now than I did about the data system. But you get into specific records by having keys. I've cracked a few of them. Not all. *Not* the policy level. Not the level where Guild orders might be stored. And the senior captain isn't about to give them up and I'm not about to ask."

"You can't *erase* a log entry, can you?"

"You'd think. But at this point—we've rebuilt a lot of the ship's original systems, over the centuries, and I'm not sure that's the truth any longer. At my level of expertise, no. Not possible. If there's a key that allows that—it rests higher than I can reach. Maybe it sits in some file back on old Earth, that launched us. Maybe Sabin has it. I don't."

Jase was *Ramirez's* appointment, and Sabin hadn't approved his having the post.

And the crew, the general, non-bridge crew—who'd all but mutinied to get them launched on this rescue mission—if they saw this tape, they were going to be far faster on the uptake than a groundling ambassador. There was a reasonable case to be made that the Pilots' Guild itself, in charge of Reunion Station, was behind all the trouble and all the lies and all the deception. There was a reasonable, even a natural case to be made that the alien hostility that had wrecked the station was directly the Guild's fault, and not Ramirez's. But believing the old Guild was the sole culpable agency required suspending a lot of possibilities, because the station wasn't mobile. The station wasn't gadding about space poking into other people's solar systems.

And the ship's executive hadn't talked. Hadn't breached the official lie that Reunion Station was dead.

Nine years without talking? Nine years for that many people on the bridge to keep a secret from their friends and relations among the crew?

Mospheirans never could have done it, Bren thought. Then: atevi . . . possibly. And ship-folk—

He watched Jase watch the tape, thinking that all the years he'd known Jase hadn't gotten him through all the layers of Jase's reticence. Even with friendship. Even with shared experience. In some ways ship-folk were as alien to Mospheirans as a Mospheiran could imagine.

And the ease of lies in this sealed steel world of the ship . . .

They continually heard reports that told them where they were. They imagined stars and space. They imagined progress through the universe.

The ship docked with a station mast, and went null-g. The *ship* would have been perfectly normal, null-g, even while the station wasn't. Surviving relatives could have been just the other side of the hull, and crew might not have known.

A very, very different set of perceptions, from certain consoles on the bridge, to those that weren't involved with that reality. While certain other techs, deep in the inner circles of the ship's operations, kept secrets until told otherwise—policy. Policy, policy.

The Pilots' Guild had once run this ship. It was a good question how much it still ran the upper decks. Did the ship work *with* the old Guild? *For* the old Guild?

Or for itself, these days? The Pilots' Guild hadn't actually consisted of pilots for centuries. Supposedly they'd gone stationside at Reunion, and let the ship's captains go their way, under their authority in name, if not in fact.

Jase touched a button. Sound came up, the ordinary hoarse whisper of a man's exerted breathing. *"Almost there, sir,"* a voice said.

"They know where they're going," Jase said. "They never ask. They're about to pass a working airlock. They know in advance certain of the lifts are going to work. There's no mystery about this, not to them. They're representing Ramirez and they're going in to meet with the station authority."

"And that *is* Jenrette we're hearing. The one with the helmet cam."

"Affirmative."

Sabin's man now. Sabin's sympathy for a man decades in Ramirez' service, a man too senior to be on a despised junior captain's staff?

For Jenrette, with, maybe, a whole raft of executive secrets on his conscience, a much more comfortable assignment, that with Sabin.

"Presumably," Jase said, "Sabin's thoroughly debriefed him by now, even the things he wouldn't want to say. So I assume she knows as much out of Jenrette as her imagination prompts her to ask and his sense of the situation lets him answer. Presumably, once we raised the possibility this tape existed, Sabin immediately reviewed it and questioned Jenrette. What else she may have gotten out of Jenrette, I wish I did know."

"She's going to know I came up here. She's going to ask why."

"True." Jase picked up a disk from off his desk and gave it to him, *tape* being in most instances a figure of speech on this ship. "This is a copy. Your copy. Consider—I was aboard when we docked at Reunion. I was belowdecks being lied to like all the rest. I *remember* how it was. I *remember* the announcements that we were going in. I remember the solemn announcement that we were going back to Alpha to find out if the rest of the colonists we'd scattered out here had survived—with the implication things were going to change and we were going to patch everything and find a friendly port and then prepare against the possibility of alien invasion at Alpha. Right along with crew, I got behind that promise. I was young. I'd had a peculiar course of study, and I understood I was going to be useful in that approach. I had a notion that was the reason I existed at all; and all during that voyage I bore down on my studies: French and Latin and Chinese and history, a lot of history. Yolanda and I were all impressed, because Ramirez was so incredibly wise as to have had us going down that path in the first place. Wise. . . . bullshit. I'm thirty years old. I'm relatively sure I am. Tell me: why was he so incredibly ahead of the game?"

Thirty years. A human who lived among atevi, to whom numbers were as basic as breathing, twitched to numbers. He immediately dived after that lure, wondering. Attentive. But answerless.

"What have you found out?" he asked Jase.

"I don't know what I've found out. I wanted you to come up here in human territory, where I'm not thinking like atevi. Where it's a lot easier for me to remember what happened, because, dammit, I should have been asking questions. Thirty years old. That's question number one. Ramirez had me born out of Taylor's Legacy, and picked me a mother who's now found it convenient not to have been on this voyage, for reasons I can fairly well understand are personal preference, or maybe a desire to live to an old age. Or maybe to avoid questions I'd ask when we got closer to our destination, who knows? Maybe it was Sabin's order. I know Ramirez had me studying French and Latin and Chinese, *he* said, since humans might have drifted apart from us over the last several centuries. So I was created to contact Mospheirans, before Ramirez had any idea Mospheirans existed . . . because he was a student of history and he did know that a few centuries of separation can make vocabulary and meanings drift, and we might not understand each other. Isn't that brilliant? That's what he told me when we headed back to Alpha."

"It's factually true—at least about linguistic drift. But I don't buy the prescience."

"Nor do I. And *maybe* I was created to contact humans—maybe to contact atevi, too, because Ramirez did, of course, know there was a native species. Contacting them had been at issue before *Phoenix* left Alpha two hundred years ago. Bet that humans were likely to go down to the planet and learn their language and change fairly radically. All true. I was born for all those reasons, let's suppose, *twenty years* before aliens showed up and hit Reunion Station. But that's assuming what later became useful was useful twenty years earlier, isn't it? Why? Why do you suppose Ramirez was thinking about going back to Alpha for the first time in two hundred years? Guild orders? Guild orders that didn't have any foreknowledge that there was going to be any alien attack?"

"It doesn't make sense."

"It doesn't. I don't know what's behind any of this. I'd like to know why Ramirez *really* wanted me born."

There was a *lot* of pain behind Jase's quiet statement. The part about remembering human things better up here in human territory—Bren well understood that. The curiosity about his own birth—a man without natural parentage could well ask. Jase was born out of genetic deepfreeze, the Legacy, the stored genetic material of the original crew. Of *no* living father, and maybe not even of the woman he called mother. That was one personally disturbing matter.

But the intersection of Jase's birth with Guild intent and Ramirez's intent, coupled with an education suiting him for nothing practical in ordinary terms: those were scary, scary questions.

"I've always thought it was a reasonable precaution,

your peculiar education," Bren said, "if Ramirez always meant to come back to us."

"Always meant to come back," Jase echoed him. "So figure: I'm thirty years old, give or take the games travel does with time. My years are mostly on this ship, so hell with figuring planetary terms: I think my answer is on this ship, the same way my life has been on this ship, and I know *when* Ramirez ordered me born. But then I'm up against another wall. I don't know *how long* he planned it. I don't know *why* he planned it, and I don't know what was the triggering event, but at some point, clearly, my existence was going to be useful to him. Twenty-some years later, the aliens show up. And did that *change* my purpose— or satisfy it?"

For any human born *why was I conceived* was an interesting question, to which the answer might be as simple and human and serendipitous as *we didn't plan on it*. But for Jase, Jase being definitely planned, his genetic code extracted from the frozen genetic legacy of dead heroes—the first crew, the legendary Taylor's crew, who'd saved the ship from sure destruction in a radiation hell—if there was a god-among-mortals, Jase was born with that cachet. He'd had done everything possible since to duck the job, but he was born disconnected from modern ship families and he was born of a dead hero . . . maybe of Taylor himself, the legendary Navigator. Point one.

Point two: being disconnected from modern families, he was naturally up for grabs. *Ramirez* had appropriated him, no other word for it—appropriated him and dictated his life, not quite father, never that available. No emotional attachment—nothing close, at least, except a boy's human need to attach to something.

Ramirez created Jase to mediate with the colonists

the ship had left at Alpha? And with the possibility of atevi involvement? Brilliant thinking. Except this tape, this lie, and the fact he hadn't trusted his own heir with the truth of survivors abandoned at Reunion until he was on his deathbed.

Magnificent planning, that was. Up to that point, the crew had thought all they had to do was tuck in at Alpha and build defenses in a very remote chance of unfriendly visitors turning up on their track. They hadn't thought their remote cousins and occasionally closer relatives had been left alive. They'd mourned their dead and gone on and adjusted to a new reality.

Then they'd heard what Ramirez said on his deathbed. The crew, when it heard the station was still alive, had downright mutinied and demanded to go back; atevi allies had thought about it and decided to back that request, for fear of aliens tracking humans from Reunion to their own world. And *Mospheirans* had insisted on joining the mission, to get human records cleared from Reunion for exactly the same reasons. A remarkable three-way alliance had leapt into action on what they thought was a rescue mission—or at best a critical mop-up of dangerous loose ends of information left behind. Find out the situation, shut down anything still left, and get out, destroying *any* record that could lead an alien enemy back to the atevi home-world.

Now, one move away from their destination, Jase was saying they'd better rethink Ramirez's whole path of action? Someone who lived by numbers should have been looking at the equation that was Jase Graham's life a long, long time back.

"I'm listening," Bren said, chagrinned. "What *does* add up? What do you think the truth is?"

"Earliest," Jase said somberly, "earliest I remember, I was supposed to view tapes and learn languages.

Yolanda and I," he amended his account: Yolanda Mercheson, sister in event, but not in genetics. Likewise one of Taylor's Children, Yolanda had been his partner—his lover, in a match that hadn't worked out. Now she was back at the atevi station doing what a paidhi did: translate and mediate with atevi authorities, and try to keep the three-way alliance stable. "Understand, I'm not complaining about my abnormal childhood," Jase said. "But grant I wasn't stupid. God, no, it wasn't remotely my heritage to be stupid. I did know I was abnormal, and I did wonder. Most of all I wondered why everybody else studied things you could put a name to on the ship—they were going to be engineers, or techs, or nav, or bio; and they got together by tens and twenties and made ball teams, that sort of thing. I just had Yolanda. And she had me. And we didn't know what we could call what we did. But we studied what we were supposed to, because the Old Man said so, because our mothers said so. Because the seniors on the ship expected it of us, and *they* thought we were doing the right thing, even if our peers thought we were strange."

One couldn't imagine such a life. He'd had his own oddball passion—to see the rest of the world. To understand the exotic lands of the atevi. But it had been *his own* passion that had led him to the University and a career in the Foreign Office.

Jase had been assigned an ambition. Issued one, like a uniform. And was ruled from above, by Ramirez's decisions.

That was, Bren thought, fairly horrific.

"So," Jase said, "Here I was, doing what was interesting enough, but peculiar—I mean, Yolanda and I could speak Chinese to each other, but no one else, and we hadn't a clue why. And the next minute of our lives, something went way wrong. The last mission was going as usual: we were at a star, looking around, making notes, taking our usual survey, as if we were going to carry out our mission and find some trace of old Earth—big chance that was, and we all knew it, but it was what we were supposed to do, so we did it. Then, bang. Alarm sounded. Everything was secrecy and we were ordered to quarters, headed home to the station via a point where we had a minor, uninhabited base. That fast. Total change of direction. Total change of plans. I heard senior crew talking about it when I was going to quarters, but no one talked to me. Ramirez certainly didn't call me personally and explain.

"But you know how it is, now, when the ship moves. You travel and you stop and refigure, and while you're inertial, you hear all the theories floating the corridors if you just keep your ears open. Ramirez didn't talk to me. Rarely did. My mother didn't know any more than anybody else. The same with Yolanda and her contacts. But rumor was, on that voyage, that we'd seen something that wasn't confined to the planet we were observing. An alien ship. So we were running hard, getting out of that place and going back to report to Reunion. Via an indirect route. That was the idea." Jase was quiet a moment. On the desk, the tape played on, four men walking through corridors mostly dark, but not as ruined as one might think. "Talk was, in the lower corridors, the ship had acted hostile. But no one knew details. And when we got to Reunion, again—something definitely wasn't right. Information didn't come down to the corridors when it should. We were confined to quarters. That part's normal on an exit. You know. But we moved closer, still without information. And linked up with the station. And took on fuel. And during that process we were shown the view outside, the station damage, while Ramirez broke the news we'd seen aliens and now they'd hit the station and killed everybody. And he said all we could do was go back to Alpha colony, where we thought there might be support we needed, and resources . . . oh, give or take a couple of hundred years of neglect. So we went. Ramirez called me and Yolanda in privately during the voyage, and he talked to us about how people changed into nations and accents turned into languages in a couple of centuries. Yolanda and I being the only ones who'd studied any other language and who really knew on an operational level— on a mindset level—how that sort of thing worked, we were critical to what was coming. And wasn't it marvelous and lucky we existed? We didn't know what to say. We didn't ask him, 'So how did you know in advance you'd need us?' That was our best chance to ask why we existed, and we were so overwhelmed with finally having a practical purpose we didn't ask that question. Didn't even ask each other, until I guess, between us, the time for questions passed. And after that—I don't know: maybe I was scared of the answer. Maybe I was just too focused on the future to question the past."

"And you think now?" Bren asked. "What *is* the truth?"

"My innermost guess," Jase said, "my middle-of-the-watch-and-can't-sleep guess used to be that he'd had us born because there always was some secret plan to go back to Alpha, some scheme either the Guild had cooked up, or something he meant to do secretly in a breach with the Guild. I was sure he intended for us somehow to figure those cross-cultural differences he foresaw. Ramirez studied history. He knew about cultures outside ship-culture. He created *paidhiin* without ever having seen one. Without ever knowing atevi had gotten in charge of the situation back at Alpha—he was prepared."

"You *used* to think that. And now?"

"He had us born and set to the course he wanted long before aliens were in the picture. That tends to exclude them as a cause—so far as I know. So maybe he *was* thinking about Alpha. Second—he shoved me into a captaincy I begged him not to give me and tried to get rid of. And he wouldn't give it to Yolanda, who wanted to be on this ship. She got left behind on this trip, and I got ripped away from the world I wanted more than anything, to be on a ship I can't run. Ramirez wasn't crazy and he wasn't arbitrarily cruel. But it seemed unfair. And you know——when something's not damn fair, it does make you mad. And you don't think straight. You ask why, but you constantly ask the wrong why, and you don't go back to first questions. And ever since we'd gone back to Alpha and the atevi seemed our only hope, Yolanda and I had forgotten all about the whys we *used* to ask. We had a job to do. Dealing with outsiders was work Yolanda flat hated, and work I really took to, *really* took to— and both situations were just as distracting. I was lucky enough to draw the atevi side. Yolanda had humans trying to use her to get at each other. So the two of us grew apart. And then Ramirez had the gall to give *me* the captaincy, for God's sake, permanent ship assignment, at the same time he used Yolanda secretly to do translation, bound to the planet, keeping major secrets from me. It wasn't fair."

"And?"

"So on this voyage, maybe I've gotten some mental distance, enough to deaden the emotional charge in that situation. I think about Ramirez frozen down there in storage—and I think about what I should have asked him. Questions I wish I'd asked Yolanda, to the point, that she might not have thought to tell me before we left. What she might have assumed I knew.

"And at the same time, I was after this tape. Without the right keys. Denied the right keys, by Ramirez and by Sabin, both. Is *that* somehow to the good of us all? So in that mood of executive curiosity, and during that search, I've dug into everything I could get, things that aren't a restricted record. Like what files Ramirez got out of the Archive—what books he read. History. Earth's history. That's no surprise. Ancient, recent, didn't matter to him. He *studied* the world he was trying to find, as if somehow the coordinates were going to occur to him, as if somewhere in the Archive, the actual location might be buried—or some necessary navigational cue. Never was going to happen."

"Never?"

"We lost the signposts. The stellar signposts that should have been a clear marker for us. If you can't see the noisiest stars in space, either something's between you and them, or you're way far from where you thought you were, so far lost that finding old Earth's not even possible. No, it's never been possible, beyond the original accident."

"That's not what the ship told my ancestors."

"The great search. Along with a lot of other myths. But without an elaborate arrangement of fuel depots and far more ships, by what the navigators say, it wasn't ever going to happen, and somehow the Guild never got around to building other ships or arranging any fueling stations. Whatever their reason, we can't *reach* a point of vantage without traveling a lot farther than may be prudent, counting everything that's happened, and we don't know what direction to start looking. Take it from me, that never was really the reason we left Alpha. I think you know that by now."

"I know the ship's *current* story."

Jase was silent a beat or two. "Fair enough."

"The ship wanted to take the colony out of Alpha, set up in deeper space, and the colonists—my ancestors—wouldn't go for it. Is *that* still true?"

"The Guild was for setting up further out in space. Building a place that would be just human, and just spacefaring. We weren't supposed to live on a planet. Weren't supposed to *contaminate* ourselves with what wasn't human."

"Small choice atevi ever got about being contaminated."

"The Guild. The Guild's decisions. The Guild split over Alpha. The faction that prevailed didn't *want* your ancestors going down to the nice green, inhabited planet. No. And once it happened, even the solar system was too close for comfort. They were diametrically opposed to atevi contact—not so much to protect the atevi culture, though that was a consideration; but to protect our own."

"From us."

"Us. Which *us?* We were so few. The universe is so big. It's an article of faith that original Earth exists somewhere—but from the Guild viewpoint, we're the sole true custodians of the Archive, the guardians of human culture. Your ancestors wanted to dive into an alien gravity well and give it all up."

"That's not all there was in the decision."

"You know I agree with you. But Guild *leadership* was obsessed with establishing a secure base where only human ideas had currency."

"It was a human idea to go down to the planet."

"But not a solely human idea that came back. In that they were right, weren't they?"

"Does it matter?"

"To them it matters. It's still going to matter. When they couldn't control Alpha, they took the ship and left."

"To preserve their *purity*."

"And as soon as Guild leadership found a likely spot, they built again, not near a planet this time, not near any attractive, living world where people could escape by a low-tech dive to a living world, oh, no, not twice. They built Reunion out where everyone would be under their orders, always, totally, dependent on them and their orders. And the Guild leaders got off the ship. And established their rule over Reunion. And then—then I'm guessing here—I think after they'd built up their population a while, after they'd educated the population the way they wanted, they might try to terraform a moderately liveable planet, and keep it only human. I think the Guild couldn't *find* Earth. So they were going to *create* Earth."

Mindboggling. "You're kidding."

"Give them some credit. They weren't going to do it to the atevi planet. Give them that much virtue, that they were looking for somewhere they could claim for themselves."

"You keep saying *they, they, they*." Aboard ship, the term was *we*. Crew. Family. And it hadn't been *we* at very critical points. "The ship, I take it, held a different view in the proceedings."

"The ship is the ship. The Pilots' Guild went ashore and became something aside from the ship's executive. The Guild began to run station business. It *became* station business. It had done *that* from way back at Alpha. So, yes, there was a schism between the ship's executive and the Guild—at least—there was an increasing division of interests."

"And *we*, meaning the ship, weren't as interested in Reunion?"

"We had relations on Reunion. We refueled there. They mined fuel for us. It was all interconnected. You know there's an emotional connection. But no, we weren't Reunion. We were *Phoenix*. We'd never stopped being *Phoenix*. And we never trusted the way the station was run. We just couldn't do anything about it."

That was the universe as he'd speculated it existed. Populations achieved self-interest, and wider interests cooled. Only the ship had stayed footloose, traveling. Capable of change. And ominously so, of meddling in new things.

"So," Bren said, "the ship created Reunion, and used it, and thought of it as home away from home. And the ship never came back to Alpha. But still reserved that notion for itself."

"Reunion we knew was safe. We were loyal to Reunion."

"Was Ramirez?"

Jase might not have anticipated that question. He blinked. He keyed. The image on the screen froze.

"Good question," Jase said. "Useful question."

"Was Ramirez loyal?"

"He created us. Me and Yolanda."

Back to that same pathway. "And you were—what?"

"I think," Jase said slowly, "and this is a difficult thought—I have this niggling suspicion, sometimes, that, the same way I suspect the Guild had its notion of defining humanity, Ramirez meant me and Yolanda to out-human the rest of the Guild—filtering the human Archive through our perceptions. Being able to challenge their concepts. We were learning Latin and Chinese. The ship was still working for the Guild, cataloging planets, investigating likely ones, ones that met their criteria. Purely scientific, they said. Increasing the human database. For what? For what logical purpose were we going about, that had the station devoting so much energy to *our* energy needs? But not for us to ask, I suppose. There was always fuel. We'd dock, we'd go. We'd explore and refuel. That routine was my whole world. You don't question the world—not until the plumbing fails, isn't that what you said once?"

"And now?"

"Now that the plumbing's really failed? I don't believe pure scientific curiosity had anything to do with it. I'm sure the Guild sent us where we went, or they wouldn't have gone on refueling us. Maybe they simply wanted to have us gone as long as possible, to keep our influence out of the station. Maybe they wanted the unification, the symbol, of us as the focus of community effort, the pressure valve. The reason for sacrifice. And they could control us. Fueling was always the sword over our heads. And while all that was going on, I'm sure we were gathering information that would eventually be useful, investigating other solar systems, and fuel sources. But Ramirez—I have this tenuous theory—didn't ever mention his two linguists to the Guild, not that I ever was aware. And I wonder—did *he* mean to create what he was looking for? He knew about *diversity,* which wasn't quite the Guild's insistence of everyone walking in step. He didn't know the lost languages, but he knew he couldn't create a new Earth on a ship where everybody is cousins and brothers and sisters, and living the same lives and doing the same jobs. He couldn't do it on a space station the Guild's running. But he *could* do it if he ever found a place where he could get supply that the Guild didn't control, and where he could establish an orbiting base that wouldn't hold fueling as a sword over his head. He had the genetic storage. He had the Archive. Fantastic as it is on a human level—I think he was hoping to find a place where he could build another station and ultimately set down an unregulated colony."

"A green planet."

"Another green planet. One without a population. I think, in that, Ramirez and the Guild were after the same thing."

"Not to have a population, if it could support humans?"

"Bren, my friend, what educated ship-folk know about planetary biology fits in a lifesupport tank. I know I don't know as much as I should. But let me tell you, I *do* know the British monarchs and the Alexandrine Empire. I know Darwin and Eberly and Teiler. Yolanda knows German history and Bantu. I'm really keen on the Shang Dynasty. Hell, we're diversity incorporated. We're culture in a plastic pack. I suspect going back to Alpha wasn't Ramirez's real plan. He had every opportunity to do that. No. I think Ramirez's ideas were pure Guild—humans only. Ramirez wanted the Guild's plan—but he didn't want current Guild leadership in charge of it. *He* intended to run his version of it. And poking around in various solar systems, looking for life-supporting planets to drop us on, I think he got more than he bargained for."

"Angry aliens."

"Their planet, is my guess. At least something they owned and cared about. They'd probably been watching us for a while. They showed hostile and we made a feint off to another destination. But when we got home, home had already been hit. So they knew damned well what they were hitting. They knew us, knew where we'd come from, and we didn't know them—not even know which of various systems had been the trigger for the attack. But I think, whoever hit us, they very well knew the neighborhood we've only been parked in for a couple of hundred years."

"Seems very likely," Bren said. "Based on all you say."

"So back to our question—why do I exist? Hell if I know. But Ramirez was up to something that blew up on him and took out the Guild's home base, whether it was his idea or the Guild's. It was a thorough catastrophe. What bothers me in all of this is where Sabin fits. And what kind of politics went on between her and Captain Ogun, when he stayed behind at Alpha and sent her to manage a rescue neither of them thinks is likely? You'd think she'd at least give up her antagonism toward me. But she won't—as if she thinks I'm still following Ramirez's agenda."

"Might you be?"

"Not that I know."

"What could you do against her?"

"I don't know. Until I know what I was for—I don't know what she thinks I might do."

"Not that many choices, are there?"

"There still may be choices. Like—who's running this ship on the way *back* to Alpha . . . if anyone's alive."

Guild getting in charge of the ship was a very, very grim scenario. Not one they'd actively considered, in the bright lights of Alpha Station and the full steam ahead of their own planning. But a year later, out in the vast dark of the universe and closer and closer to Reunion, it did prompt a sober reflection—on people, on old loyalties, on their prospects.

If they got there and there was no fuel, they had that covered—in Gin and her robots. If they got there and found a still-potent Guild in charge—and Sabin much too sympathetic toward them—

"They'd want the ship, wouldn't they?"

"Oh, damned right, they'd want it," Jase said.

"You think Sabin seriously might lean their way? Give up her own authority? I don't read her that way."

"Or if she became part of theirs," Jase said, and drew a breath. "At the start of this voyage I had some doubts about her. But this last year, this voyage—I don't know what she thinks."

A last year of being de facto senior captain. Of working with Ramirez's unwanted appointee.

Of having a section of her ship in atevi and Mospheiran control, an arrangement not to her liking. If the Guild didn't like "contamination," what did Sabin think?

"Have you seen any shift in her opinions?"

"I can't read her. I do think whatever went on between Ramirez and the Guild, she's on a completely different agenda. And keeping me out of the log— that's said something, too, hasn't it? She never was on Ramirez's side. Always the contrary vote. Always outvoted. And Ogun put her in charge here. Why, Bren? Why in hell did he do that?"

"Admittedly putting her where she didn't have to deal with an entire nation of atevi and diverse politics on the planet. Aboard a ship that's dead set on its mission—a crew that's going to be pretty hard to argue with if it gets this tape in hand, among other points. You talk about the Guild possibly taking over. But that's not the way the crew feels about past decisions, if I have it right."

"A two-edged sword. If Ramirez was *against* the Guild, if blame for this goes against *him,* I was born part of it. And that's the critical detail I don't know.

I don't know when it could blow up and I don't know what's going to be the issue."

"You've got the tape. You could release it. You could take your position from that."

"And that could blow wider than I intend. *Stranded* is a hot enough word with Mospheirans, but let me tell you, abandoning survivors at Reunion—that nearly fried the interface. And things don't make sense. The *way* the lie was constructed, right from the start of the ship coming into Reunion, how do you read that? *I* can't answer it."

"Plain logic: Ramirez stopped the situation, froze the tape until he knew what he'd do."

"Until he'd made up what his story was."

"Ramirez didn't know what he'd find going back to Alpha. He knew things might not be optimum. As they weren't. Ten years getting refueled was a miracle, as was. If the crew had known, they still couldn't change things, but they'd have sweated and fretted harder. And crew can understand that."

"That's logic. But it's not emotion. There've been too many lies, Bren. The depth of deception in this one event has too many layers. Tamun's mutiny was only one manifestation of the *poison* of lies that's run on this ship."

"There's only one layer in this lie. Ramirez needed the crew to take orders without division of opinion."

"And if the crew hadn't ever found out there were survivors? Would he *ever* have told the truth?"

"He'd had the ship fueled. Priority. He'd had the ship fueled. We're going where he prepared this ship to go. That's a fact, isn't it? I think he sweated the situation he knew he'd left."

"The *fact* is, he told us for all those years we were the last human outpost, there at Alpha. The last hope for humanity. The sole planet for atevi. That we were all preparing a planetary defense. That we were building another starship for a counterstrike, if we had to. *Then* we get the facts. And this crew's wild enthusiasm for this venture ran out in the first month of this voyage, far from civilization. Now we're down to grim determination and the very real likelihood we're going to find the station dead after all this effort. Things aboard are quiet. They *will* be quiet, until there's some result. But if I take this to the crew—"

"You're a captain. Equal to Sabin, on your watch. You have the authority to decide the course of this ship, the same as she does."

"I'm a captain who knows less about the operation of this ship than the average maintenance grunt. I'm a damn linguist, Bren! That's what I am. That's *all* I am, and I'm not even competent at that."

"You are competent. What you can do is always invisible to you. From outside perspective . . . you don't have to sit a technical post. You can command the techs. You can say, go here, or go there. That's all the captains do, that I've ever observed."

"And what do I do when we come charging in to Reunion and I haven't any of the Guild computer keys?"

"As *surviving* ship's executive," Bren said in Ragi, "might one not say—the keys weren't passed?"

Jase stared at him. Outright stared. Maybe took an internal moment to translate that twice. But Jase had been in Shejidan, and knew the atevi court, and the use of daggers and plots. The paidhi-aiji was steeped in that culture. And at a pinch, could more than *think* in Ragi.

"The full range of alternatives," Bren said, again in Ragi. And in Mosphei': "A question. Merely a question."

"Too much unknown," Jase said in Ragi. And in ship-speak: "And I'm human, and I'm holding a bomb, in this record. And I respect Sabin. I do respect her. I didn't start this voyage that way, but I do."

"Granted. Not incompatible considerations."

Maybe Jase needed a dose of Ragi. Maybe he added, not subtracted, possibilities and solutions. But it remained an uncomfortable situation.

"You respected Ramirez," Bren reminded him, in Ragi. "And by all you say, nadi, who knows? Maybe he was about to execute the plan you used to think he had. He released the Archive to the planet. He wasn't that worried about contamination. Or he'd reconciled himself to us. Maybe he really did refuel the ship as a defense. He planned for another starship . . . but that's going to be atevi-run. The aiji's help could provide him his widest ambitions. A developed planet, all those resources. Maybe he wasn't, in his own plan, going back until he'd prepared a base that wouldn't fall under Guild control."

Worth considering, at least. Jase steepled his hands, thinking, and thinking. "He deployed me, and Yolanda."

"Yet put *you* back in space, but not her."

"It's a damned circle, Bren. Everything runs in a circle."

"He wasn't getting any younger. The Tamun blowup took his health. He didn't plan, perhaps, to be overheard in what he told you."

"About the Great Lie? Betraying the Guild?"

"I'm betting, though," Bren said, "that at least by then, the other captains knew what had happened back at Reunion. It would have been irresponsible of him to know there was a Guild authority surviving out here in that critical situation, and not to tell those who'd succeed him. He was dying and told you the biggest secret aboard to make you equal to them. And maybe he wanted to know, for one thing, how you'd take it. And whether you forgave him."

"Emotional answers. Not logical ones."

"The man was dying. At that point, maybe emotional answers mattered."

"Wanting me to make the decision? Me, but not Yolanda? Damn it all!"

"And Ogun. And Sabin. It would be their decision, too, when he was out of the picture."

"I'd be the deciding vote. *Damn* him!"

"If they split. As they didn't."

"Most days I forgive him. I suppose I forgive him. I suppose we're doing the right thing in coming out here. And if we show up and the Guild does what's ultimately sensible, and boards the ship, and take orders, so many things will become moot. But by all I know about what's happened in the past—I don't think that's highly likely."

"I never thought it was all that likely, where the Guild is concerned. If they'd wanted to leave Reunion, they'd have left, wouldn't they? But they've had nine years now to get worse off—or better. If they're stronger and more recalcitrant, we may have decisions to make."

"Sabin's going to decide those issues. That's the fact I can't change."

"Crew may decide," Bren said. "And *you* have that tape."

"I'll confess," Jase said, "I've had it for the last month."

"Not surprising you'd think about it before showing it to me."

"I'm out of time for thinking. I had to show it to you. We're coming up on the last move."

Last move.

"Before Reunion."

"This next one I really think will put us there."

A small inner shiver. "You know, I never get used to this *I think* business."

"Space is lumpy," Jase said.

"All that. But I still don't like to hear *I guess* from the navigators."

"Or from your partner in this mess?"

"Some things you can't figure with a computer. Jase, we'll make it. We do what we'll do when we get there. It's all we *can* do at the moment, but we just plot alternate positions, if it doesn't work. Same as I suppose your navigators do. Which is why I think you called me here."

Jase gave a wry, one-sided smile. Started the tape moving again. On the screen, the exploration reached a corner.

"The fact is," Jase said, "the one reconciling fact, in all the Old Man planned, is that he wanted me in some kind of authority over my own destiny. More than that, I think he'd be happy you're here. And honored that the dowager is here, with all she represents. I think you're right. Contamination no longer frightened him. He'd reconciled himself to the blended civilization he'd found. I think, all his old Guild notions to the contrary, he'd found the universe a far more dangerous place than he'd ever imagined, and before he died, he'd learned to take allies where he could get them. Yolanda kept her standoffishness from local culture. I didn't. I fell far more deeply not just into downworld culture, but into atevi culture, and the one thing that both infuriates me and encourages me is that Ramirez appointed *me* to succeed him. Me. *My* view of the universe. My atevi-contaminated, impure view of the universe humans have to live in. It's not a degree of importance I ever wanted, I'll tell you.

But the thought that Ramirez meant to do it, that he actually approved what I am—is what gives me the courage to get out of bed and go on duty." Jase pressed a button and skipped ahead, to a point where the helmet-cam view reached a sealed pressure door. In rapid motion they locked through, and then . . .

Then the record ended. Stopped.

"That's it?" Bren asked.

"That's it," Jase said. "That's all we have. It's absolutely not regulation that the tape stops like that. It's very much against regulations. And maybe Sabin knows what happened next and maybe she doesn't, but certainly, based on that tape, you and I don't. And that's the other reason I wanted to talk to you. You're the diplomat. My outrageous instinct says have the inevitable confrontation with Sabin about this tape right now, before we get to Reunion Station. Tell her what I know, what I suspect, all the structure of tissue and moonbeams. If it's going to blow up, let it blow and let's talk about the ship's great secret, and Ramirez's crazy ideas, and settle it before we have another crisis on us. Let me add a fact to keep between you and me. We've run with a little excess of fuel, ship's rule. Enough fuel reserve to get out to a place we know if things aren't optimum or if the Guild tries to take us. *If* Sabin's disposed to do it—she can get us away from Reunion. The name of the place is Gamma. And you're right—I can order that, if Sabin is in some way incapacitated. There are resources there. It would take us years, but we'd get home that way. On the other course, if we do go into Reunion, and dock, and open the hatch—by then we're dealing with somebody else, with Sabin involved, with people she'll know and I won't—who are going to outright outnumber us. Not to mention the crew may be in a very foul mood, once the truth starts coming out. As it still may. If they start talking to remote cousins and the stray mourned-for-dead uncle, all sorts of truth is *going* to come out, this time."

"You're the number two captain," Bren reiterated. "You decide what to do. You always had the authority to go after that log record. A little more questionable extension of authority, I suppose, that you show it to me. More, to show it to the crew. But by Ramirez's decision and Ogun's concurring vote, you are the number two captain. So I'd think you do have that authority to break this secret wide open—if you choose. It's your watch. Isn't it?"

"Clearly my watch. And the burning question still remains—what else do we do with it?"

"When you show it to me, you clearly know you're showing it to my security. And the dowager's. I might have given you special privacy. You didn't ask it."

"*You* keep secrets. So does the dowager."

"Secrets again?"

"That's the eternal question on this ship, isn't it?"

"Tell Ginny Kroger," Bren said. "She's tied into our information. It's hard to keep her apart from anything."

"And her staff circulates on three-deck."

"And if they know—crew's not far. You're right. Everywhere we turn, there's another question how wide to take this, and it all runs in a circle . . . once you tell one other individual, it all leads eventually to the crew."

"You understand my problem," Jase said. "And telling Gin Kroger, who's next to telling you, eventually leaves everyone on the ship *but* the crew knowing what's in this tape, which has got to be another psychological statement, so far as the crew's concerned, doesn't it? Pride. Trust. And how *do* we admit, this late in the game, that Ramirez lied to them twice? I'm just beginning to figure out how long Ramirez lied to *me*."

"Secrets," Bren said, "never, ever served *Phoenix* well. But letting them out just before making port is going to be difficult."

"So here we are—trying to shut Reunion Station down and keep the aliens from tracking us back to Alpha? That's a secret, isn't it—and one we're not going to confess to the Guild on first meeting. Secrets are our whole existence. Maybe some of them have to be kept. Even inside. I have scraps of facts that lead under closed doors. And what do we do? Fling wide all the doors? Open just one, thinking we can limit the damage? Restrict images during docking again, and hope that crew won't think to ask until this has all worked and they're too happy to lynch their officers?"

"We don't even know for an assured fact," Bren said, "that Sabin herself has a clue what's on this tape."

"She's got Jenrette to ask."

"Maybe she's never *asked* Jenrette. Or maybe Jenrette didn't tell her everything."

"She knows there's a question. Yes, she's seen this tape, no matter when she saw it. She knows, by now. And knowing all she knows, knowing that I've been after this tape, she's kept it to herself, letting me hunt for it—and ultimately letting you and me go into a situation on arrival without the information, if I didn't get it. I think that, and I get very angry. And then I reason," Jase said quietly, not looking at him, "that she hasn't failed to tell me yet. Not yet. And I keep waiting, day by day, for a briefing on what happened at Reunion—and on a dozen things I don't even know to ask."

"And it doesn't come," Bren said. "And it hasn't

come. And we're running out of time. And you're mad about that. And getting madder."

"It's that emotional cloud again."

"You're not sure you're thinking straight about it?"

"I'm not sure I'm thinking straight about anything. A check on the thought processes is useful. So after a suitable time of sweating it alone—on the eve of our last ship-move—I asked you in on it . . . knowing . . . knowing, unless she does exactly what Ramirez did and freezes the station image . . . crew will see it, first glance. They haven't thought to ask. No one's thought to ask. But if it's laid in front of them, they won't take five minutes to figure it out."

"It's been nine years. Station could have repaired themselves. Wouldn't they?"

Deep breath. "True. And the natural expectation would be, yes, just expect any survivors would have gotten rotation established, on a fairly high priority, to assure there *is* someone alive and healthy to meet us. So we might get through that. But not once information starts flowing, between stationers and us. Then we'll get the questions—and I have a dire suspicion there's more to it than we know."

"You're likely right."

"I think crew could swallow the worst suspicions— if it's on a soaring expectation of success. But having *lived* down in the lower decks, as, mind, none of the other captains have done—I think if we let the rest of the crew find out in the middle of a crisis that they were lied to like this, they'll blow, and this time—God knows. God knows whether mutiny is a possibility, but it's happened once, and we don't forget that. Sabin's not overly concerned for crew opinion—never has been. So here I sit, thinking yes, no, go this way, go that way—I've put myself in a position, digging this out, an uncomfortable one, but I've found it. And now I have to sit on it or let it loose. Either's a decision."

"No question."

"Third choice. Do I confront Sabin?"

"Truth is a fair start for a complex operation. Truth—at least between two captains of the same ship."

"So you think it's a good idea to ask her?"

"I'm sure truth may precipitate certain things."

"I'm sure of that, too. But do you advise me to do it?"

"The idea has a certain merit. And certain downsides. Are you *going* to do it?"

"I want you in on it."

"I'm less sure that's a good idea. My presence is provocative. Distracting from the issue."

"To the good. I want you there. I want *Banichi and Jago* there."

Bren was dismayed. "A threat?"

"A reminder to us humans we need to settle this quickly and not bring our unguarded tempers to our atevi guests or, for that matter, to the Mospheirans. I want all I've got on my side, environment, plain environment, not verbal argument. Sabin absorbs facts. She doesn't listen to arguments worth a damn. What she sees in a confrontation, *that* impresses her. If she sees the two of them, she'll know the scale of it. She'll know there's no secrecy possible there. Period."

It was, in certain particulars, a fair assessment of the senior captain.

"So," Bren asked, "when do you want me?"

"Now."

"It's four in the morning. Enthusiasm for the truth aside, is she going to be happier being waked up in the middle of her night?"

"Sleep-cycle," Jase reminded him. "We have sleep-cycles. Only you planetary types have nights. You run a ship, you get odd hours. And her cycle's closing out pretty soon. A moderately urgent *technical* consultation. I think that's the way to put it . . . a step short of an operational emergency. That'll get her on deck. If I say I just want to talk theory at this hour she'll tell me go to hell. And if I bother her in her duty hours she'll be on edge from the start and anxious to get back to schedule. *This* is an emergency."

"I'd at least offer tea," Bren said dryly.

"I don't think she'll stay for breakfast. Tea it is." Jase punched buttons and sent away the schematic. The tape started over. Jase punched another button, this one on his collar. "C1. Captain Sabin to my office at earliest convenience, technical consultation. Wake her."

"*Yes, sir,*" the answer came from the desk unit.

That fast. He'd agreed. They were in it.

2

"**B**anichi-ji," Bren said under his breath, sitting in the office chair, and using the pocket com while there was still time, "please advise security everything's under control and proceeding well."

Advise the atevi establishment, that was, and *under control* was tolerably true. He sat in Jase's office waiting for Sabin to show up on a small hours of the morning, on a minor emergency call, waiting for all else that might fall out—and the second worst situation he could think of was that Cenedi might have waked the dowager to advise his ultimate authority what was going on upstairs. The second worst. The *very* worst thing he could think of, outside of a complete malfunction of the ship's engines, was the dowager deciding to come up here in person to have morning tea and reason with Sabin.

Tea was not a word of fortunate history, under those circumstances.

Kaplan, however, had indeed come into Jase's office just for that purpose, to make tea . . . a nominally Mospheiran herbal item, one of those light mass planetary amenities that the ship's crew had taken to as passionately as they took to fruit sugar.

Polano and Banichi and Jago made a living wall of security outside . . . that sense of presence Jase deemed a very good idea.

Sabin had gotten the message from C1, and hadn't objected to Jase's office as the venue. She might, Bren thought, have breakable objects in her own.

It was a level of not-quite-critical summons that meant she could take a decent amount of time responding. She *might* even stop for breakfast, if only to try Jase's patience, but they made strong tea, all the same. It was pushing five hundred hours, not too far off first shift's ordinary waking.

Bren's pocket com beeped. So did Jase's desk unit. *She's here,* was the general advisement. Heads up.

A few beats later the door opened and Sabin walked in. She was a thin, past-sixties woman with close-clipped gray hair, uniform sweater and uniform coat. She didn't walk into a room: she invaded it— gave an habitual scowl to their security, who folded in after her—their security, then her security, two men, Collins and Adams, intent on coming inside if the rest were bent on it.

Bren stood up, a courtesy. Jase poured a cup of tea and set it on his desk edge.

She didn't take it. She didn't sit down. "Nature of the emergency. I trust there is an emergency."

"A fairly major one," Jase said. "The tape, captain. The tape. And I'm not about to let Mr. Cameron go out of here seeing what he's seen without hearing your side of this."

"*What* in hell have you done?"

"Well, looked for answers, for a start." Jase's eyes could be perfectly innocent, on demand. "Unfortunately I've stirred up more questions than answers, but I have every confidence you had a reason for restricting the tape record. I'm equally confident that you were testing me to see if I could get it. I did. So I'm not sending our ally below with half the truth to work on. I'm certainly not having our allies wait until they get to the station to see what any eye can see— that Reunion was under an immaculate one *g* rotation nine or so years ago, while we were docked and refueling, contrary to the image provided belowdecks; and certainly the crew will see it, and recall all too keenly that *isn't* what we all saw on our screens, so there's a whole other question. So I think we ought to talk about this, captain, and I'm sorry about waking you early to do it, but Mr. Cameron's knowledge of the situation—for which I take full responsibility— provides a certain urgency. Unhappily my watch falls during your sleep, and I apologize. Considering the hour, I at least made you some tea. My aides will provide whatever else you might want."

Dead silence. Sabin was fully capable of wishing them in hell and walking out, all questions hanging.

She didn't. "So you got into the log."

"It took some work, captain. I trust you knew I'd do that. I took it rather as one of the many tests of competency you've set me. I did it. Now Mr. Cameron's seen it. So has his guard."

They'd provided a chair for Sabin in the scant room there was left. She turned it on its track, took the tea from Kaplan, and sat down.

Bren sat, having been prepared to intervene, glad he hadn't had to. But the crisis wasn't past. Sabin often operated on a delayed fuse.

She had a sip of tea—she took it dark, strong, and unmitigated, ignoring the condiments, ignoring the hazards of one past poisoning.

"So?" she said to Jase, likewise ignoring the crowd of security and the sure knowledge the atevi representative was wired.

"I've a lingering few critical questions," Jase said. "I can certainly understand why you didn't release this to the crew at large. Captain Ramirez faked the monitor output, and he did it before he ever had clear contact with the survivors. Am I right?"

Sabin sipped her tea and didn't say a thing.

"When crew finds out," Jase said, "if they find out when they're in a good mood—that's one thing. If things aren't going well when they find out, I ask myself, what else are they going to doubt?"

Sabin shrugged. "You have all the answers. You've made the decision to view this with Mr. Cameron. I'm listening to your reasoning."

"Excuse me, captain," Bren said. "Our section is disconnected from these events and capable of discretion, if that's the ruling here."

"I'm sure you're capable of a good many things," Sabin said. "Including seeking your own advantage. I take it the dowager now knows, too."

"If it isn't the case, I'm sure it will be as soon as she wakes. At least her staff knows. So does mine."

"Marvelous," Sabin said dryly, swallowed the tea and held out her cup to Jase. "Another cup."

"Yes, ma'am," Jase said moderately, without a ruffle, and handed it to Kaplan to fill, which menial task Kaplan did with dispatch. "And in the reasonable assumption," Jase said, "like other matters you've left me to find for myself, that this tape and the technical way into the log was a matter of my education in command, for which I'm grateful, I certainly learned a great deal more about ship's operations than I expected, as *you* knew I'd learn, I'm sure, all to the good. So I doubt you're entirely surprised that this tape Mr. Cameron suggested was important at the start of the voyage remained an issue with me. I did note you never cautioned me against finding it—and considering my peculiar position in this office, I've also spent some time wondering about reasons you may have had for remaining the perpetual dissenting vote on the Captains' Council. Voting on principle, I take it. Possibly opposed to my very existence."

"Go on." Sabin took the second cup from Kaplan's hand. "This is actually interesting."

"As to why I brought Mr. Cameron in on the matter, it's precisely the consideration of a foreign state of mind that we on *Phoenix* don't quite understand. The very thing my education prepared me to deal with. You sent me down to the planet . . ."

"Correction. *Stani* sent you down to the planet." Ramirez, that meant.

"With your dissenting vote, granted. As, very likely, when Ramirez proposed to get into the gene banks to create me and Yolanda in the first place, you weren't highly pleased. But all that aside, the captains voted, and I exist. It was the ship's executive that sent me down to the atevi world, unprepared as I turned out to be—but having at least the basics of an understanding what I was up against—what Yolanda and I were up against. Then Mr. Cameron took me in hand and shook new considerations into me. Set me out on an ocean and let me contemplate a whole wealth of new input."

"This is far less interesting."

"Like everything not bounded by this hull. I'm aware that's your view, captain. It's not your job. But I assure you it's mine, to understand things external. And that's my use to you. I was born to acquire a certain expertise—enough, in my executive capacity, now, to know what Mr. Cameron's knowledge is worth, and enough to consult him when the executive of this ship is as entangled as it is in Guild deceptions, and burdened as it is with past decisions, and sitting on an ocean of information far deeper than we may think it is."

"Meaning you brought him in here hoping his presence will moderate my response to what you've done."

"*Meaning,* captain, I recommend hearing his input where it regards diplomacy, including internal diplomacy, particularly that of our allies, whose reaction is not to be taken for granted—and I suggest we listen to him particularly carefully, because if a first viewing of this tape touched off his ground-born suspicions, it's certainly touched off mine on certain major topics—such as whether Captain Ramirez deceived the rest of the executive or only half of it; or whether Pratap Tamun was specifically after this tape when he staged his mutiny; or whether this crew should worry about the integrity of command; or whether Mr. Jenrette, whom you snatched fairly precipitately out of my security team once this tape turned out to be an issue, is going to be available to me to fill in where this tape stops. And as to why Captain Ramirez ordered me born twenty years ahead of the mission I ended up being uniquely suited to perform, I don't believe in coincidence. He knew something. He intended something. You've spent twenty years of my life voting no on every single issue I've been involved in, and probably before that. So I'm asking if you had good reason to vote that way."

"Good reason." Sabin seemed surprised, even amused, somewhere in the outrage. "And we're to discuss these delicate situations with Mr. Cameron present and his security wired to the hilt. Do you intend to provide a translation to your staff, Mr. Cameron?"

"If you ask my discretion, again, my particular interests involve the dowager's safety and the mission's success. We won't jeopardize this ship. Personal issues between members of the ship's executive are likely outside our concern or interest. But serious questions are posed here, captain, and the tape is disturbing. I'd suggest even at your level you suspect Captain Ramirez *didn't* tell you half what was going on, and that what happened at Reunion on your last visit didn't involve unanimous decisions of the executive of this ship."

He hadn't put that the most straightforwardly possible. He'd backed around the issue and given Sabin the broadest possible avenue to maneuver. And Sabin took a moment, thinking.

"Not bad, this *tea*."

"A planetary gift," Jase murmured.

"Addictive," Sabin said.

"An easy habit to form, at least."

"Like a hell of a lot else that's insinuated itself aboard! Hype up on sugar, calm down with tea, never ask what it does to the body. *Poison's* at least decently evident in the aftermath."

Sabin rarely brought up the unfortunate dinner party.

"This *isn't* poison, is it?"

"No, ma'am," Jase said. "This is my personal store. And lest we ever forget, you're in command of the ship getting there and getting home again, while I'm not remotely confident I could do that. So I'm extremely determined you should survive in good health."

"Home," Sabin observed. In fact it *was* a curious word for *Phoenix* crew to use about any destination besides the ship itself.

"Yes, ma'am," Jase said. "*Home* to the atevi world. After which I'll resign this post and leave your command unquestioned and forever untroubled by my existence."

Sabin's gaze strayed up past Jase's shoulder, to the barren shelves, the single framed photo, the fishing trip.

Snapped back, and hooded in speculation. "A captain of this ship wants to live on a ball of rock."

"I'm Ramirez's appointee," Jase said. "An interim solution to a specific problem, in no wise approaching your expertise or your talent, I've no question."

"Yet you get into the ship's log and distribute information on your own authority."

"I do specifically what I was trained to do, senior captain, which is to figure whether smart people are saying what they think they're saying when the words reach somebody not on their wavelength."

"You're determined you'll never lack employment."

"And I hope I'm useful, captain. Question: Tamun got into the captaincy and immediately mutinied, and died. Was it all about this tape?"

"Why would you suppose that Pratap Tamun has anything to do with this tape?"

"He was bridge crew. And how many of the crew that watch were sworn to secrecy, and how many of them had to hold onto suspicions for years, watching the executive lie to their cousins and mothers?"

"Lie?"

"Lie, captain. It's clear the images fed throughout the ship—maybe even to the bridge—were a lie. And the common crew is going to find out, now or later, assuming there's anyone alive on Reunion Station."

"Make it later. Once the mission's succeeded they won't care. If they find out before—it certainly won't serve this ship."

"On the whole, I've reached the same conclusion."

"Oh, I'm gratified."

"But if we can tell at a glance that that station's alive, so could anybody else coming here over the last nine years, and if someone has come calling, and if they're the same hostile aliens, the station won't have fooled them by playing dead and using spinner chambers way inside, which somehow some of us were left to assume. As good as put up signs saying *we're here.*

Let me pose you this, captain: let's assume—let's outright *assume* we're going to get there and find the station in ruins. Let's assume worse than that. Let's assume we're going to get there and discover humans don't own it any more. What's left for us? We should have told the crew the truth back at dock. If we don't tell them now and they get there and find trouble, where are we going to start telling the truth?"

"And I'm saying if that happens, crew's going to be too busy for questions. Stow this information and don't make trouble."

"What *did* you see when you were there last? What was Ramirez poking about in when the ship tucked tail and ran back to Reunion in the first place?"

"Stop at the first problem. Other operations aren't in your capacity."

"Why did Tamun finally turn on you, captain? And while you're at it—why was I ever born?"

"Both deeper questions than you ever want the answer to."

"Ramirez meant to double-cross the Guild years ago. Didn't he?"

"He had a lot of crazy notions."

"And you voted no every time."

"We have witnesses, Captain Graham. Maybe this is best said between us."

"Maybe it's not. Maybe at this point I'm done with secrets and having him here will save me the trouble of explaining it all. So treat him as family. Why? What were you voting against? Why were you always opposed to me?"

"Your ignorance isn't enough?"

"You can't provoke me out of asking the question, Captain. Why do I exist?"

"What's your guess?"

"That Ramirez had a private notion of a colony of

his own, one that the Guild might not find out about until it was too late."

Sabin didn't respond at once. She sipped cooling tea and set the cup down. "Well, you're smarter than I thought."

"It doesn't tell me an answer, what he wanted."

"Oh, you're fairly well on the track. He kept nosing about until he found trouble and until trouble found us. Then he had the notion of going back to Alpha colony. And when we did go back, and when he found what he found, it set him back, oh, for about an hour. By then, of course, we had limited options. And no fuel. And we knew that the island was founded by rebels against ship's authority; and that the atevi continent—having all its drawbacks—had natural resources the island didn't. So right from the start we had our problem—and we weren't that sure the trouble that hit Reunion wasn't coming on our tails. I didn't vote against refueling at Reunion. I didn't vote against refueling at Alpha. I didn't vote against cooperation with the atevi, for that matter. It was all we had left. It's all we still have left. I tell you, if I ever have to plant a space station, I'll do it in a populated, civilized region, not out around some remote rock with a disputed title, where you don't know who the owners are."

"That's what happened?"

"We haven't a clue what the aliens think. We're pretty sure we went where they objected to us being. Violently objected. As far as I'm informed, they didn't consult the space station to lodge an objection: they just hit it, took out half the mast and did major damage to the ring, fortunately missing the fueling port. End report. We hope, in the nearly ten years we've been building a space program and refurbishing Alpha Station, that Reunion has managed to patch itself up and gather in a load of fuel for us. If, as you say, worse isn't the case. That's the truth, pretty much as it's always been presented. Except the fact, evident to me, at least, that our chances of finding the station in one piece are minimal, for exactly the reason you cite, and our chances of convincing the crew we ought to give up on that station are nil until they know there are no surivivors. We *are* a democracy, junior captain, at the most damnedly inconvenient moments."

"I'm glad to hear it's not worse."

"Oh, it can easily be worse, sir. I assure you it can easily be worse."

"What *was* Captain Ramirez up to when he had me born?"

"Stani kept his own counsel," Sabin said. "Or he confided in Jules." That was Ogun, who was sitting back at the atevi station, managing a small number of ship's crew in technical operations—and in the building of another starship. "Frankly, Stani had a lot of pipe dreams involving what we could build out here. I'm more pragmatic. *Where* we are is *what* we are. And Taylor's Children aren't anything better than what *we* are."

"I'd agree, ma'am. Quite honestly, I would. What I do have for a resource is unique training."

"And, curiously enough, a certain divorcement from the past—as well as unique entanglements. You're Stani's pet project." From hostile, Sabin had become downright placid. "And by your own qualities, you're liked. It's occasionally useful to have a captain the crew likes."

"Crew's gotten rather fond of you, as happens. And they'd take the truth from you—now, if not before."

"Bull."

"Crew knows how you work, senior captain. Doing my job and yours. And they're grateful."

"You'll have me shedding tears."

"Truth. It's *my* skill, remember, to figure out what people are really saying about the powers that be."

"Doesn't matter what the crew thinks."

"I differ with you on that one."

"Differ all you like. You say you just know what people think. Fine. You don't figure me or you wouldn't have to ask."

"You're not simple, captain."

"I don't play your games. I don't give a damn. And don't plan to."

"Yet you took a chance and sponsored Tamun into office. You believed in him."

"He was qualified."

"And collectively, Ramirez and Ogun agreed and voted him in. And he turned on you. I take it he turned on you."

"You're asking if I sponsored the mutiny."

"I'm asking if you have any special clue why he turned the way he did."

"I'm a lousy judge of character."

"I still suspect it was about these tapes."

"You want to know the deep-down truth, second captain? I don't know and I don't give a damn at this late date. Tamun turned out to have an agenda I didn't know he had, and Stani and Jules didn't know he had. They took my advice. It was bad advice. A bad decision approved by all three of us. And since he's dead and the ones still with us that followed him have stepped sideways as far as they can, it doesn't matter these days, does it?"

"I hope it doesn't," Jase said. "I truly hope it doesn't. I want us to get there, grab any survivors we can find, and get out of the neighborhood forever, as fast as we can."

"And if there's other occupancy?"

"Just get out of the neighborhood as fast as we can."

Sabin leaned back, cup cradled in a careless hand. "You really want your question answered, why you were born?"

"I'm curious."

"It's possibly germane. Stani had a notion of contacting the civilization he thought he'd found. But it contacted *us,* didn't it? So much for reason and diplomacy."

Contacting the civilization, Bren thought, and felt cold clear through. Jase's instincts were right, if not his exact suspicions. Stani Ramirez had stepped *far* outside Guild rules—long before he returned to Alpha.

"I hope not to do that," Jase said, "contact the other side, that is."

"I'm glad you hope so," Sabin said, "because where we are and what we're doing, and where we're meddling, can bring all hell down on our heads. The short answer is—Ramirez had a plan. *You* were to advise him in his projected alien contact, whenever the chance came. And that didn't ever happen, did it?"

"I'd say," Jase said quietly, "that I never had the question posed. Ever. And if I had had it posed to me, senior captain, maybe things wouldn't have gone the way they did."

"You were a green kid. You couldn't do anything."

"And a year later he dropped me on the atevi planet. The point is, senior captain, he answered without me. Anything he did with the aliens was an answer. Leaving the scene was an answer. Maybe totally the wrong one. And anything we do in the future is under the same gun, with a bad start, because of things Captain Ramirez did that we may not even know about. I *need* to be on the bridge when we arrive in system. And log records that might tell us *what* he did would be extremely useful."

"Oh, now you want to give the tactical orders."

"In no way, senior captain. Advice. First thing I learned in the field: you don't have to speak to strangers to carry on conversation. Staying's an answer. Running's an answer. Shooting's a statement *or* an answer. Before the conversation gets to missiles, the ship needs a second observer. Another opinion. I may not belong in a captaincy—but I was competent enough in Shejidan that at least you don't have a war with *that* species. You need me there. You need Bren."

Sabin listened, give her credit. Bren found himself holding his breath, wondering dared he say a word, when a woman who controlled their ship, their movement, and the decisions the ship would make, considered all possible options.

"He's right, is he?" Sabin asked Bren suddenly.

"He's quite right," Bren said. "A good translator and an experienced cultural observer. The dowager's side of this agrees with him, and you, and I assure you we have no interest in exacerbating the situation."

"Gratifying."

"It would be a good idea for me to be on the bridge when we reach our destination."

"No."

Deep breath. Reasonable tone: carefully reasonable tone. "If you should confront a situation you don't expect, captain, you might not have time to send for us and brief us. If everything's as you expect, you don't need us and we'll know that. If it isn't, you'll have a second immediate analysis from me and from Jase, with what *we* know about talking to strangers, granted we have no choice. My immediate advice is . . . don't talk without analyzing the situation."

Sabin raked him up and down with a glance, turned to Jase. And back again.

"And if we have to move suddenly, rather than talk, Mr. Cameron, you can dent the wall. You stay belted in belowdecks until we call you."

Amazing. Astonishing. *That* was an agreement.

"My staff would likely agree with that, Captain. But expert advice in a dicey situation—"

"*After* we arrive. We'll come in far enough out, we'll be searching for our destination. Plenty of time. Take it or leave it."

"Accepted, captain." He *had* won access, unexpected, and a good thing, in his own summation: time to stop asking. Time to get out of the crossfire.

"So, Captain Graham," Sabin said.

"Ma'am," Jase said.

"You're going to offer your sage advice."

"I appreciate that, senior captain."

"You were always supposed to be the expert. You and Mercheson's kid." Yolanda. "Taylor's Children. Nice symbol. The completion of the ship's mission. The holy mission to spread human culture. Ramirez didn't trust what might have happened at Alpha. Not because of the aliens—because of the humans. Because they hated the Guild. Because they'd be numerous, if they'd survived at all, and they'd be hard to direct. If he'd gone to Alpha in the beginning, everything might have been different, but he didn't. He had this notion of *controlling* the change he was going to make in human affairs. He had this notion of keeping his maneuvers secret—and it couldn't be a secret if he took the ship back to Alpha and opened up that old issue. Guild would find out where he'd been and they'd want answers. Controlling the contact of aliens with the Guild—sitting in charge of everything—that was his notion. Quietly becoming a power the Guild couldn't control. But his venture brought retribution down on the station, and he ended up going precisely the direction he didn't want to go—toward Alpha. This was the set of decisions that put us where we were. And he and his faction still ran the ship. You ask about Tamun. Tamun sounded good, to answer your question. He was my chance to get another no vote on the board, a counter to Ramirez and Ogun. But when a captaincy came up, no, the situation out here wasn't one of those pieces of information we immediately discussed with Pratap Tamun. We were more concerned with problems where we were—the battle to keep some kind of balance against Ramirez's unilateral decisions. Maybe I should have raised the Reunion issue with him before he got the seat. I didn't. What I did know—he didn't accept where Ramirez had led us. He wanted separation from nonhuman influences."

"Separation from the atevi?"

"Separation from the atevi. Building up the Mospheirans. Helping humans take over the mainland."

Appalling. Evidencing a vast lack of understanding. "Mospheira wouldn't have any interest in ruling the mainland," Bren said. "They wouldn't have the manpower to run the continent if they had it handed to them, and they don't see any reason to want it."

"The way they didn't have any interest in fueling the ship or maintaining the station."

"They're farmers and shopkeepers," Bren said, "and no, their ancestors didn't have any interest in doing that for your ancestors. They still don't."

"Which is why atevi are running the place," Sabin muttered. "Which is all well and good. At least someone's running things. And not doing a bad job of it, as turns out. But Tamun was a humans-only sort, vehemently so. I've come toward a more moderate view, but in an unfriendly universe—I still don't trust books or faces I can't read."

From hate and loathing to pragmatic, even educated, acceptance? No, it wasn't an easy step. More, Sabin had always shown a canny awareness of that ambiguity of signals that was so, so, dangerous between two armed species. In her way, Sabin had dealt intelligently with the hazards of interspecies cooperation, reasoning out a caution the Mospheiran fools trying to yacht over to atevi territory in friendship or on smuggling missions didn't remotely grasp.

"Was Tamun Guild?" Bren asked bluntly.

"He never said. What mattered in the long run was exactly what you originally said, Mr. Cameron. The man was so blinded by his agenda that he couldn't count. He couldn't get it into his head that atevi had all the numbers, and when it turned out atevi would do what we needed and get us operational and that we *could* deal with them, he couldn't change his views. That change was where *I* stopped voting no, as you may have noticed. When it came to getting the ship up and running, when it came to the station having power and a viable population, well, then I *could* deal with my personal reluctance—my *regret* that some of those historic human skills you were born to learn, Captain Graham, were, in that very process, becoming irrelevant. But I wasn't so regretful for dead languages and lost records that I'd kill the last chance we had to keep the ship alive out here. I wasn't that enthusiastic for the Archive, that *I* had time to sit down and learn old languages, so in the end I suppose they don't matter that much."

"One person *can't* learn the Archive," Bren said. "But one person can save it. *Ramirez* saved it, when he sent it down to the planet. And you know that the part of it Jase knows *isn't* irrelevant. A language freights its history, its culture, inside itself. Its structure is the bare-bones blueprint for a mindset. Know one, gain insights into another. That's how we repair the damage Ramirez did."

"Blueprints for another starship. That's the relevant part of the Archive," Sabin said. "A starship and the guns to defend ourselves from Ramirez's mistakes."

"As a last resort," Bren said.

"I'm only interested in one thing," Sabin said harshly. "Running through this charade of a rescue mission as fast as we can, having our look around and convincing crew to give up, without dragging an alien armada back on our tail. If I was going to lie, gentlemen, I could *lie* to the crew without going all the way in there. But we will go in. I want this question actually settled and done with. If they're dead, they're dead, and we go on."

"The Archive at Reunion," Jase added, "has to be deleted. No matter what."

"We do what we can."

"Senior captain, a piece of history, one of those irrelevant bits: Earth had a very famous piece of rock called the Rosetta Stone, a translation key that put two languages together in the same context—one known, one hitherto undecipherable. If the aliens get a live human and that record, captain—and we don't know what they have, at this point—"

"Hell with your rocks. If some batch of aliens track our wake, we're dead and Alpha is dead. End of relevance to anything. We take out the Archive if we can. We have a look around and we go back to Alpha. It's the recent knowledge that matters. Getting the ship refueled, finding out what's going on there and getting out unobserved is number one priority. Granted there's fuel convenient, which I personally doubt. I'm not an optimist."

"Can we reach Gamma?" Jase asked.

That drew a quirk of the brow. "Maybe. Maybe *that's* been hit. So, between you, me, and our guests," Sabin said, on that sober note, "if I have to form a completely cheerful concept of where we're going, it involves a functioning station with a full fuel load and nothing more exotic, thank you. So you can remain irrelevant. So we can rescue enough people to make the crew happy. Or prove it's impossible. This always was a crackpot mission, purely on crew pressure, nothing more.—Mr. Kaplan, another, if you please."

"Yes, ma'am." Kaplan moved instantly, filled the cup, gave it back.

"So if you ask me what you haven't pressed, would I fake a new tape? No. But I'll use this one. Am I going to deal politically with the Pilots' Guild if we find anyone alive? Damned right I am, and if we're lucky enough to have fuel, we're going to be very correctly Guild until the ship's fueled and ready. Do we have that, Mr. Cameron? If we do find a live station, you're going to take orders and keep your alien aristocrats under tight orders and out of sight."

"I perfectly follow your reasoning, captain. Though I'm not the one who gives the orders in that department."

"I deal with *you*. What's your diplomacy worth if you can't persuade your own side?"

"Point taken, captain. Meanwhile—can we get the log record from the incident that sent your ship running off to Gamma?"

"*Second,* we're not disseminating log records among the crew. Or to the Mospheirans. That's *my* diplomacy. Hear me?"

Somehow Sabin had rather well hijacked their agreement. Their security already knew and wouldn't talk. The dowager was the soul of secrets. Gin would inevitably find out. That left only the ship's crew still in the dark. And Sabin was still the autocrat she was determined to be.

"Give us the log records, captain. I'd think you'd want all the information you could get out of that incident. We can extract it. We can possibly give you information you don't know you have."

"We're in transit, headed for a ship-move, Mr. Cameron. Am I going to abort that operation for some piddling records search?"

"You might well," Bren said levelly, "if informing your own resource people what you might have done wrong the last time saved you all those small inconveniences you name."

"We'll see," Sabin said.

We'll see, by experience, could take forever. But it was what they had. Sabin sipped her tea and talked about the day's schedule as if there was nothing in all creation out of the ordinary, a rapidfire series of hours and acronyms that made only marginal sense to an outsider, but that Jase seemed to follow.

"Well," Sabin said, then, reaching the bottom of the small cup, "some of us go on duty at this hour." She set down the cup, got up and gathered up her security. "Thank you for breakfast, Captain Graham. Good night to you. Good morning, Mr. Cameron."

"Good morning," Bren murmured, as Jase murmured the same, at the edge of his night. Foreign habits. Planetary habits. Sabin used the expression consciously, in irony, Bren was quite sure, and after the door shut, with Jase's security and Sabin and her security on the other side of it, he realized he'd just held his breath.

"We're alive," he said.

"Don't joke," Jase said.

"Do you *believe* that?" Bren asked.

"That she took it that well? I don't. Meanwhile what you do with the tape is in your discretion. I trust you."

They'd reached, as Sabin had observed, the end of Jase's day and the dawn of his. The information was in his hand. The map and that record and the pieces of information he'd gathered were going to keep his staff and the dowager's very busy for the next number of hours. If only, God help them, they could get those log records on what Stani Ramirez had done. But if he went on pushing Sabin, they might lose the cooperation they did have.

"This the last time I'm going to see you before we move?" Bren asked.

"Likely." Jase offered his hand, a quick, solid grip. "We'll work on it. I'll nudge her about those records, much as I can. Likely one more day's work before the move, but unless something comes up, I'm going to be seeing to details up here on one-deck . . . for days."

"Same below," Bren said, and let go the handshake—wishing, after a year of numbing tedium intermittent with bone-shaking anxiety, that they'd had this information at the start of the voyage, not at the end. At the start, back at Alpha, things had seemed cut-and-dried simple: go back, fulfill what the crew thought was a plain promise of rescue of their stranded relatives, if the station survived, and pull the old Guild off Reunion, destroying all sensitive records in the process. Only on the voyage the wider truth of the senior captains' assessment of the situation began leaking out, bit by bit, incident by incident. The only senior available to them here was Sabin. The other, Ogun, was back managing things at Alpha— presumably not pushing relations with the atevi further or faster than prudent.

And typical of any dealing with *Phoenix's* original

four captains—he wished he knew which half of all Sabin said *was* the truth, or what resources she held that had made her willing to agree to this voyage, and what secrets she still kept close. More fuel reserve than they'd ever admitted to their allies who'd filled their tanks? A potential fuel dump at a place called Gamma? On both accounts, very reassuring news, though it would have slowed refueling efforts back at Alpha and given political ammunition to those who hadn't want to fuel the ship at all.

But both the possibility of repair to the station and a fear of finding alien presence there? Was that Sabin's natural voyage-end pessimism at work, or a long-held conclusion based on more information than they'd yet laid hands on?

Jase had to work with the woman, had to maintain cooperation and simultaneously keep alert for sudden shifts in Sabin's intentions—about which they were *still* not convinced.

"Take care," Bren wished him.

"Take care," Jase said, too, and added, pointedly, counting the aiji-dowager down on five-deck, full of justifiable questions of her own: "Good luck."

3

There was no extended comment from Banichi and Jago, even in the lift: there, the ship's eavesdropping was a given. There was no comment, at first, as they crossed toward the closed door of their own section, through that foyer they shared with Kroger's corridor.

But for the first time it was moderately safe to talk, in Ragi. "You followed most of it," Bren said, "nadiin-ji."

"Certainly important points, nadi-ji," Banichi said. "But not enough to be confident of understanding Sabin-aiji." Banichi let them through the closed section door and into the long corridor that was their own domain. The dowager's staff stood guard, as always, and passed them on without a word.

"No one understands Sabin-aiji," Bren muttered. "She deliberately obscures her actions."

"One perceives," Jago said as they walked, "that there may have been a falsified television image when last the ship visited this station. That more secret records may be at issue."

"True in both instances." He gathered his breath for an explanation. Didn't even know where to start, about Ramirez's actions and Jase's suspicions, that ran back for decades.

A missile from out of the galley hit the corridor wall.

Ricocheted to the floor.

And skidded toward them on the tiles.

A red-fletched, blunt arrow.

With a whisper of leather and a light jingling of silver weapon-attachments, Jago bent down and gathered it from their feet.

A young atevi face peered from the dowager's galley, down the corridor. Gold eyes went very wide.

"No, we are *not* the indulgent side of staff," Jago said ominously. "I am Assassins' Guild on duty, young aiji, escorting the aiji of the heavens to his apartments in dignity fit for his office, young aiji. I react quickly to threat. Fortunately for you, young aiji, I react as quickly in restraint, a lesson which in future might prove more beneficial than archery. Do you know what your *father* would say if he saw this arrow at Bren-aiji's feet?"

The future aiji exited the door, bow in hand, and stood contrite . . . as tall as a grown human; but far shorter than adult atevi. "Jago-ji, I put another lamina on the bow."

"Evidently." Jago strode to the point of impact, which bore a slight dent. Young muscles as solid as an adult human's had put a fair draw on a bow that had grown thicker on this voyage—a bow with added strength, since the boy had tinkered with it. "You have damaged the ship."

"It's only a dent, Jago-ji."

Oh, we *are* getting bold, Bren thought, wondering what his staff *was* going to do with this burgeoning personality, if they all lived so long. That sullen look was his father's. Or—one dreaded to think—his grandfather's.

"Dare you say so?" Jago was not daunted. And

towered over the boy. "*Dare* you say so? Did you
build this ship? Did you place those panels? Do you
command those who can?"

Clearly the answer was no. Cajeiri didn't command
anything about the ship.

"So?" Jago said. "Do you fancy going to Sabin-aiji
and asking someone to repair it?"

Set of the jaw. "I would go to Sabin-aiji."

"That would hardly be as wise as an aiji needs to
be," Banichi said in his deep voice. "Do you know
why?"

Clearly that answer was no, too. But the boy was
not a complete fool, and lowered the level of
aggression.

"I was seeing how hard it would hit," Cajeiri said.

"And did not intend to dent the ship?"

"I beg pardon, nadiin."

"Wrap the points," Jago said shortly, "aiji-ma. Be
wiser."

"Yes, Jago-nadi." The young wretch set the offending instrument of war butt-down on the deck, its
heel in his instep, and unstrung it. He took the arrow
from Jago. And bowed to authority, attempting charm.
"Good morning, Bren-nandi. Is Jase-aiji coming
down?"

"Little pitchers with big ears," Bren translated the
human proverb, which Cajeiri understood and thought
funny. "I have had my meeting with Jase. It was very
nice, thank you."

"Grandmother wants you to come to breakfast,"
Cajeiri said. "But the hour is past breakfast."

One could imagine she wanted to hear from him.

"She has not yet invited me, nadi."

"I told Narani. I brought the message."

"Staff does these things quite efficiently on their
own," Banichi said dryly. "If you can shoot at lord

Bren, you can manage beyond the children's language, am I correct?"

"No," Cajeiri said defensively. He was only seven. Consequently he spoke Ragi without the architecture of courtesies and rank and elaborate numerology of his seniors. He had liberties appropriate to his age—and was bored beyond bearing, being the only seven-year-old aboard. Ship's crew had left their minor children, considering it was not a safe voyage.

But the aiji in Shejidan had sent his son on a voyage that should teach him more than bad behavior and dangerous familiarity.

"I shall see the aiji-dowager," Bren said. "Go beg Narani-nadi to arrange some graceful hanging on this wall, to save the servants asking each other who could have damaged our residence."

"Yes, Bren-aiji."

"And regard security's advice. Aijiin do not defend themselves with bows and arrows—"

"With guns, Bren-nadi!"

"Not even with guns, Cajeiri-nadi. Their staffs defend them. The very humblest servant who locks a bedroom window at night defends them. Not to mention the Assassins' Guild, who do carry guns, and whose reactions are very quick, and not to be trifled with. Please live to grow up, young aiji. Your father and mother would be very disappointed otherwise. So even would your great-grandmother."

Cajeiri's eyes . . . they looked at one another eye to eye . . . grew very large.

"And by no means forget," Bren said, "that I am several times your age. So your father would remind you."

"Yes, Bren-aiji."

He *liked* the boy. And *like* was for salads. *Love* was for flavors of fruit drink. It wasn't an emotion one could even translate for a species that operated by hierarchies and grouping and emotionally charged associations.

"You are within my man'chi," was as close as he could come. "No matter you behave like this. But be careful. The ship is going to move soon. We're going into a place of considerable danger."

"Are we?" Eagerness. The boy *was* seven. "Is it the lost station?"

"It may be. Meanwhile—wrap the arrowheads. Don't shoot my staff. And see me later. I'm sure we can find some new videos for the trip."

"Some human ones!"

"Some human ones, too." They had a store of them. A large store. In consideration where they were going and the risks they ran, they'd dumped a great deal of the human Archive from the ship, entrusting it to the planet and the station of their origin. But they'd kept a few useful bits. "Now apologize, and then off with you to tell Narani."

"One is very sorry," the scoundrel said, with all his father's winning ways, and bowed to him and to Jago and Banichi. "One is doubly sorry, nadiin-ji. And begs to be excused."

"Go," Banichi said, and the boy escaped.

Galley staff had watched all this from the open door.

"One is equally sorry, nandi," the cook said—the dowager's men, all young, except the cook; and bet that Cenedi, the dowager's chief of security, had had an immediate report about the dent that had sprung, likely without much warning, from the depths of their premises.

"One very well understands, nadi," Bren said. Never turn aside an atevi apology: they came when due. "One is informed the dowager has sent for me?"

"You were expected at breakfast, nandi," the cook said. "The aiji-dowager is now in her study."

"I'd better go there immediately," he said to his staff.

"One will inform Narani," Jago said, and they turned back toward the dowager's main doors, their own unvisited—well, except by a boy on a life-saving mission. The dowager was not long on patience.

Several doors back, in their relatively compact living arrangement, this linear, human-designed interlock accommodated what should be roughly circular routes, by atevi habit. Atevi ingenuity did manage: the dowager's household accessed the bone-numbing cold of a service tunnel running behind the cabins' back walls for brief, discreet trips past the dowager's front door, where a guest entered.

He rapped softly—a shared custom—rather than use the signal button. The door opened. Cenedi had a small, highly electronic secretary desk in the curtained-off foyer. Cenedi was often at work there, and Cenedi was on the spot at the door, right behind the dowager's major domo. Expecting them—no miracle, given their ubiquitous communications links.

"Welcome," Cenedi said. "Welcome, nandi."

"Indeed, thank you, Cenedi-ji.—I shall keep the coat, nadi." This for a servant who silently offered to take it. The dowager's favored temperatures were too cold for comfort—this, the woman who preferred a drafty mountain fortress with minimal plumbing to the luxury of temperate—and political—Shejidan.

He retained his coat, left Banichi and Jago to their ordinary social interface with the dowager's security, and followed the servant's polite lead to the service access, a bone-chilling walk three doors down, a duck of the head to get into the comparative heat of the dowager's underheated study.

They could have gone back into the main corridor. The dowager did otherwise. The staff did otherwise. So her guests, once admitted to her premises, did otherwise.

The dowager occupied a chair in what was, given the carefully restrained objects on the shelves, an office-study cumlibrary—in short, all those functions that in the dowager's establishment were sanity-saving and civilized.

The dowager, knitted shawl about her, read. And looked up from her book.

Scowling. Darkly scowling.

"You coddle the boy."

Where *was* her communications link? He had never spotted it.

"He's bigger than I am," Bren said, and it struck the dowager's humor. She laughed, and laughed, and moved her cane to tap the other chair.

He sat. He didn't begin a report. He waited about two breaths.

"So," she said. "And how is Sabin-aiji?"

"Well," he said.

"Have you broken your fast?"

"No, aiji-ma, but—"

"But. But. But. Will you have breakfast? Or tea?"

"I fear my stomach could by no means deal with a breakfast, aiji-ma, and I have had tea upstairs."

"And your estimate?"

That was the formal invitation. "Aiji-ma, you know the ship-aijiin lied to the crew."

Impatient wave of the hand. "Estimate of Sabin-aiji."

"A difficult book to read, aiji-ma, a palimpsest of several regimes on this ship, and to this hour I cannot know precisely which layer has the truth. But she acts as if she expected Jase-aiji to find that tape. She is aware that it was falsified. And in my own opinion, that deception may have served us all. The crew would have been very difficult for the aijiin to manage over the last decade if they had known from the start that there were survivors back at the original station. They would most surely have diverted all energy toward refueling the ship precisely for this voyage, and subverted all construction toward that end. Neither Mospheirans nor atevi would have agreed with that as a priority, one is sure, and one is convinced Ramirez foresaw that. If there were no particular haste to return, the crew would take any order. Pratap Tamun's attempt to take power—this is my own guess, aijima—might indicate a certain suspicion within the certain levels of the crew. He may have used his suspicion to blackmail the other ship-aijiin into conceding to his demands—but he lacked proof. His kidnapping of Ramirez instead of killing him suggests he wanted something Ramirez could give. I used to wonder what. Now I strongly suspect it was an admission of information on this tape—or beyond it, from some meeting of Ramirez's men with station authorities."

"And this tape shows?"

"Corridors lacking power or air . . . in which the search team walks—walks, with the appearance of gravity, which, aiji-ma, cannot be created without stable rotation, and stable rotation of a damaged station is no accident. That is the sensitivity of this record, on a pinpoint. At a certain point they disappear into a working airlock and the tape ends. Which is also against regulations, Jase-aiji informs us. That record should not have terminated, but it does. They preserve the secrets of their negotations with their Guild."

"Shall we be surprised at this?"

"No, aiji-ma. In retrospect, one thinks not. But that raises another question: *did Ramirez act on his own?*

Jase suspects the timing in which he and Yolanda were created, decades before their usefulness in Shejidan. Jase suspects Ramirez had ambitions to create yet another colony, secret from the Guild. But Sabin suggests Ramirez meant to contact foreigners—spacefaring foreigners, and that his intrusion into sensitive foreign territory prompted the attack on Reunion."

"Bypassing atevi? How were these persons preferable?"

Trust the dowager to see to the heart of a matter. "One believes, aiji-ma, that it was not so much fear of atevi as fear of detection, if he diverted the ship to a known and forbidden destination—the old colony; and fear that contacting humans once hostile to the Guild would be very difficult to manage. He had no idea of the technical advances atevi might have made. He wanted potent, spacefaring allies. And found potent, spacefaring enemies, as seems, from some place he visited."

"And where is this place?"

"Out among the stars. Sabin-aiji strongly suggests Ramirez disturbed and alarmed a foreign world."

"As Mospheirans dropped down on us, abusing our hospitality. Is once not enough?"

"One hardly thinks Ramirez's intentions were to land. In this case, aiji-ma, the owners of the planet were out in space and armed. And resented his intrusion."

"Bad habits will get one in trouble."

"One concurs, aiji-ma. In this—very likely they did."

"Why run such a risk, counting its previous failure?"

He had no clear answer, even for himself, on a human level. "Desire to throw off an oppressive authority, one might surmise. The Pilots' Guild is that. Desire for alternatives. Atevi, to his knowledge, had only mastered the steam engine. He thought, mistakenly, that contact would be easy—it had been easy, with atevi, before the ship left. It lent him false confidence. In seeking allies, he found an enemy—or made one, by error. He never had a chance to engage Jase in the contact—Jase was, at the time, quite junior. He was unprepared, and fled. This may have been a grave mistake."

"So. This fills in the shadows of the image, but only slightly. Ramirez was ambitious. Are we utterly surprised at his ambition?"

"We are not, aiji-ma. Not wholly. But he was desperate, perhaps, as desperate as ambitious—wholly dependent on the station for fuel. Everything he did found limits on fuel needs. I surmise they continually planned his missions and kept the ship on a tight rein precisely because they lacked confidence in the captains' man'chi. A powerful ally would have utterly upset the balance and given the ship alternatives, resources, everything at a stroke. And patience is not a ship virtue. He looked elsewhere than Alpha, continually niggling away at something he could do undetected. A second contact, with those he might deal with in secret, changing the ship's man'chi, establishing himself as aiji, making his power firm before challenging his Guild."

"History has sharp teeth, Bren-paidhi. Both our species have found that true." Ilisidi took a placid sip of tea. "So. So. One always wondered what lay within Ramirez's energetic and open-handed approach to us."

"Not only to you, as now seems, aiji-ma. But you were by then used to humans."

"A truly reckless man. So we read him in his deal-ings. If the paidhi-aiji had not intervened—who knows what his contact with us would have been when he returned? A disaster. Clearly a disaster."

"He had prepared Jase to deal with outsiders. This time, Jase and Yolanda having had intense prepara-tion, he did engage their services—having more fore-sight than his ancestors, on a year-long voyage toward that meeting. I respect him for that act of foresight, aiji-ma, but, yes, he was reckless. Utterly. And naive in his approach to outsiders. He should have consulted them when his contact with outsiders went wrong—although possibly the incident proceeded too rapidly to brief newcomers to the situation. One has no idea."

"He was reckless. He offended strangers. He brought ruin on his Guild. And what shall we do with this knowledge, Bren-paidhi?"

"Little else we can do, now, aiji-ma, but go to the station and hope to find what Ramirez left in no worse condition than it was."

"And if there are worse conditions?"

"Jase-aiji tells me we have resources to pull off to a nearby refuge, one where Gin-aiji and her robots can work, though it would be chancy and slow. One suspects Sabin-aiji has had that contingency very much in mind. I confess I have increasing misgivings about the planning for this venture."

"Which we have left in human hands."

"I have requested more information on Ramirez's past actions, aiji-ma. Jase is attempting to learn, and he takes our view. But Sabin forecasts a ship-move tomorrow. The *last* ship-move, so they think, before our destination. We are forced toward this event, pre-cipitately so."

"Inconvenience," Ilisidi said with a grimace. "Uncomfortable, these transitions. One wearies of them. And far too much to hope that these remote station-folk at our destination dine better than we."

"One greatly doubts it, aiji-ma." His misgivings on Sabin's misdirection of his request were heard. Not discussed. Not discussable, since there was nothing, in the dowager's opinion, to be done, except to note the fact against Sabin. Therefore she changed the subject. "One doubts we will find much comfort there."

"We equally doubt that Reunion has entertaining sights to see. We have extensively *seen* a station."

Be brave, she was telling him. Steady on course. Be calm.

"I fear we could never promise the aiji-dowager grand entertainments there."

"Ah, well." The dowager adjusted her laprobe. "We have seen very curious things on our voyage, all the same. Whatever the outcome, we have learned the names of two hundred stars and seen one eat another—Grigi-ji will be envious."

"That he will, aiji-ma." The Astronomer Emeritus would have given his aged life to be on this voyage—but health and duties and the pleas of his students had, the dowager had said, dissuaded him.

"Do you suppose Sabin-aiji plots revenge on this household?"

Back to the Sabin matter. Back to questions of reliability of human authority in charge of this ship—a logical question, since she'd served Sabin poison at her dinner-party, letting Sabin choose it, to be sure: baji-naji. And in that chaotic revolution, she'd made sure that Sabin would *not* dictate to atevi where they spent the voyage, and *not* restrict atevi movements or communications on a ship on which her grandson might have designs of ownership—if atevi had one species-wide bad habit, it was that tendency to take for themselves anything they could lay hands on, if there was no preventative civilized agreement . . . and ship-humans had never quite established their willingness to defend their own ship.

Now the dowager asked, having been informed about Sabin's ignoring his request for information—has Sabin a lingering intention of revenge?

And he had to say, with far too little information—"One doubts it would be related to that, aiji-ma. She seems to take the matter of the dinner as a known hazard in dealing with foreigners."

"And her opinion of the situation?"

"By her history, she might decide to favor the Pilots' Guild for certain reasons, in some attempt against Ogun's authority, on our return to our world. But as regards the incident of the dinner—with this one particular woman, I believe a decision to act against atevi would be a policy decision, no personal vendetta. *Humans* find this woman difficult to predict. It is a trap to find some of her actions atevi-like and reasonable."

It was wry humor. Ilisidi was wryly amused. But took the information behind those lively eyes and stored it.

"A grudge is not efficient," Bren added. "And very few of Sabin's acts carry inefficient ornament."

"One finds it very tempting to think one understands this woman."

"A trap, very certainly a trap. I remind myself daily not to view her as, say, a miniature Tatiseigi."

That did amuse Ilisidi. The aiji's wife's uncle, Cajeiri's former guardian, possibly Ilisidi's lover, was a notorious stickler for tradition, often offended in this era of fast food and faster transport—and a notorious participant in various schemes.

"Ah," Ilisidi said, "but Tatiseigi would have invited us all to dinner."

True. And made them sweat every minute of it, likely doing nothing at all.

He was amused in turn.

"And do you think she may yet invite us?" Ilisidi asked.

"Her customs are by no means atevi, aiji-ma. But this is how I read her. Ramirez deceived the crew in his pursuing alien contact. He kept that secret from his Guild. And from the moment he saw the station in ruins, he knew he had to persuade his crew to leave the ruined station behind, or embroil himself in the rebuilding and defense of the station, which would, I believe, have been a mistake—binding the ship to a hazardous location, and not using the assets he had—notably Jase and Yolanda. He lied quickly and efficiently. One suspects he grieved not at all for the Guild—but he had to refuel, and he lied to Guild authority, telling them that he was going to our world to find out if there were useful resources there. Perhaps he even offered them the chance to board, and they refused. One suspects so. And failing the Guild's delivering themselves to his authority, he maintained his deception of his own crew and left, with or without his Guild's permission. And of course once he reached our world, it became necessary to deal with atevi instead, and to take nearly ten years making Alpha Station viable. Then . . ." On this point he was far from certain. "Then he did something curious, given all the rest. He refueled this ship, as his health failed, and in dying, told Jase the truth about survivors at Reunion. He also managed to talk where someone could overhear: whether that was intentional or not, it certainly put the heat under the pot, as the proverb runs." All of this latter history Ilisidi knew as well as he, but he was aiming the arrow of logic at a particular point and the dowager listened with remarkable patience. "So the crew, once they heard, demanded to go back, and of course, the ship being fueled, the surviving captains found it expedient to concede to this voyage—Sabin protested being the captain in charge, but Ogun-aiji ordered her to go—logical, since he communicates far more easily with the planet, and Sabin-aiji is far more skilled with the ship. Sabin-aiji undertakes this mission under protest . . . she finds herself poisoned before the ship leaves dock, and accedes to the arrangement that atevi will go where they like—as human crew can't, on this ship. Understand, aiji-ma, that very, very many who work aboard have never set foot in the control center—persons whose jobs run ordinary operations, maintenance, cooking, cleaning—lately, opening and provisioning the three decks of the ship that can take the population of the space station and feed and house it, as if we shall indeed find survivors—which Sabin now avows she very much doubts. Yet all this work proceeds."

"Keeping the populace quiet."

"Indeed, aiji-ma. A very few at top who know everything, and a great many common folk who have to trust their aijiin to make good decisions . . . and who may waver in their man'chi if previous lies become evident. Therein the ship's authority has operated in some fear of discovery. And Jase has uncovered one lie. One suspects there are others."

"Insurrection?"

"The crew's patience is fragile. Their expectations come closer and closer to the moment of truth. Jase now knows the image they were shown belowdecks was completely, deliberately falsified. If they see the same sight as we come in, they will know they were deceived. And that will lead them to question Ramirez, whom they hold as their great aiji. If that reputation cracks—indeed there will be a crisis of man'chi—

partly grounded in the fact that Sabin already distrusts the crew. She affects to choose her isolation from those of her man'chi—not as mad as it sounds, for a human, aiji-ma, even a sign of strength—but a fragile strength, once the crew becomes disaffected and rebellious. And that could happen: the old Guild is very generally blamed even by the crew for past bad decisions, and crew has abandoned that Guild, blaming it for whatever dangerous situation exists. In their view, innocent persons could have been rescued from the station immediately if the Guild hadn't ordered Ramirez to the contrary."

"This, you say, is the popular rumor. Is it, however, true?"

"We have no idea. We suspect even Sabin lacks information—she avows that Ramirez created Jase and Yolanda to deal with aliens he hoped would give him a means to defy the Guild. One listened to Sabin say so—and remembers at the same time that Sabin herself may have stronger man'chi toward the Guild than any of the other captains, living or dead. Jase, on the other hand, lacking other information, believed he and Yolanda were created to deal with the Mospheiran colony. But the plain truth is, we have no knowledge what Ramirez promised the Guild before he left for our world. He may have lied to everyone, top to bottom."

"Ah, what a lovely nest of contrary intent."

"Ship's records might clarify this. Jase persists in trying to obtain them—but the ship-move will give us no time to deal with anything we learn at our best advantage, even if he can get the records from Sabin. And they may not be relevant when we get there. This ship has been away from Reunion for a decade. Anything could have happened there."

"Certain things have happened on this ship, have

they not? We will not, as a start, recognize the authority of this Guild to be above our own."

Could one ever doubt the dowager's resolve? And that *was* the order of the universe he served—the point at which he and Jase might diverge, the point at which he had to be what he was—and Jase had to; and that was the way things would be.

"I know Gin-aiji will very strongly join you, aiji-ma. The Guild comes to us begging resources, after having mismanaged human affairs for several hundred years, and Mospheira has relations with the ship-aijiin, but *not* with the Guild at Reunion. Have no doubt that the Presidenta of Mospheira will stand behind you. Conceivably the crew of this ship might stand behind you, in any falling-out with their aijiin—though I would never predict that."

"Have you explained this state of affairs to Gin-aiji? Or to Jase?"

"I came straight to you, aiji-ma."

"Flatterer."

"Prudence, aiji-ma. Among humans, keeping one's subordinates in the dark is sometimes a matter of common sense and security—as long as one fails to mention it openly, Gin will take it for secret."

"A very tangled skein."

"For Gin's pride, if nothing else. She knows Sabin holds her in complete disregard. It's a sore point with her, but fails to provoke her."

"Sabin does not highly regard Mospheirans in general," the dowager observed.

"Sabin still views Mospheirans as rebels from ship authority, aiji-ma. She respects Tabini-aiji and she respects you, aiji-ma. If she wanted something from the planet, I'm sure she'd go straight to the aiji and negotiate without even thinking that the Presidenta of Mospheira—or Gin—might be able and willing to give her what she needed. Sabin doesn't want them here—far more than she suspects atevi intentions, she suspects Mospheirans. Ramirez's reasons for avoiding Alpha and courting outsiders were not only his."

"Curious," Ilisidi said. "Very curious thinking."

"Our ancestors were extremely hostile to their Guild."

"One sees a certain grounds for suspecting a hidden man'chi, paidhi-ji."

"Old feuds die harder than old loyalties, aiji-ma. Even Sabin might not realize how strong the old opinions are in her. And one worries, too, about attitudes among the population we mean to rescue. Who knows what the Guild told them—or what the truth is? *They* may have been told Ramirez refused to pick them up. I find it entirely possible he did refuse, in favor of first establishing his own authority at Alpha—which even Jase may not suspect. Mospheirans would not take that behavior well, if that were the case. Let alone the crew's opinion."

"Madness."

"Certainly a tangled mess, aiji-ma. I advise only keeping the lid on that pot."

"Never examine a stew too closely. It offends the cook. Consult your clever islanders. If Gin-aiji says anything useful, advise us."

He gave a wry smile. "I shall, nand' dowager." Half-frozen in the temperature the dowager favored, he took it for leave to go.

"Don't coddle that boy," she snapped.

"Yes, aiji-ma." He reached the door, slipped out. Servants, waiting all this time, breaths frosting in the chill, conducted him back through the labyrinth to the foyer.

Banichi and Jago had passed the brief interval at

tea with Cenedi—doubtless the eccentricities of the ship-aijiin had been the topic of the hour. And likely the dent in the hall had been a small issue. Last week it had been a spring-gun, and a sailing-plane launched from a slingshot prior to that.

"I need to speak with Gin, nadiin-ji," he told them, once they stood in the warmth of the main corridor. *I'll call her,* he'd almost said, meaning the intercom. He'd been an hour upstairs and that unacceptable notion just leapt out. He thought instead about going to her office, but that venue was not as secure, and if he was going to violate Sabin's clearly expressed wishes for secrecy, he wanted not to risk spreading the news to Gin's team. "Suggest to her staff she would be welcome in a social call."

"Asicho hears," Jago said.

"One will advise Narani," Banichi added.

Done, then. His arrangements moved with many more parts, but well-oiled, efficient. A dinner event of adequate size and service would happen if Ginny Kroger's staff and his managed to communicate. He could imagine it. *Yo! Gin! It's the atevi,* gracelessly shouted to Gin's office, would get a cheerful Mospheiran answer: *Sure I'll come. What time?*

Mospheirans viewed themselves as fussily formal.

They walked back to his apartment, where he shed the coat in favor of a dressing-robe. He was able to sit down and take notes, while invitations to Gin percolated through the vents, and while Banichi and Jago consulted Asicho in the security station, catching up on any untoward bit of business that might have gone on—the dent seemed the notable item on five-deck. He made a file, meanwhile, out of the upstairs conference, neatly indexed for points of particular interest, robotically translated, down to the point where the mindless machine couldn't tell the difference between like words and where his staff couldn't be expected to figure the meaning.

Noon passed. He skipped lunch. Jago brought him the transcript of the verbal exchanges upstairs, and he traded them Jase's tape.

"There's not too much to translate here," he said, "but index it carefully, nadi-ji."

"Yes," Jago said, and added, just as the door opened. "One believes that will be Gin-nadi and one of her staff."

"Excellent," he said. They hadn't disturbed him with the report, but the mission was accomplished. And as Narani showed Ginny into his makeshift study, Jago deftly picked off the aide and requested him, in passable Mosphei', to come for a separate, far less informative briefing.

"It's all right," Ginny assured her aide, who had to be used by now to the concept that when lords talked, aides made themselves invisible.

"Tea, Rani-ji," Bren requested. "Do sit, Gin. I take it you've heard a bit from my staff."

"At least the topic and the source." Ginny settled— sixtyish, no different than he'd first met her: thin, gray, with an inbuilt frown that hadn't been an instantly endearing feature when they'd first met. Nor had the habit of challenging him. He'd come to treasure that bluntness, and her. "I take it the senior captain isn't supposed to know we're talking."

"She knows she won't prevent us talking. But it *is* sensitive."

"Our problem or hers?"

"Both. I think in this we ought to accommodate her. If this does get out at the wrong moment, it could cause problems." Narani provided the tea, aromatic, safe for humans, tinged with fruit and spice. "Thank you, Rani-ji. We'll manage."

"Nandi." Narani politely withdrew—not the microphones that assured everything would be available for reference, but withdrew, at least, his visible presence. Ginny assuredly knew they were bugged, and came here without objection: it was just procedure, and she came.

And came, not infrequently, for the company the stuffy Mospheiran notion of hierarchy didn't give her within her small technical staff. Back on Mospheira, or in Shejidan, one held short, sharp meetings. Onboard ship, with far less diversion—meetings lasted, especially in the atevi section. Lasted through the afternoon, if need be. With tea and refreshments.

"So?" Ginny asked him, and he told her in great detail.

"Lied to the crew, too," Ginny said with a shake of her head. "Lied to the Guild, lied to Jase—lied to everybody. Not surprising."

"On Ramirez's side, there was some reason. It was a useful lie. And one Ramirez could have predicted would give him maximum maneuvering room with us. But still—"

"But still. But still. But still." Ginny, the guest, lifted her cup for a refill. They'd gone through one pot and were on their second. "You know, you always wonder what things would be like if there weren't these diversions into deception. Unvarnished truth never seems the ship's first recourse. The expectation that the crew would be rational. The expectation one's allies might just realize that ship command hasn't told the whole truth on any major point in the last three hundred years . . . I mean, don't they figure we'd figure, sooner or later? That crew would?"

Bren poured the bottom of the pot for himself. "I think they figure we'll figure they'll be lying and they'd only confuse everyone if they told the truth."

"Point," Ginny agreed. "But from the absolute start. From the very start of them going in, Ramirez, faking that image. Damn him. Chasing aliens, for God's sake. And he's the *good* guy."

"We assume he was on the side of the angels. Jase assumes he was. These days, Jase isn't any more sure of that than we are."

"Hell on Jase, stuck up there with Sabin-bitch for company. You think he can get those other records?"

"We're moving ship tomorrow. He's sticking close to Sabin. He says he'll try." Jase didn't know a thing about ops, or rather, knew as much as he'd been able to pick up by hearing, but he'd never so much as been on the bridge for a look around before being named captain by the aforesaid Ramirez. "I won one thing. I've asked—insisted—both the paidhiin should be on the bridge at arrival in system."

"And Sabin said?"

"Oh, she's not totally in favor. But she agreed."

"Good God."

"Sabin is not optimistic about this mission."

Ginny sipped the dregs of her tea. "I insist on optimism at this point. I'm ready for the alternative—at least the one that gets us out of there fast. But I hope there's fuel waiting for us and my robots and my staff don't have a thing to do but connect the lines and suck up the good news and load survivors. At a certain point I don't care what Jase's ancestors did. I want to get home. I want to win this."

A lengthy mining operation out in a stellar wilderness was one alternative. There were far worse ones to contemplate.

Like running straight out into alien guns.

"Let's hope," he said. "Let's hope for a fast, simple homecoming at the other end."

"It's springtime back home," she said meditatively, Mospheiran-like pouring herself another cup. "Did you know? Tourists on the north shore. Nice little bar in Port Winston. Orangelles. That's what I imagine. Orangelles, orangettes, limonas and chi'tapas. You can smell them in the air."

Fruit flavors. Flowers. Orchards in bloom.

"I'll settle for salt air and the waves," he said, since they were indulging fancy. Best air on earth. Best sound in the world. In his memory, he discovered, it was less Mospheira's north shore and more the sound of his own cliff-shadowed beach, a strip of white sand under the balcony wall, a little floating pier, lord Geigi's huge boat tied up there.

And the faces. And the voices. *Bren-ji,* they'd call him. And they'd all understand when he wanted to go barefoot at low tide.

But they were there. He was here. Lord Geigi was running the station they'd come from, trying to keep relations between atevi, Mospheira, and the ship's technical mission functioning smoothly. A vacation at his own seaside estate was a pipe dream.

"I'll take a sunset on the beach," Ginny said cheerfully. "Mind, no tourist shops. I erase those."

"Oh, we're editing."

"Privilege of being out here in hell's armpit. There'll be this nice little bar, white fence, blooming vine— chi'tapas petals on a sea breeze, while I'm at it, so sickening-sweet you could just choke. Sunset, just one of those orange ones."

"Touch of pink," he said.

"Clouds and sails. Lights of the boats on the water, right at twilight."

"I'll go with that." He liked that image. It wasn't

really maudlin. Ginny wasn't a maudlin sort. She edited that out, right along with the tourist shops and their shell boats and paper flowers. In favor of chi'tapas. "I'll give you one. Big stone fortress on a stony hill. Huge wall and a gate. The ground's so steep grass won't grow in a solid mass, just sort of little shelves of grass and bare ground between. Thorny brush. And it's one of those gold sunsets above the hill. There's light in the windows, and there's supper waiting, and you're riding in on mecheita-back."

"You're riding in," Ginny said with a laugh. "I'm walking on two feet."

"Most dangerous place to be." Mechieti had fighting-tusks, short ones, and didn't mind stepping on a pedestrian or knocking him flat, at very least. When the herd went, the individuals went, the dreadful fact of an atevi cavalry charge—unstoppable as an avalanche; forget steering. "But there's roast something or another for supper—"

"Oh, stop. I'm going to die. Roast, with gravy."

"Brown gravy."

"Hot bread. Fruit preserves and real butter."

"Egg pudding. With chi'tapas."

Sigh.

"We'll get back," Ginny promised him doggedly. "We'll get back. I can't deliver you roast and gravy in a castle, but I'll buy you dinner at Arpeggio."

"Date."

"Jago's not possessive?" Slow wink from a woman as apt as Ilisidi to be his grandmother.

"Totally practical. Well, mostly." It was good to exchange human-scale jibes and threats. He'd come very much to appreciate this woman's steady, slow-fuse humor in recent years. "All this talk of food. God. Want to drop in for dinner?" He'd halfway thought Ilisidi might propose a supper on this eve of change.

But she hadn't. Staff hadn't contacted staff, which was how lords avoided awkward situations. "Can't promise roast and gravy either."

"Deal. Absolutely. Your cook—your food stores— I don't know what you do to it, but it sure beats reconstituted egg soufflés and catsup."

"Don't say catsup near Bindanda's egg dishes. He'll file Intent."

"Anything for an invitation. Can Banichi and Jago be there? I'll practice my Ragi."

"Delighted. You *might* have 'Sidi-ji as a fellow guest; and we might end up there, instead, but I swear you'll get dinner. Trust me."

"Either will be glorious. Believe me."

A dinner.

It posed a pleasant end to a day that overlooked a sheer drop. He *hated* the ship moving. He hated that whole phase of their travel.

He hated worse the anticipation this time. He needed company, he found. He pitied Jase. He wished he could find the means to get him back—if only for an hour.

But hereafter Jase belonged to the ship. Had to. That was the way things had worked out . . . at least for the duration.

4

In the end it was his cook in collaboration with the dowager's, and a table set in mid-corridor—anathema to ship safety officers—and *both* staffs and the lords of heaven and earth at table. *Pizza* seemed the appropriate offering, a succession of pizzas, with salad from the ship's own store, and atevi lowland pickles, and the dowager and her staff delighting in salty highland cheese on toast. The aiji's heir adored pizza, and was on very best behavior. A new hanging adorned the hall, which had had all its numerology adjusted for the occasion. Cajeiri's reputation was safe.

There was adult talk, translated, and a fair offering of liquors, and a warm glow to end a rare evening.

"An excellent company," Ilisidi pronounced it.

"One applauds the cooks," Cajeiri piped up—an applause usually rendered at the main course, but it was still polite and very good behavior, and entirely due.

Bren offered his parting toast. "One thanks the staffs that lighten this voyage—for their cleverness, their hard work, their unfailing invention and good will."

"Indeed," Ilisidi seconded his offering.

"I also thank all persons," Ginny said—in Ragi, a brave venture, "and one offers sincere respects to the lords of the Association and to the aiji's grandmother and to the aiji-apparent."

That called for reciprocal appreciations, before they went to their separate sections and their several apartments.

Over all, Bren said to himself, it was like the voyage itself—an astonishing event, a mix of people on best behavior and divorced from those things of the world that usually meant diplomats working overtime to take care of the agitated small interests. An event that would take a month to set up—they managed impromptu. They had very little to divide them, at least on this deck.

Pizza, that food of sociality and good humor, had been the very thing.

A social triumph.

The dowager had genteelly remarked on the change in the hangings, without remarking on the dent. Cajeiri had surely realized she knew, or he was not her great-grandchild.

Ginny had gotten her company of engineers through an evening mostly in Ragi, without a single social disaster and even with a triumph of linguistic achievement at the end. She'd likely polished that speech for hours.

And, as Cajeiri had very aptly pointed out, the joint efforts of the two staffs had turned out a success. In a long and difficult service aboard, there had to be some moments to cheer, and this was one.

We should have done this before, he thought, and wished Jase had been able to come down. That would have made the evening perfect.

But Jase had had—one hoped—a night's sleep by now, if Jase dared sleep. It was near the end of Sabin's watch.

One day, one very long day, at the end of which, guests all departed to their separate venues, Bren could sit in his dressing-gown and review his notes, by a wall on which two potted plants had run riot. Gifts from home, those were. They'd seemed to grow with more vigor during ship-moves. Humans didn't like the state they entered, but the plants thrived, given water and food and light enough.

He read until he found his eyes fuzzing, then took to bed. Jago came to bed shortly after and they made love . . . well . . . at least that was what Mospheirans called it.

Atevi didn't. Jago didn't. He didn't care and she didn't. There was no safer companion, no one who'd defend him with more zeal, no bedfellow as comfortable in a long and difficult night. She came to distract him *and* herself, and it worked. He did sleep.

And waked, and finding Jago asleep, he slept again, thinking muzzily of station corridors and of the petal sails of his ancestors, dropping down and down through the clouds of a scantly known world, onto atevi struggling to master the steam locomotive.

God, who'd have thought, then, where they'd all be, now?

"Stand by," a voice said at oh-god in the morning. *"Ship-move in one hour."*

Now? They weren't waiting until watch-end? It was Jase's watch. The ship didn't move on Jase's watch. But the robot maintained night lighting. It had to be.

Sabin was likely awake to supervise. And it was Jase's techs and officers that needed, one surmised, to exercise their skills in—for the first time this year-long voyage.

"Shall we be on duty, Bren-ji?" Jago asked out of the pitch darkness.

"One hardly knows what we could do," he said, and then did figure what they *could* do with an hour to wait, because they couldn't go out into the corridors, rousing staff to risk their necks.

At the end of that hour the count went to audible numbers, and he and Jago counted, and tried to time themselves to the ship's curious goings-on.

It felt strange when the ship did go. It made a giddy feeling, and after that life went on, just a shade light-headedly.

"It's very strange," Jago murmured.

"Well, if anyone asks, we can say we did it." Bren burrowed his head into her shoulder, and tangled unbraided hair, gold and black. He had the illusion of the verge of downhill skiing. It was like that.

Top of the hill. Big long slope below. Biting cold. Right now he was warm, but if he got out of bed and moved about, he'd be cold—everyone was, continually, when space was folded and the ship was where things from the workaday universe didn't like to be.

Space did fold. That was what Jase said. He didn't understand it, but atevi mathematicians were intrigued.

Long, long slope.

Downhill on the mountain. A streamer of white and a whisper of snow under skis.

Toby would be on his heels.

Except he and his brother Toby had left the mountain a long, long time ago.

A world ago. Their mother had been in hospital when he'd left the world, uncertain whether she'd live. The aiji had called him to duty and he'd gone, leaving Toby to deal with the world . . . as Toby did and had done, all too often. As Toby's wife and kids did and had done, but it grew harder and harder. Another kind of steep, steep slope, and he couldn't help Toby or his mother, and he couldn't patch things, and he couldn't turn back time.

He was lost, and confused for a while, and seemed to dream. The world became a veil of spider-plant tendrils, branching to more and more little worlds, and he wasn't sure which one he wanted. But one of them Jago was in, and that was where he went.

He moved, and she moved. "It's very strange," she said. And it was.

It was, however, possible to go about a sort of a routine while the ship needled its way through folded space. Bindanda managed to create a basic but very fine breakfast, and it was possible to get a little work done, at least of the routine and non-creative sort, translating files—approving what the computer did— that being about the height of intellectual activity he trusted himself to manage.

That was the first day. Jase had indeed been captain of record during that transition. Sabin, it turned out, had gone to her cabin and wished him and his crew luck.

Maybe it was a sea change in relations—a statement to the crew at large that she trusted him that far, since below-decks was sure to have learned that Jase had been in charge. Or maybe it was a subtle strike at Jase's confidence, meant to scare him. One thing remained certain: the navigators, the pilot, and the technical crew ran matters. The trade-off of authority and the alternate crew hadn't risked the ship.

Presumably, at the same time, Jase attempted to persuade the senior captain to trust outsiders with the log files. It remained to be seen whether that would ever happen.

The staff watched television.

The dowager stayed withdrawn in her cabin, her standard practice throughout these voyages through the deep dark: no invitation would tempt her. No one was at his best, and the dowager had no interest.

The heir, however, took to racing wheeled cars, which Cajeiri had seen in videos out of the human Archive, and which he had made for himself out of pieces of pipe, tape, pieces of wire, various washers and gaskets, and beans for ballast. One early model exploded on impact with the base of the section door and sent Cajeiri and the servant staff searching the hall for errant beans—not so much for fear of the footing as the certainty that any ship's maneuver would turn them all into missiles.

Over the next number of days Bren produced the briefing tape. No one on the ship was at his sharpest, but Bren judged his wits adequate at least for a summation of the situation, and he reviewed for the entire security staff, in careful detail and with numerous questions from Cenedi, exactly what he knew: the surmises of various authorities, the history of the Guild, the physical details of the station's structure and, not strange to his own staff, the station's necessary and critical operations, especially as regarded the fuel port, the mast accesses, and the damage the ship had previously observed.

Then the staffs—his, the dowager's men, and Gin's—put their heads together. In a meeting of their own lethal Guild, they listened to the briefing tapes, then considered the structural charts, reviewing approach, docking, and the refueling protocols. No one would deceive them. No one would confuse them by telling them lies. And no emergency would overtake them unanticipated.

Bren wished he could say the same for himself.

"Any luck on the records?" he asked Jase, in a social call.

"She says she has it on her list," Jase said.

So, well, damn, but not surprising. That could go on for days. And doubtless Sabin intended it to take an adequate number of days.

He helped staff where he could. Security came back to him ready to discuss their situation and their potential situation for muzzy days and evenings of careful reconsideration. He informed himself on finer technicalities about ship-fueling that he had never intended to know, but a translator necessarily learned, and relayed that information. He fell asleep of nights with Jago, their pillow-talk generally dealing with the same worrisome contingencies and potential operations as occupied their days.

And he slept and waked and slept and waked, day upon quasi-day, with diminishing conviction about the accuracy of time-cycles in their automatic world.

No luck, Jase still informed him, regarding Sabin and further records. She still says she's thinking about it.

Watching *them*, Bren began to think. Watching their reactions. Maybe waiting for Jase to make a move . . . but maybe, at last, questioning her own universe of rights and wrongs and consulting her human conscience. He assumed Sabin had one. But hope for it daily diminished.

He visited Ginny for one lunch of quasi-egg sandwiches on something that passed for bread, and arranged to bring an atevi-style dinner to their section.

Then the notion took them of holding a truly formal folded-space supper in the Mospheiran corridors—Cajeiri wanted to come, and gained permission from the dowager. He even demonstrated his best car for Ginny's engineers and mechanics.

Immediately there were notions for improvement

and a proposal of bets. An electric motor. Remote steering.

"No," Ginny chided her engineers, but one suspected *no* would by no means suffice.

Well, Bren wrote to Toby, in a letter that couldn't possibly be transmitted until they were within reach of docking at their home station, at mission end. *Well, brother, the advisement from above claims they have seen some sign the ship is nearing exit, whatever they know up there.*

If you're reading this, it worked. And it's about the umteenth day, and I'm tired of this muzziness.

Tired and a lot scared at this point. I can't string two thoughts together. I tape them in place, laboriously, or they slide off and get confused.

I think about you a lot. I hope everything's going well for you. I think about you and Jill and the kids, with all kinds of regrets for chances not taken; and of course there aren't any answers, but I can't survive out here thinking about things that could go wrong back home. I have to hope that you're out on that boat of yours enjoying the sunshine. And that those kids of yours are getting along. And that Jill's all right.

He didn't write a great deal about Jill and the kids, not knowing what sort of sore spot that might be by the time he returned. He'd left Toby in a mess, their mother in hospital, Toby's wife Jill having walked out in despair of Toby's ever living his own life, the kids increasingly upset and acting out, in the way of distressed and confused young folk. He wasn't utterly to blame for Toby's situation—but he regretted it. He wished he'd seen it coming earlier. He wished, with all his diplomacy, he'd found a way years ago to talk Toby out of responding to every alarm their mother raised—or that he could have talked their mother, far less likely, out of her campaign to get him out of his job and Toby back from the end of the island he'd moved to.

Their mother was one of those women who defined herself by her children. And who consequently cannibalized their growing lives until, ultimately, the campaign drove the family apart.

He patched nations together. He made warlike lords of another species form sensible associations and refrain from assassinating each other. And he hadn't been able to impose a sense of reality on his own mother. That failure grieved him, his grief made him angry, and his anger made him feel very guilty when he thought of how he'd left the world, without that last visit that might have paid for so much—that would have turned out so opportune in his mother's life.

No, dammit. There *was* no final gesture with someone who was only interested in the next maneuver, the ultimate strategem, the plan that would, against all logic, work, and get her sons home—no matter what her sons wanted or needed. If he'd gotten there, she'd have taken it for vindication.

Toby, unfortunately, was still in the middle of it all. Toby had still been trying to figure it all out. And even if their mother had passed—as she might have— Toby would still be struggling to figure out all out.

Well, what are we up to? he wrote to Toby. *A lot of things that I'll tell you when I get there, because I can't write them down, the usual reasons. And today I tell you I'd really like that fishing trip. Jase would be absolutely delighted with an invitation from you. He's done so much. He's existing in a position he doesn't think he's able to hold. He even supervised this last ship-move. He does a thousand things Sabin would have to do if he wasn't here. I think he's why she's sane.*

But besides that, there remain some few questions we'd like Sabin to dig out of files, questions we've asked. I wonder sometimes if maybe she's putting more operations on Jase's back because she really is doing something—or thinking about those answers. Maybe she's found something she didn't expect in those records and she's considering her options. I hope. I don't know.

Remind me to tell you about exploding cars when I get back. For the future aiji's reputation I don't want that one in print either.

When we last folded space I thought about Mt. Adams and the slope that winter—remember the race? Remember when I went off the ledge and through the thicket and lost my new cap and goggles?

I remember hot tea and honey in the cabin that night and us making castles out of the embers in the fireplace. And I'd turned my ankle going off the cliff and it swelled up but I wasn't telling Mum and I went on the slope the next day, too.

We tried to teach mum to ski, remember, but she said if she wanted to fall down on ice there was a patch in front of the cabin that didn't involve long cold hikes.

It was an exact quote, and one she'd stuck to. But she'd brought them to the cabin—well, brought them up to the snow lodge ever since the time he'd lost himself in the woods and scared everyone, so she'd changed vacation spots. And she hadn't liked the ski slopes, either, and had been sure he was going to fall into some ravine and die of a broken leg. Their mother was full of contradictions.

He was sure there was an essential key in that set of facts somewhere, a means to understand her, and consequently to understand himself and Toby, if he knew how to lay hands on it. But no thought during ship-transit was entirely reliable.

I was thinking about you and the boat today. You know, in his office up on the bridge, Jase has just one personal item—that photo of him and the fish. Clearly he thinks about getting through this alive and getting that chance to come down—maybe for good, he says, though between you and me, I think he'd get to missing life on the ship, too. He has a place here. And there. I know he remembers you and the boat.

I have learned a few things in the last few days. I'll have to tell you when I get there. But then this letter and I will get there pretty much together, so you'll at least have a chance to ask me first hand.

Here's hoping, at least.

He had another running letter, this one to Tabini; and to that one, too, he appended a note:

Aiji-ma, we have moved the ship on toward the station. Your grandmother has taken to her cabin as is her habit during these uncomfortable transitions. Your son is taking advantage of the opportunity to undertake new experiments, not all of which have predictable outcomes, but he is learning and growing in discretion. We fill our hours with plans and projections and take a certain pleasure in his inventions and discoveries.

Dared one think Tabini would understand? This was the boy who'd ridden a mechieta across wet cement.

One believes you will approve, aiji-ma.

Concerning Sabin, about the missing files, he withheld statement. If the letter ever got to Tabini, all their problems would have been solved—one way and another. He damaged no reputations, created no suspicions that might later have to be dealt with.

He held misgivings at arms' length. Viewed suspicion with suspicion, in the curiously muzzy way of this place. He waited.

*   *   *

Besides his letter writing, he took daily walks, around and around the section. He worked out in their makeshift gymnasium. At times the suspension of result and the lack of outcome in their long voyage simply passed endurance, and he pulled squats and sit-ups until he collapsed in a sweating, sweatshirted heap.

He had nothing like Jago's strength, let alone Banichi's, but he'd certainly worked off all the rich desserts and sedentary evenings of the last ten years during this voyage. He no longer rated himself sharp enough to downhill Mt. Adams, but he figured if he fell in the attempt, he'd at least bounce several times before he broke something.

And, like the transcript-translation and the two letters which had now become individual volumes, exercise filled the hours, mindless and cathartic. Unlike the transcript and the letter-writing, it didn't force him to think of dire possibilities or to fret about records on which he could spend useful time, if he could only get them.

He resurrected old card games out of the Archive and translated those for his staff, with cards made of document folders. Whist became a favorite.

Cajeiri, deserted to his own young devices, built paper planes and flew them in the long main corridor, where they took unpredictible courses. Cajeiri said the strangeness of the journey made them fly in unpredictible ways. It seemed a fair experiment and a curious notion, so Bren made a few of his own, and greatly amused the dowager's staff.

Their designs were dubious in the flow of air from the vents. The properties of airplanes in hyperspace remained an elusive question. They were at least soft-landing, and the walls were safe.

And there was the human Archive for entertainment, such of it as they still carried aboard. The servant staff assembled with simple refreshments and held group viewings in the servants' domain, occasionally of solemn atevi machimi, but often enough of old movies from the human Archive. Horses had long since become a sensation, in whatever era. Elephants and tigers were particularly popular, and evoked wonder. *The Jungle Book* re-ran multiple times on its premiere evening. "Play it again," the staff requested Bindanda, who ran the machine, and on subsequent evenings, if the other selections seemed less favorable, they ran and reran the favorite..

On a particular evening of the watch, Bren passed the dining hall to hear loud cheers go up. He wondered whether there was a new sensation to surpass even *The Jungle Book.*

He looked in. The assembled audience was, indeed, not just the servant staff. Banichi and Jago attended. He saw Cenedi and the dowager's staff, and Cajeiri, his young face transfigured by the silver light of the screen—of course, Cajeiri had inveigled his way in.

A black and white, the offering was—odd, in itself. Color was usually the preference. As he stood in the doorway, a scaled monster stepped on the ruin of a building. Humans darted this way and that in patterns that atevi would search in vain for signs of association.

Men in antique uniforms fired large guns at the beast, which slogged on, to atevi cheers and laughter.

Hamlet, atevi had appreciated and applauded, when he'd brought a modern tape to the mainland . . . appreciated it, but felt cheated by ambiguities in the ending. They'd been puzzled by *Romeo and Juliet,* but were both horrified and gratified by *Oedipus,* which they conceded had a fine ending, once he explained it.

Now . . .

A building went flat.

The great Archive. The unseen dramas, manifestation of the collected human wisdom, the possibility of every digital blip the storage had carried on its way to build an outpost of human civilization. And this fuzzy black and white delighted the audience.

Laughter. A light young voice among the rest, the future aiji.

He couldn't begin to explain this story. He considered going in, tucking himself in among the rest, trying to figure the nature of the tape—but he'd likely disturb the staff, who were obviously understanding the story quite well without him—or at least finding amusement in it. He drifted on to his own quarters and ran through the Archive indices for himself, looking for entertainment, for diversion, for edification— and finding absolutely nothing in the entire body of work of the human species that appealed to him this evening.

Which somehow told him it wasn't really a tape he wanted.

What he *wanted* was to be absorbed and equal in the company out there, watching a mythical beast flatten buildings.

What he most *wanted* was to sit surrounded by congeniality and supplied with something munchable and something potable, having a good time—but the staff, even including Banichi and Jago, could only do that when they thought they had a moment off, and if he showed up, it could only make them ask themselves who was minding the things that had to be minded.

And they would get up and go see if there was anything he needed.

He was feeling human this evening. He was feeling human, strange, and somewhat melancholy.

So let them relax, he said to himself. Staff worked

hard enough to assure his relaxation: let them have their own enjoyment without his crises of identity and visions of an uncertain outcome.

And if Cenedi included the aiji's heir in the security staff's dubious amusements, Cenedi judged it was probably good for the boy. He himself sat at his desk solo, and played computer solitaire, in complete confidence that if he should ask, tea would arrive. But he chose, again, not to disturb staff. He was human. He was Mospheiran. He could very easily go to the galley and make his own tea. He thought he could find a pan and the tea-caddy . . . but he hadn't the energy or the will to attend his own needs. He felt sorry for himself in the numb, dull-as-a-rock way the transition let anybody feel anything.

And he kept losing the games, which in itself was a good barometer of his mood and his muddle-headedness with the basic numbers of his situation.

Nearing the end of this long voyage, and no information, when he blackly suspected Sabin had by now seen it, formed a conclusion, and denied it to him.

He was nearing the point at which his ideas had to work—if he had any; which he wouldn't, until he got a view of the situation at their exit.

God, he *hated* improvisation. The older he got, the more he distrusted gut instinct and initial impressions—and he used his instincts, or he had used them, and they'd worked, but they'd worked with people he knew, and often on blind luck—*baji-naji*, atevi would insist: actions in good awareness of the transitory numbers of a situation flowed *with* a situation, and luck and chance themselves flowed along discernable channels. One only had to understand the numbers to ride the current and improve one's luck in moments of change.

But one had to know the numbers. And he didn't.

The ship-folk were more alien to planet-bound humans than atevi were—while ship-folk had queasily found atevi easier to deal with than they found Mospheirans. And nobody, not even Jase, understood the Pilots' Guild—or the senior captain.

He wanted Jase to rush down to five-deck right about now with a handful of log records assuring him there was a quick, even brilliant answer to what Ramirez had agreed to with the Guild, and it was all fine, but that scenario wasn't going to happen. By now, he understood the dowager locking herself in her cabin and refusing to come out.

Fragile, that was what he was feeling. Fragile and entirely in the dark.

Stupidity might help. The simple disinclination to ask what came next.

As it was, his mirror and his computer and his steadily lengthening letters home asked him that question, every morning and every evening of their arbitrary, diversion-filled days.

On a certain morning Bren opened his door, bound for breakfast, and a motorized car whizzed noisily past his foot, destination right, origin left.

He looked left, at the future lord of a planet on his knees, control unit in both hands, looking entirely sheepish.

"I'm testing new wheels," Cajeiri explained, and added in frustration: "They aren't working right. But one thinks it's the ship moving."

"It may well be," Bren said numbly. "Or not."

Cajeiri scrambled up and chased down the corridor after his car, where it had swerved and stalled against the inner wall.

"May one go ask Gin-aiji's staff, nandi, about the wheels?"

Oh, now one knew why the aiji-to-be raced his car past authority's door.

"If Cenedi agrees." One suspected Cenedi had just said no to the young wretch. And that diversion was in order. "My breakfast is likely waiting . . . a simple one, aiji-meni." One never, except through staff, *invited* a person of higher status to share a meal. One could, however, suggest that breakfast was available at a whim. "I'm sure Bindanda could manage another place."

"I already had breakfast," Cajeiri said. And confessed the ultimate catastrophe. "And I'm *bored*, Bren-nandi."

"Well, there you have the dreadful truth about adventures, aiji-meni. A great deal of adventures is being bored, or scared, or cold, or wet, or not having breakfast *or* information on schedule. But adventures often improve in the telling."

Cajeiri belatedly saw he was being joked with. And took it with an expression very much his father's when things didn't go well—not angry, more bewildered at the universe's temerity in trifling with his wishes. And next came, unmistakably, great-grandmother's tone.

"Well, I *detest* boredom, Bren-nandi. I *detest* it. I brought my own player, and I want tapes, and nadi Cenedi says I have to have your permission to have them."

"That's because it's the human Archive, nandi-meni, and what's human is very different, and some of it confuses even humans who aren't ten yet."

"I know. But I'm *very* intelligent."

"Well, one supposes one could go back to the computer and find something. If the young aiji were interested, he might watch." One didn't ask an aiji under one's roof, either. One suggested there might be something of interest under that roof and the great lord went, if he wished.

Cajeiri wished. He all but tumbled over himself in longing to be somewhere new and entertaining, in a generally off-limits cabin where he hadn't yet put a dent in something or scratched something or met local disapproval.

So, well, with Bindanda's forgiveness and given the staff's devious ways of knowing where he was, the lord of the province of the heavens decided breakfast could wait a few moments.

"The nearest chair is comfortable," Bren said, sitting down at his desk, and opening up his computer. "Tapes, tapes, tapes."

"Cenedi doesn't have to know," the young rascal suggested. "I want the *war* ones."

"Oh, but Cenedi is extremely good at finding out, aiji-meni, and I am *Bren-nandi,* and dare I say that the young aiji's latest statement held an unfortunate two?"

"Bren-nandi." Cajeiri was occasionally experimenting in the adult language. "And it was not two, Bren-nandi."

"Mode of offer, young aiji, was the implied infelicity of two, since though I trust you were speaking regarding my action, you nevertheless omitted my courtesy." He could be quite coldly didactic when his fingers were on his keyboard. But one didn't dwell on an aiji's failures. He called a list of film titles to his display. "Ha."

And sifted them for classics as Cajeiri leaned forward, looking . . . as if Cajeiri could even read the list.

"Ahh," Bren said as enigmatically as possible.

"Where?" Cajeiri asked sharply, and immediately, under threat of no tapes, remembered the courtesy form: "What does one find in this list, nandi?"

Another sort through the list. Children's classics. One owed the aiji a proper response for his newly-discovered courtesy. "The very best of stories, aiji-meni." He considered *Tom Sawyer* and *Connecticut Yankee*—no, problematic in approach to authority. And one had no wish to see Cajeiri discover practical jokes *or* paintbrushes. *Robin Hood* . . . no, not good: not only defying authority, but promoting theft.

"Ha." *The Three Musketeers*. Satisfying to most atevi principles: the support of an aiji's wife by loyal security personnel, the downfall of base conspirators.

The education of a young man with more ideas than experience.

He copied it and gave the lad the disk. "Your player will handle this, aiji-meni. One believes the piece is even in color. One is advised to set the switch to second position."

"Thank you, Bren-nandi!"

"A pleasure, young aiji." God, he'd forgotten the story himself. And remembered it, once his mind was on it. The whole notion of youthful derring-do came like a transfusion. Oxygen to the blood.

Dared he even think age came on with a little stiffening of the backbone, a little too much propriety, a few too many situations that numbed the nerves?

"Perhaps it would suit the young aiji for me to examine that racing car, after all," he said. "After breakfast, that is, which the young aiji might still attend."

Cajeiri happily changed his mind.

And handed the car to him under the table, in a hiatus of service. He had a look at the wheels. And in lieu of a consultation of Gin's engineers, he proposed an after-breakfast investigation of available possibilities, which ended up providing bits of plastic tubing to stand the wobbly wheels off from the sides. Which was how, in this transit between places in the depths of space, the dowager's security happened to find the lord of the heavens down on his knees at one end of the corridor with the future aiji similarly posed down by the galley.

And that was how the dowager's security ended up, with Banichi and Jago, designing a remote-controlled car whose wheels did not wobble. One understood there were secret bets with Gin's staff. And a proposed race date.

The staff's new passion became Alexandre Dumas, books and tapes alike, even the dowager requesting a copy, via written message. Bren began reading the works himself, amid the growing tendrils of Sandra Johnson's plants, which now formed a green and white curtain from their hanging baskets, and writing daily to his brother.

Banichi and Jago have a chess match going, was one entry. *The staff is laying bets.*

And at the resolution: *Jago is trying not to be pleased with herself; Banichi is trying not to notice. They've started another game.*

I think there was a car race. And I don't think we won. I haven't heard a thing, but Banichi is building a small remote control device of his own, and bets on that are secret, but not that secret.

Jase turned up at one lunch, Jase's midnight snack, and for an hour they sat and discussed nothing in particular—the merits of cork fishing and the currents off Mospheira's south shore—whether or not Crescent Island development had ever taken off and whether a small yacht dared try the southern sea.

No, the log records had not surfaced, Sabin was growing peevish, and he had found no key to the information.

Damn.

I had lunch with Jase. We talked about Beaufort Bay.

We'll have to talk about the exact plans when I get home. That's how crazy we've become.

God, Toby, I want to get home. I want to get home—and it comes to me that it's not just the chance of waking up somewhere we didn't ever mean to go that scares me spitless. It's that I want to get home, I, me, the me that's going to have a home when I get back. I changed when I went to the mainland, but not so that I didn't recognize home. I changed when I began to live on the mainland, but not so that I didn't dream of trips to the north shore. I changed when I went to live in space, and the situation was always hot, and getting back to the island meant running a gauntlet of press and politics that just wouldn't let me alone. It's so strange out here—not that we've seen anything or done anything but sit in our cabins for a year and read Dumas and race toy cars—but it's still strange; and it can only get stranger, and I think so much of home. I'm a little desperate today. I wish I had answers I don't have.

But I can't govern the changes that have already happened.

I can't govern what happens to me on the way. I never could. And every change has been away, not toward, and every change makes the circle of those who've been through this with me smaller, not larger, until at this moment I think I'm becoming a sort of black hole, and I'm going to pull everything I know into a pinpoint so none of us can get out, and then I'll stop existing at all in this universe. I'm terrified of never getting home, that you'll never get this letter.

A few people still on earth matter. You. Tabini. And if you are still speaking to me, and if I can get there, I'd like to take about a month sitting on the beach and telling you all the things most people on Mospheira wouldn't at all want to hear about. I don't know if you're curious or if you're just that patient, but for either reason, I think you'd listen and nod in the right places, even for this. I love you, brother. I miss you. And one part of me wishes you were here and the sane part says thank God you're not. Thank God something I remember is still there.

By the fact I'm now panicking, you can guess this is the scary part of our trip coming up. This is where I need every scrap of courage I've got, and I wish I had more information of substance. I think about Banichi and Jago, and if they or the staff ever doubt our success in this crazy venture, they don't let me know it. The dowager—she won't spook, no matter what. Meanwhile I'm thinking this is the scariest thing I've ever contemplated, and there's a six- or seven-year-old kid down there playing with a toy car and thinking it's all fairly normal for a kid to be racing cars in a starship corridor. He's not afraid. He doesn't imagine the trouble we could be in . . . or he does, but at his age everything's an adventure. Being alone in the dark scares him. The thought of dropping into deserted space just doesn't faze him. I'm not sure anything scares Banichi and Jago but the thought of losing me somewhere out here. So is any fear real? Do we become self-focused cowards by measures as we get older? Or am I the only one on this deck who really knows the odds?

Jase is likely as scared as I am. Ginny hasn't got nerves. I don't know what drives her. She's just busy seeing to her staff, and that's what she does. But my staff sees to me, not the other way around, and I suppose that leaves me time enough to think, way more thinking about the consequences of various things than I find comfortable.

The beach and the sound of the waves can take all that away. I'd say, the deck of the boat, but right now, considering just stringing thoughts together is like swimming in syrup, sitting very still on a planet's solid skin sounds good to me.

On a certain day he'd had entirely enough.

He left his computer, left his notes, gathered Banichi and Jago without warning, and headed for the lift.

"Is there an emergency, Bren-ji?" Banichi asked.

"A conference," he said, and neither Banichi nor Jago asked further questions.

Nor did they evidence any surprise whatsoever that he ordered the lift to the bridge and strode out and past working operations on the consoles, down that screened aisle. He was bound, since Sabin's bodyguards, Collins and the rest, were sitting watch down in the executive corridor, for executive offices.

The guards got up from benches—not quite hands on weapons, but close.

"I'm here to see the senior captain," Bren said in Mosphei'. *"Now."*

Jenrette happened to be part of that group of five. But the seniormost of Sabin's guards, Collins, was a man who'd been Sabin's for decades before Jenrette came into the picture. The lot of them might have had orders of one kind about crew coming up here—but they likely had special orders about care and coddling of their alien passengers, too, and those separate trains had suddenly intersected, headed for collision.

"I'm not going back down," Bren said plainly, standing a little out of hearing of techs on the bridge behind him. "She won't want an incident, I can assure you."

Collins looked at him, looked at Banichi and Jago, a solid dark wall behind him.

And they were indeed about to have an incident:

he was set, however muzzily, on course, and stood his ground.

"Captain," Collins said to the empty air. "Mr. Cameron's up here saying it's urgent business."

Whatever the answer was, Collins opened the door.

"Kindly wait here, nadiin-ji," Bren said quietly to Banichi and Jago, facing Sabin at her desk, Sabin—who leaned back in her chair to have a look at the intrusion into her day's problems. "Senior captain, good day."

"Mr. Cameron." No invitation, not a cue or a clue. Sabin folded her hands on her spare middle. The door shut behind him, securing their privacy.

"The record we mentioned, senior captain."

"Record."

"You want my help . . ."

"I don't recall *requesting* your help, Mr. Cameron. I do recall your request. I've reviewed it. Hell if I'm giving you our log to play with. Go find other amusement."

"I want the record, captain. I'm sure it doesn't take you eleven months to find a log entry. I'm sure you had it that same shift we discussed it. I take it you view your survival as a matter of some importance. I want the record."

A lively, analytical regard. A pursing of the lips. One thing about long-time crew—they adapted to the mental conditions of folded space, did it far better than planet-dwellers. *Sabin's* thought processes at the moment might far out-class his. "You do."

A little caution might be in order. "Politely put, *please,* captain."

"You want it." Sabin moved her chair so suddenly assassination-honed reflexes twitched. Inwardly. He didn't budge as she opened a cabinet. And took out a tape. And held it up to his view. "You think this holds answers."

"If you know what you were looking for, with your accustomed ability, yes, I hope it does."

She flipped it to a landing on the desk. Making him reach to pick it up, a petty move. He wasn't inclined to object to that.

"Good luck," she said.

"More than this," he said, and pocketed the tape. "More than this record, captain, what's *your* estimation of the facts?"

Momentary silence. And cold irony. "Forty years and someone finally asks the question."

"I'm asking, captain. You've had, all along, a very keen sense of the risks involved in contact. If we'd had you in charge of the original contact with the atevi, we might not have fought a war. Let me guess— you've tried to figure this without my input. *You* wanted your own uncontaminated assessment, uncolored by my opinions. You have some opinion of your own. What do you think?"

Cold, cold stare. "I want *your* uncontaminated assessment, Mr. Cameron. Enough is there. Beginning to end. You figure it. You tell me. Five days likely to system entry. You've worked miracles, so they tell me. You figure this one."

"You weren't going to give me this."

"I lead a full, busy life," Sabin said. Then, less provocatively: "I was still asking myself whether I was going to give it to you, to Jase—or not at all."

"Copy to him. I won't consult him until I've seen this."

"Done." Sabin shifted the chair and punched one button. "Good *luck,* Mr. Cameron. Go do your job. And *don't* do this again."

"Only to mutual advantage, captain. Even *you* need a backup."

He walked out. He gathered up Banichi and Jago and walked back the way he had come, to the lift, and they rode it down.

"Was it a success, nandi?" Banichi asked him.

"One waits to see, nadiin-ji," he said to them, and felt of the tape in his pocket to be sure it was there, that his muzzy, half-dreaming brain hadn't dreamed this gift.

Folded space wasn't a place to try any complex analysis. Sabin, having a keen brain, being used to these conditions, surely, even so, observed a certain caution about critical decisions. Maybe that was why she made this one belatedly, to hand him the record.

And the ship went, and space bent.

Five days out, Sabin said, five muddled days left, in which, without his going up there and confronting the issue, she might have laid it on Jase's desk, and might not.

Now he took himself back to his computer, and back to software, Jase's gift, that could unravel the ship's image-output or plain-print files.

It wasn't image. It was text, a sparse, scattershot text that Ramirez had recorded—in Ramirez's unskilled, demonstrably flawed notion of what to record.

There was a small file of personal notes—that, to a casual scan, revealed nothing but coordinates and dates and a handful of cryptic symbols.

Bren's heart sank. What might the man have left out, that might be absolutely critical? What was the second record? A notation of where they'd been? What sites the ship had looked at, at vantages far removed from station?

Granted there was something Ramirez hadn't wanted the Guild to know, the record was disappointingly . . . useless. Useless without Ramirez's living brain to explain the memories, the intentions, the actions he associated with those cryptic references.

But there was also the minute-by-minute telemetry report, the autolog, another kind of text, mostly numerical, and huge. *That* was there. Thank God. Thank Sabin for including it. It *was* a fair record, best impartial record they seemed to have of those encounters, right down to the chaff of information from the air quality units, reams of it.

One could arrange. And filter. So he filtered. He filtered for hours, going through every internal system's chatter, dumping the chaff and lining up the log record for the sparse useful facts, all with a brain packed about with cotton wool and unaccustomed to the kinds of data he was trying to sift. He wouldn't attempt to organize a social dinner in his current state—and here he was put to figuring out an alien contact gone wrong, and figuring what in the data had still changed when Ramirez gave a no-output order.

Fact: Phoenix had spent a decade founding a space station to supply her and spent most of the next couple hundred years poking about in various neighborhoods likely to have supply—*supply* that came to the ship most conveniently when it came in space—planetoids, not deep planetary gravity wells that the huge and fragile ship had no means to plumb. That fact, he had heard from Jase over a number of years.

No gravity wells—being so fragile: so the choices a Mospheiran or an ateva would logically think of first were excluded. *Phoenix* had arrived at the atevi world not only with no landing craft, but, embarrassing as it was, and admitted much later, the ship had no atmosphere-qualified pilots who *could* land on a planet and get off again—well, except by brute force and massive lift, something that didn't rely on air and weather—and which they couldn't soft-land in the first place. He wasn't, himself, qualified to pronounce on the feasibility of just lighting a powerful rocket and aiming it straight up; but such a craft had no ready reusability, nothing to enable mining and agriculture on a regular basis, so, from the ship's point of view, relying on anything in a gravity well was a damned inconvenient way to run a space program.

Not to mention the fact that ship-folk floating in orbit didn't in the least know what to do with crops outside a hydroponics tank, and weren't inclined to fall down a gravity well to find out, either.

So scratch landing as an option, and as a basic intent of Ramirez's illicit explorations. Mospheirans had landed on a no-return basis—and taken two hundred years getting back into space again. No, definitely *Phoenix* had been interested primarily in space-based resources. Asteroids. Comets. Floating real estate. They'd mine, occasionally, gather, occasionally . . . that was the way they'd lived.

The ship had had mining craft once upon a time. Which the ship hadn't had when it showed up at Alpha. They'd lost their resources of that sort. Or maybe the ship usually had them and just hadn't carried the extra mass on the voyage in question. It *was* a lot of mass.

And where would they have left them? At a remote star, when they'd pulled up stakes in a hurry?

At Reunion, when they'd come in and found a station in ruins?

Would they have left them as station relief, an aid to rebuilding? Or had they just not been carrying them?

Thoughts slid willfully sideways, into lunacy. Into human behavior that hadn't, no, been wise at all. They were not figuring out *right* behavior, even rational behavior, in tracing the history of station and ship decisions. They were second-guessing a senior captain who'd done some peculiar things wrong, including arriving in atevi space with no way to refuel.

Damn, damn, *damn.*

Question for Sabin—exactly how much mining the ship had been doing in Ramirez' tenure as senior captain? *Did the ship have mining 'bots?*

If not, where did you leave them—and when? And why?

Risking stranded themselves? Risking exactly what *Phoenix* had run into in the disaster that had stranded them? Was it at all sensible, not to have had that capability, when they'd learned their historical lessons?

Something didn't add up. Or something added up to mining craft either not loaded for the mission, or deployed and not recovered, or left to aid Reunion in a critical situation.

The Guild held refueling as a weapon, hadn't Jase said?

So was it a Guild decision to keep all possible refueling operations under its own hand?

Worrisome thought.

Had the Guild begun to be suspicious of Ramirez's intentions, his activities when he was out and about? Or suspicious of the ship's independence, from the time they built Reunion Station, centuries ago? They should have foreseen the ship would develop different interests. If they were wise.

Four times damn. He called Jase.

"Jase. You have a *record* you're working on? Did she give it to you?"

"Affirmative."

"No queries into your line of thought—but did the ship ever have mining craft? And where did they go?"

"Weren't loaded," Jase answered. There was a long pause. *"Never were. Guild monopoly."*

"Fuel at Gamma, possibly?"

"Ported out there. Occasionally there was. Such as there was. If there still is any, I have no knowlege. If the aliens haven't hit it, too, by now."

"But fuel exists—in its raw state—at Gamma. One could mine."

"If we got into that kind of situation. Yes. That's the option. What are you thinking?"

"No comment yet," Bren said. He *didn't* want to prejudice Jase's thinking, or change its direction. But he was muzzy-headed with folded space. With things that didn't make sense. With fears, that got down to station's power play, holding that mining machinery to itself. It *hadn't* trusted Ramirez, dared one think? "Ramirez's personal notebook. Without useful comment from Sabin. Does it make any sense to you?"

"It's all coordinates. Bearings. I think he could have been *watching* something come and go. The points given don't match up with past destinations that I know about. We didn't ever *go* to these points. He only wrote them down, outside the log. There's absolutely nothing else I can get out of the notes."

Scary implications. Spying on the aliens. Wonderful. Visitations that frequent, and station not aware of them? "Want to come down for lunch? I swear social only. No contamination."

"Can't," Jase said. *"Wish I could. Sabin's set me an administrative job. Have to. You take care down there, Bren."*

"No question."

Conversation ended disappointingly, a conversation kept entirely in ship-speak, nothing to worry Sabin or make her question what the former paidhiin had been up to—nothing to make Sabin doubt them at a critical moment yet to come—the way the Guild might have doubted Ramirez. Everything was too fragile. Everything depended on Sabin's judgement of them. And Jase hadn't risked her opinion by coming down to consult.

Their lives all depended on that brittle thread of Sabin's judgement. And the solution to Ramirez's actions relied on brains that couldn't work at maximum efficiency. So, just to help out, Sabin had loaded Jase with something extra to do. Maybe necessary, maybe not. He was annoyed. Frustrated. But he didn't want to push Sabin further, not yet.

Conclude one thing for a fact. Ramirez hadn't had mining capability on the critical run into trouble. He wasn't likely to get it from a station that didn't trust him. And he hadn't been after material gain at that star—not immediately. Information. Data. Scouting things out. Maybe for future mining, if he could beg, borrow or steal a craft. Maybe not. But by what Jase said, he'd been nosing about where he was, possibly watching some sort of activity—without, he thought, getting involved, without going to those destinations.

Wasn't ready yet. Was still collecting data. Still training Taylor's Children to be his go-betweens, his eyes and ears for another world.

But the list in the notes, if it was observation of alien craft—was that observation a notation kept aside even from the auto-log? Difficult, one would think.

Log recorded the last arrival at star 2095 on chart, G4, small planets. A great deal of data on all the planets. But the second, temperate planet . . . *temperate* planet . . . had atmosphere. Liquid water. Abundant water. Moderate vulcanism. A single, modest moon—old enough, perhaps, to have swept up all its competitors. A human's natural interest turned to that world—ignorant as his interest might be.

Resources useless to the Guild, again, at the inaccessible bottom of a gravity well. *Guild* interest might well be piqued by the data, far more abundant, on the debris in the outer system. Ices. Iron. Nickle. A radiation-hot fourth planet gravitationally locked with an overlarge satellite and surrounded by an unstable ring—that was no place a sensible operation would like to conduct business. That world's well held a rich debris cloud; but from the Guild's point of view, not because of that hellish place, but because of that inconveniently attractive number two planet, the whole solar system was less attractive to them—a temptation all of history indicated the Guild wanted to avoid like the plague. Both a rich hell to mine, and a quasi-paradise sitting within potential rebels' reach.

The Guild had had that situation once, at Alpha. And colonists and workers there had staged a rebellion that worked only because the green world allowed a soft landing. Consequently that gravity well wouldn't give up a single craft, not for centuries—placing all local resources offlimits for a Guild that had forgotten atmospheric flight—so the Guild could whistle for obedience: no one had had to listen, and finally the station had folded, oh, for a couple of centuries.

Interesting, that beautiful green world. Decided temptation, as a Mospheiran saw matters. Temptation for an atevi ruler. Temptation for anybody interested in population growth—

Even for a Guild captain who should be doing his Guild-bound duty and avoiding another planet-based colonization?

A captain with questionable loyalty to the Guild—a captain legally obliged to convey his log back to close Guild scrutiny . . . and who might not want to tell them everything.

So said captain heaped up piles of data on the hellish fourth planet. Stayed there weeks, observing that fourth planet. From a distance. Which argued to a suspicious son of rebels that the fourth planet wasn't all Ramirez was observing and might not be the focus of Ramirez's real interest.

But if there had been notes on his intentions, they weren't in the log. And they weren't in the little file.

No evidence of any foreign occupancy around that green world . . . no evidence that Ramirez chose to record. That was all the soft tissue of memory, attached to those simple numbers in the little file. And all of that was gone, evaporated, when Ramirez died.

But there were witnesses. Sabin said Ramirez had found something somewhere. Said Ramirez *sought* alien contact—had *wanted* to find somebody to deal with, somebody excluding atevi and their own troublesome rebel colony at Alpha. And where was Ramirez to find that, except near such a green planet? And might natives of such a green world, if they had an installation in space, have the supplies Ramirez needed to break free of the Guild?

What foolish thing had Ramirez done?

"Nandi-ji." Bindanda presented a tray. Tea. And sandwiches. Bren looked at them as alien objects until, a heartbeat or so later, he recalled dismissing Bindanda's last request for attention. Bindanda was absolutely determined he eat.

"Thank you, Danda-ji."

"Your bed is also prepared, nandi."

Was it that time? He wasn't prepared to consider ordinary routine. Not now. Not given what he still didn't understand. The sandwiches he was grateful to have. "I shall manage to sleep here, Danda-ji. Please don't let my schedule disturb staff. See that Banichi and Jago rest. My orders. And you rest, Danda-ji."

"Yes, nandi." A bow. The tray stayed. Its contents

disappeared bit by bit as Bren worked, considering one piece of non-fitting data and the next . . . in this gift freighted with every blip and hiccup of the ship's operations in those hours, and on the other hand lacking all human observation that might have informed him on Ramirez's state of mind, on what he thought he saw, on what he hoped.

What had Ramirez done to contact outsiders? Nothing that involved Jase—or Jase would have known more. Nothing, one surmised, that involved Yolanda, who'd been equally a novice when she'd landed on the atevi world, to try to deal with disaffected humans. Neither of them had had any experience of outsiders—not to mention planets. Ramirez had prepared them for some venture, but they were still junior; and they weren't well-prepared for planets. And they were, at that time, just very young.

And for that reason he hadn't asked them. Hadn't used the tools he himself had prepared. Hadn't *planned* the encounter. It had come on him. And he'd simply—

Perceived another ship. That was the first fact in the data log. Another ship. A huge ship.

Another ship—just sitting there. So Ramirez had gone to passive reception, no output. Dead silent.

Then . . . then Ramirez had recorded one cryptic note: *A massive ship has appeared in the orbit of the second planet. We have received a signal. Three flashes, no other content apparent. We are holding position without answering.*

Without answering.

Next entry, forty-eight minutes later:

No movement. No signal.

And after two hours:

No movement. No signal. Retreat seems most prudent at this point, in a vector that doesn't lead home.

First vector to Point Gamma, then wait for the wake to fade. After that, home and report.

The log record broke off there.

He didn't have any record of their arrival at Point Gamma, whatever that was, however useful that record would have been. But Jase had stated they'd gone to that place. Trying to obscure their origin, one guessed.

The segment ended.

No record of further output from the alien before departure. Nothing.

Bren wiped his face. Went through the record multiple times, looking for any chance output that might have generated a misunderstanding.

Running lights had been on. Those stopped when Ramirez ordered no-output. Nothing but cameras and passive reception, gathering signals in, putting none out.

He couldn't find an active cause prior to that silence. Couldn't find it.

He realized he'd slept, head down on the desk, neck stiff from hours of bad angle. He rubbed his face and tried to gather up all his threads, found the pieces of last shift's thought—no wiser than before.

Narani, missing nothing, provided breakfast, offered a dressing-robe instead of his rumpled clothes. "One can think in the shower, nandi. One does suggest so."

That, Bren thought, might be useful to clear his head; and he tried, but the warm shower only tended to put him to sleep. He came to himself leaning against the wall, and all but fell asleep a second time when Narani was helping him into his bathrobe.

His brain, past experience told him, was vainly trying to assemble diverse parts of a pattern, one that, thanks to missing bits, wasn't willing to make sense. Conscious thought was timed out while the hindbrain tried its own obscure pattern-making out of the bits and pieces; but it wasn't getting anywhere, while his waking forebrain came up with images of Jase, younger Jase, sitting in his cabin in those days wondering what was going on.

Those progressed to remembered images of Ramirez himself sitting at his desk, hands together in that deep thinking attitude of his, Ramirez asking himself, in those hours, whether he ought to engage his two translators, whether it was time, yet, to risk contact.

And what could he do? Initiate the plan he'd been building for over twenty years, with two junior and necessarily inexperienced translators who hadn't finished their educations . . .

Ramirez, hesitating and hesitating, asking himself how much of this meeting he could now keep out of record, how much of his resources he could keep the Guild authority from laying claim to, if he brought them into the question and entered something of their activity on record . . .

Like the Guild snatching Jase and Yolanda onto Reunion, grilling them for every detail of that encounter, and finding, perhaps—clues that led under other doors.

The Guild appropriating twenty years worth of preparation into the Guild's hands, with its demonstrably isolationist theories.

Ramirez would find his precious program stopped. His ideas quashed. Twenty years tossed down a black hole. The Guild never had released what it laid hands on. If Ramirez engaged Jase and Yolanda in a contact he wasn't ready to pursue, the Guild might then take them and never let them go—or not let them go until they were thoroughly Guild, on a Guild mission. A senior captain who'd invested twenty years in a project knew he didn't have another twenty years to rebuild from scratch, and wouldn't have the resources to get ahead of the Guild. He had to get through this, lay his plans, try a second time.

Guild—and ship. Two authorities running human affairs.

Guild—and ship. One wasn't necessarily the other, but ship depended on Guild—and hated its dependence on the Guild for fuel, the lack of mining 'bots. Ramirez wasn't independent. He couldn't make a total break from the Guild's authority.

But in this system he had his fuel source and he had a green world—if he could have used it. He'd flirted with alien contact—so Sabin said—maybe before this. He hoped to break out of Guild control. He hoped to get a source not dependent on the Guild.

But here the aliens confronted him.

So what was prudent?

Sit still. Hope it didn't notice?

It noticed. It waited.

Awaited contact? Wanted some gesture? Theoretically a civilized entity ought to realize the signals under such circumstances wouldn't be congruent—but grant atevi and humans, highly civilized, had very clearly botched their own contact well into the process, and nearly killed themselves before they straightened matters out.

Ramirez left. Ramirez had left the confrontation. That was the conclusion of the affair. That was the one rock on which he could build a theory. Whatever his surmises about Ramirez's reasons and Ramirez's thought pattern and what a civilized entity on the other side ought to expect—the fact was Ramirez had unilaterally broken his freeze-state, and left in a vector other than Reunion.

That redirection hadn't fooled the aliens for a minute. Had it? So they had an idea where he came from. They'd been watching.

Silence. Then a deceptive vector.

Touching off, perhaps, as Jase said, *emotional* responses—those sub-basement responses and assumptions that clouded thinking, those gut-level conclusions that were beneath clear thought.

If he put himself as, say, *ship-human*, in the aliens' position—how would he react to seeing an intruding ship pull out without responding? He had no clear idea.

If he put himself as *Mospheiran* in that situation—he'd—well, he'd find a superior and give a report. And if he was President of Mospheira—he'd call his ally and ask what his ally Tabini thought. He'd get a committee together. He'd fund a study. He'd be paralyzed until the committee report came in. A Mospheiran had a thoroughly despairing view of official decision-making. On the other hand, the average Mospheiran tourist could be an incredible fool.

If, next thought, he put himself as atevi in that situation—

He thought he knew what he'd do if he were atevi. He thought he knew what responses would follow, acted-upon and otherwise. But he had the opportunity to ask someone whose nervous system had those other answers. He called in the least warlike ateva on staff. He called in Jeladi.

"What would one believe that meant?" he asked, having explained the situation, "if the stranger ship left, under those circumstances?"

"It went to its associates," Jeladi said, "by a devious route."

"And, nadi?"

"It will return with weapons, nandi."

He was not particularly surprised. Several thousand years of atevi experience led to that conclusion. He gathered himself up, in his bathrobe, and went to Banichi and posed the question. Jago arrived, and he repeated it. "What would you expect?" he asked them collectively.

"A lure to an ambush," Jago said.

"We would not take that bait," Banichi said.

Atevi were not the most peaceful of species. Hadn't been, even before the petal sails dropped down. There was a reason the Assassins' Guild mediated the law, a civilizing force in the society.

There remained a third source of information. "I shall dress," he said to Narani, and began to do so, thinking of begging the dowager to receive a petitioner, no matter that none of them were at their mental best.

But before he had quite donned his coat, a message cylinder arrived.

We have heard your question, Ilisidi said—God, how did she manage? *Even my great-grandson has an opinion in this case. One should not follow, except with superior force. One should lie in wait. My great-grandson believes we should blow it up immediately and fortify against general invasion. His great-grandfather would have concurred.*

Go to bed. We order it.

Bren stood there with his limbs wobbling, half-dressed and chilled, thinking—well, now he need not call on Ilisidi. Now he should call Jase with his multi-sided answer and inform Jase how provocative Ramirez's apparently prudent actions could seem.

He should call Jase—when he had a brain. And when it wasn't the middle of Jase's night. Jase was still asleep. At the moment, he thought, sleep in his own case might produce more intelligence than study would.

He didn't want to fly his theories past Sabin until he had his wits about him.

He undressed as meticulously as he'd dressed, thinking, thinking—how the ship had gone off its direct track home. But the aliens hadn't wasted time. They'd known where the human base was.

One assumed an advanced civilization wouldn't be mindlessly, pointlessly violent.

One assumed that, based on humanity's rise from the caves. Based on atevi's general progress—toward television and fast food. On the whole it tended to be true, for these two species. Any two points made a straight line. But a third—felicitous third—wasn't guaranteed to be anywhere on that line, was it? Not at all.

He was losing his train of thought. Points that didn't lie in a straight line.

Aliens had gone straight to the station. What they'd done before they hit it, what the station had done— no record.

Ramirez had left the encounter. That didn't say, on the other end, what the station had done. Or not done.

He lay down in bed. Thinking.

Did the ship observe a pattern in the three blinks from the alien craft? A variation of color, of duration? No information on that score. No image.

One *assumed*, humans being sensitive to visual input, that Ramirez would have recorded any such anomaly in the signal—*if* he hadn't tucked all the really useful notes somewhere outside the official log.

But then, if Ramirez had known enough to take the right notes, he'd have stood a chance of taking the right actions. Wouldn't he?

Eyes were already shut. Brain drifted toward dark.

He felt the give of the mattress. Felt a familiar warmth, smooth skin against his.

"Jago-ji." He'd been thinking back and forth in Mosphei' and Ragi. At the moment he didn't know which he spoke.

"Have you reached a conclusion, Bren-ji?"

"Not that I trust."

"Ramirez's actions were peculiar," Jago said.

"Not for a human," he murmured. Senses were leaving him. He settled against Jago's warmth, still trying to think through Ramirez's actions and beginning to suspect his thinking had gone off the edge of reason.

He felt Jago's hand on his face. Felt a caress on his shoulder. He tried desperately to reconstruct his train of thought. Everything was dark, dark and the touch of a familiar hand, the whisper of a familiar voice: "Rest, Bren-ji. Rest now. You try yourself too much."

He did sleep. He was sure he slept, because, *"Bren,"* the intercom said, Jase's voice, in the middle of his night, and he had to wake. He groped for the side of the bed, momentarily forgetting that he was in a steel and ceramics world, where words were sufficient. He thought he was in the tall bed in his own apartment in Shejidan, and was shocked to meet the floor sooner than he expected.

"Lights," he remembered to say, and thoughtlessly blinded himself and Jago. He held a hand up to shield his eyes. "Two-way com.—Jase? What's up?"

"Looks like we're finding an interface," Jase said. *"Not certain yet, but take this for a warning. Whether we're there or not is always a question, but the navigators think this should be a straightforward entry."*

"Thanks," he said, muzzy, out of breath. "Thanks." And tried to organize what he knew. "We're not done yet. Jase, I'm not done. I've learned things—"

"I've called the senior captain. My chief navigator estimates one to three hours, big give-or-take."

"Have you got an answer yet out of that tape?"

"Makes no sense," Jase said. "No sense."

"I have theories—at least about the contact."

"We'll have to solve those questions on the other side. Drop's going to happen whether we're ready or not. It's in progress. You've got leave to be here just as soon as we make entry. Get ready. You may have a very small safe window to move."

"Understood," he said, rattled, and translated that in more detail for Jago. Jase was thinking in shipspeak at the moment, not Ragi, and small wonder. They were going in and he and Jase weren't ready. But the navigators guessed . . . *hoped* . . . this would be it.

And God knew what they were about to meet.

"Advise Narani, nadi-ji," he said to Jago. "Advise Cenedi. I'll advise the dowager myself." He dragged his chilled limbs off the bed and flung a robe about him as Jago hastened about her orders.

Bren stumbled to the table that served as his desk and penned a quick paper note:

Aiji-ma, we may well have arrived at our destination. As ever, there is the possibility of imprecision, but I am proceeding to the ship's central command immediately after arrival to assess the situation. One hopes for your approval as ever. He dimly remembered, on the other side of sleep, the dowager's unlooked-for response to his query. *One appreciates beyond expression your felicitous response to my question. One is grateful. I shall represent your interests with all my efforts.*

He rolled it, slipped it into the cylinder, took the risk of omitting the seal, the reception of which informality depended on the state of Ilisidi's nerves.

"To the dowager, Rani-ji," he instructed Narani, who had appeared in the door to assess the state of affairs, and while Narani undertook that diplomatic errand, Bren headed for his shower, for a minute of warm steam and a dry towel, no waiting for the vacuum. He scrubbed violently, trying to rub sensation into his skin; he toweled his hair, hoping for clear thought.

Scared. Oh, he was that, no question. He attempted to finger-comb his hair, breaking through the snarls. He put on trousers and boots, trying not to show absolute terror.

"Haste, nadi-ji," he told Asicho when she began to comb his hair. "We may be surprised by events. Never mind it pulls." He would have welcomed a sharp pain, anything to define the space, the time, the event, some keen sensory input to sting him out of this foggy-headed limbo of the ship before space straightened itself out again and dumped them into a situation none of them could predict.

Bindanda and Jeladi both showed up to assist him. For the important event of their arrival, Narani had provided a shirt that had to go on with its coat, the lace so starched it could cut cake.

Asicho finished his pigtail with breathless haste. Narani arrived to supervise Bindanda and Jeladi and be sure of the lace. Banichi and Jago were, meanwhile, managing for themselves, he was sure, while he accepted the help a lord needed, all of them hurrying, accurate, calm in the way his staff had been calm dressing him for court warfare.

One assumed the cylinder had by now found its way to the dowager's attention at such an hour; one very well knew Cenedi knew, and that courtesy was done. Handled. One thing of all the things on his agenda was done and nailed down tight.

A siren blew briefly. Space, that had held them in a mind-fogged grip for day upon day of perceived time, was about to unfold itself, taking them back into reality with it.

Not his favorite thing. God, no. A lot like landings in airplanes. Or space shuttles.

He was, however, formally dressed. Ready for whatever happened.

"Fifteen minutes to drop," the intercom informed them.

He received a vexed message from the dowager. Could not the ship-aijiin arrange such events at a more civilized hour?

"This is the captain speaking." Sabin's voice, not Jase's, in dead calm, near monotone. *"We are beginning procedures for arrival. All non-essential crew to quarters. Take hold, take hold, take hold."*

Official, then. Sabin was in charge over their heads and crew, all the great majority of personnel that maintained non-critical stations and operations, was to tuck down and remain invisible and out of the way for the duration.

Jago arrived, dressed in her best—armed, though what good that did against their current situation he had no idea, nor, surely, had Jago. The weaponry was an expression of support, of professional attention to detail.

"One believes we should take our seats," he said calmly, and settled down in a broad, comfortable, bolted chair, carefully arranging his coat tails. Jago took the other. The rest of staff had such accommodations in the security station, where Banichi likely sat; or in their own accommodations, where they could ride comfortably belted down in bed.

"Stand by." C1's advisement, the calm clear voice of senior communications.

The slight muzziness of their days of transit increased, convinced the senses that the ship was sliding sideways, then forward.

His staff took it far, far better than he did. His stomach felt very queasy, and he didn't want to shut his eyes: sense-deprivation only made it worse.

Boarding a plane. He was scarcely out of his teens. Scarcely out of university.

Coming in at Shejidan, ahead of a cargo of tinned fish and electronics, all the tiled roofs spread out below him. It rained, common enough in spring. The tiled roofs became more textured, more real, slicked and shining, while the surrounding hills veiled themselves in rain and cloud.

The Bu-javid sat on its hill, mysterious, indistinct in blowing rain. He'd live there one day. He hadn't imagined it, then. But he'd have an apartment high on that northern wing, just that window . . .

Explosion of gunfire, amid golden fields. They were shooting at targets, and Tabini-aiji, tall, slender, skilled marksman, popping branches off a dead limb, while a novice human paidhi tried to figure why the unprecedented invitation, and trying to hold his own firearm steady and not shoot the servants. Illegal for him to have the gun, but the aiji invited him, and he asked himself what the motive might be.

Shot in the dark, in the spring night, with a shadow outside the blowing draperies and the smell of djossi flowers on the heavy air.

A very foolish, very young human interpreter diving out of bed and behind the unlikely cover of the mattress.

Banichi had found him there. Found him, and traded guns with him, and covered what might have been a deep secret among atevi lords.

Keep him safe, Tabini had ordered Banichi and Jago, and who could have known they'd one day be guarding his life this far from home?

Keep him safe. Was ever a man luckier in his associates?

Breakfast on a balcony, in a thin coat, freezing, drinking burning-hot tea before it chilled to ice. Breakfast with the dowager, who hadn't needed a coat.

Breakfast and a broken arm.

And an end of all easy assumptions, all confidence in what humans believed about atevi intentions and the atevi's choices for their future.

That breakfast had led him here, wherever *here* was beginning to be.

Down, now, increasingly down, an illusion of falling through space faster and faster, weightless for a moment.

Then here.

Here.

Suddenly at rest, when intellect knew they weren't: that the ship was still going faster than a planet-bred imagination easily grasped.

But down felt down again, as if it had never been different—at least a planet-habituated stomach felt very reassured by the current state of affairs. The safe universe had fractured and someone had fixed it. Very nice, very reassuring.

That meant they had arrived. Space had straightened itself out. And he had to move. Quickly, by Jase's advisement.

He got up, and Jago got up.

"We'll go up to the bridge," he said, as if he proposed a trip down the hall at home. Thoughts were suddenly easier. He *remembered* things. One didn't have to nail every thought to the wall.

But now he wasn't sure any of his prior reasoning about the log records made thorough sense.

Jago tugged her jacket smooth. He adjusted his coat. They went out to find Banichi. Staff had turned out into the corridor, too, understanding that events would flow rapidly in this arrival.

"This is the senior captain speaking," the intercom speakers said suddenly. *"Early indications indicate arrival in Reunion System. General crew will stay in cabins until further notice."*

They *had* arrived. Banichi met them at the security center, where Asicho waited, ready to take up her watch at the boards. Narani had accompanied them down the corridor. So did Bindanda and Jeladi. They all gathered outside the security station, all his household, all awaiting information and instructions on which their safety might depend.

All relying on him.

And in the same instant he grasped that distressing thought, the dowager's apartment door opened and the dowager exited her rooms—*with* Cajeiri in tow. In court dress. It was not a casual expedition.

Ilisidi, Cajeiri, Cenedi. One of the senior staff carried a fair-sized packet wrapped in a tablecloth— lunch, one greatly feared.

They had notions where they were going.

Cajeiri, too, had a small wallet tucked under his arm, which Bren feared was not lunch.

And had he somehow implied, in his general muzziness, that the senior captain had cleared *them* to come up? There was nothing that stopped a tidal wave *or* the aiji-dowager once assumptions had gone this far. She was dressed. She was in motion.

And, granted Sabin was going to have the proverbial litter of kittens, the dowager was a resource the paidhiin could well use close at hand if things came unhinged.

"Go," Ilisidi said with an impatient wave of her cane, as if she were not the one arriving late. "Go, go, nadiin. For what do we wait?"

"Nandi." Bren stood aside to prefer her and Cajeiri, and both their bodyguards folded in behind.

5

The senior captain would be too busy to lodge strong objections, Bren said to himself, watching the lift level indicator flick numbers past. And the captain did expect him, and expected help.

"The ship-aiji believes we have indeed arrived at our destination, aiji-ma," he said as the lift rose. "One isn't quite sure how they know, but one supposes they find familiar indications."

Ilisidi gave an indelicate snort. "High time."

The lift stopped at its appointed level. The doors opened and they walked out into that neck of the lift foyer that had no view of the bridge, only of the administrative offices beyond.

So far, so good.

Jase stood in view, beside the short screening wall. The lift noise had not gone unnoticed. Whatever his opinion, Jase kept perfectly deadpan, poker-stiff as they walked toward him, beyond that curtain wall and into full view of the bridge. Captain Sabin, in those narrow aisles of techs at consoles, stood there, watching over the situation, occupied, at the moment, at a console in the middle aisle.

"Four jump seats to your right," Jase muttered in Ragi. "Emergency cabinet is next to them. Go there if alert sounds."

Bren spotted the seats and the access—the takehold

cabinet was, in effect, the curtain wall itself, and their party certainly exceeded the safety seating.

Then Sabin passed a cold glance over the atevi invasion, and strode toward them.

"Mr. Cameron." The voice of doom.

"Additional opinions, ma'am. A valuable point of view."

"The *kid* is a point of view?"

"I assure you there'll be no disturbance, Captain." Bren fervently hoped so, and said, in Ragi, "One must wait in patience, aiji-ma. There are seats over there for you and the young gentleman, should you wish, and one advises their use. This may be hours in progress."

"We shall undoubtedly avail ourselves of the chairs, paidhi-ji." Ilisidi leaned on her cane and looked about her. There was no general image view, except one small screen forward, which was uninformatively black, and Ilisidi scanned it, and the general surrounds. "So. Hardly more than a security station. And where will Reunion be?"

"Far distant, nand' dowager," Jase said, interceding. "Even so the ship is going very fast in the direction of the star, about which one will find three very large planets. Reunion orbits the one nearest to the sun."

"There are no persons on these planets, is this so, Jase-nandi?"

Ever so careful of the protocols: a considerate honor from the dowager in Jase's native territory—to which Jase gave an ever-so-little bow, Ragi-style. "The dowager is of course correct. They're hardly more than balls of natural gas and nitrogen."

"Fertilizer." The dowager gave a wry laugh. "So. So. Let us not interrupt your work, ship-aijiin."

"Nand' dowager." Correct address for a great lady no longer *his* lady: Jase used the remote, not the personal *ma*—and drew aside to continue, as Sabin did, a slow patrol of the aisles among the four rows of technicians.

Everything was going well. Very well. They were still alive. Sabin had, with a baleful stare, accepted their help. But there was noise from the lift nearby, unregistered in the moment.

The lift had gone down: not unusual. The car resided in mid-levels. But now it ascended a second time, opened its door and let out, God help them, Ginny and her chief engineer, Jerry; and one now had to ask how many they could cram into that emergency cabinet if the ship had to move.

"What's this?" *Sabin* had stepped into line of vision, too, and confronted the Mospheirans. Jerry had also brought, one saw, a sack lunch—like Mospheirans on holiday, Bren thought, the pernicious national habit. Dared one say it lent a very surreal feeling to the moment?

"Moral support," Ginny said. "And advice, where needed."

"Hell," Sabin said sharply, gave Bren a withering look—*I didn't* was the gut-level response, but he kept that useless protest behind his teeth, and Sabin forbore to order the lot of them off the bridge. "Keep it quiet. And keep out of my way."

"Takehold shelter," Bren advised the newcomers quietly, with a gesture toward the cabinet. Ginny and Jerry took a look and had that information.

So they were all represented here aft of the bridge—all there but the residents of the ship, the run of the crew who ran the systems that didn't have to do with conditions outside the hull.

The ones Ramirez had lied to so early, the last time they'd made this approach.

One wondered if there was, this time, a live video

feed belowdecks—or—so basic was the supposition that what one saw on the monitor was real—one had to wonder if what was up there at the moment in front of the bridge crew was real.

Jase would know. Surely Jase would know.

And one reminded oneself that Sabin, with all her other faults, had taken a stand in favor of truth. At least she had advertised that to be the case.

She wouldn't possibly lie about that.

Would she?

"Mani-ma." Whisper from Cajeiri. "May one see the screens up close?"

"One certainly may not, great-grandson."

"What are they doing, mani-ma?"

"What the ship-aiji bids them do, young sir, and a wise young sir would leave them to do it undistracted before they crash this ship."

"One would never distract them, mani-ma. One only—"

Thump! went the ferrule of the cane against the deck. Ginny and her companion jumped. Technicians jumped. Both captains turned to look.

And, meeting utter atevi and Mospheiran propriety, the two captains turned back to their work. The technicians never had looked away from the screens and instruments, not a one.

Bren took a deep breath.

"Is everything all right?" Ginny asked.

"Oh, ordinary," Bren said. "The young aiji would like to see the view."

"So would we all," Ginny said.

Presumably the image above them was indeed valid as it shifted . . . magnified, became centered on twin points of light.

A star? A planet?

They stood in silence a lengthy period of time, Cajeiri fidgeting with his pockets, and his parcel, and finally receiving a reprimand.

The view shifted again, and the points of light became larger, and resolved into a disc and a dimmer point, dimmer, flickering, and resolving, and resolving again as Sabin and Jase moved routinely from station to station.

The next resolution shut out the brighter object entirely. The smaller light source became very likely a space station, rotating, showing one great dark patch.

"Is that where we're going, nandiin-ji?" Cajeiri asked.

"One believes so, young sir," Cenedi answered him.

"Is—"

"Hush," Ilisidi said sharply, and added: "If waiting tires you, you may go sit in your room, young sir."

"No, mani-ma."

The image grew clearer, slowly, slowly. Jase drifted near in his patrol of the room.

"The crew is seeing this, nadi?" Bren asked in Ragi.

"One believes so," Jase said under his breath. "One hopes so. What we're seeing is what we hope to see at this point. The station doesn't know we're here, yet, unless there's an alarm we don't know about. They'll respond soon, if there's anyone alive, but we're two hours sixteen minutes and some-odd seconds out from their answer, nadiin-ji. You'll see a counter start to run on that screen once we know our initial signal has reached them. We have transmitted a focused signal, aimed tightly at them."

Jase moved off. Bren translated for Ginny and her companion, quietly.

"The ship's ten years late," Ginny muttered to him. "No big surprise if whoever was listening is on tea break."

"No big surprise," Bren agreed, and translated the

remark for the dowager and the rest, who thought it funny. Even Cajeiri got the joke, and wanted to know when the promised numbers would turn up.

"One will point it out," Cenedi said, and just then the numbers did appear in the corner of the screen. "There. One has *that* long to wait."

Cajeiri looked. And fidgeted.

"Will we do nothing else, nandiin-ji?"

"A small boy could go back to the nursery," Ilisidi said sternly, and Cajeiri clutched his packet and stood stock still for a remarkable fifteen minutes before he heaved a sigh.

Another before the feet had to move.

The dowager's cane came down gently on the offending foot.

"One regrets, mani-ma."

"Good," Ilisidi said sharply.

They waited. And waited. A quarter, then a half hour crawled past with no movement at all from the boy.

One hesitated to suggest again that the dowager sit. She was veteran of the court in Shejidan, where standing was a test of endurance and will. She had the boy for witness to any weakness.

But the cane was not all for show.

They stood another half hour and more. Bren tried to think of a courteous way to suggest again they rest, and found none.

Then Ilisidi lifted her cane and pointed to the jump seats against the takehold cabinet. "We shall sit, Cenedi-ji."

"Yes," Cenedi said, and certainly with relief. They moved to let down two of the jump seats.

Ilisidi sat down. Motioned to Cajeiri to sit. There were three other seats. "Paidhi-ji. Gin-nadi."

Persons of equivalent rank might sit. Bren accepted

the honor gratefully, and relayed the invitation to Gin, who sensibly did come and sit down, accepting her lordship, leaving Jerry to stand.

The numbers ran on the screen. Jase and Sabin continued their slow patrol of the aisles and C1 made a brief status report to the general crew: *"Situation normal on the bridge. Still awaiting response window relative to station. We have Reunion Station in long-view. Channel one is currently providing that image."*

They sat. Cajeiri's packet proved nothing more dire than a book, which evidently the dowager approved— or accepted as a necessity for young nerves. Bren found himself trying to see the book title, trying to see any information at all to distract an information-hungry brain, but he couldn't quite manage. So they all waited. Distances were large and information crawled over inconceivable dark spaces.

Jase and Sabin spoke together for a moment. The station image suddenly grew more distinct. No exterior lights showed, none of the navigational blinkers operating on the mast. A source of flicker showed as trailing debris from a massive dark area of destruction.

The clock ticked down toward the reply window. Anticipation on the bridge was palpable.

The clock entered negative territory; and time ran. Anticipation began to curdle.

"Is it not past time?" Cajeiri asked—having learned perfectly well to read human numbers. He had closed his book and held it against his chest.

"It is, indeed, young gentleman," Ilisidi said. "Which may mean many things, including the possibility that we are too late to effect a rescue. Or that the one person on watch has decided to read a book. Hush, and listen."

"What if—?"

"Hush."

Cajeiri hushed, and with worried looks at the display, reopened his book and buried himself in it. The sentiment was much the same among the techs. And the captains. Gin Kroger frowned, saying not a word. Bren exchanged a worried look with Banichi and Jago.

"Might we have sandwiches?" Cajeiri asked eventually, in the long crawl of time.

"The aiji's heir alone may have a sandwich," Ilisidi said, "while his elders worry."

A small silence. "I no longer feel hungry, mani-ma."

"When the crew has refreshment," Ilisidi said, "*then* would be appropriate."

"Yes, mani-ma."

Cajeiri dutifully returned to his book. Bren longed to get up, to pace the deck, to ask Jase what he'd said to Sabin and what Sabin had said to him—but his questions did no good, no more than Cajeiri's, and he kept them to himself.

"*This is C1. As yet there is no response from the station. Stand by.*"

Natural caution, Bren said to himself. The station, if there was anyone receiving, had likely to advise its own officers, review the situation, decide to respond to a distant signal.

"Captain." A communications tech flashed a signal. Sabin was over there in an instant. So was Jase.

They looked like two rescuees from a drowning.

"We have signal," Sabin said aloud. "A simple hail." And to the technicians: "Put me through. Put two-way communications on general address, bridge excluded." She lifted her personal comm to speaking range. "This is Captain Sabin, *CS Phoenix,* inbound, ETA in your vicinity sixteen hours fifty-six minutes. Hello, Reunion."

Distantly, from the administrative corridor, as it

would on every deck, breaking centuries of precedent, her voice echoed, marginally time-lagged.

No time lag at all within the corridors . . . compared to the astronomical distances involved in their communication.

Atevi, however, needed quick information.

"A signal has come from the station," Bren translated the situation quietly, as he sat. "Sabin-aiji has identified herself vocally and given, human reckoning, sixteen hours fifty-six *minuta* as our arrival."

"Sixteen and thirty-eight," Ilisidi said, instantly converting the awkward number . . . not felicitous, but certainly transitory, as the ship was rushing toward that goal, making the gap tighter and tighter. *He* hadn't been able to reckon that far that fast, and should have, he realized to his chagrin, if his brain weren't overladen with human concerns and racing in a dozen directions at once.

"We contain the numbers of all the world," he murmured, "which *are* fortunate, aiji-ma."

"And *we* are not superstitious country folk." Ilisidi sat with hands about the shaft of her cane, in a human chair that would have been inconveniently low for the majority of the atevi staff. A seat on his scale and Ginny's. And Cajeiri's. "But do they then trust this reply as genuine, Bren-paidhi?"

"I don't think Sabin-aiji necessarily trusts anything in this situation," he said, "but yes, aiji-ma, there's a certain rush to accept this welcome as reasonable and expected."

"And?"

"The station authorities may well view us with suspicion after years of delay in our return. We don't even know for certain Ramirez-aiji left here on their mission—or on his own."

"The residents should have left this inconveniently located outpost and saved us the bother. And they chose not to vacate."

"Yes, aiji-ma."

"Unreasonable, by any logic."

Indeed, not the first time atevi had posed that nagging question. Not the first time they'd discussed it on this voyage.

"One certainly wishes one knew why before we arrive," he said. "I have some doubt that even Sabin-aiji is confident that things are as Ramirez-aiji recorded them."

On the other side, Reunion must have concluded, from their nine year delay, that there hadn't been fuel waiting, indicating a political situation or a technical failure, or possibly the loss of the ship itself. If things had gone ideally, from the station's point of view, the ship would surely have coasted up to the station at the atevi star, gotten fuel as fast as possible, and been back in short order.

In the nine, ten years counting Ramirez's transit to Alpha, depend on it, any survivors at Reunion had had ample time and motive to implement options that no longer included *Phoenix*.

And now, suddenly, here was *Phoenix* back again to upset their efforts at self-rescue, efforts potentially involving power struggles and reputations. More, in their eyes, the ship would come freighting in God knew what business from Alpha, with all its questions. On one level, if things were less than disastrous here, Reunion authorities might question very closely what *Phoenix* had found. And *that* didn't help their mission run smoothly.

Figure it. If there were two humans, there were two sides, and if both had a pulse, politics would be at work somewhere in the business.

Getting here involved one set of problems. Now

that they were down to another set, the politics of the station itself, he discovered his heart beating as if he'd climbed a tall, tall flight of stairs, nothing to do with physical exertion and everything to do with decades of preparation that had brought him into this situation. It wasn't a high-speed train of events—or it was, as planets saw time—as nations changed and rose and fell; in human terms, it moved like land-creep, but in terms of finite human beings supposed to be wise and to make the right decisions, time both dragged and flickered past, and Sabin's stated number of hours was far too long to worry and far too short a time to do anything creative.

He *could* represent the colonists, or pretend to: he had been the island representative once upon a time. Atevi weren't the first surprise they should spring on the residents of Reunion: Ilisidi would surely agree to that.

And he assuredly was about to have a job to do, if talk had begun to flow.

"The ship has begun to talk with the station, aijima. I think I should place myself at the ship-aiji's disposal." He said much the same to Ginny Kroger: "I'm going to go stand somewhere in Sabin's easy reach in this reply cycle. I think we're running stable enough."

He got up and walked into the aisles. His purposeful approach to the operations area brought a glance from Sabin. An answering slow approach on Jase's part intercepted him for a private word.

"How do you think we're doing?" Bren asked him quietly.

"Too well at this point," Jase said. "Scarily well."

Sabin walked over, hands locked behind her, muscle working in a lean jaw. "Holding conference, gentlemen?"

"Offering my services where useful, captain. As a start, with all due respect, I'd advise not telling station authorities everything about us."

"Oh, I'd certainly concur there, Mr. Cameron. By a long way not half about us. And if we're really lucky we can refuel before we have to tell them a thing about our passenger list or our intentions."

"One believes they'll have long since taken their own survival measures, invested reputations and effort, developed an emotional charge on their own course. Resentment of us for not coming back immediately. Suspicion now that we have come back. I wouldn't be surprised at that."

"You're just a prophet of all kinds of trouble, aren't you, Mr. Cameron?"

"Certainly best we don't rush out of the ship and hold a farewell party on dockside."

"I don't think I had any such intention."

"I'm sure not. Here's another item. They'll contest your command versus their authority."

A little silence and a sidelong look.

"You know I'm right," Bren said.

"You're just full of opinions, Mr. Cameron."

"I advise the aiji in Shejidan, who's outlived all expectations. I advise you defy any order to meet them outside the ship."

"Son of a *bitch*, Mr. Cameron."

"Yes, ma'am. At your service. Continually. They're the authority that's run human affairs for the last several hundred years. Their ideas haven't worked damned well. We all think it's time there was a new authority. And not even for fuel should you give a step backward."

"Go on, Mr. Cameron, as if I have no imagination of the situation."

"I'm sure you do, captain. And if we assume they *ordered* Ramirez to go to the original base, secure it, refuel and get back, we can assume they don't plan to be taking your orders when you show up, do they?"

"Keep going."

"Two, they expect Ramirez. Three, they've had all these years to figure out things didn't go according to plan back where we come from. So they'll immediately ask you what happened to Ramirez and what took so long. If you say, refueling, they'll know immediately that the station we come from wasn't exactly waiting for your return. If you say we had to get the locals back into space and build the whole apparatus to refuel, they'll wonder what else went on. They know the planet is inhabited. And that leads step by step to other questions, such as the reason I suspect Ramirez was courting aliens rather than go to Alpha's colonists in the first place—I think they're scared of finding an alternative *human* agency set up back at Alpha, offering opposition to them. And numerous hard-headed humans, tending to subvert the Guild vision for humanity. I'm willing to be your token colonist authority and lie through my teeth, and try to diminish those fears."

"A whole lot of help we've got," Sabin said. "Help from your alien allies, and pushy help from a self-appointed advisor."

"Yes, ma'am," Bren said, "exceedingly pushy. I have a vested interest in having you in charge, not them."

"You think so, do you?"

"You've told us Ramirez was up to something. I'm sure Ogun knew it. I know you knew it. I know you and Ogun aren't precisely on the same program. But if you like the idea of turning yourself and your ship and crew over to the people that have gotten this station in need of a rescue, you're flat crazy, and I don't think that's the case."

Sabin lifted one eyebrow. And looked at Jase. "Does he talk to the aiji that way?"

"Yes," Jase said.

"The fact is, we haven't won. We won't be halfway toward winning this until we're fueled, loaded, and on our way back. Reunion could have solved all of their problems and ours simply by boarding *Phoenix* on your last call here. They didn't do that. So they have another plan, involving some linkage to Alpha, and Alpha's position is very blunt: fold operations, come under ship rule, and stop bothering the neighbors. Do *you* think you're going to get what you want out of them?"

"Go entertain your aliens."

"Advice, captain, simply advice."

"No place for a damned atevi kid," Sabin muttered. "No place for the whole damned lot of you. You have your assumptions. But we can't go blazing in there laying down conditions to the Guildmaster, Mr. Cameron. Fuel first. *Then* we read them the rules as they're going to be."

"If there *is* fuel."

"If there is fuel. If there isn't, then I'll most certainly call on Ms. Kroger to take our own measures and you'll doubtless have a word on that, too. Meanwhile, we're not near docking yet. Go sit down and don't distract my crew with your predictions."

She hadn't asked the station about the fuel situation. She hadn't presented any long-distance chatter, nothing friendly, nothing as ebullient as long-lost friends meeting. Was he surprised they weren't leaping up and down and cheering on the bridge, either?

Sabin walked off.

"She appreciated the advice," Jase said.

Bren raised an eyebrow.

"I work with her," Jase said. "She's on alert. She's glad we got here, but she's spooked. She's not trusting anything she sees. She appreciates a cross-check of observations."

Sabin wasn't stupid. Thank God.

He went back to the small gathering of atevi and Mospheirans, relayed the gist of the discussion and his own speculations, in Ragi and in Mosphei'. And sat down and waited.

"Is the stationmaster still talking to us, nandi?" Cajeri asked.

"We ride so very far from the station that we have to wait for their answers to reach us. Like seeing lightning and listening for the thunder. This distance is ever so much farther than we ordinarily consider on a planet. So the captain talks and waits; the station talks and waits. By the time the station answers the captain's questions, the captain has had time to sit down to tea and think about it."

"This could take all day!"

"And tomorrow, too, young sir, but remember the ship is moving, no matter how it feels. We're going there quite steadily. So the interval between question and answer grows shorter and shorter."

"Astonishing, nandi."

The dowager had thwacked *that* respectful courtesy into the young rascal.

"It is, young sir. Astonishing to us all." He recalled his own boyhood, sitting through adult feuds, intimately involved in the outcome and unable to read the signals passing over his head. "Translation: matters with the station are going better than we expected. There are people on the station and they can talk to us. If we're *very* lucky everything will be in order and we can do what we came to do and go home."

"But I want to see the station first!"

The dowager boxed a young ear. Gently so, but sternly. "Your elders have more serious business to consider, young sir."

"Yes, mani-ma."

One could understand. The dowager herself likely shared the sentiment. The atevi delegation was on formal manners, sitting and standing. Ginny and her companion were uncharacteristically quiet and solemn.

"Going too well," Ginny said, next to him. "Worries me."

"If it goes this easily," Bren said under his breath, "it's the first time in this Guild's history."

Ginny cast him a look. She was Mospheiran. She knew.

He sat. He waited. Eventually a station response came in and Sabin queried back, giving little information, but asking for the condition of the mast where they would dock.

Jase came to them shortly after. "The captain is ordering up food and drink for the bridge. The shift is not going to change. Would you wish anything, nandiin?"

"Hot tea," Ginny said.

"We have our own resources, ship-aiji," the dowager said. "But one is grateful."

"Nand' dowager." Jase bowed, and went back.

The galley order arrived in due time. Bridge crew ate at their posts. Atevi and Mospheirans opened up their small picnic lunches and ate, standing and sitting, in decorous quiet.

Information regarding the mast seemed to have come in: zenith mast was undamaged: one couldn't say as much for the nadir.

"We go on routine approach," Sabin said.

After so much, so long. Routine. That in itself was surreal.

Bren was thinking that when a technician moved suddenly and a red blinking quarter hit at least half the screens on the bridge.

Sabin leaned to look more closely at that intrusion; Jase did.

Bren stood up and in the same instant saw Sabin pass an order he couldn't hear. He walked back across that intangible line, back into aisles where screens still blinked red without explanation.

Jase met him, while Sabin stayed in close conference with the senior navigator.

"Armaments have been called up," Jase said in Mosphei'. "Something out there just pinged us. *Not* from the station."

"Damn," Bren breathed.

"Damn, for sure. Maybe a mining craft. But it could also be targeting. We've been spotted by something."

Triple damn. He'd just been settling into the comfort of their success and now they might not exist another hour.

Not that he hadn't asked himself for the last year what they ought to do if this happened.

"Any evidence of mining operations?"

"It's a big solar system. We haven't gotten any word from station about other activity. More to the point, the origin isn't in a region where we'd expect mining." Jase was scared too. It was in his eyes.

"Moving source, or something that's been there, all along?"

"Seems stationary. Our wavefront apparently just reached round-trip, us to them, them to us. Whoever it is. We've got continual signal now, and it's not showing motion."

"Did we ping them back?" All the while he was thinking about Ramirez's response, the dead-ship silence. "What's Sabin ordered?"

"We're waiting in silence," Jase said, that damnable word, *silence,* that governed their whole situation. That governed the Pilots' Guild's approach to the universe.

Deep breath. "No. Broadcast a hail. Noisy as possible. No more tight focus."

"Your advice is noted, Mr. Cameron," Sabin said. She could come up silently. She had, almost at his elbow. "It's one option. But we're closer to station than to it. I've queried station. They'll answer. We'll brake early. If it's a missile response we get, that creates a targeting problem."

"Yes, ma'am, but I'd prepare a broadcast in the event we need it."

"We can broadcast *Mary Had a Little Lamb* and whatever's out there won't know the difference."

That happened to be true. On the verbal level. "Send a pattern response. Three blinks. As they did the first time they met Ramirez. Something that at last sounds like an attempt at communication."

"We'll consider that option. Meanwhile, gentlemen, we're doing a take-hold."

"It's going to be evident when we brake, captain, won't it, and maybe they'll take it for a hostile act if the engines show activity . . ."

"We have to brake to dock, Mr. Cameron. They may want to critique our approach path, too, but in the meanwhile we hope station has an answer for us, what that noise source is. Advise granny, there. Siren will sound."

"Yes, ma'am," he said, and walked back to the dowager. "One should prepare, aiji-ma, for a maneuver of considerable strength and suddenness. I would advise the safety cabinet at this time rather than the seats. Some other presence is out beyond the ordinary limits of station activity. One suspects a hostile presence."

"Are we going to fight?" Cajeiri asked, rising.

"Hush, wretched boy." Ilisidi leaned on her cane and rose stiffly, to take his advice. "Prudence should lead valor. Have you never heard that?"

"Gin," Bren said. "Inside. We don't know if there's going to be emergency action, but they don't want loose bodies flying about."

"I'll skip that experience," Ginny said, and ordered Jerry into the L-shaped enclosure.

They still had a view: the screen at the end of the safety compartment, on a padded wall, showed the bridge, and in a window overlaid on that image, the image from space—the station. They likewise had audio, Sabin's low voice, and the flow through C1.

"What are they saying?" Cajeiri wanted to know.

"The captain is giving technical instructions, young sir," Bren answered, setting his back against the padded wall, hoping at the same time that their whole mission didn't come to a sudden end.

Siren sounded.

Then Sabin's voice overrode the chatter, loud and clear, on general address: *"We're beginning a series of small maneuvers preparatory to station approach. Stand by."*

Lie. Damned *lie*. Bren drew a sharp breath, all but exploded out of the safety zone, out where, if they hit the brakes, he could go splat against the other bulkhead, or up on that nice big viewing screen, untidy objection quashed. But he stayed put. He didn't go argue the point, on the bridge, in front of all the techs, that truth to the crew might be a good policy. It was reflex, was what it was. Given a situation, given a choice between truth and shading it—it was still the same choices.

One hoped to God Sabin's current maneuver with the ship was the right one. Braking wasn't exactly what Ramirez had done. Not quite. And could it look hostile?

"What have they said, paidhi-ji?" Ilisidi asked him.

"The ship-aiji claims this is all preparatory to docking. This may even be partially true, aiji-ma. But it is also maneuvering so as to confuse a possible enemy. Whom they refuse to contact. And one does not believe this silence is wise, either regarding the crew, or the watcher out there."

The ship braked. Hard and fast, as he'd suspected. He braced himself. Held his breath.

The invisible hand lifted. Let them breathe.

"Shall one not advise the ship-aiji of this opinion, nandi?" Cenedi asked.

"I intend to, nadi-ji." He was more and more set on arguing his point. Ramirez had been wrong. *Silence* had been wrong.

Another gentle nudge.

And silence continued from the speakers.

"Are we there yet?" Cajeiri asked. "Nandiin, are we—?"

Hard braking.

"Mr. Cameron to the bridge."

Sabin was calling *him?*

He didn't hesitate. He simply turned to the side against the padding and dived out into the open bridge, already planning his next hand-hold, on the end of the third row of consoles. He made that, and the ship stayed inertial. He made his next move halfway down the aisle, where Jase and Sabin both stood, not using handholds at this particular moment.

Safe. Free. If one believed it.

"Mr. Cameron," Sabin said, and to someone else-where: "Put the transmission through to station fifteen."

Station fifteen was the console nearest. That screen display changed and became a set of numbers and geometrical figures. It looked like navigational problems.

"We're instructed to come ahead and hard dock at the masthead," Sabin said. "Ordinary procedure. Guild authority says, quote, that there's been an ob-server lurking out there for years doing very little. Unquote. It's waked up on our approach, made its first active assay of the station in a long time. They're receiving that output, too. Passive input and long-range optics would be just as efficient observation for its ordinary operations. It was sitting out there lis-tening, it heard us pass, and heard station answer—and woke up. We're not sure why whoever it is needed first to come alive and betray their presence if they don't mean to talk. If it's targeting, and if there's something on its way, it's likely going to have fired on the expected path toward docking. Which we're be-hind. There's no reason, either, why they wouldn't just fire at the station if they were going to—take it all out. What's *your* best observation of the situation, Mr. Cameron?"

Good question.

"How many pings?"

"Single."

"Single output. Last time, three blinks. If it *was* the same entity." He dealt with atevi so exclusively he began to think the numbers themselves had signifi-cance. And one couldn't assume that. Daren't assume it. "A, they're a robot. B, they're more interested in watching than in destroying. C—they're wanting our attention and they want to see if we're smart enough to have learned anything in ten years."

Sabin nodded slowly. "Captain Graham would agree. Next question. A's possible. Why B?"

"Why B? To see what kind of traffic this place gets . . . one ship, two, a hundred . . . and where those ships come from, and where they go."

"The atevi planet," Jase said in a low voice. "They'll have that pegged, at least what vector we've come in from. Long range optics can do way too much once they start looking."

"How long can have they been here?" Bren asked. "Were they here, for instance, when *Phoenix* did her last lookover and left toward Alpha? Is that possible?"

"Good question," Sabin said. "I don't know. If they were, they weren't in our pickup. But I wasn't on the bridge that day."

"C, captain. C. *Have we learned anything?* I advise we go toward them. Slowly. Go toward them."

Sabin shot him a dark and frowning look, then turned her back and started away from him.

He wedged himself past a seat, past her, and firmly blocked her path. "On review of the log, captain, my conclusion. My *best* advice. Issue a signal. *Approach* them. It's exactly what the Guild hasn't tended to do. It may be the one thing you ought to do. Be forthcoming."

Sabin turned, glanced from him to Jase. And around them, not a single tech had taken eyes from their work to see argument around the senior captain.

"I agree with him," Jase said in a low voice.

"Then what?" Sabin asked. "Do we have a conclusion for this adventure? Perhaps we rush over there and stir up something we don't know how to deal with."

"Your predecessor stirred something up, got a signal, refused to respond, left on a diversionary track, and they didn't take one of those manuevers kindly. Atevi say—and I asked them—that Ramirez gave a hostile appearance in his behavior, simply by remaining mute. Then by leaving and trying to deceive. So let's at least do something else."

Sabin looked at him. Poised, on the brink.

"So maybe they're going to ignore us," she said. "By station's information, they've ignored the station for years."

"Imitating Ramirez? Imitating *his* actions?"

"After blowing hell out of the station," Sabin muttered.

"Maybe preparatory to blowing hell out of us if we just cruise over to the station, dock, and sit."

"So we're going to go over to the alien ship and do *what*?"

"Play it as we meet it, captain. It's why we're here. I'm not afraid to board them, myself, if that's what it comes to." Not afraid was a lie, but it was an offer he saw no recourse but to make. "Get me over there. I'll do it."

"The hell you say. Get you there, but we're all there in the same ship."

"Don't ignore the contact we just had. My best advice. We were touched. They asked a question. Give back the same. Three blinks. Same frequency, same pace as before. You want to bet it doesn't have a record of the last encounter? Or that there's no cultural logic behind that output? I'd rather bet on that course of action than on going into dock right now."

Sabin stood still, at least, gazing dead at him. "You're crazy."

Bren shook his head. "An opportunity. An opportunity. What do we do? Go in there, tie ourselves down at dock and diminish our range of responses? Including getting out of here, captain, as I understand is still a possibility right now."

A long, long stare. "You think so."

"You asked my opinion. I base it on all the information I have. Can we *see* this ship? Do we know how it's shaped, what it looks like, how it's configured?"

"Not damned informative. C3. Give us image, central screen."

A dim image flashed up. It could have been a rock. If it had color, it was brownish black, a collection of irregularly arranged panels suspended around a core of indefinite shape, showing no lights at all at the moment.

"Does it tell you anything?" Sabin asked him.

"No," he had to admit.

Sabin folded her arms, gazed at the screen. Then at him. "And how are you going to talk to this ship once we engage it?"

"I'll have to find out," Bren said. *"That's* what I do, captain. That's what Ramirez trained Jase to do, and Ramirez made a fatal decision when he decided to back off and wait for another try, when his translator was older and better prepared. *This* is that next opportunity. If we don't take them up on that invitation to communicate—if there's any symmetry about their actions—who knows? They *may* hit Alpha, the way they hit here."

Sabin looked at him, a sidelong glance, on that last. Looked away, then. And back. "A basic rule of intelligence, Mr. Cameron—you can chase just one more certainty and one more piece of information just one fatal step too far. At a certain point you have to quit listening and go with best guesses. We don't *know* the situation on the station, do we? And we don't know the situation out there."

"We need answers," Jase said. "We're not going to get them on the station. If we get that far."

"Oh, I'm in favor of answers, second captain. We're on our original course, not quite on the original schedule, so if that ship out there fired a few minutes ago, we'll more likely be spectators to a fire show. If we do get a strike, Mr. Cameron, at the first sign of a siren, dive under the nearest console and brace, because we'll move long and hard; and you haven't felt movement yet. Not in this entire trip. Not in your *life*, Mr. Cameron. Right now you have time to get to a takehold and time to get granny to shelter, and I advise you do that.—Mr. Carson. Docking spot number one, three bright flashes toward our spook. Stand by for braking, Jorgensen."

"Yes, ma'am," Bren said. And moved, not even pausing for a glance at Jase. The ship was acting— God save them, Sabin was taking the action Ramirez had ducked.

He reached the shelter and repeated that warning in Ragi, for the company. "Prolonged strong movement. Everyone must stay in the shelter, nadiin-ji. This situation may continue a while or change suddenly." Five-deck would hear. Trust Asicho for that.

A siren sounded.

"Sabin here. Take hold, take hold, take hold. Alien contact. We are manuvering after sending signal to alien craft. Stand by."

God, *truth* from a *Phoenix* captain.

Bren wedged himself back in among the rest. Kept his breathing calm and steady.

"Sabin-aiji has sent a signal to the foreign ship," he said as calmly as he could manage. His breath seemed inadequate. And the braking hit. The signal had gone. Three blinks of the ship's powerful docking spots.

Braking let up. *"Mr. Cameron."* Jase's voice. *"Mr. Cameron to the bridge."*

"Aiji-ma. Nadiin-ji." He groped for the padded edge of the cabinet and moved, not sure of his safety, but he answered the summons, as far as Jase's position, against a padded wall. "Jase."

Sabin was there, too, braced with her back against the same surface.

"Mr. Cameron."

"Yes, ma'am."

"Atevi are hearing that advisement below, too?"

"Yes, ma'am," Bren admitted.

"Efficient. Keep it that way. *Don't* get in my way. Stand by to answer questions."

Sabin left the takehold position, walked off, resuming her continual tour. Jase stayed close to him.

"Scary," Bren muttered.

"You noticed," Jase said. "We've signaled it. We've changed our position in case they fire on our signal."

"Which also tells them we fear hostile action."

"Shouldn't we?"

"By our logic. They should figure we thought of it and preferred to talk, not shoot. One hopes they think that way."

A small moment in which he could scarcely believe he'd just argued with Sabin on her bridge and urged the ship to take an aggressive response—but there wasn't a reasonable alternative. There simply wasn't, within anything he could think of.

And even in that gut-deep human and atevi dislike of turning their backs on an enemy, in their choice to deal with the situation rather than go on in, ignoring the presence, there was animal instinct at work . . . a good instinct, an instinct viable in every situation that two similarly wired species could jointly think of, but that didn't say definitively that no other answer had ever evolved in a wide universe. It only said their behavior was statistically likely to be understood, based on a sample of two and based on the limits of the translator's own imagination.

"Likely this maneuvering will drag on now for hours," Jase said. "It might be an opportunity to persuade the dowager below. Tell her it's for comfort. Comfort, at least."

"This is the woman who sleeps on stone several times a year. Who rides mountain trails in thunderstorms. Who took on Cajeiri as a ward. I don't think we'll persuade her easily, Jasi-ji."

"Days, Bren. It could be days working this all out. With terrible forces, if we have to move. Hard on the whole body, even in shelter. Tell her that."

"One will pose the question." He made the short trek to the security cabinet, quickly, economically.

And met a row of dark and light faces all with the same wary, determined expression.

"Jase-aiji suggests this maneuver will be extremely long, even days, and that for comfort and dignity—"

"No," Ilisidi said abruptly. "We will not go below."

"Nand' dowager . . ."

"Interesting things happen here. Not there. If I were reckless of staff safety I would send after hot tea," Ilisidi said. "I forego the tea. In that, I have *taken* my personal precautions and my staff is settled in safety. We are very well. Gin-nandi is very well." This with an all but unprecedented nod toward Ginny Kroger, who gave a nod in turn—a unity of appalling, infelicitous two, give or take the ship itself—a welding of Gin's notorious obstinacy to the dowager's, which was legendary. *Somehow* there had been basic converse in his absence.

"I convey the respects of the ship-aijiin," Bren said

with a little bow. "And urge you all make yourselves comfortable, but sit warily, aiji-ma, nandi. One hopes this matter will work itself out peacefully."

He caught Banichi's eye, and Jago's, and they extracted themselves from shelter, with relief, he was sure. He left, with them in attendance and within easier reach of information at the moment—atevi presence re-expanded onto the bridge.

He found Jase where he had been, next the take-hold just outside their shelter.

"The dowager declines. Gin declines. I used the word 'days.' They've formed an alliance."

Jase didn't look at him. Jase's eyes, like Sabin's, roved continually over the aisles, where techs sat waiting for response. "We have what facilities we have up here," Jase murmured. "We can't change them. But if she grows weary, offer my office, my cabin, my bed, for that matter."

"One will do so, nadi-ji, with thanks."

"For yourself as well. I want you rested, paidhi-aiji."

"One understands that as well."

Jase reached to his ear and handed him the communications unit, warm from his skin. "Use that. I want you current with our information flow."

"One concurs." He positioned it in his own ear, beginning to receive the very limited cross-chatter of station with station, Sabin's low-key orders, the ordinary life's pulse of the bridge. Jase secured another unit for himself, meanwhile, from one of the endmost consoles, adjusted it, became available.

"I am now in direct touch with ship's communications," Bren muttered to Banichi and Jago. "Make clear to the dowager Jase's offer of his own cabin, which would afford more comfort and security. Tell Cenedi first: he may have more luck in argument."

"A very good idea," Banichi said, with a side glance at Jago—their information had simultaneously gone to Cenedi and to five-deck. And one hoped the dowager would hear reason.

A desk, a chair and a bed within easy walk of the bridge, it turned out, was an acceptable idea. There was not only Jase's cabin and Jase's office, but Ramirez's and Ogun's, unoccupied, ample room; ample means by which experience could be available and out from under foot, and the dowager was *not* opposed.

The station, meanwhile, answered an earlier time-lagged query. *"The spook's been out there for years. It may be robotic. We instruct you, ignore it."*

"What grounds to believe it's robotic?" Sabin fired back. "Be advised we are taking measures for contact."

That was all the communication that could flow in that exchange. There followed, from the station, a few further queries. *"What kept you?"* was one particularly significant, along with: *"Who's in command at Alpha?"*

"Fuel load wasn't ready," was Sabin's immaculately honest answer, along with, "Local control, local politics, but negotiable." That could cover anything, including armed conflict. "What changes here? What's our fuel situation?"

There was the prime question.

Meanwhile galley served more tea and sandwiches, and Narani and the dowager's staff sent up delicacies for the dowager *and* for humans on the bridge—weary bridge crew, crew who'd stayed far longer than their own shift, while below, crew chafed to be out of confinement in quarters. Officers of the next shift sent wary inquiries, briefing themselves, a busy, busy flow of conversation on several channels, C1 to C12. One had never appreciated how much went on, not even counting the flow of atevi communications aboard, which was another several channels.

The dowager took possession of Jase's quarters. Bren meanwhile stuck close to the bridge, eating a sandwich while wandering between the atevi settled into the executive corridor and the human crew in constant activity on the bridge.

Jase had suggested, not for the first time, that they might take advantage of the moment to go to shift change. Bren's own knees began to protest he'd stood long enough; and he had no doubt Sabin's older bones had to be aching far worse than his as she kept up that slow, mostly silent patrol, occasionally commenting into the communications flow.

Waiting, he was sure, for some answer, from some quarter, not likely to rest until it did come; and now the reply-clock was thirty-two minutes into negative territory.

Bridge crew took intermittent rests, a few at each console moving about on break, or, by turns, head pillowed on arms, resting weary eyes, waiting, waiting, waiting.

"Request you proceed with approach, captain. Explanation after you dock."

It *wasn't* the positive fuel answer they wanted. It wasn't, *we have everything in order, proceed toward the fueling port.*

"They may not anticipate the alien craft can understand our conversation," Bren murmured—wishing that were so, wishing that the Guild had miraculously turned cooperative—or that the alien out there did understand a common language. There was no proof of either. "One might distrust this request to dock first."

"C1, repeat the last query." That was Sabin's answer,

cold and calm, as if they hadn't just waited the lengthy time for the last inadequate answer, as if she weren't, like all of them, aching to have basic questions settled and to know for certain they had fuel. But: *do it again*, was the response, in essence. *Do it again until we get an answer we like.*

And meanwhile, be it admitted, they weren't doing what station wanted.

Bren felt his own knees protesting. And he walked, and paced, trying to think of all possible angles, and finally went back to Jase's office and sat down in a chair opposite Banichi and Jago's seat on the floor.

"Station has failed to answer Sabin-aiji's simple question regarding available fuel, nadiin-ji. She has therefore reiterated her question. This give and take of answers will take, at least, another two hours."

His bodyguard absorbed that information, respectfully so, noting clearly that Sabin-aiji had not backed down, and showed no sign of it.

"If it should be a lengthy time, then you should nap, Bren-ji," Jago advised him. "It seems we are not yet useful."

It was reasonable advice. He had been observing every micro-tick of information flow, fearful of missing some critical interaction, but found no further advice to give. . . . He *didn't* like the reticence on the station's side. If the alien didn't understand, Sabin was right: they could transmit nursery rhymes and targeting coordinates with no difference in that ship's behavior—and if it did understand—then they had a very different problem, at once an easier one, but one in which the station would participate, and in which, in the fuel, it might hold a key bargaining item. Most of all he didn't like the picture he had: a third party, themselves, arriving in the middle of a long standoff, an arrival recognizably allied to the station, talking with it while signaling the alien presence out there. It looked all too much like a schoolyard squabble, politics on that primitive a level, and the imbalance of power since their unexpected arrival here could tip things over the edge.

It would do it faster if they made a wrong move. *Two* powers had to be refiguring the odds at the moment, and he hoped the apparently bullied party, the station, didn't suddenly decide to shove things into a crisis with some demand for action, the rationality of which they couldn't assess at a distance.

"Shift change," C1 announced then, over the general address. *"Crew will go to second shift."*

Belowdecks had waited long enough.

"Sabin speaking," came a smooth, routine murmur following that. *"Situation remains much the same. We have not received adequate answers from station. We have not received a response from the alien presence. As you move through the ship, bear in mind the location of nearest takeholds. We will specifically notify crew of any change in the level of alert."*

Sabin *was* continuing to inform crew. Give her that. They were going to the second of the ship's four shifts, one that properly was her own crew. And evidently she wasn't going to rest now.

"We might rest," he said. Jago was right. It was only sensible. "The both of you—one wishes there were a bed, nadiin-ji."

"The floor is adequate, Bren-ji—room for one's feet, at least. Will the chair suffice?"

"Admirably," he said, and they rested—Banichi and Jago in full kit, with room to stretch out, at least, himself in a partially reclined chair, hardly daring shut his eyes, because of the buzz of communication in his ear. It became a white sound, and it was too easy just to go out.

He concentrated all the same, aware from the flow of communications that Sabin, still linked, had gone temporarily to her own cabin. That there was a shift-change in progress on the bridge.

The ship still waited for response, still waited.

"Guildmaster Braddock speaking," came suddenly, clearly, the station's answer, a different voice. *"Affirmative on your last query, captain. Don't take any action toward the outlying ship. Repeat, take no action. We estimate it's a robot outputting its observations to some more remote presence, which may or may not be manned. Your arrival has lit a fire under the situation. Come in immediately."*

That did it. He wasn't going to lie there after that answer, rational and sensible as it might be on the surface. He was sure Sabin would head back for the deck like a streak.

Faster. An answer came immediately. *"C1, repeat our former query as a response."*

Sabin hadn't budged an inch.

Damn, he thought. But he approved her obstinacy. If there was any doubt about the fuel situation and they weren't talking about the alien, he was just as glad she wasn't taking *Phoenix* in to become part of a larger, predictibly orbiting target.

He heartily wished there were better answers out of Reunion. But going out there at the moment wouldn't help matters. He had nothing to say.

"Senior captain," he heard Jase say, and he tried to stay in his semi-rest, expecting Jase to concur in the response, or to report the shift change complete. *"We have a flash response from the alien. Three bright pulses."*

That was it. He flung the chair upright, and moved.

6

He and Sabin came out into the corridor at the same moment, Banichi and Jago close behind him, Cenedi exiting the dowager's cabin, Gin and Jerry not far behind.

"It's not a damn group tour," Sabin muttered, ahead of them only by virtue of her cabin's position in the corridor. Words floated in her wake and echoed in Bren's earpiece. "Advice, Mr. Cameron. Advice!"

"Repeat their signal sequence at the same pace as our answer. Not upping the bet. Duplication, we can hope, is perceived as neutrally cooperative. I hope it gains us time, maybe a further signal to compare."

"Second captain. Do you copy? Implement."

"Implementing," Jase's answer came immediately.

Bridge personnel had all changed. Every seat was filled, all the same, every head directed absolutely to console screens and output.

"If that should be a robot," Bren said as they arrived in Jase's vicinity, "we might try to calculate the position of any outlying installation by any significant lag in their reply."

"Ahead of you, Mr. Cameron," Sabin said. "We'll be working on that information."

"Or it could just represent the lag-time in their decision-making," he said. "We've already told them we're independent enough that *we* generate answers

when station doesn't. Contact station and get them to join us in another response. Indicate their cooperation with us."

"The hell they'll do that," Sabin muttered, but: "C1," she said. "Transmission to station. Quote: Request you also transmit three bright flashes, identical duration, toward spook source. Critical you comply."

Bren suffered cold shivers. He'd tried to rest and the body hadn't quite waked up. The mind, however, had, calculating possibilities that began to branch and multiply untidily. *The hell they'll do that.* Clearly, by this demonstration and others, the *Phoenix* senior captain didn't expect to give the orders to her Guild. It was becoming critical, and the Guild still thought it ran matters. Not a surprise.

But that the *Phoenix* senior captain meanwhile prepared to act and make a statement, a simple, light-flashed statement to match the ship's singular: *I*—that was going to have its effect later in their dealings with station, and they couldn't help that. Not in their present situation. They could only hope for station to comply, if only it would.

And they had to wait more than an hour to get station's yes or no. Were they unified *we?* Or not?

"Visual senses dominate in that species," Bren muttered. He'd studied the processes of contact—historically—with the atevi. He couldn't swear another living soul aboard had that background. And he'd spent eleven months reading on that topic. "Visible spectrum overlaps ours. Brain architecture has that in common, at least, with us and atevi."

Jase and Sabin alike shot him a look as if he were launching into prophecy.

"The ship out there won't know the station refused you," Bren said, teeth chattering in a persistent edge-of-sleep chill, and it sounded like fear, and he couldn't stop it. "But if our own station won't cooperate, it tells *me* something about the Guild, while I'm unraveling alien behavior."

"Screw your suppositions, Mr. Cameron. Confine your speculations to that ship out there and give me facts, not guesswork."

"Best I can, captain. The only thing we've said to them so far is *I* and they've answered *me, too.* Useful if we could get the conversation to include a demonstrable *we,* but we don't expect to have a *we* with station, do we, so that's likely out." Where *did* a dialog start, without sea and land and sky for conversational items? Series of lights? Sequential blink used as a pointer?

And a pointer aimed at what? At the noncooperative station, which might pot-shot the alien and start a war? *That* was no good.

"It may be a naive question, captain, but are we moving toward the aliens at the moment? Or toward station?"

"What are you getting at, Mr. Cameron?"

"I'm trying to figure out what we're saying in relation to where we're going. *Everything's* a word. Where we're going is a word."

"We're splitting the difference at the moment. We've veered off from station signal. We haven't gone on a heading directly for the alien craft. We're not going directly at either."

"Good decision."

"Thank you," Sabin said dryly, and he ignored the irony.

"Can we stop? Stand still?"

"Relative to what, Mr. Cameron?"

"I don't know." He was totally at sea where ship's movements were concerned. "Just, once we go on toward the station, now or hours from now, we've involved the station. If our own station will cooperate with us—then, yes, we could slow way down, sit out here and maybe work this out. I'm assuming the Guild's not going to be helpful. So if we could, relatively speaking, just stop or slow way down and talk with this outlying ship—if we could say, by our motions, *we're going to deal with you rationally and calmly, no hurry here . . ."*

"We don't even know if there's intelligence aboard."

"But something somewhere in control of this is rational. We have to believe that, or there's no hope in this situation—and percentage, captain, percentage in this is all with *hope.* If we can get to talking, if we can get them to accept a slow closer contact and occupy their attention with communications—we may just possibly shift decision-making from their warlike to their deliberative personnel, if there should be that division of power aboard."

He saw the little frown grow. Sabin was at least listening. And the next part of the thought he didn't like at all—but it was, personally applied, the hope equation. Percentages.

"If we can do that," he said further, "if we can just calm down and sit out here increasing our ability to talk to them, then we've over all increased the likelihood they'll talk in all other circumstances. They'll have invested effort in talking. At least on economy of effort, they'll reasonably value that investment. Individuals will have committed work to the idea. We may gain proponents among them. We could be several *years* sitting here unraveling this, but the immediate threat to the station will be a lot less down this path. We might be able to defuse this situation and get their decision-making well away from the fire buttons and over to the communications officers."

"And you think you can accomplish this fantasy of cooperation."

He didn't know what to say. Then he shifted a glance over his shoulder, by implication the array of atevi and Mospheirans—and back. "My predecessors certainly did."

Sabin's glance made the same trip. And came back. "You can do it and take my orders, mister."

"I respect your good sense, captain."

"What do you propose for the next step?"

"Ignore my ignorance about ship's operations. But we've answered the aliens. Where's the clock on that, relative to our request to station?"

Sabin checked her wristwatch. "That's thirty-one to station reply and forty-six to alien reply."

"If station agrees to signal with us, we do a unison approach. If station doesn't agree . . . how many lights can the ship manage in a row, to signal with?"

"Eight."

Infelicitous eight. Was it mad for a human mind to think in those terms—to have numbers make a difference at all?

"I'll give you a blink pattern with those eight. I'll think of something."

"I'm sure that's very useful, Mr. Cameron."

"We can signal an approach. If we can make an approach to them."

"You're recommending this."

"I'm recommending this."

Again a long stare. "I'm not expecting station cooperation. Get me your blink pattern, Mr. Cameron. Let's just see what we can learn."

Half an hour. He had other minds to consult, and he went and consulted, the aiji-dowager sitting ramrod stiff in an upright chair in Jase's cabin, Ginny sitting on the bed, security standing about. He sat down and made his proposal, talking to two individuals: the human one of which didn't remotely understand his craft; but the dowager understood the problems. So, even, did Cajeiri, who stood by his great-grandmother's chair and listened very solemnly, not a word from him, but a lively spark in his eyes, not a reasonable ounce of fear.

No more than in his great-grandmother. "So," Ilisidi said, having heard him out. "What does Jase-aiji think?"

"One will surely consult him in this, aiji-ma." He had a keen awareness of passing time. Of the impending reply window. He hastily took his leave, gathering Banichi and Jago and Gin—almost Cajeiri, but for the dowager's sharp command restraining the rascal.

"Answer?" Bren asked Jase, arriving beside him on the bridge. The communications flow in his ear was momentarily interrupted, for sanity's sake. He was screwing the earpiece back in as he asked.

"Station says their policy is no contact. They repeat their order to come in."

His heart thudded for no particular reason: he'd expected worse—but the citing of policy under present circumstances hammered at his nerves. The communications chatter was back in his ear. He watched Sabin stroll over.

"Negative," she said. "So?"

"I suggest, then, unless the alien initiates some new pattern we can work on—blink all lights sequential toward the endmost, toward that ship. Then slow. And turn. Blink all lights toward the center. Then steady light, and go toward them."

"That's *it?*"

"Works in downtown Jackson traffic," he said, beyond being defensive. "Communicates to our species. Atevi intuitively figure it on Alpha station."

"A damn stationside *turn* signal?"

He shrugged. "We're not going to communicate the whole dictionary, captain. Simplicity. The most universal things we can think of: *we're turning* and *we're coming toward you very, very slowly.*"

Sabin swore under her breath.

"What would you do, captain, if they sent that signal to you?"

"I'd uncap the fire button, plain truth."

"Would you fire?"

Sabin thought more soberly about that. Expressionless, walked over to the third console and gave an order.

Another transmission-wait clock showed up on the main screen.

They'd signaled.

"Takehold, takehold, takehold," the intercom warned the ship.

Maneuvering. His plan was in full, precipitate operation, not waiting for answer.

He looked uncertainly toward Jase. Jase looked to *him,* that was the panic-producing realization; and there wasn't time. "Nadiin-ji," he said to Banichi and Jago, "take hold. Advise the dowager. We three shall use the alcove."

Where he had at least the hope of contributing advice—if the aliens didn't construe their movement as attack, or simply prove intractably hostile.

"Bren-ji." Banichi insisted he enter first. Jago followed. They made a sandwich of him within the protective, padded closet, and he tried not to shake like a leaf. *They* rather expected the lord of the heavens to have a notion what he was doing. And not to shiver.

An hour and more until the aliens knew they were

slowing and turning—and signaling their intentions. Which might also make a shot miss them, if the aliens pissaciously fired before they considered the blink signal.

Head against the padding. Eyes shut.

Final alarm. The ship began to maneuver. Ships that traveled such vast distances so fast were rather like bullets. They weren't meant to jitter about, changing course, making loose objects and passengers into pancakes. *Phoenix* certainly wasn't designed to do it.

But she did.

Long change of direction. Time for thought, which he tried not to use, except on his next step.

Suppose the other ship echoed the signal, including the ship movement. Supposing they came forward.

Suppose they offered some different signal.

Suppose, on the other hand, they sat inert, not doing a thing. Could *Phoenix* detect it, if they did? Or if, sitting still, they fired?

A certain degree before a physical missile reached them. No detection if hostility traveled at the speed of light. One thought ever so uncomfortably of very bad television, back home, death rays from the heavens, shadow-creatures menacing whole towns—

Such naive images. And so unwittingly prophetic if he couldn't think of the right answers.

He felt the living warmth on either side of him, steady, absolutely unflinching.

Calm, calm, calm. Panic didn't serve the cause, not at all.

"How are they down on five-deck?" he asked.

"Very well, nandi," Jago answered.

"And the dowager?"

"Very well, too," Banichi said on his other side.

"Well," he said, "nadiin-ji, we have at least gotten one signal out of these folk, whether or not it comes from something like Gin's robots—which hardly matters: if signal is being offered, signal is being offered, dare one say? So we orient ourselves toward them. We have offered a signal stating our proposed motion, which we hope does not look like stealth or offense." He *had* the Assassins' Guild right at his elbow and hadn't asked them their opinion of the captain's precipitate execution of his plan. "How would you manage a peaceful approach to them, nadiin-ji, figuring a complete dearth of cover?"

"One would stand at distance and signal in plain sight," Banichi said, "except that distance places this inconvenient lag between responses, and one seems therefore not to be quite in plain sight."

"One hopes, if nothing else, the signals continue to flow," Jago said. "We have every confidence the paidhiin will manage matters very adequately in that regard. But does there not remain the small possibility, Bren-ji, that there have been other, surreptitious messages from the station to the ship?"

Trust the Assassins' Guild to entertain truly disturbing thoughts—it was their job. "One hardly knows," he said. "We cannot guarantee Jase has all the information, nadiin-ji." He had Jase's communication device muttering in his ear—but that channel only carried voice transmissions, and only what C1 opted to put on that channel.

Jase was on the bridge, nonetheless, moderating Sabin's reactions, if nothing else. And Sabin, so far as they saw, responded to their arguments, and met the station's with anger.

But his security reminded him: one couldn't, here or in Shejidan, just watch the noisy things that were going on. Atevi lords died of mistakes like that. Subtexts mattered. Plans advanced by moves not apparently related to the objective. God, one could go crazy in the levels of distrust that existed between ship and station and that transmission-source out there.

A queasy motion. Turns on any axis were subtle, mere reorientation. They'd shed velocity as they bore. Then what seemed a turn.

They accelerated briefly, modestly, he thought, eyes shut, trying to read the ship's motion.

At a certain level, biological organisms trying to get within proximity without touching off fight or flight mostly did the same things, at least on the evidence of atevi and humans. One could call what they did an approach. Or, even being human, one could call it a hunter's moves. Stalking the prey. One hoped—hoped—

The all-clear sounded.

He moved. His bodyguard moved. He followed Banichi out of their refuge, Jago following him as he looked for the principals in the case.

The bridge seemed calm. Sabin and Jase were back on slow patrol of the aisles of consoles.

Banichi meanwhile spoke quietly to Cenedi and Asicho, advising them of the current situation.

The reply-clocks ran on the display, independently, computer-calculated, one supposed.

Bren heaved a deep breath, went and stood at the end of the middle row of consoles, his bodyguard with him, all of them quietly watching the display for information.

Station's answer arrived first. *"Don't contact the alien. Don't meddle with the outlying ship. It's been quiet for six years. Let it alone. Do you read?"*

Late for that.

Station *wasn't* taking Sabin's instructions, that was clear, and thought Sabin should take theirs.

"Captain Sabin," he heard Jase say, amplified by the earpiece, "we should proceed on Mr. Cameron's advice."

"We're on course, second captain."

"If the spook's been out here six years, it may have gathered something of our language—if it's picked up any station chatter. If, God forbid, it's gotten hold of any personnel."

Jase's mind was clearly working. Chillingly so—convenient as it might be to their mission to meet an opposition that could be talked to. The blink-code procedure wouldn't carry that. Direct transmission might.

Dared they risk breaking pattern with what seemed the alien's own chosen mode of communication?

Not wise, every experience informed him. Not wise to push the envelope.

"We should stay to the blink-code, captain, unless they initiate another mode."

"We'll try Mr. Cameron's notion," Sabin said grimly, and gave no window into her own thoughts.

Neither, one noted, did she show any inclination to answer station's orders at the moment.

They stood. They waited.

The clock ticked down.

"Repeat," the word came in from Reunion, *"do not contact the outlying ship."*

Sabin's lips made a thin line. "I believe we're having transmission troubles," she remarked to all present. "C1, put me on general address."

"Proceed, captain."

Sabin picked up a wand mike from C1's console. *"We have now signaled the alien craft and diverted course toward it in what our planetary advisors suggest is a reasonable approach. We remain on high alert. We are not releasing crew from cabins. There remains a likelihood of sudden movement which may exceed takehold safety. In other words, cousins, we may have to get the hell out of this solar system. Stay smart, stay put, stay alive."*

Bren translated that for his allies down in the executive cabins, and for five-deck. And waited. And sweated.

"Captain Sabin." A deeper voice, this time, from Reunion Station. *"This is Guildmaster Braddock. If you insist on this change of course, you risk our lives. We have this information for you. This is very likely a robot. It's sat there for years without moving or responding. We have no indication of it being controlled from outside. Optics have turned up nothing in outlying regions. We detect no transmissions and no active probes. Our experts believe it's a failed piece of equipment dating from a second attack on us and we urge you reconsider any approach to it. If it's dormant, it does us no good to wake it up. Abort whatever you're doing in regard to it. If you're on Ramirez's orders, abort. You don't know what you're messing with. You may get a robotic response and it may be lethal and unstoppable. I urgently advise you pull back."*

That, Bren thought, that was interesting . . . not least regarding a *second* attack, in the ship's absence. And interesting regarding Ramirez's relations with his Guild, if they'd had overmuch doubt. Station hadn't trusted Ramirez. And they'd had no way to remove him from command.

Sabin looked at him, eyebrow arched.

He looked back, looked at Jase, looked at her. *"Second* attack."

"We continue our transmission difficulties," Sabin said without comment.

And the clock ran down toward the alien's reply window.

"Second attack," Jase echoed, walking near him on his right. Jase and Sabin alike showed the hours they'd been on duty. Jase's voice was ragged.

"Things haven't stood still here."

"They're right, six years of patience doesn't sound organic. But . . ."

"Can't assume an alien behavior," Bren said.

"Can't assume an alien machine is set the way we'd set it, either. The thing could do any damn thing."

"There is that," Bren muttered. "But it's signalled us. Machine or not, it had that pre-set in its routines."

Flick-flick-flick of the reply window numbers.

Into the negative. Ten, fifteen seconds. Thirty. Forty-odd.

"Signal from the alien," someone said, audible in Bren's earpiece.

Sabin and Jase moved to the nearest consoles. Bren, Banichi and Jago a massive shadow behind him, watched over Jase's shoulder, hearing the details. The signal was a series of six lights—was there significance in six?—mirroring their action.

It made an analog of their signal, it mirrored what they sent, and it didn't need to slow down, just point its bow their way.

Then a steady central flash. One light. Blink. Blink. Blink.

"It's coming toward us," Sabin said quietly. "We're now mutually approaching, Mr. Cameron. One could say a leisurely near-collision course. *It's* moving toward us."

There were numbers involved on one of the screens. One assumed they had something to do with that movement. Bren held his breath, then decided oxygen was useful.

Deeper breath.

"I think I'll go have a cup of tea," he said, "and get my wits online."

Sabin stared ice at him. Then, curiously, gave an accepting nod. "You go do that, Mr. Cameron. If the ship out there doesn't blow us to hell, we may need your services in what you've gotten us into."

"I'd advise a pause," he said, "a conversation at convenient distance."

"If it won't interfere with your tea break."

"I'll manage, captain. I *don't* want to push the body-space issue with them. Just a mostly conversational distance. This is ours to set."

"We're not a dock runabout, Mr. Cameron. We don't jitter about with any ease. And we don't pick the interval, now. *They're* enroute to *us*."

"Yes, ma'am. But we signal when we'd like to. With luck, they'll do the same."

Sabin just stared at him. Then: "Takehold in forty-five minutes, Mr. Cameron, given they don't fire or accelerate. Go have your tea."

He had outraged Sabin. He hoped not to do the same for the crew. He gathered his bodyguard and walked back to the executive corridor, straightening his coat and cuffs, asking himself did he need a new shirt run up—the brain was, oddly, going into court-mode, and Shejidan's instincts rose up, ridiculous as some of them might be. He became nand' paidhi again. He *worried* about his wardrobe. And with it, the signals they might be sending. It wasn't just a tea break. It was a way of life.

He rapped gently at the dowager's door, and discovered the dowager, in the most comfortable chair, held court with a fruit drink in hand, and Cajeiri sat on a mattress beside Gin Kroger. They'd taken the cabin apart and put it back together in a more felicitous configuration, Ilisidi sitting centermost, Cenedi and his men occupying the corner, standing.

Bren bowed. "Aiji-ma. We have now issued a set of signals which the foreign ship is mirroring. The current course will bring us to conversational distance and the ship will manuever briefly and slow down, although the possibility of violent evasion exists. Please be prepared for quick action. In the meanwhile, I shall retire to my cabin to think."

"Pish," Ilisidi said with a careless wave of her hand. "This is a mattress. That is a wall. We do as we can, nandi."

"One observes so, aiji-ma." He made a little bow. "I have secured Sabin-aiji's cooperation and seen felicitous numbers on the bridge. One hopes for a little time, yet, aiiji-ma. Do take care."

"If you need help up there—" Gin. Dr. Gin Kroger, who understood machines. In Shejidan that move intervening in the dowager's conversation would have had hands reaching for sidearms, and Cajeiri looked up, mouth open.

Ilisidi simply waved an indulgent hand. "*Tea,* one believes the paidhi-aiji requested."

Oh, *someone* understood more ship-speak than they routinely admitted. Someone closely monitoring his doings on the bridge. Nothing was news to the dowager.

"Go refresh yourself, nand' paidhi. Tea will arrive here, at your convenience."

"One is honored." He bowed, turned and went to his own makeshift cabin, more fortunate than Jase, more fortunate than Sabin, whose code was endurance and who never understood the loyalty of her crew.

His staff's solution to impending disaster was to set their *lords* at a problem, which meant assuring themselves their lords had their wits about them—and meant that the lords had ultimately to make a return on the investment and perform a miracle. He'd thought of having time to himself—but now he did draw an easier breath, it seemed to him that a little space in familiar context was what he did need.

He returned in due course, paid his quiet courtesies. And with the dowager, with Gin, Cajeiri advised to non-participation and silence—he sipped a cup of tea, how gotten, whether it was part of the picnic supplies, he neither knew nor cared. It was enough to be here, with Banichi, with Jago close at hand. With all the strong, quiet surety of their Guild, very different than the human one that opposed them.

"So," Ilisidi said, "have we thought of an answer to this conundrum?"

"Several things have become clear, aiji-ma—that while this ship was absent, the aliens returned. That Ramirez may have earned his Guild's distrust and disapproval in seeking out contact with foreigners. Third—that the stationmaster refuses to take Sabin-aiji's orders."

Why was he going through the list of new information? The job involved only the foreign ship.

But did it?

Something bothered him, beyond the obvious detail of goings-on in their absence, Ramirez's subterfuges, the Guild's historic autocracy. He wasn't sure what nagged at him.

But the dowager listened, waiting for him to put it all together. And he—

He sipped his tea and looked from the dowager to Gin, the third leg of the homeworld tripod, met a sober, on-party-manners look: and the thought of Gin and the colony the ship abandoned—troubled him.

Why should it?

His job was the ship out there. The ship now moving toward them and them toward it.

And what was he going to say, that he *could* say? Hail them in ship-speak as if they were supposed to understand? Continue with the blink-code?

Sitting out here *six years* meant observation or a stubborn ship's captain.

Or damage.

"One learns, aiji-ma, that the ship has sat quietly out here, they claim for six years, doing nothing. Station thinks it may be robotic." He rendered that in Mosphei', for Gin, who looked as if he'd posed her a personal question. "With control at some remove off in the dark peripheries of the solar system. Which is a very large place."

"So," Ilisidi said. "And what shall we do if it is robotic?"

He translated that for Gin, too.

"Or it might be stuck, without fuel," was Gin's instant assessment. "If it's a robot, either the other side lost track of it and it's out of instructions, or they know it's here and it's doing a job. If it is a robot. Personally, I wouldn't wholly trust a robot to avoid a war. I think they'd be outright stupid to leave diplomacy to a machine, and to leave a weapon sitting out here ready to explode isn't the way a smart government would carry on, is it? We could be some very powerful non-participant."

Another translation.

And a thought. It might be sitting there waiting, as robots did so well, for input. And *they* could well be that input, couldn't they?

Or if it might be doing a job—what job, beyond observing? Communicating?

Gin was right. Robots weren't outstanding at avoiding hostilities or at finessing interspecies communication.

He sipped his tea, thinking, it came here, hit the station, and it parked. Odd behavior. Behavior that, however alien, didn't seem to have a constructive outcome—unless there was some piece of information missing.

"Ramirez arrived," he said slowly. "And left." Translation. "Perhaps it waits for the ship." Translation. "And here we are." Translation. Grim, cold thought.

"These are not reasonable people," Ilisidi said, "to fire on persons who have not fired on them."

"Would a wise and civilized entity fire without more provocation than that? One hardly knows, aiji-ma. Within the possibilities of truly alien behavior—it might." Translation.

Another sip of tea.

One fired—if.

If one's culture was to fire on strangers.

If fired upon. That was a big if.

Sip of tea. Very basic thought. One fired to stop an attack. Or what one construed as an attack.

Then one ran for one's life. If fear was the guiding principle.

Primary mistake to make any third species behave like humans or atevi. But a third point, a third species, could close a geometric figure, make an enclosure, bend lines back to intersect everyone's positions, over and over and over. Three points could close a circle. Two points might be part of that circle—but one had to guess where the third might land.

Primary mistake to expect them to behave the same. Primary mistake to think there was no logic—that *their* behavior didn't make sense within their culture. Give them the same set of circumstances and they'd always do the same thing. Chaos and chaotic response didn't get a species out of the swamp and into a space program. There was logic in the behavior. That there was any willingness to signal at all was a fair indication that they expected response in kind.

He drew a breath. "One is grateful, aiji-ma.—Thank you, Gin-aiji."

Nods from both. To that extent, Gin had taken in the adjacent culture. And both understood the value of a tea break.

"Takehold, takehold minor, takehold, three minute warning."

He stood up quickly, turned over his teacup—bowed, and with Banichi and Jago, headed back to his borrowed quarters.

Braking. What the senior captain called a gentle braking. One hoped the teacups were safely put away.

7

The bridge was calm when he arrived, the captains momentarily converged at the edge of the corridor. "It's braked," Jase reported. "It's braked, we've braked."

"Excellent news." It was. Thank God, he thought.

"Our courses are not head-on. Closest approach in three hours fourteen minutes. We signaled with all lights, then braked. They mirrored all actions."

"Good. Very good."

"Glad you approve," Sabin said dryly.

"It *was* the right answer, captain," Bren said, deliberately oblivious. Then: "Is the station armed, captain?"

Sabin gave him an odd look. "Yes. I would be, wouldn't you?"

"We're human. We're both human. I can say atevi would be, too. We don't know what it expected. What would Reunion have done, back then, if something like this just showed up and came close?"

Small silence. "I frankly don't know."

"They could have fired?"

"I have no way to know."

"They're human. They could have fired."

"Not ours to estimate, Mr. Cameron."

Near white-out of thought. It *was* possible. "We have to be careful not to give that impression, captain.

My advice—last thing we want to do," Bren said, watching that central monitor, "is send anything substantial outside our hull. If, on the other hand, they do it—don't shoot at it. Evade." He had no desire to divert any energy into a debate with Sabin. He had more faith Jase was on his side—if sides there were. The train of actions from the alien craft so far mirrored theirs, all the way. Now they paused. Waiting, both ships careening along a converging diagonal, facing one another.

They had to do *something* before someone made a frightening move, something one side or the other might misinterpret.

"Blink lights one and eight," Bren said. "Any possible confusion of communications with attack, if we try to talk to them in a voice transmission?"

"At low energy," Jase said. "Not likely."

"I take it that it still hasn't transmitted." He heard traffic via the earpiece: blink sent. And very quickly answered. They were that close.

"Negative," Sabin said.

"They've been sitting here for six years. I'd think they'd have learned something about our communications. At least our frequencies."

He didn't know the capabilities of the equipment.

"Nandi," Banichi said. "Our line is thus far infelicitous eight. Multiply by felicitous nine. One has television."

"Television, nadi?" Line by line transmission. Black and white, yes/no. Blank space off. Object area on. Or reverse.

Damn. *Yes.*

"I have a proposition," he said to Sabin. "Banichi suggests a matrix. Line by line. Like television."

Jase had already heard. Now Sabin listened, frowning intensely.

"Tell it to C1," Sabin said, and he went to that console and made his request, not even betting the alien's hearing was compatible. Light was. Bright dark. They had a matrix of eight by eight, and a black line. Then a new image.

He made a block of eight by eight, image of a man.

"Transmit," Jase said.

A delay. A delay that stretched on into seconds. Half a minute.

Flashes came back. Image of a man.

"Do you suppose they get it?" Jase asked.

There was no way they could do a matrix entire. It had to be assembled to be read.

"Try sound," Bren said. "Can we transmit a series of beeps, imitating the lights? Eight by eight? Simultaneous with the lights?"

C1 looked at Sabin, who nodded.

They transmitted.

Beep.

"Again," Bren said.

They beeped. It beeped. Series of eight.

"Long beep. Short beep."

It mirrored.

"One long. Forty-nine fast and short. Do that three times." He didn't wait for confirmation. "Give me our ship and their ship in pixels. Nothing fancy. Forty-nine wide by forty-nine high." Felicitous numbers. Entirely arbitrary. His choice. And he hoped to God the opposition didn't have the atevi's obsession with numbers.

"C2," Jase said. "Create an image."

"Yes, sir." The next man keyed up. A real image appeared—broke up into largish pixels, became a shape.

"S3," Jase said. "Alien ship image to C2. Stat. C2, form the image."

Bren drew a deep breath. Banichi and Jago were

near him, Jago in low and quiet tones informing Banichi and their other listeners the gist of what they were doing. Sabin watched as they created their pixel-image. Couldn't rely on perspective-sense, not on anything fancy. Step by step and no assumptions.

"Transmit?" Bren asked. Sabin nodded.

It went. It came back. The alien mirrored their transmission.

"There was a bird called a parrot," Bren said quietly. "It mimicked. Didn't understand all it repeated. I don't know if they'll understand us. Transmit: one short, forty-nine long. We see if they figure this. Get me a station image."

"What when we've got it?" Sabin asked. "Attach labels?"

"We're going to animate our image," Bren said. "Old-fashioned television. We give them our version of history. We see what they have to say."

"Do it," Sabin said, and for a worrisome few minutes, with a flurry of instructions and corrections, several stations scrambled to produce their images. Reunion Station appeared, a simple ring. An alien ship approached. A jagged dotted line went out from the alien craft. Station showed damaged. Alien ship went off and parked.

Their ship arrived.

Diverted to confront the alien ship.

Now what? Bren asked himself. It was his script. They reached present-time. They were real-time with events. He had to script the next move. And he was petrified.

"Nadiin-ji. How shall we address these strangers? Shall I offer to go to their ship?"

"By no means," Banichi said. "By no means, Bren-ji. But we would go with you."

By all means they would. And could they look unwarlike?

"Invite one of them aboard," Jago suggested.

"We have no knowledge even what they breathe," he said, sweating, resisting the impulse, uncourtly like, to mop his brow. "We should tell them what we intend," he said. "We should propose our actions to them."

"Reasonable," Jase said.

"Do you mind," Sabin asked, "to conduct the affairs of this ship in some recognizable language?"

"Pardon," Bren murmured—bowed, his mind racing on the problem. "I need to sketch."

"Sketch."

"If you please."

He'd puzzled Sabin. The ship had no paper, to speak of. Didn't work in pen and pencil. *Jago* came up with a notepad, from an inside pocket, and he never asked what was on its other pages, just sketched a rapid series of images and tore the paper free. "This," he said to C2. "Can you render this sequence? That's a ship. That's the station."

"Yes, sir," C2 said with a misgiving glance toward Sabin for permission: C2 produced the figures: the two ships. *Phoenix* left the alien ship for the station.

Arrived. Established a link. And a line of human figures appeared one by one, moving from station to ship.

The last human marched aboard. *Phoenix* sucked up its connection. Dotted lines came out from *Phoenix*. The station exploded in a series of traveling parts. *Phoenix* then exited the screen, leaving the alien.

"This is dangerous," Jase muttered, in Ragi. "This is very dangerous, is it not, nadi?"

"One can hardly assume anything, nadi-ji." He remembered the senior captain's requirement and changed to ship-speak. "Dangerous, yes, assuming that they're assembling our images instead of trying to decode. At least I don't think they can put them together wrong."

Sabin shrugged. "Can't be worse than sitting here mute. Transmit."

It went.

All in high and low beeps.

Off/on, black/white on a field limited by a burst of black pixels. Next screen. Next image. One didn't even know if the eyes weren't compound, but if they communicated in light they had to have some sort of light-reception, which all his reading said added up to eyes of some sort.

Light-sensitive patches didn't get a species to communicating starship to starship in light pulses. He hoped.

They waited.

And waited.

"These delays," he murmured finally, "don't seem robotic. There's some sort of thought process that takes time. Living creatures take time. And they're not transmitting otherwise, are they? I'm assuming they're doing things on their own, no consultation outside."

"Maybe. Maybe they'll blow us to hell in the next second," Sabin said. "Is the dowager still passing out hot tea?"

"She—" Bren began to say.

Then a series of beeps flooded back.

"Display!" Jase said.

One/forty-nine. One/forty-nine. One/forty-nine.

Then variance. A row with two separated black dots. Like theirs.

Next row. More image.

Third row. Image taking shape.

Techs glanced surreptitiously from their consoles, violating the inviolable rule.

"Eyes!" Sabin snapped. All motion stopped but the building of that image.

Two ships met in space.

"It's not our image," Bren said. The ships were further separated. "They're not mirroring. They're innovating."

Next frame. Next and next and next, and on and on.

"Display in sequence," Bren said. "Eight frames a second."

Ships blinked into proximity.

"Two per second," Bren said more modestly, and the screen gave back a sedate approach, two ships approaching one another.

The image came in three times.

"They've got the idea," Jase muttered.

Then a pause.

Then another series of animations.

Not theirs. Again, not theirs.

Station in space. Ship approaching. Approaching. Slowed. Stopped.

Stayed stopped. Stayed stopped. Stayed stopped. Blinked. Blinked numerous times.

Emitted slow-moving black dot toward station.

Station emitted fast black dot.

Convergence. Debris tracks. More black dots coming fast.

Ship emitted fast dot.

Station emitted debris.

"Damn," Bren said. "Damn!" He had no need to translate that. The images spoke for themselves. "What they sent out first wasn't a shot."

"We don't know that," Sabin said.

"They've drawn a distinction. What they sent wasn't

what station sent back. And they're *talking* to us, Captain: they're not lunatics. They're trying to communicate what happened ten years ago, and they don't know *we're* not dangerous."

"Good. Let them keep thinking we are dangerous."

"Their send is repeating," Jase said. "Shall we answer?"

Deeper and deeper into the maze. And one wrong step meant a whole wrong branch—one that might lead them all to destruction.

"Repeat our own first sequence." Station evacuation. Departure. Station destruction. He held the pen and the notebook and tried to think what else mattered in the meeting. What else two ill-met species possibly had to say to one another that could reassure, after the disaster . . .

If they didn't have fuel—if they couldn't follow the program he laid down, simply because they'd have to stop for years and mine—what he proposed might be impossible. Might lead the alien to attack.

"We don't have fuel enough to get to Gamma if we take the station population aboard," Bren said. "Am I right in that?"

"We can't," Sabin said, with a sharp, estimating look at Jase. "If we go in, and they don't have fuel for us—we have to mine, Mr. Cameron. With all that means. Once we take a significant number of people aboard, we're a sitting target."

"Rock and a hard place," Bren muttered, and still didn't know what to draw.

Transmission was coming in.

New one.

Black round shape. That developed downward into arms. Snowman shape. Short, thick legs. Alien ship beside it.

His heart beat fast.

"That's them," he murmured. "That's *them.*"

"Wait on any answer," Sabin said.

"We daren't hesitate. They've asked. They're not shooting. We need to answer them. Give them the man-image again. Refine our image. Make more frames. Make it more lifelike. Stall!"

"Station may hear this. *Don't* mention atevi in your pictures."

A lie. The first hour of dealing with a new species, an unknown civilization with unknown parameters, where the ability to show there were two species united here might be a potent argument toward nego-tiation, and he was supposed to start with a lie that wouldn't ultimately blow up all communication they might establish once the aliens *did* find out.

Of course. The Guild was involved.

"Transmit the human silhouette," he said with a sinking feeling at the pit of his stomach. "Then repeat the station evacuation sequence."

"Do it," Sabin said. Quick job. They did that.

"Amplify that to men, women, children. Refine it."

"Yes, sir." This time without looking to Sabin for confirmation. Several consoles worked, dividing up the task, hauling images out of archive, converting them to silhouettes, to basic animations.

Meanwhile the alien had been silent. One hoped someone over there on the other ship was applying constructive thought—and not that some sort of poli-tics was debating. They couldn't penetrate that veil to know which was true.

"Image ready," C1 reported.

"Transmit," Bren said, and at Sabin's nod, that happened.

More silence.

Ominous silence. At least a pregnant silence. *Some-thing* was going on over there. One envisoned a furious debate of creatures more or less people-like. Stocky. The images they had showed that. *Dared* one show a human face in their graphics? Or might it frighten them right out of the dialogue?

A new transmission began to come in, faster than before, a step by step sequence, a skewed design. More pixels.

Their techs compensated. The image of human ship and the alien ship refined itself, then refined itself again.

"They're pushing a clearer image," Bren said. "More detail. More data from us. Or to give more *to* us."

"I'm not enthusiastic," Sabin muttered. "More detail, more information."

"Listen to him," Jase said. "Senior captain, at a certain point this is psychology. A rhythm of cooperation. Don't break it if he doesn't advise breaking it."

"We get as we give, captain. Silences mean something. They're thinking, over there. It's *not* a robot, I don't think. Data density means something. They want more. They'll give more to get it. It's all communication."

"Do it," Sabin said, not happy.

Pixels had quadrupled. Animation ran the old image, the ship's approach to the station. Showed—

Showed a figure getting into a small craft. Backed off. Showed the craft going toward the station. Showed a missile strike. The wreckage going every which way. A figure spinning toward the station. Beep. Beep. Beep.

"Hell!" Bren said. "Hell! They sent a manned probe in. Station blew him up. Station blew him to *bits*."

Sabin said not a thing. Neither did Jase.

Then: "Mr. Cameron," Sabin said calmly, "I believe this sort of mess is your specialty."

Counter that just-transmitted charge with contrition? Regret? The occupants of that ship weren't guaranteed to feel anything remotely compatible. There was no telling what they felt about the situation.

But they offered this image, their version of history. They *offered* it, evidently passionate about it after some fashion, and they weren't shooting. For at least six years they'd sat out here.

Enigma. Passionate in their obstinacy. Watching.

"Banichi. Jago." He turned to his bodyguards, to impassive atevi duty-faces. "Advise us, nadiin-ji. What are these individuals saying?"

"They say," Banichi answered, "that they have approached in minimal force and have been attacked, nandi."

"Why have they waited?"

"To find out what ships come and go here," Jago said. "To listen. To learn their enemy and his purpose."

"What would *you* answer them, nadiin? What would you do?"

"*We* are not paidhiin," Jago murmured, "nandi. Our Guild has only certain answers."

"On your own. What would you advise a lord in your protection?"

"We would not advise attacking them," Banichi said solemnly. "One would advise making a further gesture."

The Assassins' Guild not only delivered redress, among atevi. It delivered justice. It made cold, clear judgements. And Banichi, in his sense of truth and right, had judged this one, that attack against an enigma was folly.

"Captain. Answer: our ship. Seated human figure." Communicating non-aggression, he hoped. "Head bowed."

The image needed building. C2 wasn't up to the figure. C3 involved herself, built a seated figure in profile. C2 composed it with the ship. Sent. All in a matter of moments.

Bren folded his arms and waited, hoping to God it had been the right move, the right expression. Hoping it *hadn't* looked like surrender. "Send again. Our ship going in. Evacuation. Destruction of the station. Our departure." Restatement. *We intend to do a job and leave with all humans.*

Which might not matter to an alien fact-finding mission that had been waiting out here, aggrieved and looking for redress in a situation that had started, perhaps, with Ramirez's intrusion into places he shouldn't have been and that had gotten far worse in the station's reception of what might have been an inquiry. It *wasn't* a robot over there. And it hadn't given up. Hadn't moved. Hadn't communicated.

Maybe ten years wasn't that much to this species. Maybe they were just stubborn. Maybe they'd set up shop and, as station thought, occasionally contacted some higher authority outside station's view.

And if this situation had gotten to a second round six years ago—what had been the truth behind the initial damage to the station?

A reply started coming in. Echo of their own last transmission. But the ending differed. In this version, the human ship took aboard not their string of human figures—but a notably stocky horizontal form, a body.

"They want him back," Jase said in a low voice.

The new ending: the human ship voyaged from the station back to the alien craft. Sent over the body.

Rites for the dead?

A determination to get their own back?

If the station had found the craft was occupied—he could see it—they'd have taken the body for study. They'd have tried to learn from every piece and fragment. There might not *be* a body in any reasonable condition. Maybe the aliens suspected that to be the case. And notably, the sequence didn't end, as theirs had, with them collecting the station occupants and leaving.

It ended with them parked opposite that ship.

He didn't like that.

"Refinement," he said. "Capture their sequence. Repeat it and splice on our approach to the station, boarding passengers, destroying station, leaving." *We'll get back your dead. Let us do our job, destroy this outpost, and go.*

Jase gave that order. Sabin simply held her position, arms folded, face grim.

He waited. They all waited.

Image came in. Repeat of the former sequence: *give us our dead.* No mention of evacuation and departure.

"Do we have a problem, Mr. Cameron?"

That, from Sabin. And, yes, he'd say they potentially had a problem.

"We well may. They aren't getting beyond that demand. *Give us our dead.* Nothing beyond that. They won't negotiate until we do that. I think it's pretty clear."

"Hope the station's got fuel for us," Sabin muttered between her teeth. "Agree. Tell them we'll do it. What we'll really do is go in, get our business done, see what the situation is, and prepare to run for it. *If* we have fuel. If we don't, we can't board the station population. Then we see about negotiating our way out of this."

An unthinkable dilemma, then. Destroy the station—

destroy the Rosetta Stone. But that did no good if they couldn't get themselves out. If they couldn't avoid leading a vengeful alien presence back to the atevi planet . . .

"No matter what we do, we're going to have to negotiate this, run or stay, captain. They can track us. Wipe out the Archive, yes, but that's not all that's at risk. Everything back at Alpha is at risk." A terrible thought came to him, that in some measure, *Phoenix* itself could survive, alone, fugitive that it might be. And Sabin was the *ship's* protector, nothing less, nothing closer to her bedrock loyalties. "They're talking, captain. We can solve this. But we've got a hellacious puzzle here. Station was hit ten years ago. *If* that's the truth. We don't even know for sure that this ship represents the ones that did it. We do know this ship's been involved for six years. That they came here and sent in a probe. And station blew it up."

"Four years making up their minds sounds like a committee decision to me."

"It may, captain. It well may. It may be a hundred planets making up their minds for all we know, and do we want to take that on?" He wanted to undermine any notion of survival on their own. And took his chance. "Can we say where in this whole universe is safe to run to, if we make a mistake here? We *start* by cooperating with them, far as seems reasonable."

Sabin gave him that patented stare, straight in the eyes. And he gave his own back.

"And if you're wrong, Mr. Cameron? What you propose means approaching them after they've got what they want."

"Can we defend, if they launch an attack while we're at the station?"

Lengthy stare. "Point of fact, no. We'll be as vulnerable as the station."

"Then I'm right, captain. Last thing we ought to do is run without satisfying these people."

"People," Sabin scoffed. While Banichi and Jago stood at his shoulder.

"Yes, ma'am. Whatever shape they come in. Whatever their faces look like. The outline's of a person."

"And the minds, Mr. Cameron?"

"There's thought. There's insistence. There's forbearance. There's regard for their dead. There's an inclination to communicate. That's all a foundation."

"As I recall, you and the atevi lived side by side for quite a while before you went at each others' throats. The War of the Landing, you call it."

"We learn. We come here, my bodyguard and I, the dowager and Gin and I, with all that experience—at your service, captain."

"What, then, Mr. Cameron?"

"Is station going to cooperate with us?"

"I'm not a prophet."

"Station hasn't sent us anything else."

"Not another word," Jase said.

"C1," Sabin said. "Replay the sequence as Mr. Cameron suggests."

"Yes, ma'am," C1 said, and it went out.

Lengthy wait then.

"Sequence showing us going to the station," Bren said. "Let's not get deeper in. Let's just go do what we can, captain. Let's try it."

Sabin gave him a cold, speculative look. Then: "Give me general address."

"Confirmed," C1 said, and Sabin took up a mike.

"Sabin speaking. We've conducted a short conversation with the alien craft. Seems it sent a probe to the station and had it blown up. It thinks station has one of their dead. We want answers. We're going to go over there with a reasonable expectation the alien craft is

going to stay off our backs in the meanwhile, and we're going to find out what the fuel situation is before we make any further decisions. So we're going to takehold in a few minutes, cousins, and we're going to move very, very slowly about this, so as not to alarm the neighbors. Don't take anything for granted. Second shift is now in charge. Likely next shift change will not be on schedule, but technical crew, continue to brief yourselves on channel 10. General crew, feel free to get some sleep if you can—

God, Bren thought, exhausted—and very far from sleep.

". . . and stay to your cabins until further notice. We might still have to move ship far and fast on a few seconds' warning, but right now, we're going to start in toward station and see whether refueling is at all an option."

The message from the alien craft meanwhile came back, identical to their output.

"Looks as if they agree," Jase muttered. "For good or ill."

"It secures our backs," Sabin said. "It gets us there."

Sabin was being uncharacteristically charitable. His action wasn't all a success. It might be a grave mistake to have conveyed regret. Belligerence and indifference wasn't his native inclination, and he'd mistrusted the notion, incapable of playing the hand the way Banichi, perhaps, would have done. At times Tabini had wisely shoved his translator aside and said, in effect, let me deal with it. And Tabini dealt, hard and fast and with nerves that didn't flinch at a frown from the opposition.

Tabini's opponents fell into Tabini's sense of timing and didn't ever recover their balance—ended up negotiating peace because they couldn't ever get their feet under them. Figuratively speaking.

He envied that ability. He wished he'd found his

balance in this exchange for any given moment. He wished most of all he'd found a way to get a confirmation out of the alien regarding their leaving the scene.

That could be the greatest failure in his life. Absolutely essential, and for a critical moment he'd doubted he could get it, and balked. Mistake, mistake, mistake.

"Mr. Cameron." Sabin.

"Ma'am."

"Good job."

Did one tell the plain truth, in the middle of the bridge, if not in the midst of the below-decks crew? "I have lingering concerns, captain."

"A no-go, Mr. Cameron?"

Did he then undermine administration's confidence in the outcome, when he was negotiating with his own side as well as the other?

"No, captain. I'm sure we'll solve problems as they come."

"Best we can ask, Mr. Cameron. Take a tea-break."

Take a tea-break. Get your interference out of my thought processes.

"Yes, ma'am." He wasn't going to be provoked, not here, not now, not with what they had hanging off their bow. He did walk away, Banichi and Jago close on his heels.

"Takehold, takehold minor, takehold," hit the speakers. They were about to back away from the confrontation.

He took hold, in the corridor, where there was a safety nook and a recessed bar for handholds. Banichi and Jago braced him within the lock of their arms, and scarcely swayed to the ship's gentle push.

Sabin might be halfway satisfied with what had happened.

He wasn't. The longer he reviewed his performance the more he doubted what he'd done. They'd lied to the aliens about who they were. They'd lied about their possible intentions.

Now they went to the Guild to lie to them about their ultimate intention to destroy the Archive and shut down the station the Guild had built and defended. And where did the truth start?

The all-clear sounded. The alien ship hadn't, apparently, fired on them, confirming he'd interpreted the signals well enough. They were still alive. He straightened his collar, arranged his sleeves and walked on to the dowager's cabin.

Best steady his nerves and quit double-thinking what he'd done. Decision was decision. He might yet get a chance to finish that letter to Toby, and the one to Tabini. He might yet get a chance to send them.

What would he write about the last performance? *I guessed? I did my best guess. They didn't shoot at us.*

Better than the station authorities had done, at least.

At the moment he owed the dowager and Gin a personal presentation of the facts, beyond what they'd have picked up from their communications. He removed the noise from his ear, pocketed the device as Banichi rapped at the dowager's door.

One of Cenedi's men opened to them, and they walked in on that most uncommon of sights, the dowager's small court and Gin and Jerry sitting together, faces all turned toward him.

He bowed. "Aiji-ma, Gin-ji." They made a fortunate number, together. He was never so aware of settling back into the comfort of that system, every detail considered: baji-naji, but the chances of chance were limited in the dowager's company. "We've sent a sort of animated cartoon to the foreign ship, aiji-ma, an illustration of past behaviors and present. We've received their version in reply, and their information indicates they approached the station, sent a probe, and the station blew it up—retaining the remains of the occupant. The aliens have offered no further explanation of their long wait here, but they declare, as best the images indicate, that they want the remains returned, along, I would assume, with all bits and pieces of the craft. They may be concerned, as we are, with information that may have fallen into human hands. One could surmise they have identical concerns about an enemy researching their home planet."

"Understandable," the dowager pronounced it. "These seem reasonable demands."

"They haven't, however, agreed that we can take the stationers away. We put forward that proposal and they failed, as best we can understand, to consent. This remains a problem for future negotiation. Sabin-aiji wants to dock with the station and find out whether we can refuel. If we have fuel, we have numerous options." He hadn't translated for Gin, but Gin followed a little of it, and had heard the original events in ship-speak. "If we have none—we have a further problem."

Ilisidi lifted a thin hand, waved it. "Pish. Running is no choice. It leads home. And will Sabin-aiji lie to these strangers? A bad beginning."

"A very bad beginning," Bren agreed, inwardly cringing at his own responsibility.

"A hard choice," Ilisidi said.

"But," Cajeiri said, hitherto wide-eyed and silent, "what do they look like?"

"A little like us," Bren said.

"Bren-aiji is tired," Ilisidi snapped. "Pish on your questions. Let him sit or let him go to his quarters."

"I should indeed take a rest, now, aiji-ma. They haven't requested we go below. I rather think we should all rest, and be on the bridge as we approach the station. I may go there earlier, and be there when the captains communicate with the station."

"I can go forward and observe," Gin said.

Good idea, he thought. He trusted Jase to tell him what was going on as the ship glided away from the encounter. But he didn't trust himself to stay awake. He took the earpiece from his pocket and handed it to Gin. "Just listen for me from here. Saves arguments. I'm going to try to sleep an hour."

"You got it," Gin said, and laid a hand on his shoulder as he started for the door. "Good job."

"I wish I'd gotten more from them," he said. It was hardest of all to present a half-done job to his own associates. But he bowed to the aiji-dowager, to the young aiji, and left, Banichi and Jago in close company with him—went to his temporary quarters and sat down in the reclining chair.

He shoved it back all the way. Banichi and Jago settled where they could find comfort for their stature, next the wall, one corner of a square.

Quiet, then. His ear still itched from the long flow of communication. When he shut his eyes he saw black and white figures, the animated docking with station, the embarcation.

The alien ship putting out a probe. The explosion.

Had the alien ship initiated fire on the station ten years ago? Had the station possibly blown half *itself* away trying to hit a ship that came close, and deceived Ramirez about the event—in the same policy of secrets and silence in which Ramirez had shown a lie to his own ship?

Or was it one ship that had hit the station ten years back and another the station had hit six years ago?

God, it was getting far more convolute than a simple lad from Mospheira wanted to figure.

The plain fact was, they and the alien craft had an agreement—and a lie he had to keep covered, namely the atevi's presence with them.

Now he was going to lie to the station. Aliens aboard? What aliens? Oh, the Mospheiran gentleman . . . a jumped-up colonist negotiator. Never mind the slightly odd clothes.

He wondered if Jase or Sabin was going to get the leisure to sit down for half an hour—let alone sleep. It wouldn't improve their chances to have the ship's captains on duty through shift after shift after shift.

Four shifts, still. Two captains. It was all fine when they were careening through folded space, puttering half-wittedly about their duties. At the moment, he desperately wished there were relief for them. *Sabin* wasn't about to turn anything about this over to Jase and Jase wasn't going to leave her alone to deal with whatever came up. He had that pegged.

Distrust. The habit of lies. And now this Pilots' Guild, that wove its own walls out of lies.

Not easy to sleep on that thought. But he did his best. He had the two bravest individuals he'd ever known not a few feet away. He had their wit, their steadiness whenever he faltered. They wouldn't flinch. He couldn't. When he lost sight of everything else—they were there.

He thought of home. Of his mother's dining room. A cufflink, gone down the heating duct. Gone. Just gone. He'd pinned his cuff, rushing off to the plane, rushing to escape the island.

He wished he'd made a visit there before he left.

He'd get together with Toby when he got back. He'd drag Jase down planetside to take that fishing trip. They wouldn't bait the hooks. Just bring a week's worth of sandwiches and a case of beer.

8

It wasn't enough sleep before Gin came across the corridor.

"I hate to wake you," Gin said—the door opening had already roused Banichi and Jago, who had sorted themselves out and got up immediately. Bren found a harder time locating his wits, but he straightened the chair and set his feet on the floor.

"Sabin's talking to the station," Gin said. "They're asking questions like what did we just do out there with the alien? What took us ten years getting here? Sabin's stonewalling them. Says since they didn't help out with the alien confrontation, she sees no reason to talk to them about what we said until she gets there."

There might have been a better answer, but he couldn't think of one yet. It certainly set the tone between ship and Guild. He was very much concerned about Sabin's short fuse, and Jase's, not inconsiderable, both of them running on no sleep whatsoever.

"I'm going," he said, standing up, and, too incoherent to explain his wants, held out his hand for the earpiece. She gave it to him, and he stuck it in, immediately hearing the minor traffic of the consoles. "They haven't changed shifts."

"No. Overdue, but she's keeping her own people

on. I think she's getting just a little punchy, if you want the brutal truth."

"What's our ETA?"

"Not sure. About an hour. We're headed for the slope."

A lot like skidding on ice. That was how he conceptualized maneuvering in space. Sometimes you were facing one way and going another, and if you got onto a gravity slope you slid very damned fast, accelerating without doing a thing. He could almost understand Sabin's viewpoint: she hated planets, wasn't fond of stars, didn't at all mind the dark, empty deeps.

Reunion was situated high up on a gravity slope. Stations had to be. And a station was a scary place to navigate, so he gathered. High toehold above a deep plunge. Like wi'itikin coming in for a cliffside perch, a lot of tricky figuring best done by computer brains, humans not having the wi'itikin's innate sense—or wings, if something went wrong.

He was fogged. He managed a thank you to Gin.

"Ignore them," he heard Sabin say to someone. *"I'm busy. They can rant all they like."*

Sounded like high time he got to the bridge. "Go rest," he said to Gin, and headed out the office door with Banichi and Jago in close attendance. His face prickled. He wished he'd thought to bring his shaving kit topside. He'd foolishly believed the dowager's sack lunch was excessive.

The bridge looked no different than when he'd left. Those at work took no special note of his return.

Jase, however, walked over to him as he stopped to survey the scene.

"How's it been?" Bren asked.

"Station's not pleased with us," Jase said. "Senior captain's not cooperating with them. They want us to do a hard grapple at nadir of the mast. We won't. Fueling port's zenith. That's where we're going."

"They want us *away* from it. That's not encouraging."

"The fuss is," Jase said. And held a little silence with a glance across the bridge at Sabin, who wasn't looking at them. He gave a hand-sign, the sort that Banichi's and Jago's Guild exchanged on mission. It was a warning. "Angry," he said in Ragi. "Overdue for rest. I lack the skill to bring us in, and I lack the rank to argue with the Guild. Which she *is* doing."

That was good news. "I need your advice in what's coming. I need you sane and rested. Is there any reason you can't go off-duty and take an hour?"

"She won't. I won't."

"What are we? Kids in a schoolyard, egging each other on? Take a break, Jase. If she won't use common sense, at least you'll be sane."

Jase shook his head. "She's pushing herself. She won't trust me to handle the smallest things. And if I want her to pay attention to my advice over the next handful of hours, I can't fold, now, can I?" They were old friends, and there was adamancy, but not anger, in the argument. "And matters are too critical right now to worry about my state of mind or the fact my back's killing me. We're dealing with the Guild. You want non-reason in high places? We're dealing with it."

"What do you read in them?"

"I'm not the expert."

"In ship-culture, in Guild mentality—you very much are." He changed to Ragi. "Your professional opinion, ship-paidhi."

Rapid blinks—total change of mental wiring. Moment of mental blackout. Then, in Ragi: "Understandable. They disapprove Sabin-aiji's defiance of their authority. They refuse talk until we get into dock."

"Then?"

"Then—they and we will be in closer contact."

"They intend to board."

"A question whether Sabin will permit that, nadi-ji. But perhaps."

It was *not* good. He began to read the psychology of it through an atevi lens, and pulled his mind away from thoughts of association, *aishi* and *man'chi*, the social entity and the emotion—which, after all this voyage, began to seem logical even on human terms. Two metal motes with humans inside *wanted* to come together. Like magnetism. Like *man'chi*. But once they met—

Human politics were inside those shells. Not just two metal shells. Two grenades gravitating toward each other.

"Do they trust *her* at all?" he asked—meaning Sabin.

"One doubts," Jase said, and added, in ship-speak: "She's just ordered an outside operations team to suit up immediately after we dock."

"Boarding the station?" They'd have to turn out the whole crew to take something as large as that— and still might be outnumbered.

"To have our hands at the refueling port."

"That's not standard operating procedure, is it?" Of fueling stations in the vast cosmos, there were only two he knew. And one, Alpha, ran operations from a stationside control center.

"It's not. I know that much. The captain's preparing to have us do it ourselves, from outside. I don't know what she's going to say to them. Being Sabin, she may not say a thing. She may just do it."

Aliens waiting in the wings and the captain outright preparing to commandeer a fuel supply from the people they'd come to rescue, who at the moment weren't cooperating—at least their officials weren't. He'd thought his heart had had all the panic it could stand in the last few hours. He discovered a brand new source.

"And we haven't gotten word from them yet that there is fuel." That was the prime question at issue, and Jase slowly shook his head.

"They're not talking about that and we're not asking. If they can't fuel us, we have a choice to make."

"If we run," he said, "there's every chance that ship out there can track us out to Gamma and hit us there. Isn't there?"

"So I understand. Starring down a gun barrel while we scrape what we need together out of space isn't attractive."

"We can get the alien remains out of the station and negotiate. I *don't* recommend running. We have a reasonable chance so long as we seem to be cooperating with that ship out there."

"That's your advice."

"To keep all sides talking while we spend the next few years gathering fuel. Running's only going to make matters worse. We'll have none of the passengers we came here to get, we won't have destroyed the Archive, and we still won't have any fuel."

"I'd tend to agree with you."

"Most of all—most of all we have to get some sort of calm."

"Calm." Jase's laugh held stress, not humor.

"Whatever situation has existed here for six years has been destabilized by our arrival. And we don't know what's gone on here. We have to ratchet down the stress on this situation. And she—" Meaning

Sabin. "—has to be reasonable, right along with the Guild. First and foremost, we have to show good faith with that ship out there. That's a priority, even ahead of the fuel, toward getting us out of here and keeping the Archive to ourselves, with all that means. *Hang* the fuel situation. We can solve that with Gin's robots."

"Over years."

"Over years and I'd rather not. But that ship out there represents a more critical situation. We get locked into a push-pull with the Guild and we can lose sight of what's going on at our backs."

"We have guns."

"We have guns, they have guns—we also have a potential chance to *settle* this mess before it comes home with us, Jase."

"*I* agree with you," Jase said, leaving hanging in the air the implication that the other captain was at issue. "And I'm asking you, Bren, stay up here. Be cooperative with her, whatever it takes. The situation needs you *and* the dowager with your wits about you, and it needs us all with as much manuevering room as we can maintain with Sabin, if we're going to have to negotiate our way out of this. She's not a diplomat. You've given her information. *Don't* assume she'll use it diplomatically."

"I'd better talk with her," he said, "before we go much closer."

"She's several hours less rested." Jase gave him that look. A plea for extreme caution.

"We have the chance now," he said. "It's only going to be less sleep if this goes on."

Jase said nothing to that, and he walked on down the aisle, quietly intercepting Sabin, delicately as if he were picking up a live bomb. "Captain. A moment, if you can spare it."

"We don't have many moments, Mr. Cameron."

"In private, captain, if you will. I have something to communicate."

She grudgingly yielded, as far as the end of the console, where the general noise of fans overcame the small noise of low voices. She hadn't cut off her communications pickup. But if one talked to her, as to him, discreet security personnel were inevitably involved.

"I take it," she said, "we're about to receive a personal confidence from the dowager."

"A message from me, captain. A further offer—with the Guild. I *am* a negotiator, if the Guild turns recalcitrant. I'm offering, in all good will—so you know your hands aren't empty. For a start—in spite of my distaste for secrets—I don't advise spilling everything the aliens out there said, if there's any likelihood they didn't overhear it."

"They're asking. Likely they didn't get it."

"That's to the good. Second point: never mind Gamma. Get in control of whatever alien material the station's holding. That's critical. We can solve a fuel problem. But if they're not put off our trail, we're in deep trouble."

"Oh, I am so gratified to have that advice, Mr. Cameron."

"Fuel be damned, captain."

"I don't recall you got a confirmation from that ship out there that we *can* leave if we jump to their orders."

"I can't swear to their customs, their attitude, or their morality. But I know ours. If there's a way not to lead them back to Alpha, *that's* a priority. It's common sense, captain."

Sabin's mouth tightened. "Priority is *options,* Mr.

Cameron. Yours is one on a list. Fuel, passengers, *then* their little errand."

"Station's not cooperating with you."

"Tell the second captain keep his advice. I've heard it. Trust me that I've heard it."

"Captain, it's *cooperation* I'm offering. To convey *your* viewpoint to station. To get what you want."

Sabin gave a short, grim laugh. "You say. You know the dowager's a bastard. So am I. And so, in your sweet, stubborn way, are you, Mr. Cameron. Tell the second captain I'm *fine*, and I can deal with the Guild. Now go shut the hell up and leave me to my job."

He'd walked into this trying to get ahead of the situation. Numb as he was and remote from full-tilt feeling, his brain uneasily advised him the paidhi was not truly functioning at his utmost, either. And he didn't know what he'd accomplished. Sabin took advice without telling the advisor she was taking it. And one never knew what she'd do.

"What did she say?" Jase asked, in Ragi, when he drew back into range of him and Banichi and Jago.

"She is at least maintaining our secrets from the station," Bren said in Ragi. "She refuses to accept the alien mission ahead of our own. And hopes, one believes, that there might be fuel. If the station had any time at all to prepare itself before this second incident, they ought to have thought, if *Phoenix* comes back, fuel is essential to our own safety. Therefore it would be very highest priority. Would it not be, Jase-aiji?"

"One certainly hopes," Jase said. Meanwhile the image forward was a rotating, damaged station.

Sabin paused by C1 and gave an order. And spoke on general address.

"Sabin here. This is the situation: we have contact with the station and we're on track for our high berth,

contrary to their instructions. I've ordered a team to suit and connect the fuel probe from the outside. Communications with the station have been limited: considering we're not alone here, that's understandable. But due to numerous unanswered questions, these are my orders. We'll refuel as a priority, and if station has other ideas, we'll hear them afterward. You'll have a ten minute break coming up as soon as I sign off. Do what you need to do and get back to a secure bunk. Second watch crew will maintain current assignment. Third watch will take station after docking."

Damn, Bren thought. She wasn't letting Jase's crew take station. She was driving her own past a due change. Had driven herself for hours.

"We don't know the situation on the station," Sabin said. *"And so long as we don't know, we don't let our guard down. Keep on alert. This isn't a time for any celebration, and nobody will attempt to contact station communications. Evasive action remains a moment by moment possibility. I'm giving you a ten-minute break off strict precautions, but as you value your necks and the necks of those around you, don't get sloppy.*

"Ten minutes. Starting now. No excuses."

"I need to translate that for my staff," Bren said to Jase, and relayed the information in Ragi, above and below decks, that they might move about for a very few moments.

Banichi and Jago had stood by quietly the last while, translating occasionally on their own, always there. That was a relief to him, too, as if, while they were not by him, even by the width of the bridge while he was talking to Sabin, he had been somehow stretched thin. Now that they were close, all of him was there . . . curious notion for a Mospheiran lad to get into, but that was the way his nerves read it.

Bridge crew, half a dozen at a time, took the chance

for a break, a mad rush for the available facilities. Those first absent returned, and gave immediate attention to business while partners made the same rush.

Sabin herself took a small break: "You're in charge," she told Jase in passing. "Don't start a war. Evade if there's a twitch out there. Nav knows."

"Thank you, captain," Jase said quietly. Jase changed none of her orders, did nothing but walk the aisles on Sabin's routine. When Sabin got back, he simply made a small salute, continued his own patrol and said not a word.

She did approach, however, and talked with him somberly in low tones that failed to reach Bren's ears. She'd trusted him, however briefly. Jase hadn't failed her.

The dowager and Cajeiri, meanwhile, took advantage of the moment to come out, with Gin and the rest, and, unopposed, resumed their seats along the bulkhead. Cajeiri was wide-eyed and watching, the dowager grim, while Gin—Gin watched everything that moved. Neither captain seemed to note their arrival, but Bren waited, assured both captains had very well noted it, expecting that if Sabin had had any comment, Jase would soon wander by.

Jase did.

"When we go in," Jase said with a little bow, "we're going to maintain rotation. It's a power drain, operating like that, and it means we don't grapple—we tether. Senior captain's ordering it to make life more comfortable here. The tether dock means more security for us. That's a cold, uncomfortable passage that only takes two at a time. It's a deliberate bottleneck. It *doesn't* accommodate boarders."

"She's not letting crew off."

"No. No way. Crew's not going to get communication with the station."

"Prudent."

"Also significant—maintaining position on tether gives us the excuse to keep our systems hot."

"So we can move at the drop of a hat."

"If a hat should for some reason drop," Jase said. "Yes."

"But in that state—we can't board passengers."

"Not rapidly," Jase said. "We can easily hard-dock from that position, for general boarding. But the thing that may be most important, soft-dock slows down the rush to the ship. She wants our fuel load. Her priorities. And it's sensible. We don't want to depopulate the station all in a panic."

Any Mospheiran knew what had happened to the station at the atevi star, once the inhabitants had decided their futures lay elsewhere, on the planet. They'd deserted for the planet below, a trickle at first, then a cascading chain of desertions and station services going down, until the last few to leave the station had just mothballed it as far as they could and turned out the lights.

"God," Jase said then, while input pinged and blipped at the consoles, "I hope this whole business goes fast."

"Fishing trip's still an offer," Bren said, deliberate distraction—but that offer seemed to strike Jase as more unreadably alien than the communication out there in the dark. A different world, that of the atevi. A different mindset, that required a quick, deep breath. But it offered stability.

"If I survive this," Jase said shakily, "I swear I'm going for Yolanda's job. Frequent runs down to the planet. Court appearances. Estate on the coast. Right next to yours."

"I'll back you. Big yacht, while we're at it. We'll go take a close-up look at the Southern Sea."

"I'll settle for a rowboat," Jase said in a low voice. "A sandy beach and a rowboat."

While the numbers went on scrolling on the screens.

"Don't let your guard down," Jase said suddenly. "Keep ready for takehold."

9

No touch. A gentle shock a little after the takehold ran out: alarming, to people who'd just given up their handholds. "That was the tether line," Jase said, and Bren translated for the dowager and party.

They sat and stood, atevi and humans, on that division between corridor and bridge, meticulously out of the way, and watching.

Jase stood next to the lot of them, buffer, translator, reassurance.

"We have fired a tether line toward the station mast, nandi," Jase said to the dowager in Ragi. "This is to stabilize connections for essential lines. The ship's computers will keep us positioned relative to the station by small adjustments, which we will feel occasionally while docked, none of which should require a handhold. That tether line will keep the fueling probe and communications lines in good order, as well as carrying information within itself, now that it has contacted the reciprocal port on the station."

"So we should hear from these persons," Ilisidi said.

"More often and more clearly, nandi, and in communications protected from bureaucrats," Jase answered.

"Eavesdroppers," Bren corrected. The words were akin. Jase's Ragi occasionally faltered, even yet.

"Eavesdroppers," Jase said with a little nod, a slight

blush. "Pardon, nandiin. The tether also provides a person-sized soft tube which permits one to come and go, rather like an ordinary boarding passage, but very cold, very much smaller, easier to retract or even break free in case of emergency. Sabin-aiji is preserving our freedom of movement. We expect a clear understanding with the station before we establish any more solid connection, nandi."

Sabin meanwhile, not far distant, gave rapid orders establishing that connection; Bren heard that with the other ear.

"Tether line is established," C1 informed the crew belowdecks, in that operations monotone. *"Links are functioning."*

Sabin appeared in a far better mood now than an hour ago. She looked to have aged ten years in the last few hours, but there was a spark in her eye now— more like a battle-glint, but a spark, all the same.

"Now we have a physical communications linkage," Jase said, hands in jacket pockets.

Mechanical whine and thump. *Airlock,* Bren thought on the instant, with a jump of his heart. They hadn't heard *that* in at least a year.

"Someone is going outside," he muttered to Jase.

"Fuel access, belly port. We are not asking their permission, nandiin. We will see what our situation is. But this process of arranging the port connection may take hours.

"One *might* take the chance at this point to go back to greater comfort below," Jase said.

"And when will the captains do so?" Ilisidi asked.

"Perhaps soon, nandi." Jase looked wrung out, at the limits of his strength. "But we shall go to shift change soon. One anticipates that Sabin-aiji may declare it her night, and when that happens, I shall likely sit watch up here claiming I know absolutely nothing, should the station have questions. We may well start fueling under that circumstance, granted there is fuel. It may cause a certain distress, but Sabin-aiji will not be disposed to listen."

"A diplomatic situation, then," Ilisidi said.

"But a human one, aiji-ma," Bren said quietly. "I should stay up here within reach, but there is clearly no reason for the aiji-dowager to miss breakfast."

Clearly it tempted. Ilisidi rarely admitted fatigue, except for show. The harsh lines of her face were not, at this point, showing. "One might consider it, if this ship has ceased its moving about."

"One may trust that, aiji-ma."

"This bloodthirsty child will go disappointed that we shan't raise banners and storm the station, I'm sure, but if matters have reached such a lengthy wait, I shall appreciate a more comfortable chair. And this boy needs his breakfast."

"One understands a young gentleman's endurance is very sorely tested. I don't know what other young lad might have stood and sat for so long."

"One makes no excuses," Ilisidi said sharply—though the young lad in question, eye level with a human adult, looked exhausted. "A gentleman *offers* no exceptions, does he, rascal?"

"No, mani-ma." It was a very faint voice. "But one would very much favor a glass of—"

Click. Softly, Ilisidi set her cane down in front of her feet.

"At convenience, mani-ma."

Ilisidi's hand lifted. A disturbance had just rippled across the bridge, Sabin and C1 in consultation, nearby stations diverting attention to that conversation. Technicians' heads actually turned, however briefly.

Something unusual was going on.

"A moment, nandiin." Jase excused himself toward the epicenter of the trouble.

"Excuse me, aiji-ma." Bren took Sabin's tolerance of Jase in the situation as a similar permission and went, himself, to stand and listen.

The team from *Phoenix* had reached the fueling port. Video from a helmet-cam showed a yellow and black band and a hand-lettered label stuck across an edge. It said . . . God! *Lock rigged to explode.*

"They've locked the fuel port," Jase said under his breath. "With a sign out there for *us* to read."

"Evidently there's something to protect," Bren muttered, "from us."

"Get me station administration," Sabin said in clipped tones, and C1 acknowledged the order.

A sense of unease welled up. Banichi and Jago hadn't followed him into the sacred territory of the operations area, but he felt a Banichi sort of thought nagging at him. "Jase. If we plug into their systems to talk, can they possibly get into our systems?"

"Two-way," Jase said. "I don't know the safeguards. I assume we both have them."

There had to be safeguards—had to be, *if* the captains hadn't trusted the Guild. *If* the Guild had doubts about the captains. Or had they? "Captain," he began to say to Sabin, but Sabin leaned forward on C1's console and said, "Get me the stationmaster. Now. Asleep or awake, rout him out."

A loyal ship turned up after a decade-long voyage, there was a lock on the fuel and the stationmaster wasn't saying glad to see you as it docked? Granted station wasn't glad they'd approached the alien ship out there—it ought to be happy they'd gotten away alive.

"Anybody bothered by this silence from station?" Bren asked under his breath.

Sabin shot their small disturbance a burning look, intermittent with attention to the console. On the screen, some sort of official emblem appeared, links of a chain, the word *Reunion.*

"Stationmaster's answered," C1 said quietly. "Stationmaster, stand by for the senior captain."

"Stationmaster," Sabin said abruptly. "Sabin here, senior captain. We're tethered in good order. Speaking on direct. What's your situation?"

C1 had the audio low, but audible.

And below that circle of links, the screen now held the old Pilots' Guild emblem, a white star and a ship, superimposed with *Pilots' Guild Headquarters, Louis Baynes Braddock, Chairman.*

Nothing inherently terrible about that image. But seeing it actually in use, not pressed in the pages of a history book, sent cold chills down a Mospheiran spine.

That image dissolved to the heavy-jowled face of a middle-aged man, white-haired and balding, in an officer's uniform. *Louis Baynes Braddock, Chairman.*

"Stable at the moment, Captain Sabin," Braddock answered. *"Where is Captain Ramirez?"*

"Attrition of age, sir. Of the original captains, Jules Ogun is alive and well, directing affairs at Alpha Station." There was the shade of a lie, by way of introduction. "And I am senior in this situation. Second captain aboard is Jason Graham. No fourth captain has yet been appointed. We require fuel. I'd like to get that moving. What's the situation?"

"We have a full load for you, Captain."

Confirmation went through the bridge, palpable relief. Full load. Ready. They could do their job and leave. They could go *home.* But not a single face, not a single eye, shifted from absolute duty.

"That's very good news, Mr. Braddock, very good

news." No flicker of emotion touched Sabin's face, either, no rejoicing beyond that utterance, muscles set like wire springs. "And the watcher out there?"

"It never has interfered with us." Not what the alien itself had indicated. *"We tried to advise you. Your interference in that situation is very dangerous, captain. I can't stress how dangerous."*

Two lies and unanswered questions by the bucketful. The news about the fuel load was good—but Braddock lied, and Bren held his breath.

"I can report in turn," Sabin said, "that our Alpha base is secure, things there are in good order, and we're fit for service once we're fueled here—including dealing with any threat from that ship out there. Fueling should get underway immediately. I note your precautions with the fuel port. Can we get that open, priority one?"

"As soon as we've officially verified your credentials and reviewed your log records, Captain Sabin, we'll be delighted to deliver the fuel."

Not much fazed Sabin. There began, however, a sudden, steady twitch in her jaw. "Chairman Braddock, we've managed a peaceful contact with that observer out there. We seem to have a tacit approval for our approach, whether or not it's collecting targets into one convenient package, or just watching to see what we do. We don't know the extent of its comprehension. We're not anxious to postpone refueling and setting this ship in operational order in favor of a round of by-the-book formalities, hell no, sir. Unlock that port."

"Essential that we ascertain your recent whereabouts and your authority, captain."

"You haven't got damn else for a ship, sir, and I *am* the authority."

"We're sure we'll be satisfied with your report, cap-

tain. But you'll appreciate that, even considering you're clearly in possession of Phoenix, *there is a question of legitimacy of command. More to the point, there's the authority of this Guild to review, inspect, and post to rank. Those formalities we take to be important. The log records are requisite. We require you transmit them."*

Sabin took her hand off the console shelf and stood upright. There was still not a flicker of expression on her face. But she paused a moment to gather composure and reason before she leaned near the pick-up again. "Stationmaster, do I correctly gather that you're asking me to come to your offices to fill out forms and deal with red tape with my ship unfueled and a ship you can't account for already having constrained us on our way in? And that you're trying to assert Guild Council authority over *Phoenix?* I reject that, categorically. My second captain may be new, but I'm not, and I know what's in order and what's not. *Hell* if I'm putting our navigational records and the precise location of our remote base into your records when you can't even guarantee the security of your own station."

"Captain Sabin, we're asking specifically that you observe Guild law and procedures which our office, our entire reason for being, requires us to follow. You'll appreciate our safeguarding that fuel, to release it to appropriately constituted authority, operating in our interests and at our orders—"

"The hell! We *are* the ship. That's the plain fact."

"Our orders, I remind you, supercede yours, where it regards this station, and the fuel, captain, is on this station. For your convenience, and precisely to expedite this process, we have an inspection team and an escort ready to come up to the ship."

"Escort."

"To Guild headquarters, captain, where you can present your request to the Guild. This transfer of personnel would be far easier in hard dock. We have questions to ask about the encounter out there."

"After refueling."

"We understand your worry. But we have legitimate worries. We feel you've exacerbated the situation with your adventurism out there—adventurism which brought this situation on us. We are not disposed to be patient, captain, and we strongly suggest you hard dock and come in for consultation."

"Until you can present solid information about our watcher out there, I'll keep us soft-docked. I may change my mind once we're sure you're in control of the station."

"I can assure you, captain, we've never ceased to be in control of this station."

Their advantage was leaking away, utterance by utterance. "Captain," Bren said, and recklessly if gently interposed his hand between Sabin and the console.

Sabin reached past that intervention and pushed a button on the console. Held it down, preventing transmission to the station, one hoped.

"A sudden bright idea, Mr. Cameron?"

"You're senior entity. Demand the Guildmaster board and prove what's to prove. And don't let him off again once he's here."

"I'd enjoy that, but it doesn't get that fuel lock released, Mr. Cameron, and I don't want someone to panic and dump the load. Traditionally, captains *have* gone to station offices."

"And if they hold *you?*"

"Then we'll know something, won't we?" She released the button and spoke to Braddock, at the console. "I use my own escort, sir, under my own command."

Bren's heart sank. Ignored. Absolutely ignored.

"I'll expect a full explanation of the situation from your side," Sabin said to Braddock. "As for your officers boarding this ship, inspect as you like, under Captain Graham's supervision, but I've no intention of transmitting ship's log containing base location into your station records in the presence of an unexplained foreign presence, and that's the law on *this* deck. Personnel link is adequate for current business. Beyond that, I assure you *Phoenix* remains the senior entity in this organization: we are your *founders,* sir, and we don't take orders."

"We're well aware of your unsuccessful maneuver to breach the fuel port." Did one imagine a sudden, desolate chill in relations? *"When we see the documents that confirm your authority to command, we'll have more to say, Captain Sabin. Our personnel are on their way and expect entry."*

"I'll expect your escort momentarily, Mr. Braddock. Let's get this business done. Sabin out."

C1 cut the connection. Sabin wasn't happy. That needed no translation. She straightened, glowered straight at Bren, looked at Jase, at the lot of them. The tic was still pulsing away in her jaw. It wasn't a good time to argue—but, Bren thought, feeling the deck had just dropped away under his feet, it was a very unfortunate time for Sabin to shove advice aside.

"Captain Graham."

"I'll be honored to go in your place," Jase said quietly. "In that capacity, I might be more useful."

"Protocols, second captain, *protocols* say you aren't the one to go, sensible as it might otherwise be. Main security will go with me. With weapons."

"Yes, captain," Jase said quietly and Bren stepped to the background with a glance at Banichi and Jago.

"Inform the dowager and fifth deck, nadiin-ji. The

fuel port is locked with an explosive device and a sign in human language. The station demands Sabin-aiji come report in person to establish her legitimacy before the Guild chairman will release the fuel. We believe this is subterfuge. Captain Sabin is arming her primary guard to go outside the ship, but she has admitted Guild officers inside our security, expecting Jase to finesse this."

"Shall we assist?" Banichi asked, surely with a certain anticipation he hated to hold back.

"Not yet, Nichi-ji. Not yet." The troubling truth was that *Phoenix* had relatively few security personnel on each shift—they weren't a warship: they were a small town; and their advantage was they knew each other, but their glaring disadvantage was—they only knew each other. *Sabin* thought she knew the Guild better than the rest of them, and that might be true, but the move she made scared him—scared him in the extreme.

Ilisidi had moved forward, into the aisle, with Cajeiri, with Cenedi, and her gold stare fairly sizzled.

"We *have* understood. This is dangerous insolence in the absence of power, in this wrecked station. Say so to Sabin-aiji. Say that we shall lend force to her actions."

He foresaw refusal. But he went closer to Sabin and rendered that: "The dowager calls the station dangerously insolent, says people sitting in a wrecked station have no real authority; she offers atevi assistance."

"Unfortunately," Sabin said between her teeth, "and the governing fact, we have no real *fuel*."

"If you board, ma'am, they have you and the fuel," Jase pointed out. "And without you, this ship has no way home."

"On the contrary, Mr. Akers seems quite undamaged and serviceable." That was the senior pilot.

"Failing Mr. Akers, Ms. Carem and Mr. Keplinger. And they surely have *your* canny advice, Captain Graham." It was the sort of petty sniping that consistently flew at Jase and his appointment. "It also has *you,* Mr. Cameron, and the dowager and her security, and Ms. Kroger, and if the station does an explosive vent on the fuel, I'm hopeful we have machinery as adequate to recover it as it is to mine in the first place."

"With extreme difficulty, captain. With that ship lurking out there, that—"

"We can't do anything about that ship, now, can we, Mr. Cameron, without that fuel, except run to a point where we'll be definitively out of fuel and stuck, probably a place, as you so eloquently maintain, that our alien observer can find us with no trouble at all. Meanwhile we don't know the situation on station, which I mean to find out. And when I do, I intend to enforce common sense with information and observations I don't intend to pass through station's communication system. I'll be in touch. Failing that, Mr. Collins or Mr. Jenrette will be in touch."

Jase frowned. "I'd ask you not take Mr. Jenrette, ma'am. He's a resource I could—"

"Mr. Jenrette, I say, who knows the station intimately and who's a resource for me."

"His loyalty is suspect," Bren said sharply.

"By you, sir. Confine your speculations to the aliens. And I don't expect innovation aboard this ship, second captain. Wait for my orders. If things go massively wrong and you have to go to aggressive measures on your own, ask C1. If you have to take this ship out of dock, call on Mr. Akers and follow his advice meticulously. If at any time we get another flash from the observer out there—advise me *before* you start free-lancing any communications back to it; and if you can't advise me, advise station to advise me. Above all, have a clear idea what you're going to do if it all goes wrong. We don't want surviving records, second captain. *We do not want that.*"

"I understand you," Jase said faintly. And they all did understand. It was self-destruction she meant. Terrible alternatives. Even *Phoenix* had a major stake back at the atevi planet—all there was left of humanity in this end of the universe was at risk if things went wrong here.

Sabin sealed her jacket, implied preparation for cold. For passage out of the ship and into the station mast.

"So congratulations: you're in charge, Captain Graham. Remember we're very immaculately Guild and we follow the regulations until we know what our options are. And that means *you,* sir—" A glance at Bren. "Get your tall, dark friends belowdecks right now and keep them there. Aliens never left the atevi planet. Our own *crew* isn't putting their heads above two-deck to tell these inspectors differently. The inspection team will fill out their little check list, skip the log check, as per my orders, and go back to report they didn't get any more here than I gave the Guild chief on his request. That's the way it should work, Captain Graham. That's the way it's going to work. So get gran, there, the hell below, right now."

One definitely hesitated to translate that small speech for the dowager's consumption. But it was time to translate, inserting proper courtesies.

"Aiji-ma," Bren said to her, "officials of this human Guild are very soon coming aboard to inspect the ship's credentials. Sabin-aiji suggests we go below immediately. Officials are arriving at any moment. We must not be seen."

"We are here to rescue these ingrates, whose station is in grievously unrepaired condition, who appear to exist in armed standoff with an offended enemy they have no power to talk to, let alone reach, and this incompetent Guild wishes to us to dread their displeasure?"

"They do seem to have one thing: the fuel we desperately need, aiji-ma, which they have rigged so we cannot get at it. Sabin-aiji being requested to board the station, she will do it with armed escort of her choosing, and she is not pleased. One hopes she can carry her point."

"She will go. Not Jase."

"Not Jase, aiji-ma."

Complete change of expression. In such an undemonstrative species, humans might not see it. But the dowager gave him a now sweet, sidelong look—golden eyes, dark skin with its fine tracery of lines—long, long years of calculation and autocracy.

"Well, well, we shall go below," the dowager announced as if it were all her idea, and stamped the deck with her cane. "Now."

"Nandi," Jase said, who *had* caught the nuances. And understood the threat of atevi taking matters in their own hands. "There will be no foreign intrusion onto five-deck. Your residence will remain sacrosanct. One swears this, nandi."

"One certainly expects it." A vigorous stamp of the cane. "Enough of this standing about! My bones ache. I want my own chair."

"Well? Is she going?" Sabin asked.

"The dowager is going below," Jase said.

"Very good," Sabin said. "Mospheirans, too, the whole lot of you, off the bridge. Nothing left behind. And stay quiet down there, Mr. Cameron. We have enough troubles on our hands."

"Yes, ma'am," Bren said, already determined he didn't consider himself under that prohibition. *He* could change accents as easily as he changed clothes . . . and he had no intention of acquiescence in what the Guild and Sabin alone arranged.

Banichi and Jago were still with him. He overtook the dowager and Ginny and their company at the lift, got in just before the door shut and, between Banichi and Jago, set his back against the wall, heaving a deep sigh. His inner vision was all a kaleidoscope of crew on the bridge, locked fuel port, station corridors—those urgent problems and the marching dots of their communication with the alien craft. Which had to be finessed. Somehow.

The dowager was, at the moment, on remarkably compliant behavior. Cajeiri was, correctly sensing an armed grenade in his great-grandmother's quiet demeanor. Ginny very wisely took her cues.

"Damn Guild," was Jerry's opinion, and at a sharp look from Ginny: "Well, damn them, chief. We come all this way . . ."

"Jerry," Ginny said, and Ilisidi paid the matter a quiet look.

Gran 'Sidi, as the stationers called her . . . Gran 'Sidi, the atevi force that swept into station affairs at critical moments and fixed things. And to this hour when Gran 'Sidi gave a look like that—silence fell among Mospheirans and ship-folk alike.

"Sabin has something in mind," Bren said ever so softly. "Just don't rock the boat yet. So to speak. We'll have our moment."

"Anything you need," Ginny said, and with a meaningful glance at the atevi contingent. "Aiji." She managed an atevi-style bow, a graceful escape out of difficult communications, as the lift reached five-deck and let them out.

"Good," Ilisidi said, acknowledging the communication—lordly acceptance. Ilisidi walked out, her staff with her, and Bren followed, not without a parting glance to Ginny and her team, a simple shift of the eyes toward the overhead, an advisement where *he* meant to go.

Ginny understood. Ginny—who could pass for crew, herself. She returned a firm, got-the-information kind of nod.

Ilisidi's guards opened the door to the atevi section. Ilisidi's guards, Ilisidi's servants, had all turned out along the corridor, loyal support, baji-naji, come what might from the strangers proposing to enter the ship on decks above.

The section door shut. Sealed. Ilisidi, walking with taps of her cane, issued her orders, quietly, matter of factly, while she moved among the staff. "An hour to rest, *if* we are so fortunate. Security will deal with necessary issues. For the nonce, we shall not contact these intruders or become apparent to them unless they reach our territory. Bren-nandi?"

"Aiji-ma?"

"You, personally, can manage the accent and manner of ordinary crew."

She didn't miss a bet.

"Easily."

They had reached the dowager's study door. Ilisidi stopped there, hands on the head of her cane, poised. "Interesting. Apprise us of any news."

"Yes, aiji-ma."

A waggle of the topmost fingers. "Let Sabin-aiji make her attempt. Let her learn what she can of the situation and perhaps return to us. Let these officers of the Guild come aboard and lay hands where they wish on the other decks. But not on ours. All these things we may tolerate, briefly, for expediency's sake. Otherwise—otherwise, Bren-nandi, *see* to it. Use whatever resources you need."

"Yes, aiji-ma."

And with that statement, and with a belated backward look from Cajeiri—a worried look, it was—Ilisidi turned aside and let Cenedi open the door to her quarters—into which she and all her company disappeared.

Her bones, Bren said to himself, did suffer with long standing. It was well past time she took a rest. But that mind didn't rest. She was far too canny in human affairs to attempt to deal with what her human associates could far better manage. She deputed, and she sent. But she did not, one was sure, go off alert.

He walked on from that point into his own territory, with Banichi and Jago . . . who assuredly would *not* approve his plans. Who had defensive skills he could never manage.

But no amount of skill and stealth could disguise what they were.

"Nadiin-ji," he said to them, "Sabin-aiji, who has met these station aijiin before, believes she can maintain her authority, discover useful information and gain their cooperation to refuel the ship. She has refused them free access to the ship's history. They persisted and she still refused. She surely knows there is some risk to her freedom to act as she goes onto the station. Her authority there on the station is yet to establish, and one hopes she succeeds. But one still fails to trust her entirely. There is that."

"A strong possibility, Bren-ji?" Banichi asked.

"She can't compel their obedience." It might be superfluous to remind his staff what drove Sabin and the Pilots' Guild were different instincts, having nothing to do with the grouping-drive that motivated atevi, but it was still worth laying out. "We are not dealing with man'chi between her and this Guild, nadiin-ji. Each side has both merit and force to persuade the other to take their direction. But only Sabin has a ship, and I confess I wish she were staying on the ship and simply demanding they come aboard. She could compel that. She could announce her intent to the station population and create insurrection, but she refuses, and takes a security force to the heart of their establishment—perhaps for reasons of her own, perhaps that some sense like man'chi forbids she take the station apart in disorder. I fear they may ambush her—I fear Jenrette, for that matter. But she knows that from the beginning. I have speculations—even the speculation that she *is* Guild and means to spill everything she bids us conceal, laying plans to take the ship once she gets aboard."

"Do we count this likely?"

"She *has* the ship already. She could easily invite the Guild in and turn the ship over to them without risking herself aboard the station. As likely that she means to walk in and simply shoot the Guild-aiji dead at his desk. I don't know what she intends. She has taken Jenrette as one of her guards. I don't know why. Perhaps because she is Guild, as I suspect he is—perhaps because she simply wishes to get him off the ship so he can't sabotage anything. She does not trust Jase to run the ship."

"Do you so trust him, Bren-ji?" Jago asked.

"In matters of security, yes. And he has staff that can move the ship at need. We have not linked the ship within safe access of general population. A rush of population into the mast would put us in a position where we would have to open our doors or see them die of cold; and the presence of so many would increase mass that we dare not leave dock without refueling. On the other hand, if the station administration itself refuses to vacate the station, this would be a great difficulty. Sabin did reiterate to Jase the mission to destroy all the information the station holds. The computers that hold that information, on the station, are deep, and defended by the Guild. The alternatives remain—very bad alternatives. One hardly wishes to think about the possibility of blowing up the station with all those people aboard. One refuses to contemplate it."

"And what shall we first do to prevent this?" Jago asked. "Send you up undefended, Bren-ji, among officials of these strange aijiin? We protest. We very strongly protest this plan."

"Let us assist, Bren-ji," Banichi said. "We can move within the access tunnels. We can remove these troublesome individuals one by one."

He had no doubt, even given the likelihood of advanced communications and weapons. "I don't fear for my life or my freedom aboard, not with Jase in charge. I do fear the mood of the crew. We must not spread fear about—least of all any notion that five-deck intends to seize their ship and take over command. The good will of the crew is very important. And I, nadiin-ji, I am going back up there to protect Jase's authority. I have indeed learned a few things in your company. Prudence, among other things. Use of the communications equipment."

"Which they may detect, Bren-ji," Jago said sharply. "There are very many finesses to these matters."

"One will gratefully take whatever instruction you can give, nadiin-ji," he said. "I think it remotely possible that after a conference, and after reaffirming her ties to the station, Sabin-aiji may aim at getting the truth out of the Guild leadership, about the alien situation, and that would be helpful. But she remains at risk. She has refused my services and declared she is taking over the situation with the Guild herself, with armed force. One dares not fold one's hands and wait."

"One protects against threats as they come, Brenji." Banichi's professional observation was low-key, consistently calm. And calming, too. Bren drew that sense into himself, belief that, against everything else unstable, he had a reasonable chance. He would not be utterly alone.

Not alone now. In their own territory in the corridor, Asicho still dutifully sat the security station, never taking her attention from the situation, while Narani and Bindanda and Jeladi had all turned out to welcome them, to open the door to his personal quarters.

"No time for rest, Rani-ji," he said on the way through the door. "We have a situation, a successful docking on the one hand, but a very troublesome local authority. Sabin-aiji has gone ashore with ship security, ostensibly to try to deal with them, but rejecting advice. I shall need island clothes, Rani-ji, immediately without fuss, before some situation shuts down the lift system."

"Nandi." Narani asked no questions. The clothes would appear, with his staff's fastest cooperation. Doubtless, too, the dowager and Cenedi were entering on much the same endeavor, down the hall, explaining to staff and laying plans of their own, which he hoped didn't involve armed incursion into the maintenance passages.

But if the Pilots' Guild should believe it could make a move on Jase and control the ship, he was very sure the dowager would move very quickly—benignly toward the crew, so be it, but all the same, no question but that Ilisidi would take all security, all decisions, all mission direction into her own hands. Ilisidi, absent Sabin, now saw no one to stop her, no one with whom to negotiate territories directly—and what came next was as basic as gravity, as fundamental as the history of the atevi associations: a power vacuum did not last, among atevi, not ten minutes. Atevi wars most often happened by accident, when signals were not quite clear and contenders for a vacancy jammed up in a figurative doorway.

Which meant signals were already flying, humans all oblivious to the fact. Unless Jase took a strong enough stand to stand Ilisidi off in Sabin's name—it would happen. And that meant there was a very dangerous imbalance of powers developing, if he didn't get himself up there and plant himself in a position to maintain that balance between Ilisidi, the Guild, and ship's authority.

And what *would* the Guild do if the ship they relied on as their heritage, their only lifeline to the universe, their protection and refuge, suddenly turned out to be in alien hands?

And what would *Phoenix* crew do, if atevi, threatening all those traditions, moved suddenly against the Guild—which the crew increasingly didn't like?

Those last two in particular were questions he hoped not to have to answer before the hour was out.

He was exhausted despite his few hours of sleep. He wanted nothing right now more a bed to fall into.

But he did a quick change into a blue sweater and a pair of matching blue pants little distinguishable from the crew's ordinary fatigues.

The hair—well, that was a problem. He thought even of cutting it off, though common crew had varying lengths—well, all shorter than his. But he had it in a simple pigtail, like Banichi's or Jago's, and made up his mind to brazen it out.

"A jacket, nandi?" Bindanda suggested. That had, he discovered, a pocket com. He shrugged it on over the pigtail and fended off Jeladi's well-meaning attempt to extricate his hair.

Just as Narani offered him a small-for-atevi pistol, an assassin's undercover weapon.

His own gun. After all these years—staff still had it oiled and ready.

"If necessary, nandi," the old man said. "If one should in any wise need it on floors above."

He hesitated. Thought no, of course not. Jase was in charge up there. He himself wasn't a particularly good shot, nothing like his bodyguard. He was possibly more danger to their side with it than without it, relying on his wits.

And then he thought, dare I not? Dare I not go that far, if need be? If he had to take cover and got to the service accesses—what more argument, then? What far more drastic situation could develop up there, with Guild investigators coming aboard?

He took the pistol. Of course it was loaded— grandfatherly Narani, Assassins' Guild himself, was certainly not shy of such things—and went out to the security station, where Banichi and Jago doublechecked a wire antenna imbedded in his collar.

"Be quite wary of transmission near these individuals that are coming aboard, Bren-ji," Banichi said. "They may have means of noticing."

"I have the gun," he said, as if Banichi and Jago, in adjusting the connections, had possibly missed it. "I don't at all think I shall at all need it, nadiin-ji, but one supposes better to have it and never need it."

"Do use caution firing near conduits and pressure seals," Jago said solemnly, and Banichi added:

"But do so if needful. Safety systems are generally adequate and quick. Look for a door you may shut if this fails."

When had his security tested *that* theory?

"Keep the communications open," Jago said from his left. "In the general activity all over the ship, a steady signal will be less notable than an intermittent one. Speak Mosphei'. That, too, will be less evident. We *will* take this ship, Bren-ji, at any moment your safety or liberty seems in question."

"One will be very grateful at that point," Bren said in a low voice. "But one fervently hopes no such event will happen, nadiin-ji." Exhaustion had given way to a wobbly buzz of adventure. He was armed, wired, and on his own for the first time in—God, was it almost ten years?

He *thought* he could still manage on his own.

10

A quick call on Ginny—that came first. And the simple act of getting into that section proved two reassuring points: that Jase had taken care of business and that their section doors were indeed not locked to their personal codes.

He surprised one of Gin's men in the corridor. Tony, it was. Tony Calhoun, robotics.

"Mr. Cameron, sir."

"Doors are set, autolock from the outside, protection against our station examiners prowling about, but codes still work on the pads. For God's sake, don't anyone walk out and forget your hand codes. Is Gin available?"

"Yes, sir. To you." Tony thumped the door in question. Twice. Three times.

Gin answered the door in two towels. "Need help?"

"Just a heads-up. I'm up there to back Jase, if he needs it. You're down here to back me, if you'll do that—my staff's monitoring. If they need a simple look-see topside, one of your people can go up, too, right? . . . Banichi may want to take action, but I'm sure he'll appreciate an intermediate if he can get one. Meanwhile my staff may need a backup translator. Can *you* do it?"

"Best I can," Gin said, holding fast to the primary

towel. "Anything they need. Anything you need. Go. Get to it."

The airlock started its cycle, distant thump. Someone was coming aboard or going out. They involuntarily looked up. Looked at each other.

"See you," Bren said, and went back the half dozen steps down the hall and out to the lift, hoping *that* system still responded to his code, and hoping it picked up no other passengers.

It moved. He punched in, not the bridge, but up to crew level.

Deserted. Crew was still awaiting the next shift-change and nobody had gotten clearance to enter the corridors, not for food, not for any reason.

Secrets, they didn't have on this voyage, not between captains and crew. But the lockdown had to chafe, and it couldn't any longer be a question of crew safety, not with the ship linked to station.

Not a good situation. Not productive of good feelings aboard, granted there'd been one mutiny on this ship as was. And Jase hadn't released them. Jase assuredly *didn't* want common crew available for any Guild inspectors to interrogate. He could imagine the first question.

So where were you for the last nine years?

And the second.

What aliens?

Second cycling of the airlock. Bren found his heart beating faster, his footsteps a very lonely sound on two-deck.

Sabin was leaving with her guard, very, very likely, and not taking all the Guild intruders out with her. They couldn't be so lucky as a quick formality and a release of prohibitions. The Guild inspectors were aboard now, he'd bet on it, as he'd bet that Sabin no longer was aboard and that the ship's security had gone with her, leaving the techs, Jase, and that portion of the crew that routinely maintained, cleaned, serviced and did other things that didn't involve armed resistence. They were, to all the Guild knew, stripped of defenses.

Sabin, however, wasn't the only captain with a temper. Jase's had been screwed down tight for the better part of a year—but it existed. Guild investigators, up there, were going to pounce on any excuse, question any anomaly; and if they found anything they were going to have their noses further and further into business.

While a captain who didn't know the systems had to maintain his authority.

A decade ago, when *Phoenix* had come in here, had ordinary stationers rushed to board and take ship toward their best hope, the colony they'd left at Alpha? No. No more than common crew rushed into the corridors to do as they pleased. Spacers lived under tight discipline, and didn't do as Mospheirans would do, didn't go out on holiday when they'd had enough, didn't quit their jobs or change their residence. They obeyed . . . except one notable time when the fourth captain, absent information, had raised a mutiny.

Guild leadership wanted Ramirez to take the ship out and reestablish contact with their long-abandoned colony. But fourth captain Pratap Tamun had taken a look at the situation of cooperation between Ramirez and the atevi world and raised a rebellion that, even in failure, had seeded uneasy questions throughout *Phoenix* crew.

Lonely sound of his own footsteps. Closed, obedient doors. Ask no questions, learn no lies.

And what *else* had Ramirez's orders been when the Guild sent him on to Alpha?

And what did Sabin really understand about that last meeting between Ramirez and his Guild? And what did she intend to do, taking an armed force as her escort . . . some twenty men and women, her regular four, and Mr. Jenrette?

Among other points, Ramirez's orders wouldn't have *Phoenix* assume second place to the planet's native governments, that was sure.

Not to take second place to the colonials supposedly running the station, also very sure.

To take *over* the colony that Reunion believed would be running the station, was his own suspicion of Ramirez's intentions—the likely mission directive from Reunion: gain control of it, run it, report back.

Those orders hadn't proven practical, when there'd turned out not to be a functional station or a capable human presence in Alpha system. Ramirez had had to improvise. Ramirez had rapidly discovered the only ones who could give him what he wanted were atevi, and Ramirez, one increasingly suspected, had been predisposed to think answers might come from non-humans: Ramirez had chased that assumption like a religious revelation once he found a negotiating partner in Tabini-aiji, and found his beliefs answering him. By one step and another, Ramirez had gone far, far astray from Guild intent: the mutiny had gone down to defeat, Ramirez had died in the last stages of his dream.

So what could Sabin do now but lie to the Guild one more time and swear that Ogun was back there running Alpha Station's colony, everything just as the Guild here hoped?

She could of course immediately turncoat to Ogun

and all of them and tell the Guild the truth, aiming the superior numbers and possibly superior firepower of the station at an invasion and retaking of the ship . . . from which she had stripped all trained resistence.

That was his own worst fear, the one that made these corridors seem very, very spooky and foreign to him. His colonist ancestors had taken their orders from these corridors. His colonist ancestors, when they were stationers, had obeyed, and obeyed, and obeyed. Everything had gone the Guild's way for hundreds of years.

Now he was here, without escort, lonely, loud steps in this lower corridor; and he very surely wasn't what Reunion envisioned Alpha to be. The ship's common crew had mutated, too, learning to love fruit drinks and food that didn't grow in a tank.

But now they confronted authorities so old in human affairs that even a colonist's nerves still twitched when the Guild gave its orders and laid down its ultimatims. They scared him. He didn't know why they should: he hadn't planned they should when they left Alpha, but here at the other end of the telescope, Guild obduracy was real. Here it turned up from the very first contact with station authorities. That absolute habit of command.

And Sabin pent up all four shifts of her own crew rather than trust them to meet the Guild's authority face to face. Jase himself hadn't given the order to release the lockdown.

Get fueled. Get sufficient lies laid down to pave the gangway. Get them aboard and *then* tell the truth. It wasn't the way he'd like to proceed.

It wasn't the way *Jase* would like to proceed: he believed that the way he believed in sunrises back home.

But he had no answers, no brilliant way to handle the situation that might not end up triggering a crisis—and right now he feared Jase was very busy up there.

He needed to think, and the brain wasn't providing answers. Blank walls and empty corridors drank in ideas and gave him nothing back but echoes. No resources, no cleverness.

Was the Guild going to give up their command even of a wrecked station in exchange for no power at all, and settle down there in the 'tween-decks as ordinary passengers? Not outstandingly likely. They'd want to run Alpha when they got there. They'd assume they ran the ship, while they were aboard.

A damn sight easier to believe in the Guild's common sense in the home system, where common sense and common decision-making usually reached rational, public-serving decisions—and where the government didn't mean a secretive lot of old men and women bent on hanging onto a centuries-old set of ship's rules that didn't even relate to a ship any longer.

Insanity was what they'd met.

The Guild might even have some delusion they could now take on that alien ship out there, because *Phoenix* had its few guns for limited defense. Take *Phoenix* over, tell the pilots, who'd never fired a shot in anger, to go out there and start shooting at aliens who'd already seen Guild decision-making?

Not likely.

If the Guild had any remains of alien crew locked up in cold storage, they might be able to finesse it into their hands—claiming what? Curiosity?

That wasn't going to be easy. Not a bit of it.

But they had an unknown limit of alien patience involved. Whatever had blown the station ten years ago argued for alien weapons. *He* believed in them.

And while *Phoenix* had been nine years making one

careful set of plans that involved pulling the Guild off
this station—bet that the Guild had spent the last nine
years thinking of something entirely contrary.

Steps and echoes. He was up here—down here—
from relative points of view—trying to shed the atevi
mindset, trying to think as a human unacquainted with
planets had to think, up on the bridge—

Oh my God. The planet. Up on the bridge.

That *picture* on Jase's office wall. The boat. The fish.

There were no atevi in the photo, just a sea and a
hint of a headland beyond. But the evidence of that
picture said *Jase* had been on a planet, which indicated
a very great deal had changed from the situation
Phoenix had expected when it came calling at the station. More, it led to questions directed at Jase, and
questions led to questions, if Jase didn't think to shove
that picture in a desk drawer before he let the Guild's
inspectors into the most logical place on the ship for
them to want to visit: the sitting captain's office.

Clatter of light metal. A cart.

A door working.

Food service cart. He knew that sound.

Galley was operating.

"I'm walking down to the galley," he muttered to
his listening staff, and he turned down a side corridor
and did that . . . first acid test of his anonymity. Try
his crew-act on cook and his staff. Test the waters.

Maybe borrow that food cart—a viable excuse to
move about the ship during a common-crew lockdown.

He'd walked considerably aft through the deserted
corridors. And down a jog and beyond wide, plain
doors . . . one had to know it was the galley, as one
had to know various other unmarked areas of the
ship . . . he heard ordinary human activity, comforting,
common. Men and women were hard at work as he
walked in on the galley, cooks and aides filling the

local air with savory smells of herbs and cooking, rattling pans, creating the meal the crew, lockdown or not, was going to receive.

He dodged a massive tray of unbaked rolls in the hands of a man who gave him only a busy, passing glance.

Then the man came to a dead stop and gave him a second glance, astonished.

A year aboard—and he knew the staff, knew the faces. They knew him by sight. Not at first glance, however. That was good.

And without an exact plan—he suddenly found at least a store of raw material. He waved cheerfully to the man with the tray and, spotting the chief cook over by the ovens, walked casually toward him.

"Hello, chief."

"Mr. Cameron." Natural surprise. Hint of deep concern. "What's going on up there?"

"Well, we've got a little problem," he said. People around him strained to hear, a little less clatter in their immediate vicinity, quickly diminishing to deathly hush. He didn't altogether lower his voice, deciding that galley crew just slightly overhearing the truth was to the good—gossip never needed encouragement to walk about.

So he began the old downhill skid of intrigue. He *wasn't* Bren Cameron, fresh off the island and blind to the world. He was, he reminded himself, paidhi-aiji—the aiji's own interpreter, skilled at communication, skilled at diplomacy between two species—and used to the canniest finaglers and underhanded connivers in Shejidan. "Everything so far is fine, except station has locked the fuel down tight and wants Sabin in their offices *and* their inspectors on our deck, as if the senior captain had to account to *them*." That wasn't phrased to sit well with a proud and independent crew, not at all. "So do you think I could get a basket of sandwiches to take up to the bridge as an excuse to be up there, to find out what's going on?"

The chief cook, Walker, his name was, listened, frowning. "What do you *think's* going on, sir? What in hell do they want, excuse my french, sir?"

"They want us to say yessir and take their orders, and I don't think the captains are on their program. I don't officially speak for Captain Graham—but I'll take it on my own head to go up there and find out if he has orders he doesn't want to put out on general address. If you could kind of deliver a small snack around the decks and at the same time pass some critical information to crew in lockdown, it might be a good thing—tell the crew back the captain, tell them don't mention atevi or the planet at all if these Guild people ask, no matter what. If they've got any pictures that might give that information, get them out of sight. And don't do anything these people could use for an excuse for whatever else they want to do. Senior captain's taken all our security with her, trying to make a point to the Guild on station. Captain Graham's kind of empty-handed up there, worried about them taking over the ship."

A low murmur among the onlookers.

"Taking over the ship," he repeated. "Which is what we're going to resist very strongly, ladies and gentlemen. Captain Graham is worried: Captain Sabin is risking her neck trying to finesse this, and Captain Graham's attitude is, if they even *try* to claim her appointment as senior captain of this ship isn't official without their stamp of approval, gentlemen, there's going to be some serious argument from this ship. Captain Graham's worried those investigators may make matters difficult up on the bridge. And *I* want some excuse to go up there and look around and make absolutely sure the bridge crew's not being held at gunpoint right now."

Quiet had spread all through the galley. Not a bowl rattled.

"So what's to do, sir?" Walker asked.

"Back Captain Graham. Be ready, if there's trouble; if there's some kind of incursion down here, squash it. Spread the word. We've got that alien craft lurking way out there, watching everything that's going on, *expecting* us to straighten out this mess and so far being civilized about our going in here to get the answers out of the station administration. I know the aliens are waiting. I *talked* to them, so far as talk went, and right now they're being more cooperative than the station authority—who's got an explosive lock rigged to keep us from the fuel we need, did that word get down here? And a sign on it telling us in our own language it'll blow up in our faces. I don't think the aliens could read that sign. Guild won't say a thing about that ship, and now they're making demands as if Sabin was to blame for their station having a hole in it. The Guild is holding the fuel against the senior captain's agreement to walk into their offices and present *her* papers, as if they had the say over this ship, which she doesn't agree they have."

"No, sir," one man said, and a dozen others echoed.

"But there we are," Bren said. "We don't know why the innocent people we came here to rescue aren't rushing to get aboard and get out of here. Or why they didn't just board, the last time this ship docked. We believe there's people on that station that might like to board. But they're not showing up, and the only communication we've got is a sign telling us hands off the fuel. That's why the order hasn't come to walk about. I want to get up there to lend Captain Graham some help, and I figure there's less suspicion about galley bringing food in—so can you figure how to make me look like I'm on galley business?"

"Bridge wants more sandwiches," Walker growled, with a look around, and personnel moved, fast.

Then Walker asked him outright: "What's gran down there thinking about this situation? The *atevi* backing you?"

"Backing your captains, while Captain Graham's taking every measure not to let any outside inspector near five-deck. We don't want to explain the whole last nine years of our alliance to a Guild that's in a standoff with an alien ship and not leveling with us. We don't want them scared. Gran 'Sidi perfectly well understands the need to finesse this operation. Right now you're likely the only group that's free to move. You can carry messages, receive information, get it back here, carry signals, carry *plans*, if it goes that far. I can't stress enough how important it is we keep the peace down here, keep your freedom to move, and just stay ready to back the captains."

"Damn right," Walker said, and, an assistant turning up in the aisle with the requisite basket atop a loaded drink-tray, Walker took the goods and handed the exceedingly heavy arrangement to him. "Anything you need, sir. And anything your people down on five-deck need, if you're having to stay locked down. Same to the bridge."

"I'll pass that on," Bren said earnestly, restraining the habitual bow. "Thank you, chief. Thank you all."

He walked out, one more member of cook's staff on a mission involving sandwiches, drinks, and now the bridge. He didn't know a thing, didn't have an ulterior motive, didn't have a badge or an ID. No one on the ship ever had a badge, the same way they didn't put up directional signs. They were all family.

Outsiders, once the spotlight was on, stood out like the proverbial sore thumb.

But he didn't look that foreign, by the galley worker's initial reaction. And everything he'd just said in ship-speak, he was sure Jago followed well enough, at least the gist and intent of it, especially since he was sure Ginny had made it to the security station by now, to provide help with the nuances.

He carried his load down the main corridor back to the lift, not, at the moment, worrying about Guild agents inside the ship. He was just an ordinary fellow, that was all, a crewman whose greatest fear was getting his food orders mixed up.

He maneuvered his tray inside the lift, knuckled the requisite buttons, held his tray steady and kept his face serene.

One deep breath before the door opened. He walked out beyond that short partition that screened the lift area from the bridge.

A gray-armored man stepped out from the other side of that partition and leveled a rifle at him.

Well, well, *that* was different. He had no trouble at all looking discomfited, while his eye took in an immediate and tolerably complete snapshot of the situation—Jase angry and alarmed, the bridge crew sitting idle stations on a ship that wasn't moving, while four gray-armored men, one gray-haired, gray uniform, likely a technician, leaned over the number one console, the beseiged tech leaning inconveniently far over, but *not* yielding his seat.

"Sandwiches, cap'n. The chief thought you'd need 'em." Bren used his best and broadest ship-accent, simply ignored the armed threat and blundered on, presenting the tray to Jase, who waved him on—no exchange of glances, nothing but a set jaw and a situation in which an intruder from belowdecks was oh-very-welcome to walk around, the captain saying nothing about it at all.

Anxious eyes fixed on him at various places, techs recognizing him and doing a masterful job of not showing it. Hostile Guild stares assessed him as a nuisance, a fool on a job mostly below their radar, and passed him.

"Dunno what we got," Bren said to the first bridge tech, looking at the sliced side of sandwiches, while Jase resumed his argument with the Guild agents. He let the woman take a pick of fillings, then wandered over to the Guild investigator. "You're from the station." Brilliant observation. "I'll bet you're glad to see us."

"Cameron." Harsh admonition from Jase. A clear warning. "Do your job."

"Yessir." He turned a charitable face to the Guild investigator. "Want a sandwich, sir? I got a few extras here."

"No," the intruder said.

"I'll take one," the beseiged chief tech said, the one with the Guild man leaning over his shoulder.

Bren let him take a pick while the argument went on, Jase with the Guild. "In absence of the senior captain's direct order, no."

Bren started down the row, handing out drinks and sandwiches, his back to the problem. Worried eyes met his, one after the other, warning, desperately asking.

"Cook's compliments," Bren said, hoping to God nobody recklessly tried a whispered message. He was used to acute atevi hearing—and the electronics that routinely amplified it. There was ample evidence of electronics on the intruders, doubtless amplification, and he strongly suspected some sort of link back to Guild headquarters, but maybe not as good a link as they might want, given two hulls and the technical facts of their connection. He didn't need to pass specific messages. His very presence with a tray of sandwiches said cook knew, so crew below knew and atevi and Mospheirans knew. He was no threat—but atevi had a reputation for stealth and silent interventions. Don't panic, his being here said. We're aware. Gran 'Sidi is aware. The captain has armed, skilled support.

Jase's ongoing debate with the Guild—he couldn't hear it all, but it seemed the Guild inspectors demanded to see the log and Jase kept saying no, the senior captain had ordered to the contrary, the senior captain had to authorize that, and the senior captain wasn't here, so hell would have icicles before any noncrew touched a board.

"Not until she's on this deck and she changes the order," Jase said. Perfect imitation of a subordinate with one bone to chew and absolutely no imagination of doing anything to the contrary. The Guildsmen, in their turn, wanted to call their headquarters and get that direct contact with Sabin.

"Won't matter," Jase said, obdurate. "Won't matter. Until she's on this deck, no matter what she says to the contrary, I have my orders. Nothing she says is going to mean a thing to me until she's back here and she can say so on our deck."

For the first time a certain method appeared in Sabin's madness: you asked, I went, now you want it different. Sorry. You've blown your cover and I won't do a thing until I've got answers.

One hoped to God nobody had tried to apply force to Sabin and her security team. One hoped she reached the Guild offices, took her stand and explained to the Guild why they had to turn over all alien remains and materials in their custody and pack their suitcases for a long trip.

Meanwhile there seemed to have been no word from her. Jase stood his ground, heard all the arguments, nodded sagely—and went repeatedly back to a simple shake of the head and a repetition that he wasn't going beyond Sabin's orders.

Bren coasted past, dumbly made a second attempt to hand the captain a sandwich and a drink in mid-argument.

"Cameron," Jase said in warning. "Just stow it."

"Yessir," he said, as if he'd understood some silent, peeved order, and wandered off to the administrative corridor, the Guild agents' suspicious eyes on his back. One of them was going to follow. Not good.

He took his tray and basket into Jase's office, whisked the damning picture off the shelf and under the basket atop the tray, then set down Jase's sandwich and drink just as the shadow appeared in the doorway.

And came inside.

"Can't leave you in here, sir." Bren made his voice perfectly polite, a little nervous as he tucked his empty tray close. With a free hand, he waved the agent toward the door. "I got to go, sir, if you please. Can't leave anybody in the captain's office. Regulations."

The agent edged out, scowling, casting a look over his shoulder. Bren walked out and happened to lock the door in the process.

He had one drink container left. He blithely offered it to the agent—and let that cold answering stare go all the way to the back of his eyes. His only personal problem was getting back with the tray and reporting to cook. He didn't know what the captain was doing. He didn't know what the problem was up here. It wasn't his job. The galley was. Captains and officers solved the big problems. It was all way over his head.

The agent collected the drink. Bren just wanted to get back to the galley. Didn't want to lose the tray. No-damn-sir, didn't want to look any angry officer in the eye.

The hand dropped. Bren went on his way. And reaching the bridge, interrupted the captain in mid-argument. Again. "Beg pardon, sir, cook's asking when's shift change?"

"Just set it up," Jase said. *That* wasn't chance wording. "These gentlemen will be touring belowdecks very briefly—tell ops down there they have their own key."

Damn, Bren thought. *Their own key.* The captains notoriously had keys, builders' keys, that let them into anything. If they had that, nothing was defended except the bridge, where human bodies sat obdurately between the Guild men and the boards.

He carefully kept the stupid look. "Yessir." He hugged his tray to him and headed toward the exit. Past the last agent.

Whose rifle dropped to bar his way.

"What's this with guns?" he asked, quick as thinking—let Banichi and Jago know he was in trouble. Indignantly: "What's this with guns, captain?"

"You don't interfere with my crew," Jase said, strode over and shoved the rifle up, hard. "You may be almighty Guild enforcement, mister, but you don't interfere with crew carrying out my orders."

"This is the way it's going to be," the senior agent said from the heart of the bridge. "We stay aboard and we supervise. We supervise until your captain gives us access, and maybe we supervise some more. That's *our* order from *our* deck, and that's that, captain, so get used to it."

The standoff continued. Bren edged toward the lift,

remembered to cast a questioning look at Jase as the source of all law, and got his silent order. *Go.* Do something.

They were between the proverbial rock and a hard place. They couldn't afford a shoot-up on the bridge, they still hadn't had fueling questions answered—and Sabin was on the Guild's deck and vulnerable, if not already under interrogation. Not good, not good, not good. He could call his staff in, but he wasn't ready to blow the situation wide open.

"Cameron," Jase said. "Get below. Advise gran."

"Who's this gran?" the Guild senior wanted to know.

"Senior officer," Jase said. "In charge of logistics for the colony level. I take it your briefing included that detail."

It didn't. The Guild men looked perplexed, hadn't a clue that the ship was here to take their residents off the station, and Jase didn't explain what the 'colony level logistics' had to do with anything, either, whether it was full of colonials or not.

But a suspicious man could guess whatever the station had ordered or asked of Ramirez—strike evacuation of the station as part of the plan, at least as far as these lower-level officers knew.

"Well, that colony level's the mission, gentlemen." Best Sabin imitation he'd ever heard Jase launch. "It's been the mission since our last call here, and I suggest you bear it in mind as you tour the facilities. Maybe your command hadn't any inclination to tell your office what the exact arrangement was, but we're expecting their help in operations, we're expecting a certain contingent from your station to board in good order and *with* their equipment, and if general administration is trying at this point to wilt and change the mission, let me remind you that you've got an alien ship out there that's curious what we're doing. I'm well sure it has a limited patience, and if you want to prove obstructionist to our taking on a fuel load to deal with it, I have to ask whether your administration is on the up and up with you, with the station population, or with our captains."

God. Jase *had* learned something in the court at Shejidan. It was the best impromptu flight of imagination and half truths since Ilisidi's launch-day banquet.

It certainly seemed to catch the mission leader aback. At least a doubt or two flickered across that square face. Bren, on the other hand, reminded himself not to look remotely sharp, only being part of the furnishings, same as the cabinetry. He had his gun in his pocket, an open com they hadn't detected, or didn't think was out of the ordinary for crew, and a listening post down below which he had every confidence was processing all this and laying contingency plans to get control of the ship, if need be. He didn't have a word to say. No, not a thought in his head but awe of authority and a certain confusion about the situation.

"Cameron," Jase said.

"Sir."

"Conduct this officer down to the lower decks. Let him inspect on crew and colony level. Let him satisfy himself of whatever questions he has."

"Yes, sir." Eager and very glad to escape—that part was no act. He asked the agent who'd stopped him: "You want to come with me, sir?"

There was a look passed among the Guild enforcers. The rifle was still a question, not quite put back to safety. A second look.

"Stay in touch," the senior officer said, and the man moved a step and touched the lift button.

The lift car was waiting right on their level. The

door opened immediately. Bren got in, hands occupied with his trays, and freed a finger for the button, heart crashing against his ribs. He had weapons: a straight-edged tray as well as the gun in his pocket, but the best two were his brain and the awareness of his own staff and Ginny's. There were service accesses. His staff *might* move, and he wasn't ready to have that happen. Jase wasn't—or he'd surely have included five-deck in the proposed tour.

The door shut. The Guild agent bulked close to Banichi's width, given the body armor, the weapons, the equipment.

Not quite as mentally quick, however. "Thought we were going down one," the agent said.

"Cap'n said tour you around the colony deck, sir. Figured you'd want to see that, where we got all the special rigging."

The agent wasn't eager to admit he and his hadn't a clue what rigging and what arrangements were, and it clearly wasn't uncommon for Guild levels to keep truths from each other. If there was anything but a top level officer at the other end of the agent's electronics, figure that that authority would still have to wonder if there were higher-up secrets to which *their* agents were inadvertently being exposed—he gave himself about thirty minutes of administrative confusion before someone conceivably asked far enough up the chain and got an order to take action.

But the desire to see all they could see might well keep this fellow tame and following—that left three on the bridge, not four, and just that quarter less force gave Jase more breathing room up there.

The lift door opened on a bone-cold, very dimly lit corridor.

"What *is* this?"

"Colony level, sir." He was glad of the coat. Breath

frosted. Rime formed on the edge of the door. "Just starting the warm-up."

"For what?"

"Dunno, sir. Best I know, there's guys you're sending, and here's space for 'em, and we're going to save the day, I suppose, where we're going. We got the stores—you want to tour the stores, sir?"

"I'll take your word for it." The agent, breath hissing between his teeth, reached for the lift controls.

Bren hit the order for two-deck. Fast and first. First number entered was the number, unless the user used an override, and the agent didn't appear to have the key.

"What's on three?" The car moved.

"More crew quarters, sir." He still had the tray and the basket—and Jase's picture—clutched against him.

"You're not damn bright, are you?"

"No, sir," Bren said cheerfully, as the lift doors opened on two.

The agent looked disgusted. But this level was lighted, it was warm. The agent walked out and Bren walked to his right, tray clutched tight against him.

"This nearest and straight ahead is medical, sir. Just this way is crew area." Straight to the right, side corridor, a fair walk, two more corridors. Bangs and thumps came from the distance, cook's operation. Bren felt his heart thumping while his brain sorted the corridors, the charts, the not-quite-perfect knowledge of what was where among all these unmarked doors.

There was, for one thing, warm-storage here, for items various departments needed often and didn't want frozen. There were cleaning closets. He earnestly wished he dared shove the man into one and lock the door.

That firepower, however, might be adequate to blast right back through a door, and most of these doors were crew quarters. He wasn't expert in firearms. He wasn't sure. He wished he could contrive to ask Banichi and Jago that surreptious question, but he didn't know how to describe the rifle.

So he walked, opened random section doors, a meandering tour of two-deck, while the agent held his rifle generally aimed at the walls and not at him.

Elsewhere the lift operated.

The man looked in that direction, as if things he saw just weren't entirely adding up.

And stopped. Wary. Listening to his electronics.

"What's the matter?" Bren asked.

"Shut up," the agent said. And aimed the gun at him while he went on listening.

Bren had his hand on a door switch. Storeroom. He was ready, heart in mouth, to make a desperate maneuver and hope the door was adequate, if that was his only choice.

"What's that?" The agent motioned at that hand with the gun barrel.

"Service closet, sir." He punched it open to demonstrate the fact, and dropped the offending hand.

"Don't get smartass. Where's *life* in this place?"

"All these cabins. They're still waiting in quarters. Ship's rules when we dock, sir."

"What's that?"

There'd been a sound, a clank, a clatter. A cart, somewhere in motion not far away. "Oh, I imagine that would be galley, sir. The staff's delivering food around. People got to eat, no matter if shift's held over." The storeroom door shut. Doors always did, left unattended. But the agent was jumpy. Very. The gun twitched that direction. And something in the Cameron bloodstream, some ancestral fool, suddenly just had to push when pushed. "Door's automatic, sir. Watch your fingers."

"Where's auxiliary ops?"

"That's on a ways aft, sir. We can go there when you like. But there's more."

"Let's go *that* way."

He obliged the man. They walked. They saw exactly nothing. They might go to the galley, Bren decided, lacking a plan, not sure how far or how long his staff was holding off, but absolutely certain they were being tracked. He could arrange a diversion, maybe get cook's help to shove the fellow into a storeroom, his best amateur imagination of a solo heroic finish to this foolery.

But the minute he made a move on this highly wired individual, conversely, and probably what Banichi and his staff was thinking, Jase would have to answer for that action upstairs, with all the others and all that delicate equipment up there—not to mention the communications links this team of enforcers presumably had to the station's inner workings, where Sabin was also exposed to reprisals. Banichi and the rest might be maneuvering into position in the service accesses, for what he could guess—which was a cold, arduous business, getting between levels. But he wasn't alone. He was sure he wasn't alone, and that all the problems he could think of were being thought of: Banichi might have been deceived once about the sun and the stars, but the handling of an armed intrusion and a hostage situation was no mystery at all to him.

The question here was who was hostage. Bren rather thought he wasn't, that he, in fact, had this part of the problem in hand.

So they walked. And walked. Bren rattled on about safety procedures, the most boring official tour information he could muster, a compendium of the orientation video tour the crew had put together for groundlings. He clutched the trays and the damning picture against him as they walked, and he toured the man up one hall and down the other for what felt like a gun-threatened eternity, telling himself he was gaining time for those who knew what they were doing to work matters out—possibly for Gin to communicate with Jase and coordinate actions.

Meanwhile small rackets led their tour steadily toward the galley's open door, where cook's mates came and went. The armed approach drew an anxious look, but no one, thank God, reacted in panic.

"Galley, sir," Bren said brightly, the obvious, and led their tour inside, stopping just inside the door, where he set the tray and its load onto the nearest shelf and trusted no one to ask brightly what the picture was.

The agent gave everyone the cold eye. A food truck wanted out the door. The agent stood there just long enough to be inconvenient, saying nothing, asking nothing, just looking. The agent moved and the innocent cart trundled past.

"Want a soft drink?" Bren asked, pushing it way beyond bounds, at the same time cuing cook what part he was still playing. "Cup of tea, sir?" He asked himself in an afterthought whether the food menu and the planet-origin smells might give away to this man as much as Jase's photo; but most anything could pass for synthetic, if the observer were predisposed to believe everything in the universe was synthetic. "Stuff's real good."

"Not here for that," the agent said, and walked out, shoving him aside in the process.

"So what are you looking for?" Stupid question of the hour. Bren followed him. Got into the lead again. Without the damning tray.

"Checking things out," the agent said, and pointed at random. "Looking for answers. Open that door."

"It's just a door, sir. It's a cabin."

"Open it!"

"Yes, sir," Bren said, and politely pushed the entry-request, same as a groundling's knock at the door.

The door took its time opening. A couple of uniformed crewmen stood there looking confused. Alarmed, to have a stranger with a rifle standing in their cabin doorway.

"This is Mr.—" Bren hesitated, trying to keep it social, ridiculous as it all felt, and he wasn't sure what level of inanity might just be too much. "Didn't catch the name, sir."

"Esan," the agent said, giving the two occupants his long, flat stare.

"Mr. Esan," Bren amended the introduction, stupidly cheerful. "Mr. Esan, here, is giving the ship the once-over before we do the formalities. Captain Sabin's on station doing whatever's necessary. Captain Graham says I should just tour him around."

The two crewmen weren't stupid. And in this corridor of all corridors they'd likely gotten cook's warning and knew they were the lucky people to deal with a ticking bomb.

"Glad to meet you," one said, and moved forward to offer a hand.

Esan flinched, oddly enough. Didn't take the offered hand. Then did, as if the crewman were holding something objectionable . . . or contagious.

Well, well, well.

"Benham," the crewman said, doggedly cheerful. "Roger Benham." He indicated the second, younger man. "My cousin Dale. Welcome aboard, Mr. Esan. It's good to meet somebody from Reunion."

"Hard voyage?" Esan asked.

"Oh, average," Benham said. "Glad to meet you. Esan. Aren't any Esans aboard."

"We all took to station," Esan said grimly, and walked out.

Bren stayed with him. Kept cheerful. And stupid.

"Much the same with the rest of this?" Esan asked—meaning the doors. Having found nothing subversive.

"All the same," Bren said. "Well, except the store-rooms. We can go back there if you like."

"Bridge," Esan said. He seemed to be listening to someone. Muttered a quiet, "Yeah," to that someone at the other end.

"Yes, sir," Bren muttered, wondering at what time something might go very wrong upstairs and Officer Esan might simply level that rifle and shoot him with-out warning. The policy decision on this one was more than the dowager and Banichi and Cenedi: Sabin might start something, if she sent word; and Jase might, if he decided he had to move. And something up on the bridge had clearly changed.

Suddenly.

"Back to the lift," Esan said.

"Yes, sir," Bren said, and led the way, beginning to think of the gun in his pocket, thinking if things had gone wrong up there he could prevent reinforcement—but getting his electronics up to that deck could give Banichi and Cenedi direct information about the situation. He sweated, trying to figure.

The lift was quick in coming. He boarded with Esan, punched in the bridge, and kept bland cheerfulness on his face, stupidest man alive, yes, sir.

Not a word. Esan was listening to something.

"What's going on?" he asked.

"Meeting in the captain's office," Esan said.

"Yes, sir," he said, deciding not to shoot Esan through his coat pocket. A meeting. His heart settled marginally and he was ever so glad he'd gotten that picture out.

The door opened, letting them back onto the bridge. "Captains' offices are this way, sir." He stuck like glue, his stupid, cheerful presence guiding the way.

The bridge crew was still pretending to work. They drew stares. The tension was palpable as they walked the short distance from the lift area, past the bridge operations area, into the administrative corridor. Jase's men were there, Kaplan and Polano, armed, that was worth noting. Armed, but outside, looking anxious while Jase was, evidently, inside.

"Here's where, sir," Bren said, and Kaplan opened the door to let Esan in.

Jase was secure behind his desk. Two of the investigators were sitting in chairs in front of it, one standing in the corner. Esan made four.

"Mr. Esan, is it?" Jase rose and came around the corner of the desk, offering a hand. Esan confusedly reciprocated.

Then Jase turned a scowl, aimed at Bren. "Mr. Cameron."

"Sir."

"Out!"

No question. Bren ducked back for the door, fast as any offending fool.

Jase stalked to the door in pursuit. "Cameron, you stupid son of a bitch! What the hell are you doing?"

A bewildered investigator started to intervene. But Jase shoved Bren back hard, dived out after him, whirled and hit the door switch as the man tried to come out.

The door shut. The investigator had skipped back: security doors meant business. Kaplan immediately hit *lock*.

And that was, if not *that,* at least a significant improvement on the ship's onboard situation.

Bren let go his breath. Jase straightened his jacket.

"Good job," Bren said shakily, and in Ragi. "The intruders are now contained in Jase's office, nadiin-ji." He was astonished and relieved, quite astonished at himself, and Jase, and Jase's team. He didn't know what precisely what they were going to do about the morsel they'd just lodged in their collective gullet, but they'd defended the ship from capture. They'd won. Themselves. The human species had won one.

Jase gave an approving glance to Kaplan and Polano: "Well done. Well done, gentlemen." Pressman, the third of Jase's men, appeared from a little down the corridor, out of Ogun's office, with a rifle.

"Any word coming from Sabin?" Bren asked.

"No," Jase said sharply. "Her signal's quit. And these bastards aren't getting off this ship until there *is* word."

Not good news. Not at all.

"Everything all right down on crew level?" Jase asked.

"Everything but third-shift crew stewing in their cabins."

"We'll fix that," Jase said, and led the way back into the bridge area, into the middle of the bridge. "Cousins," Jase said to all and sundry on the bridge, "the problem is now contained. C1, kindly continue jamming any output or input from station. Then give me contact with my office, intercom image in my office to monitor thirty-two, with audio."

"Yessir." C1 cheerfully punched buttons, and began the process.

Jase picked up a handset and thumbed in a code. "Gentlemen."

Bren stood by, watching the monitor, on which one

saw four armored station agents battering the office door with rifle butts—and asking himself how, if they had begun jamming, they were going to hear from Sabin at all.

They would not, he feared.

"Mr. Becker," Jase said.

Battering stopped. The group looked at the desk.

"Our captain's signal has ceased," Jase said. "You are now jammed, gentlemen. Turn in all armament and electronics and cooperate with *Phoenix* authority, and we'll negotiate for your return to your own command. The same authority that established Reunion in the first place is now in charge of this station, and will be in charge, and I advise you not to disarrange my office, gentlemen, since I may be judging your case."

Bren earnestly wished he had a tap into what Jase received on his earpiece.

"That's all very well, gentlemen," Jase said, "but you're on our deck, this ship maintains its own rules, and I don't give a damn about your local regulations. Turn over your weapons and peel out of the armor. To the skin. You've far exceeded your authority and my patience, and unless I get a direct countermand from the senior captain, not likely under current circumstances, the lot of you are under close arrest."

One man moved. Leveled a gun at the door and fired. The sound reached the corridor.

Jase punched one more button. "Kaplan! Fire suppression, B4."

The view on screen clouded. Instantly.

The intruders had, Bren recalled, masks among their body-armor. They surely had internal oxygen. They surely were going to use that resource, fast.

"Gentlemen," Jase said, "I'm going about other work. Advise me when you're ready to comply with instructions. I know you're on your own air. But we can keep the office in fire-suppression for the next century or so. And if you do succeed in breaching that door, gentlemen, be assured you'll walk into worse. Would you like to negotiate at this point? Or do you want to be carried out after your air runs out? Because I'm prepared to hold out until the next century, but I don't think you'll last near that long."

Bren didn't hear what the men answered. But Jase seemed grimly pleased.

"C1," he said, "take precautions, condition red."

There was an answering murmur from exhausted crew, all the while crew locked down, pulled down covering panels for the consoles, all calmly.

Small under-console panels divulged weapons. The bridge crew armed itself, hand-weapons, a few heavier, to defend the ship's heart and nerve center if it got to that. Jase might have read his captain's training out of a rule book, but damn, Bren thought, he'd learned a few things on the planet, and he was ice calm.

Bren's pocket comm vibrated. He said, without taking the device out publicly in Jase's domain, "One hears, nadiin-ji. One believes the ship's personnel are managing the situation very well indeed. Wait."

The lift door opened. Security personnel arrived, the ship's few remaining, in full kit, with breathing assist and anti-personnel armament.

"Four Guild enforcers are occupying my office," Jase said with a hook of his thumb. "Fire suppression's engaged. Captain's signal's gone dead and they're for security confinement. My personal guard is sitting on the situation. Assist."

Ship's integrity was the ship's highest law. Ship was country and family, even if they'd had their bloody fights. And station admin was only a cousin-relationship, when it came to that. Bren didn't say a thing, only stood and watched the security team, clearly ready for some time, head down the short hall.

The executive offices security door shut across that view, protecting the bridge from whatever unpleasantness might break out of Jase's office.

Jase stood still, pushing the earpiece firmly into his ear. The spy-eye was still running, but the white fog inside the office gave way to thermal image. Four armed men, each in a corner, clear as could be.

The door to that office opened. A barrage opened up, anti-personnels bouncing all over—astonishing in a small space. There seemed to be a deal of wreckage. The intruders flinched, went down under a continuing volley of pellets that richocheted off every surface in the small office and hit from every angle.

Two attempted a breakout. Bren stifled a useless warning.

The two dropped at the door, netted and shorted out, in every electrical contact exposed. A third went down, in split-screen, clawing at a suit control that didn't seem to be functioning, and a fourth tried to bolt.

Security netted that one, too, right atop the other two, a struggling lump. It looked like Kaplan who hauled that one out and up.

It was over. Won. Bren let go a breath. His knees felt the weight of hours.

"Got the bastards," Jase said quietly.

The bridge crew breathed, too, shoulders just that degree relaxing—but they were still armed, still waiting for orders.

"You can let them out, C1," Jase said. "Get additional security to do a fire-check and a bug-check down there. Let's not have any lingering problems."

Definitely learned in his time in Shejidan, Bren thought. Banichi would declare it a fine job. Not finessed, but certainly well ended. They stood there, watching the search on the monitors, and he took a moment to report.

"Nadiin-ji, one believes the local matter is now aptly handled. Jase-aiji has done extremely well. One regrets to report Sabin-aiji's signal has ceased for some undefined reason, but the internal threat is under arrest and destined for detention. Jase remains firmly in charge of the ship."

Doors opened. Armored, masked security, Kaplan, Polano and Pressman among them, by the badges, dragged their prisoners out, four net-wrapped men, stripped of armor and weapons—men who looked far smaller and less threatening, in disarranged blue fatigues stained with sweat.

"Have medical look them over, inside and out," Jase said. "Then tank the lot and have a look at their communications."

"Yes, sir," the head of the second team answered, and bundled the problem out of view of the bridge, lift-bound.

"C1," Jase said quietly.

"Sir!" Crisp and proper.

"Once they've cleared the lift, I'll go down and address the crew on two-deck. And for bridge crew," he said, raising his voice, turning to make it carry. "Well done. Good job, cousins. Continue measures in force, pending further orders. We'll go to shift change very soon now, with thanks."

Relief went through the bridge crew on the gust of a sigh. Arms went to safety, a scattered, soft sound.

"Restore the boards for next shift and we'll carry on, cousins. That's all. I don't know how this is going to affect the senior captain's situation, but *we've* got the ship rather than losing it. And if they've got the fuel, we'll figure a way to work this. It's clear they're not going anywhere. Resume operations."

Crew began putting weapons away, clearing the safety covers from consoles. The bridge began to normalize operations.

Jase's face had been flushed with anger. Now the sweat broke out and the flush gave way to pallor. Bren remarked that. But Jase didn't offer to go to quarters, and Bren himself didn't move. His legs felt like posts. The adrenalin charge was trying to flow out of him, fight-flight instincts having incomplete information from the brain, which said, with complete conviction, *You can't quit. It's not done.* They had an alien threat at their backs and station had slammed a stone wall down in front of them.

"Prisoners are secured in medical, captain." That from C1.

"Assembly on two, C1, all shifts."

"Yes, sir," C1 said, and Jase said, from every speaker in the ship, and likely within hearing of the make-shift brig:

"Captain Graham will address crew on two-deck, all attend, all attend. Three minute warning."

"Mr. Cameron," Jase said.

"Captain?"

"You'll do me the honor, Mr. Cameron. You can explain the atevi position. I know ours."

11

Two-deck's corridors were crammed in every direction, a crowd from two-deck and likely from the crew section of three-deck converging on the lift from the moment they got off, crew standing, galley staff prominent in whites at the left, upcoming bridge crew in blues on the right, a scattering of security thrown in at random. Faces, Bren noted, were tense . . . every man and woman in the corridors having heard as much as Cook's staff had had to give.

"C1," Jase said. "Route my comm to two-and three-deck intercoms." Intercom immediately came live. Jase's next utterance went out over the speakers, making the voice omnipresent, distant as he was from the remoter rows of cousins and crew. *"You know by now the senior captain's gone to station, and that station sent on some investigators. They pushed. They're in medical. They'll be in the tank until we get the captain back."*

A cheer. That curiously rattled Jase. A cheer hadn't been in his plans. Or his self-concept.

"Mr. Cameron's here in support of ship command. 'Sidi-ji does support us."

Second cheer. Jase was further rattled. He never had been a great speaker. He didn't have the killer instinct and he never knew when to quit. He slogged on, gathering force, if not eloquence.

"So we're going to get the captain back," Jase said. *"But we're not helpless, meanwhile. We've got fuel to maneuver if we have to and remember we've got the only pilots who actually know how to handle this ship, never mind what anybody on station may have studied up in some simulator. They can't give us orders."*

Third cheer. Which threw Jase completely off his pace.

"I'm no great shakes at the boards," Jase said. *"And I'm not the senior captain by a long shot, which I know. I also know everybody aboard wants to be out there on deck doing something, and everybody wants to get onto the station, some of you with cousins to find; and everybody wishes station was what it used to be, but it isn't, and we can't, and I can't. So I'll tell you what my policy is, which is, first of all, no more secrets, so long as we're in this mess."*

Maybe Jase drew breath. Maybe he wanted encouragement here, but he didn't hear it. The crew just stood still and silent. *"So while I'm acting senior, I'm taking questions, and crew who wants to go onto the bridge and see for a fact what's going on, come ahead, never mind that protocol, just walk softly around working crew. If you've got a question, I want to hear it, in my office, in an orderly fashion. If you've got a complaint, I want to hear that, too, and I'll deal with it best I can in time-available. We've clearly got a situation working. The Guild leadership isn't cooperating, we haven't heard from the senior captain, and I'm not turning this ship over to them, I'm not giving them their people back, and I'm not handing over the log. Meanwhile we've got an alien ship out there that's got its own agenda, possibly missing personnel of its own, and we've got to finesse that, too. We've got to stay alert, and we're going to get out of this somehow, cousins. Hell if I know how at this exact moment, but we got to Alpha and back, and we've built an alliance there, and our station, with Captain Ogun, is going to back us, not them, when we go back. If we go back under any circumstances but us in charge of our ship, there'll be serious trouble at the station where this ship left its kids and old folk, among others, and I'm not going to see that happen, or come dragging in, telling Captain Ogun we've brought him a problem. We settle it here, cousins. Any questions?"*

Uneasy quiet. Maybe certain ones wanted to ask questions. Maybe others wanted to make observations. But no one moved.

Then somebody called out, "Taylor! *Taylor's son!*"

Taylor. Senior captain. Dead for centuries. But the genetic bank of those days produced the ship's special children. The special ones, born to be outside the Guild, outside politics, outside precedent.

"Taylor!" someone else shouted, and others took it up. *"Taylor!"*

Jase didn't want that. He stood there a moment, not moving, then lifted the com unit again. *"So get to work,"* he said. *"Shift change, cousins."*

Jase clicked the com off at that point, pale around the edges, sweating, maybe feeling all the hours he hadn't slept. And there was a cheer from the crew.

"Good job," Bren said under his breath, in the same moment a handful in bridge blues came through to the front, third shift pilot and backup in the lead.

"Captain." Third shift pilot and second senior navigator, Jase's own shift. "We'll back you. You want a team to go out there on station after the old lady, there's those on third that'll go, no question. We're asked to say that."

"Thanks," Jase said. Just thanks. A hand on the pilot's shoulder. "We'll see what we learn in the next hour." Jase's most urgent wish seemed to be to escape this expectation, this adoration he'd not asked for. Bren knew. He'd been likewise seized upon, made into a symbol. From that moment, however, one couldn't back down. Crew flung their support at Jase. They gathered around him, they surrounded him, they cheered him and laid hands on him in outright relief for what they thought he was.

Then Bren found hands on his own shoulders, the same officers with, "Good job, sir, damn good job."

He honestly didn't know what good job, in his own case. Jase had played the cards. His own action hadn't been a particularly good plan, only desperate, moment to moment babysitting a problem, but not at any point solving it. The situation they had left in their hands owned too many loose ends, still, leaving far too much still at risk.

Yet the crew believed in them, expected a solution.

He was ever so relieved when Jase extricated them both, back safely inside the lift.

Jase punched five-deck. "I'll get you safely home. Get some rest."

"And you."

"Got to get Sabin back," Jase said. "Not optimum, not an optimum situation. She's our authoritative voice, the only one the Guild's going to listen to in negotiations. Especially if she's told them her opinion of me."

"Is the Guild going to believe anything she does isn't a subterfuge? Don't flinch. Lull them into thinking we're stuck without her, if they'll believe that—let them think their card is higher than it is, so they don't make any further move against the ship."

"Bren, she may be on *their* side. She may always have been. I've grown up with the woman, I've taken my orders from her, and I don't know where she stands. But I'm scared to death something's happened to her, her and nine-tenths of our security team. And I don't think she'd betray *them*."

Jenrette, was Bren's thought. But in that instant the lift, having hit five-deck, opened its doors, and Bren stared, shocked, at the sight of leveled guns in the hands of two of Gin Kroger's engineers—they weren't marksmen, they weren't apt to shoot, but there they were, in case.

"We're all right," Bren said, and walked out.

"Banichi said so," their leader said. Jerry. "But he also said meet you. Captain." Belated courtesy to Jase.

"It's all right," Jase said. The ship's captain stood at the edge of foreign territory, the dowager's domain, and Gin's, and the rules and precedences down here were different. "Good job. Good job, the lot of you.—Get some rest, Bren."

"You too. Urgently."

"Intend to."

He was outside, Jase was inside. The lift door shut between them and the lift climbed, Jase's errand of courtesy was done, enabling Jase's escape to his own responsibilities. Even bed, if Jase was lucky, but Sabin's silence and Guild prisoners on two-deck didn't augur well for that chance. He wished he could relieve Jase. But protocols were in the way.

"Thanks," he muttered to Jerry, and went for the atevi section door—which opened before he could touch the switch. Staff was monitoring him that closely.

His staff met him on the other side, Banichi and Jago, who swept him safely, warmly into their own corridor and within their protection.

He couldn't say, after his brief foray up topside, *We have solved the problem.* He couldn't say, *The ship is safe.*

But he hadn't gone up there into a perfect situation,

either, and both statements might be a little closer to truth than they had been an hour ago.

Cenedi turned up, too, not a few steps past the dowager's door. Things began to pass in an exhausted blur, but Bren was relatively sure Cenedi had not been in the corridor a second ago. "Bren-aiji," Cenedi said formally, "the dowager wishes to see you before you rest."

Then, God save him, young Cajeiri, trying his best to be discreet and adult, turned up right at his heels. "Great-grandmother is very pleased, nandi."

"One is honored." Courtesy was automatic, even if the body wanted nothing more than to collapse into his own chair. The dowager reasonably wished to have the latest information, though he hadn't yet had time or coherency to talk to his own staff. So he addressed himself to Cenedi, marshalling his wits. "The parties are at standoff, nadiin-ji. One expects political postures. Communications and surveillance instruments they carried will have been cut off. That will surely bring repercussions. Jase is adamantly maintaining the ship's integrity, however, and supported by the crew." He was in the atevi world now, the solid depths of the ship, where *supported by the crew* meant that man-'chi was in good order and the ship was whole and healthy—it was the simple truth, but he grew dizzy from such shifts of world-view and reality, from reckoning what humans thought, and how atevi saw it, and what the real and objective truth was, a more fragile thing—

And reckoning, too, where the pitfalls of interspecies assumption lay, which was the paidhi's unique job.

"Has this rebel Guild changed its mind, then?" Cajeiri asked.

"No, young sir, and one doubts their sanity." Bren

answered, and saw Cenedi seize the inquisitive heir by the shoulder, diverting him firmly to the background.

"But, Cenedi-ji," the heir said.

"Hush!" Cenedi said, and the heir hushed, as they collectively approached Ilisidi's outside study door, the direct way in.

Cenedi opened *that* door, signal honor to an exhausted, chill-prone human. He was deeply grateful not to have to brave the burning cold of the back corridor.

Inside he met, still, a comparative chill, dimly lit. It had that comforting faint petroleum scent of old atevi residences, and overlain on the ship's geometries, all the curved lines and ornate textures of very old power.

And the dowager, sitting in her chair, reading by that dim light, quietly, slowly laid her book in her lap as the returning diplomat made his wobble-kneed small bow. She met him with a smile. "You play the servant very well, I'm told. Clever, clever fellow."

Alarms rang. One had to be on alert with her. Always. "My mother insisted on manners, aiji-ma."

Eyes half-lidded. "And what will the station say now that we are less mannerly?"

She was asking—without asking—shall we attack?

"Oh, likely the station will threaten the fuel, which, if it exists, we doubt they will destroy, this being their greatest asset, aiji-ma. It will have taken years of effort to gain, would take more to replace, and even in the affairs of the Guild, common folk do have an opinion—not a very important one, rarely unified. But it counts, and the Guild leadership occasionally has to fear it. The Guild should fear popular opinion on this ship, for a beginning. Crew is not pleased with the Guildmaster, and has not been, all through this voyage. Now Sabin-aiji's signal has gone silent and we hear nothing from her or her security. Therefore Jase arrested the Guild agents."

"And what has Jase-aiji told this Guild?"

"That Sabin-aiji can certainly counter his orders and release these agents once she stands on this deck and reclaims her authority from the aiji-junior. That until she does, the ship will not cooperate."

Ilisidi smiled and nodded benignly as any comfortably set grandmother. "And what will the foreigner-ship do, in the meanwhile, while we remain mired in controversy?"

"That still remains a worry, aiji-ma. No greater and no less a worry than before we restrained these intemperate agents. But their patience must grow less by the hour."

"And now Sabin-aiji has imprudently gotten herself in a difficulty, does one conclude?" Again, implied, a power vacuum.

"Likely, however, she is alive."

"Would this Guild use forceful interrogation?"

"They might use drugs on her subordinates. That might be, but one believes they would make her very angry."

Ilisidi's amber eyes caught the light, shimmered palest gold, twin moons. "She has lived on the borders of our association. She has dealt with the *aishidi'tat.* She well understands how any admission of our presence would lead to more questions and far greater suspicion. I have already sent word to Jase-aiji, suggesting that the next attempt to board will not likely be a paltry effort of inept spies. We have seen their subtlety." A waggle of fingers, suggesting that subtlety was not great. "One expects some stronger effort, and one counts armed assault a possibility, since subtlety failed. *With* this ship, the Guild, which has languished here for years under threat, has mobility. It might attack that ship out there. When will that ship attack us, do you think?"

He was too tired to think. The brain was attempting configurations of thought just too complex to chase right now. "Instinct, aiji-ma, says it's not likely. They wait. They have waited for six years, it seems, and one thinks they will go on waiting so long as we keep from alarming them."

"The station taking the ship would surely alarm them."

"It would. I'm sure it would—if they detected that."

"And this Guild. They might have made us feel welcome and easy in this meeting and then attacked. On the contrary, they have offended Sabin-aiji and now Jase-aiji. They have offended this crew. So you say."

"So it seems, aiji-ma."

A wave of an arthritic hand. "They are fools."

"They have been fools for centuries, aiji-ma. But armed and powerful fools."

"This authority is fearful of us? Or have they some distaste for subterfuge?"

"One believes they are fearful *for* their authority, aiji-ma, and know that man'chi will divert from them toward us once truths begin to come out."

"Ought we then to provide these truths?"

"*We* would frighten the population, aiji-ma, until we can provide ourselves as an avenue of escape." He was so tired he was falling on his face, yearning for nothing more than his own mattress, and the dowager, characteristically, gave him nightmares. "And we still hesitate to encumber the ship by taking a great number aboard. We have to let Jase attempt to deal with this."

"So we spend all effort on this Guild squabble. And

this Guild had rather squabble than deal with this foreign ship—after offending it by firing at it, as seems the case. This is hardly reasonable behavior. Have they a reason for confidence we as yet fail to know?"

The world swung around him. The walls did. He found no solid ground.

Dots . . . marched on a screen. An alien craft. An incursion. An expedition. His mind was trying to form a conclusion.

"Aiji-ma, I don't know. I have no answers."

"But will find out. Will find out very soon."

"I must, aiji-ma." he said, "but now, aiji-ma, I plead exhaustion, and trust myself and my staff to your resourcefulness, aiji-ma, confident in that, always."

Dots and light and dark. Flow of events.

The dowager said: "Sabin appointed Tamun."

Sometimes Ilisidi turned corners and forgot to inform those engaged in arguments with her. But this leap of logic jerked him sideways. Tamun occurred to her.

Tamun, a junior captain, had mutinied against Ramirez, senior captain, when *Phoenix* had come to the atevi world.

Why, an ateva would ask? What had changed in Tamun's mind? What was the agenda on which he operated?

That was the cliff on which Ilisidi set him to perch for whatever sleep he could get.

Sabin, not within Ilisidi's man'chi, remained a question—in Ilisidi's mind, surely. In his, too. In Jase's. In no few reasoning individuals' minds, the more since her communications had gone silent—hers and the majority of the ship's trained security personnel. But there was more than that. Sabin's relation to Tamun had always troubled them. And now Sabin, who had appointed Tamun to office, had fallen into

Guild hands. And taken twenty-odd ship's personnel into silence with her.

Had Tamun mutinied over the station mission tape? Over information Ramirez withheld from crew? Had Tamun been outraged crew? Or a Guild agent in the path of command?

"I haven't forgotten," he murmured. "I never have forgotten."

Ilisidi lifted that thin, age-wrought hand. "One would never suppose that what was true when Ramirez left this place is still true here. All things change. Persons fall from power. Persons rise. Agendas change." A second time Ilisidi waggled her fingers. "An old woman has little to do but think in her isolation, understand. These may be idle fancies. One amuses oneself. But weary as you are, you surely pay little attention to us. Go. Sleep. Rest."

"Aiji-ma." He bowed. His wits had taken one final battering. But he thought. Crazed as he was, he found his brain working.

Dicey. Very dicey, he said to himself, tired enough and bemused enough to walk into walls. He took his leave, found the door switch and exited back to the cruel, cold glare of the corridor lights, to alienly human corridors where Cenedi waited, along with Banichi and Jago.

"One is grateful for the dowager's concern," Bren said, Cenedi having every right to have some kind of summary. His voice was going. "As always, the dowager offers good advice. Utmost vigilance. She reminds us that whatever exists here was not planned for our arrival. *We* are interlopers in a situation. We may not be its most active component. And she asked about Tamun, in connection with Sabin's silence. But I have to rest. Forgive me, Cenedi-ji, I have to rest now." He was crazily sleepier and sleepier, a cascade of bodily resources all deserting him.

"Nandi." Cenedi evidenced that he understood his fatigue, and posed no challenge. Bren gave a small bow, about all he had in him, and walked, trying to make it a straight line. He had Banichi and Jago alone, now, and at the end of the hall, saw his own quarters, his own staff waiting, with Narani.

Wise, good Narani, who would do everything possible to put him to bed for a decent few hours.

"Supper and bath and bed, Bren-ji?" Banichi asked.

"Bed," he said. "The dowager has some few misgivings that Sabin-aiji may be—or become—unreliable. I confess I have similar misgivings, though tempered by a feeling I haven't—at the moment—the wit to explain." He thought it was a straggling, struggling *human* feeling trying to work its way through his brain, but he couldn't, in his fogged state, be sure of its nature. "And we should remain concerned we have only the word of this Guild that fuel is ready for us. That they would lie—yes, not even for much advantage. Their instinct is to lie, to protect all information, useful and not. There may be fuel. There may not. Things are stable, but not as I would wish, nadiin-ji. We have this offended alien out there. We have a question, nadiin, *why* Tamun once turned against Ramirez, and what Sabin knows that she never told Jase or us. She is no fool. Yet she deliberately took an untrustworthy guard and went aboard the station, leaving Jase with the ship, armed and warned, and told to heed no word from her until she returns."

"With increasing certainty," Banichi said, "we must take this station, Bren-nadi."

Mild shock. At least mild shock. Trust Banichi's absolute clear view of a situation, when his own stuck at leaping over human barriers. He had thought of taking over the ship—with Jase's consent. Banichi was far more ambitious.

Reasonable? Not reasonable? His heart gave two wilder beats, no longer quite panicked. *He* wasn't inhibited by his humanity. Or by being atevi. He had occasionally to apply it as a logic-check, as a brake on atevi actions that might be a shade excessive when dealing with humans not quite as hair-triggered as his escort.

But plan big? Banichi certainly did that.

Taking the station would solve a certain number of problems here.

Relations with humans might suffer . . . not alone of the Guild, but of the ship—

And of persons capable and willing to serve as agents, they had no more than the dowager's security, and his.

Yet for what had Tabini-aiji appointed him lord of the heavens and sent him out here? Not to sit on his hands, that was sure.

"One must rest a few hours, nadiin-ji. My reasoning grows exceedingly suspect."

"Shall we," Jago asked, "consider possibilities in this direction?"

"I believe we should. We may take Jase into our confidence. I shall have to finesse that. But I believe we may ultimately rely on Jase. On his man'chi. On the man'chi of the crew to him. On the association of our mission to all his associations." His brain veered momentarily sidelong, into human thinking. Or hybrid thinking, such as his and Jase's had gotten to be. "I don't think he expected man'chi from the crew, such as he has. They will follow him. And that is a rare and extraordinary asset among humans, nadiin-ji." He didn't know whether he was thinking straight or not, but it seemed to him he had suddenly drawn a fair bead on the situation. "That is an asset we should greatly value—this crew, and Jase."

"One perceives so, Bren-ji," Jago said, and Banichi said something of the like.

He didn't even remember reaching his room. He had the impression he'd spoken with staff. He thought he'd turned down a pot of tea. He undressed, handing the gun as well as the clothing to Bindanda and finished his muddled thought about Jase—something about the meeting with crew—while lying on his face, naked on cool sheets, with the scent and the feel of his own mattress to tell him where he was.

Only a crazed recollection of his hours above five-deck persisted to tell him, indeed, he and Jase had actually—well, if not won the round, at least had the problem locked away. Here and there were not congruent. These decks didn't match the others. The reasons down here didn't match those on upper decks, but they fit well enough. They got along.

He didn't know when he'd been as tired, as absolutely out of resources. He crashed again, beyond coherency, telling himself he had to get up and check on essentials, if he could remember what they were— involving Guild enforcers locked away, involving Sabin, involving that great hole in the station . . .

He waked a third time and crawled toward the edge of his bed in that total darkness that, with atevi, passed for moderate. "Rani-ji?"

Staff kept the intercom live, to hear such calls. It was not, however, Narani who answered the summons, but Bindanda: bulky shadow in the doorway, a merciless spear of light from the outer corridor, a glare that afflicted his eyes and comforted him at once. If there were any sort of trouble from upper decks he was sure domestic staff would wake him to report.

They hadn't. He *could* sleep if he wished, and oh, he wished. Resolution trembled. So did the arm that supported his weight.

But Jago wasn't here. *Jago* wasn't here.

"Is there any word down from Jase, Danda-ji?"

"No, nandi."

"Jase surely would tell me if there were developments." He believed it, but Jase, too, had to rest. And he daren't pin the future of two species on his faith in anyone's waking him. "Kindly see to it this happens, Danda-ji. And maintain our watch. Jase must sleep, too."

"One will surely make that effort, nandi. Do go back to sleep. I have that firm instruction, to say so."

"Where is Jago?"

"Resting, one believes."

Then it was all right. Bindanda wouldn't lie to him. "I have every confidence in staff," he murmured—and dropped onto his face.

The door closed. The light went.

If, however, Banichi *weren't* up to something, Jago would be safe in her bed, asleep, would she not? And she wasn't. And resting didn't mean sleeping. So Banichi *was* up to something.

The whole staff might be up to it along with them—whatever *it* was. Cenedi might likewise be aiding and abetting.

And any action involving foreign humans—or worse, not humans—triggered every warning bell the long-time paidhi-aiji owned.

He urgently needed, despite Bindanda's wishes, to get up off his face and get dressed and advise his staff where the limits were.

Don't assume. Don't do any of those things that had been downright fatal in interspecies relations. The Pilots' Guild on Reunion Station wasn't the President's office on Mospheira. There was no equivalency.

And most of all, none of them knew the nature of that ship out there. There were answers they had to get. A mission for *that* craft that might or might not let them leave this place: there was no guarantee of reciprocal favors—that logic didn't reach to the back end of the human spectrum and it didn't hold up as far as atevi councils, either. Expectation of like result was a box that hemmed in his thinking, that guided him toward what might be a false conclusion, when he ought to be using his head and thinking of multiple ways out.

He needed to be consulting with his staff—knowing—at least being reasonably confident—that Banichi wouldn't actually put anything into operation without telling him. He'd told Banichi that. Hadn't he given that instruction?

He couldn't quite remember. But he had confidence in Banichi, more even than in Jase.

His eyes were shut. Sleep wasn't a very long hike.

But along that short journey, he began to think critically—a sign of returning faculties.

The Guild had always been difficult. The Guild had been difficult back when the path to a unified humanity had been well-paved and lined with flowers.

The Guild, seeing the attraction of a green planet luring its crew, had doggedly held to their notion of space-based development, and attempted, instead, to force the human colony safely in orbit at the atevi planet to leave and go live in orbit about barren Maudit, instead—where temptations would be fewer.

Where the colony would be utterly dependent on Guild orders and alternatives would be fewer.

That hadn't worked. Colonists had left in droves. Flung themselves at the atevi planet and escaped by parachute.

Point: whatever the Guild had in its records about that situation, the Guild did still remember, surely, that the green world had had inhabitants. They did know that the colony they'd run off and left—and ultimately sent Ramirez back to find—was going to be to some degree in contact with the steam-age locals.

And the ship, returning to that place, had stayed gone nine years.

That things had radically changed, given a few hundred years and the remembered direction of the colony's ambition—it didn't take geniuses on the Guild board to figure that could happen. It didn't take a genius on their side to figure that the Guild was nervous about what influences had worked on the ship during a ten-year absence . . . nervous, too, one might think, about Ramirez's prior actions and what his influence might have wrought.

The Guild had wanted to talk to Sabin, alone, while their investigators prowled over the ship.

Note too, they'd wanted the ship to move into close dock—from which position the ship's airlock was accessible to them at their whim.

Sabin had cannily said no to that. She'd taken enough security to keep Jenrette in line, if she had the inclination to keep Jenrette in line—or she'd deliberately stripped security away from the ship, for whatever reasons Sabin had. She didn't say why.

The Guild tried to pretend they *didn't* have a hole in their station and *didn't* have a huge alien ship sitting out there with its own agenda. *Phoenix* tried to pretend planetary locals had never entered its equation. Nobody was saying anything to anybody.

There was a dark space in his reasoning. He realized he'd been asleep.

The door had opened. Someone was standing in the light.

Had he been here before? Had he drifted off while Bindanda was talking to him?.

"Bren-ji." Jago's voice. "One regrets to wake you, but Jase wishes to speak to you."

He moved for the edge of the bed. Fast. Too fast, for his reeling sense of balance. "Is he here?"

"On the intercom," Jago said.

He set a foot on the floor, fumbled after his robe, missed it, and went straight to the intercom without it—punched in, shivering in the cold. "Jase? This is Bren."

"Bren. Good morning." Space-based irony. Or memory of old times. *"I hope you got some sleep."*

"Did." God, he thought, teeth chattering. Get to the point, Jase. "Heard from Sabin?"

"No, unhappily. Not a word. I need answers. So I'm giving our several guests to you."

Gratefully, he felt the robe settle about his shoulders, Jago's doing. He grabbed it close. "What do you want *me* to do with them?"

"Finesse it, nadi-ji. I'm for half an hour of rest."

"Not slept?"

"Off and on the bridge all shift, with Guild messages that don't say a thing. I'm getting stupid without sleep. Which I understand you did have, lucky bastard. So go to it. I'll meet you down there. I want the truth, Bren. Or I'm going to lose my self-restraint and pound it out of them myself."

"I'm going." He had not the least idea what he was going to do. Jase was, in very fact, hoarse and on the edge, and he got the picture: the Guild was getting hotter and hotter, demanding restoration of contact with their people, Sabin was still missing—under what conditions Jase didn't know. And somebody had to move off dead center soon.

Jase clicked out. He did.

He raked a hand through his hair, exposing an arm to icy air.

"Jago-ji. I'm needed. I'll bathe." The mind was a blank. But he had to deal with humans. "Island dress."

"One hears," Jago said from the doorway. "And for us, nadi?"

He heard, too. "*Please* get a little sleep, nadi-ji. I shall have Jase's guards, and I shall take no chances, none whatsoever, Jago-ji. They should not see you yet. But I assure you. I set no conditions on your assistance if you should hear any threat to me."

"One accepts, nandi," Jago said. Not wholly satisfied, it was clear, but much mollified by the emergency clause.

"Asicho can sit duty, nadi. I *shall* need you soon. I'll need your wits sharp when I do. But one thing I shall wish immediately: have Bindanda pack a modest picnic basket for five humans. And tuck in a bag of sugar candies."

A slight hesitation. Jago could speculate quite easily that the picnic wasn't for Gin and company.

"Yes," Jago said.

Accepted.

Reassured, he dumped the robe and ducked into his shower, chilled half to the bone.

He toggled on the water and scrubbed with a vengeance, trying to adjust his thinking not only to human, but beyond ship-human and ship-speak, all the way over to Reunion Guild—trying to scrub away all the disposition of his Mospheiran heritage, all his accumulated distaste for the behavior of the Guild's officers on their deck. He had to get down to mental bedrock. Had to look at what was. Not what had been, centuries ago.

He was relatively clear-headed when he emerged, relatively calm and with his head full of tentative, Guild-focused notions.

Narani helped him dress, island-style being far, far

quicker than court dress. He omitted the ribbon, tucked the braid down his collar, as he had when he visited home, in the days when things had been easier than he had ever realized.

He clicked on the pocket comm.

"One rejects the gun, this time, Rani-ji, in close contact."

The requested picnic basket turned up, a generous container, in Jeladi's hands. A very generous container. The requested bag of candies, he tucked directly into his pocket.

The breakfast would have served a soccer team, by the weight of it. He walked down the corridor, seeing Banichi and Jago, doubtless waiting to bid him be careful—

"One will be extraordinarily careful," he said, tilted slightly with the weight of the basket. "I know their mannerisms and their threats, and I shall not be surprised. Sleep, nadiin-ji. Favor me with the effort, at least."

He walked on. By the dowager's door, Cenedi's men stood simply watching, doubtless communicating with persons inside. Definitely so. Cajeiri popped out to watch him pass, as if he were an expedition.

With the weight of the baggage, he might well have been.

He exited to the lift area. He supposed Gin knew about the proceedings, too, or would know in short order.

He got in and punched two-deck.

Armed guards met him on that level. He was a little taken aback; but it was Kaplan and Polano—Jase's bodyguard, in full kit, two men he was sure hadn't had any more rest than he had, turned out to welcome him.

"Here to help, sir. Cap'n's down there."

Jase was here. He murmured a response and walked ahead, Kaplan and Polano attending. Jase was here to meet him, maybe for a conference without a great number of witnesses.

12

Jase waited, beyond the immediate area, short of sleep and running very short of temper. Bren, having shared an apartment with Jase for no few years, saw the folded arms and the set of the shoulders and immediately recognized a man who'd as soon throttle his problems as negotiate.

Jase, however, had settled a strong veneer of civilization clamped atop his temper these days—most times.

"What is this?" In ship-speak, and referring, by the glance, to the picnic basket.

"Breakfast," Bren said. "A good breakfast, nadi, to put anyone in a better mood. Want to join me?"

Jase stared at him bleakly. Then the expression slowly changed, as thought penetrated past the anger.

"Not one of the dowager's dishes, one hopes, nadi. We need these people able to talk."

"No, no, perfectly acceptable and human-compatible. Word of honor. What's going on?"

"Oh, besides the hourly calls from Guild Headquarters informing us they're not happy, medical says we have a bug."

"A bug." Bren set the basket down a moment, dug in his pocket and produced the hard fruit candies, remembering that Kaplan and Polano were very fond of them. He gave them each one, under Jase's burning gaze. And offered one to Jase. Calm down, he was saying. Have a candy. Communicate.

It got him another of Jase's stares. A decade ago, when they'd shared quarters, a cavalier confrontation with Jase's temper would have gotten a three-day silence. But in stony silence Jase took one. Studiously considered the wrapper. "An *internal* bug. I said not to go after it yet." He changed to Ragi. "One is annoyed, nadi. One is outraged."

"An internal bug. A location device?"

"Communications." Jase tapped his head, behind the ear. "Clever piece of work. Chemo charging. Never goes dead, well, not until the body quits. Medical does thinks it can't transmit far without the electronics in the armor. Possibly it's recording. Maybe saving stuff to transmit at opportunity."

"Lovely. All of them?"

"Team leader," Jase said. "Becker." Jase had partially unwrapped the candy. Then, changing his mind, he replaced the wrapper and pocketed the sweet. "They'll be nervous about eating anything. Manmade bugs. All sorts of nastiness is possible. No telling what they've dug out of the Archive."

It hadn't been a technology the ship had used . . . among family. One could perceive, at least, the emotional outrage, the absolute outrage of a ship that *was* family. That had set family aboard this station at its founding.

"Bad."

"That's not the whole issue, Bren. If we get Sabin back—if we get any of that team back—"

Definitely bad.

"We can *find* them," Jase said, "the way we found this one. It's not a worry, per se, with Becker, but just so you know."

"I've got the picture," Bren said, and picked up his basket. "Has anyone informed Becker?"

"No. Oh, and the *other* news? We've spotted what we think are gun emplacements, down by the fuel port."

"It's not unreasonable they'd defend the fuel supply."

"From us?"

"Banichi's saying . . . we could take this station."

Startled laughter. "He's serious."

"He's always serious. I haven't said yes."

Jase drew a deep breath.

"If we don't move soon," Bren said, "the likelihood mounts that something will go wrong involving that outlying ship. I want to know how stationers *will* react to foreigners. These people. Becker, Esan and the rest. Have we got to give them back?"

"As far as I'm concerned, they're boarded for the voyage. Tell them anything you like. Do anything you like. They're in your hands. Oh, and the key they threatened us with? Bluffing. It *wasn't* a builder's key. Potent, but ours *still* outranks what they'd give to a mid-level agent."

"Interesting." It was. And the little bow, when they switched to Ragi, was automatic as breathing. "One urges you rest, Jasi-ji. You entrust this to me—*trust* it to me."

"One will most earnestly try," Jase said wearily, shoulders sagging. "Baji-naji."

Given the random flex in the universe. And Jase gave a little wave of the hand and left him in charge, Kaplan attempting to follow his captain out toward the lift.

Jase sent Kaplan back, however. So there they were. He had Jase's guards at the moment. Jase, if things stayed stable an hour, might have a little time to draw breath.

"Where are they?"

"This way, sir," Kaplan said, and led the way.

On a ship hundreds of years inbred and all to some degree related, there *wasn't* a proper security confinement. The ship had improvised. They had their four outsider problems confined in a med-tech's cabin with an oversized plastic grid bolted on for a door and the inside door to the bath locked open—no privacy, no amenities, no sliding door. A few plain plastic chairs provided ease for the crewmen sitting in charge, and the section doors at either end of this stretch of corridor were shut.

Bren walked to the plastic-grid doorway. There was a bunk, seating for two glum men, two others on the floor—chairs not being provided either. The men looked at him, not happy, but not outright belligerent.

"Brought up breakfast," Bren said cheerfully, and then recalled Esan knew him as one of the cook's aides. "Cook's compliments."

"We're not touching it." That from the gray-haired senior, Becker, that would be. The one with the bug.

"Oh, that'd be too bad," Bren said, and set the basket down and took the lid off one of the fragrant sauces. Which reminded his own stomach he'd been on long hours and little food. "But if you won't eat it, guess we can. Kaplan. Polano. Join me?"

Kaplan and Polano took him up on it without a word. They leaned near, took small plastic plates out of the picnic basket, and started unpacking food and passing shares to the crewman guards as well.

"Offer still stands," Bren said, past a first sip of fruit drink. "There's quite a bit here."

"Hell," Becker said, sounding less certain. Bet that

Guild enforcers ate as well as any tech on the station. But none of these station-bound folk would have met the smells that wafted up from the packets.

"Want some?" Bren shoved the box over against the grid. "You can pick which."

Becker moved. The others bought the offer and they all came over and scrounged, hands through the largish grid squares, for likely packets. Plates, however, didn't fit through the grid, and some of Bindanda's neat packets took a beating. Their detainees were hungry. They tasted the sauces on finger-tips, licked it off, tried small spoonfuls of it, clearly finding the flavors strong and provocative.

"Captain says don't worry about bugs," Bren said after they'd had a few bites. "The ship is family. It doesn't use such things. I suppose it's different on the station."

No answer. The finger-tasting had paused, dead still in the cell for a moment, then resumed, with baleful looks.

"Medical said one of you has an imbedded bug," Bren volunteered. "They wondered if you knew."

No answer.

"Somebody named Becker," Bren said, in his best effort at ship-accent. "What I heard."

The senior stopped eating and looked as if the food suddenly didn't agree as well. The others stopped in growing uncertainty.

"Just what I heard," Bren reiterated with a shrug. "Don't know for a fact, but they said it's up here." He touched behind his ear. "I can assure you with transmission jammed, it's not going to do anything. Medics were thinking about taking it out, but that's sort of like brain surgery, so I guess they thought not."

Becker looked green.

"None of the rest of you, though." Bren said

"Which I wouldn't like, if they were doing it to me, especially if I didn't know, as I gather you didn't. Privacy. I can't figure how you'd do without that. But I suppose it's your job. I guess they think they need to keep an eye on you that way."

"Why don't you shut up?" Esan said. They'd stopped eating. Polano and Kaplan had suspended breakfast, too, wary and on guard, and the crewmen sat still, awaiting trouble.

"No," Becker said easily, "if he wants to talk, he can talk." Becker dug in with a spoon, bravely savored a bite. "Not bad stuff."

"Smart man," Bren said, with a level look at Becker.

Esan stood up, hand on the bars. "Who are you? Who *are* you?"

"Not galley staff," Bren said mildly. Level approach deserved level approach. "You want the plain truth? You sent *Phoenix* out to see how things were at Alpha. Well, I'm from there."

That got attention.

"So you come back to see things here?" Becker asked.

"I've seen. And things there are a whole lot better than here. This crew knew. This crew, after it got the ship refueled, after it made its agreements with Alpha—" That covered an immense tract of secrets. "—decided you people back at Reunion deserve rescue. So here we are. Some welcome we get."

"You come in messing with a dangerous situation, mister."

"That ship out there? We've had more cooperation out of it than we have from Guild admin."

"The hell you say."

"Your station, whatever Guild management says,

is in somewhat serious trouble with it, don't you think?"

"Not our business."

"What—to think?"

"What has Alpha to do with it? Who gave a bunch of jumped-up colonials the say?"

"Jumped-up colonials. You're not a colony?"

"We're not a colony. We're admin."

"Sure looks like a colony to me. This is the *ship,* Mr. Becker. This is the only ship there is, the only ship there ever was, and without it, you look pretty much like a colony, to another colonist."

Clearly Becker wasn't interested in circular argument. He had his mouth full. "Not our business to say."

"It ought to be your business, don't you think? The ship's crew thinks you deserve a say. They think the innocent deserve to get out of this place alive."

That got interest. "What are you talking about?" Becker asked.

"That ship out there," Bren said. "Don't you think you need rescue? Certainly looks like it to me."

A shrug. The ship was, apparently, an old threat. A pattern on the wallpaper of the world, not even in consciousness. "We don't make decisions. We take orders."

"Do your families? Take orders, that is? You're content they should die to support Mr. Braddock's notions?"

These men didn't come out of a vacuum. They surely had relatives. At least mothers. And all four paid slight and hostile attention.

"Your parents," Bren said, "your cousins, your wives and children don't deserve the result of Braddock's decisions. But trust us. We'll get them aboard."

"Not likely," Becker said.

"I assure you, you'll like Alpha. Better food. Nice apartments. Much better neighbors." He hit somewhere close to the right buttons. He saw troubled looks, and for the last several moments, a decided lack of interest in the food containers.

"Not our business to make policy," Becker said, and took a cracker. "We just report. And the last our people heard from us is its officers being attacked. Is *that* smart policy, mister spy?"

"The ship is being stood off. Told she can't refuel. If that's the way the local Guild wants to do business . . ."

"This interview is over."

"Are you somehow under control of that ship out there?"

When the quarry retreats, throw out a lure.

"It's a robot."

"Afraid not. We talked to it. *It* says it put a probe out and got attacked. It's not happy about that. It's got you under observation. This may be the only ship humanity owns, but I'd say that's not likely the only ship the aliens have. Point blank, gentlemen, you're under someone's gun, and since we showed up, the reply clock is running, so far as that ship is concerned. Sorry about that. Refueling's become critical. And we don't think Braddock is likely to tell the station population that they're in danger."

He'd hit a nerve.

"Maybe," Becker said. "Maybe not."

"They say you killed one of their people. They want the body back. What's the story from your side?"

"I said this interview was over."

"Well," Bren said with a dismissive shrug. "Well, it's a curious point, isn't it? A hole gets put into your station and what, nobody mentions it? You do all this mining since the attack, and nobody cares there's a ship out there, even a robot, which it isn't? We came out here to rescue you. But maybe there's no fuel for us, and we can't do a thing about your situation: we'll just go off to the alternate base and refuel out there, and leave you to your problem."

"There's fuel."

"You think."

"We have our mining operations."

"Current?"

"Intermittent."

"Intermittent," Bren echoed him.

"They're not operating at the moment."

"Like since the last six years?"

A shrug from Becker. A little shift among the others.

"Not talking," Becker said.

"Well," Bren said, "dishes, gentlemen." He held out his hand for the few containers that had gone behind the grid, and the detainees reluctantly got up and surrendered them one at a time—there not being a real opportunity, through the grid, for them to make a grab at his hand, and no real chance of their success with Kaplan and Polano and the other guards there, either.

"One thing I think has puzzled everyone," Bren said, then, pausing in his packing. "Why did the aliens blow up the station ten years ago?"

"Ask Ramirez," Becker said harshly.

"Ramirez, unfortunately, can't answer that, being dead. And the answer doesn't appear in the ship's log, not that I hear. So maybe it's not the ship's fault shooting started. Or do your leaders tell you it was?"

"Not our business."

"So you think. But I wonder what truth is deep in station records, and whether the whole history of humanity out here is going to end, all because your leadership took a shot at an inquiring ship."

"No."

"It approached too close and you got nervous."

"Go to hell," Becker said.

"You know, you've had a stable situation, that watcher out there, and you, all alone. Now that we've come in, the situation's changed, and they're *demanding* to have the body from their second attempt to contact you. You haven't done that well, you stationers. You know that?"

"Not ours to say."

"Mr. Becker, with that great hole in your station, I'd think you'd suspect they could blow a second one if they were ready to. They've sat out there trying to come up with another solution, by what I see. Maybe just waiting for us to come back, so they could figure where we come from. We're not happy about that, let me say. And you're going to go on telling me your station's just getting along splendidly. It's a damned wreck, Mr. Becker, and the neighbors are annoyed with you. *We're* annoyed with you. We're telling you the only thing you can reasonably do is get out of here, which is why we've come back to save your necks, and all you can do is say there isn't any concern about the ship, it's just a robot, and the station just had a little accident. Wake up, Mr. Becker. The lot of you wake up. You're in trouble."

Becker stood fast. The rest weren't so sure, and darted little glances toward Becker. He could order Becker separated out to solitary confinement, which would only harden the resolve of the rest, if they were worth their salt—which they probably were: he'd had no indication to the contrary. And being worth their salt, they might, given a chance, apply moral suasion to their own leader.

"Mr. Becker," he said, "your loyalty I'm sure isn't to a metal and plastics station. Your duty is to flesh and blood occupants of that station, and your highest duty is to assure their survival. You want the truth, gentlemen. I'm not exactly from Alpha. I'm Mospheiran. Former colonist—*resident* of a thriving human settlement on the world below Alpha, where we maintain good relations with our neighbors. We number in the hundreds of thousands. We're building our own ship in partnership with our neighbors. We live peaceably together on the planet and on the space station, and we're extremely upset about your interfering in the stellar neighborhood and sending your problems on to us. The Guild's authority may work here. Fine. It doesn't reach us. We have governments. Thanks to Reunion, we're having to build defenses. You're sitting out here in an exposed position, having fought a patently unsuccessful action with an enemy you can't even identify, let alone communicate with. We're pulling you back to a safe perimeter. Join the far more numerous side of the human species and live in relative peace and comfort. That's the only reasonable solution."

"So give us contact with our superiors," Becker said, grim-faced. "If you want me to relay that offer to the Guildmaster, give me communication with my superiors."

Bren shook his head. "Not a chance. The captain would have liked you to settle in as passengers. Unfortunately you came here to fight, and we take it that's what you'll do if we let you loose in comfortable quarters. So you're here, and here you'll stay. Sorry about your personal baggage. We'll see if we can get someone to pack it aboard for you once we're fueled and boarding."

"The hell!"

Becker was the roadblock. As long as Becker held out, the rest wouldn't talk. Bren heaved a long, slow sigh.

And got up, picked up the picnic basket and walked away, Kaplan in attendance, out of the section and on toward the lift.

13

It was a change of clothing, at very least. Not full court dress: the modest country coat and trousers would do, a little lace, a brocade vest, but a plain cloth coat, boots that would do for a walk in the fields—God, how he wished it were a walk in the fields. The meadow just above his seaside estate, a cliff-top view of incoming waves . . . that would do, for the health of his soul.

As it was, he had a cold steel corridor and Banichi and Jago in their own country kit, which was to say, moderately armed, the lot of them proceeding down the corridor toward a rendezvous with Ginny and a consultation on the Becker problem. He had the much-abused computer that was, on ordinary days, his third arm and leg—a little extra persuasion.

He *thought* that was the plan. But as they passed the dowager's door, where two of her young men stood their habitual watch, the door opened and Cenedi intercepted them.

Then Ilisidi herself intercepted them, an Ilisidi resplendent in a black brocade with gold trim and black lace.

"And where are we going, nandi?" Ilisidi asked.

"Aiji-ma," he began, dismayed.

Whack! went the cane. "We have not heard from Sabin-aiji. The aiji of the heavens has in his custody representatives of an arrogant official who has delayed us in our essential mission. Are these the facts, nandi?"

Perfect expression of the atevi perspective.

"Yes," he said, "aiji-ma." With complete understanding, *yes,* aiji-ma. The atevi perspective was direct and essentially true, in this circumstance. "But, aiji-ma, Jase-aiji is still negotiating with this authority. He has not despaired of Sabin-aiji."

"Well, well," Ilisidi said, and by now Cajeiri had come out of the apartment and edged close to his great-grandmother. "And this authority," Ilisidi said, "intends to hold Sabin-aiji silent and threatened pending our cooperation. What of these persons that entered the ship? Have they been empowered to negotiate?"

"No, aiji-ma, they are merely to observe and report to their Guild. One fears they will never gain that much power."

"Ha. Then why have we admitted these useless persons in the first place?"

"Doubtless it seemed good to Sabin-aiji, aiji-ma, in the belief it would delay other, more aggressive moves from the Guild until she could reach the Guild-aiji. Then the Guild prevented her further communication with us, which is an extreme move. And we moved to seize these persons."

"Who are worthless, nandi. Jase-aiji definitively asserts command?"

Critical question. If Jase didn't, then someone did. They certainly didn't want anyone on Reunion taking command of the situation. Tabini sent him to act. And act when?

When *Phoenix* got into difficulty. Having the senior captain missing and an alien ship sitting at their shoulder was certainly a difficulty. Ilisidi, this backup agent of Tabini's, had survived no few attempts on her power and authority—but not by sitting still and reading the news reports.

Damned right she called their resolution into question.

"Aiji-ma." Two heartbeats for a decision: take the initiative with atevi or lose it. "One is extravagantly honored by your presence." With all it meant—including the real possibility of a dozen atevi attempting to seize the center of a space station full of humans, if he didn't come up with a better idea fast. "If I dare propose—the reaction of these four detainees to meeting atevi may well advise us how the station at large will view our partnership. This was my mission to two-deck. Dare I ask your assistance in that? We should gain something of interest."

"We *rust* in this viewless containment," Ilisidi said. He had the irrational vision of cliffs above Malguri, of a breeze rising, of wi'itikin stretching their leathery wings to find it.

He felt that breeze himself. He'd been up there on two-deck functioning in human mode, by human rules, within his obligations to Jase . . . but that *wasn't* the limit of the world they'd come from, that *wasn't* why he had come here to do this job. Sabin had left the ship to try her own best shot, whatever side she was playing. But it wasn't all the recourse they had.

"Aiji-ma." He cast a slightly apprehensive glance at Cajeiri, who showed no disposition to leave the dowager's side.

"He will understand, nandi. He is *here* to understand. And he has his own protection."

An assigned member of her guard, that was to say, who in any fracas would devote himself solely to Cajeiri's safety. A question of man'chi.

"So, well, nand' dowager, by all means. Let us go."

With which he set out in the dowager's company. Their operation was no longer quite what he'd advised Jase he would do, perhaps, but it was still within the parameters of what Jase knew existed down here . . . what Jase, maybe with a clearer vision than he had, had known might stir to action once he loosed five-deck on a problem.

He used the pocket com as he followed the dowager into the lift, punched in Ginny Kroger's channel, her messages. "Gin. The dowager's going to be discussing matters with the detainees in person. I suggest we start considering how you get that fuel back. Start considering how we get aboard the station without their being able to stop us. Things may move fast."

He was mildly surprised to get Gin's voice, live. *"Well ahead of you on both counts, Mr. Cameron."*

Deep breath. Was he surprised? Not in the least. "Good for you, then. Any result?"

"A few promising. We're up close on the images. Enhancing what's in shadow. Got one useful bit for you."

"What's that?"

"The station didn't blow. Didn't blow at all. It was slagged. We can't *do this."*

"Can't?"

"Our weapons can not *do this kind of damage, Bren. Our weapons can't do this. We're not sure what did."*

Very deep breath. And a cold that went to his heart. "That's useful. Any other advice?"

"We should do something real soon."

"Prep to do whatever we can do," he said. "I think sooner rather than later. We'll try to get facts for you." The lift arrived. Doors opened onto two-deck. "Got to go, Gin."

Cenedi and his men exited first. They always did, question of precedence. The crewman guard standing watch in the area met their intrusion with startled looks and twitches toward defense, which, fortunately, they didn't complete.

The dowager walked out with Cajeiri, Bren followed, and Banichi and Jago. He led the way back into the medical section, back to their makeshift prison, tailed by two of the ship's makeshift security into a section of corridor where Kaplan, Polano, and a handful of common crew were holding a loud and notably profane argument through the grid. "Damned fools!" was one side of it. The other side's answer was not something he'd care to translate for his companions. So much for *authorized* responses and crew on short sleep and frayed nerves.

"Gran 'Sidi." Kaplan's argument immediately gave way to astonishment, an uneasy deference to her and her armed entourage. Kaplan clearly asked himself whether his captain knew, and what his captain would say.

But Ilisidi waited for nothing. "Where are these individuals?" Ilsidi asked with a wave of her cane at the obvious plastic grid—no prisoners visible, due to the angle of the grid, but the fat was very nearly in the fire, as was.

"The dowager wishes to speak with the detainees," Bren said. "She wishes to explain matters to them herself. It *is* cleared, Mr. Kaplan."

"But, sir." Kaplan said, half whispering, as if that could insulate Ilisidi from understanding. "Sir, I'm afraid they're not going to be polite."

"She won't be greatly surprised at temper, Mr. Kaplan. Captain's orders. Will you and the rest of these people stand backup?"

"Yes, sir." Worried compliance. The company was hardly official, and likely shouldn't be here. "Yes, *sir*, yes, *ma'am*."

The several detainees, as atevi eclipsed the light outside their plastic grid doorway, backed off and stared in utter dismay.

"You damn bastards!" Esan blurted out.

"Kindly mind your language," Bren said moderately. "The Guild sent Ramirez to deal with Alpha, assuming it would give all the orders. This hasn't happened. It's not going to happen. You're dealing with Alpha *and* its alliance. I trust you recall that Alpha has an indigenous population. *This* lady is the aiji-dowager, grandmother of the ruler of their side of the civilized world. The boy, aged seven, is her great-grandson. The rest are our personal security. We have a close working relationship. We're here to rescue you."

Human eyes looked up—farther up than adult men were accustomed to look up at faces; then looked on the level at an aged woman and at a small child. And went on looking.

"This is Gran 'Sidi," one of the crewmen in the background yelled out. "And she doesn't take any nonsense from fools and she doesn't give a damn for your Guild rules."

Becker didn't like it. The Guild agents didn't like it. But Ilisidi had a certain well-savored notoriety among the crew, and if Ilisidi couldn't understand two words of what was shouted, she stood in perfect comprehension of the unruly crewman's intent and the jeering support behind her.

"Well," Ilisidi said, leaning on her cane. Then waved it at the four as if they were tourist attractions. "Are these, nandi, of that pernicious Pilots' Guild?"

"Yes, nand' dowager, one understands so."

"The Guild that opposes our *generous* gesture."

"The dowager remarks," Bren said, "that you have opposed the generosity of this ship and crew and of

herself. Possibly motivated by unsavory Guild interest." It was true. It was implicit in the infelicitous
numbers of the dowager's suggestion.

"Tell her go to hell," Becker muttered.

"Oh, I wouldn't do that, Mr. Becker. I wouldn't. If
that's your notion of dealing with foreign nationals, I
can see why you have a hole in your station."

"We're not going to be threatened."

"She won't threaten, Mr. Becker. I do assure you
that. She's very, very old, she's made the extraordinarily polite gesture of leaving her comfortable residence aboard, and done you an honor leaders of
several nations would be extravagantly pleased to receive. More, she's brought her great-grandson to let
him observe first-hand how civilized people solve
problems."

"Then get the strong-arms out."

"Her guards are with her, as mine are with me.
We don't haul you into separate rooms for processing,
which is our favor to you, and I suggest you take a
much nicer tone, sir."

"Do we hear demands?" Ilisidi asked sweetly.

"She asks if you're being rude," Bren said. "Express
your pleasure at the visit, gentlemen. Bow. I do recommend it."

Becker averted his stare, just minutely, a capitula-
tion, at least that he wasn't quite willing to start a riot.
A bow—not quite.

"Mr. Becker?"

"We demand our immediate release."

"Of course we demand contact with Captain Sabin."

"Not in my power."

"Did your leaders indicate to you they were going
to silence her communications, while you were vulnerable on our deck? If they didn't, they certainly left
you in a position. Understand, we're being remarkably

restrained—but the captain's getting some needed sleep at the moment. When he wakes up, I'm sure he's going to hope we've had a reasonable exchange of views."

Becker drew a deep breath and looked at his fellows. Then he asked, in a much quieter tone, "So what's she want?"

"A polite answer to her question."

"Look, we don't make policy."

"They claim, aiji-ma, to be lower-level agents of their Guild, incapable of initiating policy changes."

"And what is this policy, nandi?"

"The dowager asks you very politely what the policy of your Guild is, that has put you here."

There was no answer at first. Then Becker: "We came here to do a routine inspection of the log."

He translated that.

"Why has the senior captain not reported to us?" Ilisidi asked, and Bren rendered it: "She wants to know why the senior captain hasn't called in, and believe me, gentlemen, the ship's captain also wants that answer."

"We haven't any idea," Becker said—anxious, now. "That's the God's truth."

"What were you looking for aboard?"

"I think we found it," Becker said under his breath. He slid a worried gaze toward Ilisidi.

"Oh, nothing like you surmise. What you see, sir, is equal partners in an alliance of three governments, in which your Guild, gentlemen, can also look for partnership, but which I assure you it will never order or run. This ship came here at great effort of our entire alliance to rescue you from the situation Captain Ramirez reported to exist here, a situation which we find in evidence, and which you seem either not to know—or to want to maintain, so far as your answers make any sense."

Ilisidi was patient through that exchange. Becker set his jaw and said nothing at all. The others looked, at best, worried.

"Well?" Bren said.

"Take it up with Guild offices," Becker muttered through his teeth, doubtless the mantra of his service. "We don't make policy."

Bren translated: "He maintains his Guild has sole discretion to negotiate and he is ignorant."

"Then we should release these persons," Ilisidi said with an airy wave of her hand. And of course, Bren thought, if they were low-level atevi, persons claiming to be incapable of further harm, it was, in atevi terms, *civilized* to release the minor players . . . after the fracas was settled.

"One fears, aiji-ma, that they would make extravagant accusations if they were released to their own deck now. They might make the inhabitants fear the ship. And fear you, aiji-ma."

Ilisidi, the reprobate, was never displeased at being feared. "Ridiculous," she said, with evident satisfaction. "But you think they would do harm to the situation, nandi, if we released them."

"Harm of some sort," he said to her. "She wishes to release you back to your own side," he said in Mosphei', and watched disbelief and anxiety have its way with the detainees. "It's the custom. Among her people, lower-level agents are never prosecuted for the sins of their superiors. We humans, of course, advise her that you'd spread panic on the station—and that would mean people would hide instead of boarding—while others left in great enough numbers to destabilize lifesupport on Reunion. A nightmare, gentlemen. One we're trying to avoid. We want everybody off the station—*after* we've refueled. But for some reason, your government put a sign we could read on the fuel port, advising us there was an explosive lock down there. Now why would your government booby-trap our fuel?"

"To keep the ship out there from getting it," Becker said.

"They'd do what they like. *We're* the only entity that would read that sign. And we're the only ones that sign would stop, aren't we? Sounds like a bid for a negotiating position, to me."

"In case we were gone and you came back."

Listeners in the corridor hooted.

He translated that exchange into Ragi.

"Ha," Ilisidi said, and leaned both hands on her cane. "A posthumous thought to our safety. Not likely."

"The dowager says, Not likely. And I don't need to translate the crew's opinion."

Becker was red-faced and thin-lipped.

"Beck," another said, "if she's from the planet at Alpha, she's not the one that hit us. Neither's the Alpha colonists.—My name's Coroia, sir. And I've got two kids. And we're in trouble, Beck."

"Shut it down!" Becker shouted, and atevi security reacted—simply and quickly, a drawn wall of weapons. Cajeiri had ducked against his great-grandmother for shelter. And now tried to pretend he hadn't done that.

Ilisidi lifted her hand. Weapons lifted.

"Sorry," Bren said. "My personal apologies, Mr. Becker. They don't raise their voices in the presence of authority. An intercultural misstep."

Becker was shaken, the more so as apology undermined the adrenaline supply.

"You can advise them keep their damn guns safed."

"We each have our customs, Mr. Becker. Back at their world, they're taking precautions necessitated by *your* making enemies out here. They came to welcome you to a safe refuge. You haven't got any allies, as seems to me, except us, except them. As seems to me, you're stuck out here in a station with a hole in it— while we have a ship that works. So believe me: we're the only game worth playing, the only one that's going to give you any chances. I'm extremely sorry for your family, Mr. Coroia, if your Guild stands us off. You've got no defense, no agreement with your neighbors, no trade, no future, so far as we see, and we offer you all of that. But you persistently say no—not because it's sensible, but because you're blindly loyal to a Guild leadership that sent you here. The position you're taking isn't even good for your Guild, gentlemen. They've got an angry ship waiting out there. What do they plan to do about it? *We're* not going to go out and attack it for you. We've got a world behind us that's at risk if you go making wars, and we won't shoot at it."

Support in the ranks was wavering. It was evident on the other faces.

Even Becker looked less certain. "We've got only your word for what's going on."

"You've got proof in front of you, you damned fool!" That from Polano, with Kaplan, out in the corridor, an outright explosion of anger. "I've got two cousins on that station, who *may* be alive, and I don't want to leave them here, mister! Use good sense!"

"Mr. Polano," Bren introduced the complainant. "Who has a point. What's so difficult about dealing outside our species? We do it daily. We may be able to get you all out of this. But we need straight answers."

"Listen to Mr. Cameron," Kaplan said, and Polano and the crew behind him added their own voices.

"Straight answers," Becker said, and looked at his mates, and looked at him, and looked at Polano and back. And at Ilisidi and Cajeiri, with a far greater doubt. "That's a kid?"

"Aged seven," Bren said.

"Seven."

"They're tall," Bren said dryly. "That's exactly the point, isn't it? They're not us. But you're still welcome aboard. You *and* your kids. Your wives. Your grandmothers. We can get you out of here and go where your kids have a future. You've got to have somebody you care about."

He was making headway with the others. Becker, however, scowled. "The Guild's not going to approve *anybody* leaving."

"Because they've got such thorough control of the aliens out there? I don't think so."

Clearly Becker had thought he had an answer to that point, and now that it was on the edge of his tongue, it didn't taste right.

"Get us two things," Bren said. "Fuel and the reason that alien ship's out there. The truth about what happened six years ago. The remains and belongings of whoever tried to come aboard and negotiate with your Guild."

"Negotiate, hell!"

"That's what your Guild told you? Truthfulness with *us* hasn't been outstanding."

"Look," Becker said. "Look. Give me contact with my office. I'll call and tell them everything you're saying."

"And what you report won't change their basic opinions in the least, will it? What matters most here, Mr. Becker? Braddock's good opinion? Or people's lives?"

"We're not the sort to make decisions like this!"

Becker retorted. "We're not qualified to make decisions!"

"You're not stupid, either. You've been waiting for this ship. It's here. And now you think your Guild wants something else. What could it possibly want? *Control* of this ship? Your Guild's sat here for most of ten years with a hole in the station and now they need to run things? No. Not a chance."

Becker bit his lip. "Not mine to say."

"If your families don't get aboard, if nobody on this station gets aboard, do you want *that* on your conscience? Because, being on this ship with us, you will survive, gentlemen. You may be the only ones from the station that do survive, because without refueling here we can't possibly rescue your relatives. But survive *you* will, and you can remember that you had a chance. You can *think* about that fact, you can regret that fact for the rest of your lives, in safety, back where we come from."

"They've got a hostage." The fourth man, who never had spoken, blurted that out. The other three looked appalled, but that one, white-faced, kept going. "That's why the aliens haven't come back. We've got one of them. That ship out there, it's not shooting because we've got one of them alive on the station."

For two heartbeats Bren stood as still as the rest; then, having stored up his wealth of information, he finally remembered to translate. "Aiji-ma, this last man appears to have suffered a crisis of man'chi, and to save his relatives from calamity, he claims the station holds a foreign prisoner . . . a circumstance he believes alone has protected them from a second attack."

A very slight shifting of stance among listening atevi. *This* was information.

"Interesting," Ilisidi said, leaning on her cane.

"You think you've got a hostage," Bren said to Becker. "And this hostage is still alive?"

"Supposed to be," Becker muttered. Then the inevitable, "That's all we know."

"Mr. Becker, *we've* got a problem." The pieces of information began to add up, logical enough only to the otherwise hopeless, and weren't at all comforting to a man who had to make peace with the pattern they made. "So our arrival disturbed the situation you *thought* you had, and now that the currents are moving, you don't know what else to do. But my people have spent the last several centuries figuring out how to talk outside our own species. Rumor says the aliens won't attack you while you've got this prisoner. I'd say that's an increasingly thin bet, and the more we dither about it, the thinner it gets. Who is this person, *where* is this person, and has anyone successfully talked with him?"

That last was his greatest hope, that *someone* had broken the language barrier, that *someone* knew how to communicate with this species.

The listeners in the corridor waited. Ilisidi waited, hand firmly on Cajeiri's shoulder.

"We don't know anything," Becker said, Becker's answer to everything, and that provoked an outcry of absolute frustration from the human listeners. "Listen to Cameron!" somebody yelled, out in the corridor. "Idiots! You don't mess with aliens!"

Becker was nettled. "We don't know anything, dammit!"

"He's supposed to be alive," Coroia said. "But nobody knows. We guess he is, if that ship out there is staying where it is, or maybe they just don't know."

"There's supposed to be alien armament," the fourth man said. "They're supposed to be copying it."

"That's a crock," Coroia said. "If they're copying

anything, Baumann, is some popgun somebody *hand-carried* aboard the station going to stand off a whole *ship?*"

That insightful question brought its own small silence.

"You don't know even that much is the truth," Bren said. "That *is* the point, isn't it? You don't really know why you've been safe for the last half dozen years. The reason you're alive just hasn't made sense, and now that ship sitting out there, with us having stirred the pot, is liable to do nobody-knows-what. Can you tell us where this prisoner is, and can you tell us how to get to him?"

"Get families safe aboard," Coroia said. "Get the *kids* all aboard."

"That's mass," Bren said. "Is there *fuel* to move this ship anywhere if we do board the station population?"

Fearful silence. Then: "The miners went out," Becker said. "Mining went on, six, seven years ago. There's supposed to be fuel."

"And mining hasn't been going on since that ship showed. You were waiting for us with a sign on the fuel tank saying, This will explode. How did you plan to get out of the mess you're in without us?"

"We don't set policy." Becker winced as even his own comrades exclaimed in outrage, and he gave a nervous glance to the patiently waiting atevi present.

"After *Phoenix* left—" Esan had abandoned his braced, surly stance and stuck his hands in his hip pockets. "We mined. They came and poked their noses into our corridors. We *caught* this bastard. And since then they haven't tried again. That's as much as everybody knows."

"This second attack," Bren said. But suddenly he was aware of the onlookers parting.

Jase had shown up.

"I've been on this," Jase said under his breath, Jase, who *hadn't* gotten any sleep, "from my office. What's this *prisoner* goings-on, gentlemen?"

"They say an alien prisoner exists on the station," Bren said, dropping into Ragi, as if he were talking to the atevi present, but it was just as much Jase he intended. "They say they mined fuel. They maintain this prisoner, with whom the station does not communicate, is the reason the foreigners have not attacked a *third* time. Supposedly the station captured some sort of armament. But what potency it has against that ship sitting out there is questionable."

"Possession of this prisoner," Ilisidi said, with a thump of her cane against the floor. "This prisoner, and the fuel for the ship. We have disturbed this pond. Ripples are still moving. Shall we sit idle?"

"No, nandi," Jase said on a breath, in Ragi, in full witness of the detainees. "We do not." And in ship-speak: "All right. Where is this prisoner, and what does he breathe?"

Good question, that. Very good question. The planet-born didn't routinely think about the air itself.

"They wore suits when they came in," Becker said. "Shadowy. Big. Straight from hell."

Big certainly answered to the silhouettes they'd exchanged with the alien ship.

"You personally saw them?" Jase asked.

"On vid."

Anything could be faked, Bren remembered. Anything could be made up. If it weren't for the missing station section and that ship out there, Becker's shadowy aliens could be an old movie segment from the Archive, and those in charge had shown a previous disposition to make up vid displays.

"Spill," Jase said. "Spill. Now. Location of this prisoner. Location of Guild offices. Everything you know."

Becker didn't answer at once. "Guild wing is D Section," Coroia said in a low voice, in that silence, "and if you give me a handheld and a pen, captain, *I'll* show you."

"The hell," Becker said.

"Beck, I'm buying it. We haven't *got* another way to defend this station."

"Back off," Becker said to the mutiny in his ranks. "Shut up." Then, to Jase: "I'll show you, myself. But I want my people out of this cage and I want our families boarded, fast as we can get them here."

"In secrecy?" Jase asked. "You want to call your next-ofs and tell them start packing, and this isn't going to trigger questions?"

Guild might eat and breathe secrecy, Bren thought, but he didn't bet on family connections keeping a secret, not in a station where everybody was related. If Becker called his wife, would he fail to call his mother? And if the mother called Becker's sister, where did it stop?

Becker surely saw the disaster looming. He didn't entirely leap at the chance.

"We've got to tell the people," Coroia said desperately.

"And start a panic," Becker said. "There's got to be orders. Central's got to give orders, Manny."

"They have to," Jase said, "but they're not doing that. We've warned them. But our senior captain's disappeared on station. You had orders to come in here and scope us for whatever you could find. For *what*, gentlemen?"

"For irregularities," Becker said.

"For a head count. For a check on who's in command."

"Yes, sir," Becker said.

"So you've got that information, plain and clear. And *then* what was Guild going to do?"

"We don't know, sir."

"Well, I'll tell you what we're going to do." Jase thumbed four or five buttons on his handheld. "And we're not going to try to maintain this station up with an alien ship breathing down our necks. You wonder what that ship's sitting out there for? It's sitting out there because you've got one of its people and it claims this space, if you want my interpretation. It claims this solar system, it's sitting there, probably taking notes on what comes and goes here, possibly communicating with others, and we're not disposed to argue with its sense of possession. We're getting the lot of you out of here, we're establishing defenses back at Alpha, and we're drawing the line there. This station is written off, to be vacated, best gesture we can make to calm this situation down. If we can get fueled and negotiate our way past that alien craft, we're getting you, your families, and Chairman Braddock out of here." He showed Becker and crew the handheld. "This is your own station schematic, gentlemen, straight out of Archive. With the damage marked. Right now, give me specifics, where this prisoner is, where the primary citizen residence areas are, where Guild command is, and where our senior captain's likely to be, if she's been arrested. If you want your kids safe—give us facts."

Curious sight—Jase's machine, Becker and the detainees vying to figure out the diagram through the thick plastic grid, nudging one another for a better view, and to point out this and that feature, suddenly a case of Guild loyalty be damned. Atevi observers were curious, too, more about the human doings than about the image—not least, Ilisidi, Bren was well sure, who kept her great-grandson protectively by her side as her security kept hands very near weapons, all of them sensing what they would call the shifting of man-'chiin. Atevi would understand all the impulses to betrayal, all the emotional upheaval Becker and his men might suffer . . . and would not understand what pushed matters over the edge.

"Becker-nadi has seen the threat to his household, aiji-ma," Bren said quietly. "He and his associates conclude their Guild has failed them and failed to deal honestly with them."

The dreadful cane thumped down. "Observe, great-grandson. Mercy encourages a shift in man'chiin. Does it not? If it also encourages fools to think us weak, then we do not lose the advantage of surprise."

"Yes, mani-ma. Shall we now attack the station?"

A thwack of Ilisidi's finger against a boyish skull. "Learn! These are humans. These are your allies. Observe what they do. One may assume either reasons or actions will be different."

Jase's attention was momentarily for the schematic Becker had in hand, the things Becker was saying . . . the paidhiin both knew, however, the urges percolating through atevi blood and bone, potent as a force of nature: the *aishi-prejid*, the essential strength of civilized association, had to be upheld, *had* to be supported by all participants, and would survive, while the opposition's command structure was tottering, its supporters seeking shelter. Translation: a weakness had to be invaded and fixed quickly, for the common good, even across battlelines. Among atevi, the web of association, once fractured, was impractically hard to repair.

War? That word only vaguely translated out of Ragi, and at certain times, not accurately at all; but as applied to the fragile systems of a space station utterly dependent on its technicians, the atevi view might be the more applicable.

"If *we* move," Bren added in the lowest of tones, only for keen atevi hearing, "one fears atevi intervention will rouse fear and resentment among local humans. They will see you as dangerous invaders. If we are to go in to use force, it may be best humans do it."

"Kaplan-nadi and his team are insufficient," Banichi muttered under his breath. "How can they improve on Sabin-aiji's fate?"

That was the truth: if Kaplan and crew could get directly to the ordinary workers, they would have the advantage of persuasion—but getting to the common folk wasn't at all likely. *Sabin* had tried walking aboard into Guild hands, and that hadn't gone well at all. Ship-folk had no skill at infiltration.

Becker and crew, evidently the best the station had, hadn't moved with great subtlety. The very concept of subtle force seemed, in this human population, lost in the Archive—along with the notion of how to deal with outsiders.

But to risk Banichi and Jago . . . even if fifth-deck atevi *were* the ship's remaining skilled operators . . .

"*We* can move very quietly," Jago said. "We can find this asset."

"If you go aboard, nadiin-ji," Bren muttered back, "you can't go without a translator."

"We know certain words," Jago objected in a low voice.

"You know certain words, but not enough," Bren said. "If you go, I shall go, nadiin. Add my numbers with yours. I can reassure those we meet. I can meet certain ones without provoking alarm and devastation, which cannot serve us in securing a peaceful evacuation."

Banichi listened, then moved closer to Cenedi, and

there was a sudden, steady undertone of Ragi debate under the human negotiations.

"Nadi," Bren said to Jago, who had stayed close by him. "Are we prepared for this move?"

"Always," Jago said.

Oh, there was a plan. He'd personally authorized them to form a plan, but he had a slithering suspicion that, in another sense, *plans* had existed, involving the same station diagrams, from the first moment the aiji-dowager had arrived in the mix.

And meanwhile they had a handful of Guild operatives now crowding one another at the grid to point out the architecture of their own offices, pointing and arguing about the location of a prisoner none of them claimed to have seen—while crew who'd become spectators took mental notes for gossip on two-and three-deck. Openness? An open door for the crew? Jase certainly came through on that notion, and crew listened, wide-eyed, occasionally offering advice.

Jase had to be hearing everything, two-sided jumble, atevi and human. His skin had a decided pallor, exhaustion, if not the situation itself.

He listened.

And took his handheld and pocketed it. "Mr. Kaplan. Mr. Polano."

"Sir," came from both.

"Reasonable comforts for these men. Unauthorized personnel, clear the area. Nand' dowager." A little bow to Ilisidi, who, with Cajeiri, had been listening to Banichi and Cenedi with considerable interest. "Mr. Cameron. Same request. I'll see you in my office, Mr. Cameron, if you will."

Jase looked white as the proverbial sheet. Crew didn't argue any point of it. Bren translated the request: "One believes the ship-aiji has reached a point of extreme fatigue, nandi, and wishes to withdraw."

"With great appreciation for the dowager's intervention," Jase said with a little bow. Weary as he was, court etiquette came back to him. But he retained the awareness simply to walk away, not ceding priority to Ilisidi, a ruler in his own domain.

"Go," Ilisidi said to Bren, with a little motion of her fingers.

While several Guild officers, having vied with one another in spilling what might be their station's inner secrets, hung at the gridwork watching Jase's departure. With alien presence and crew resentment both in their vicinity, their stares and their thoughts, too, following the ship's captain who went away in possession of all they'd said.

They looked worried. And that lent the most credibility to the information they'd given.

14

"**M**y picture's missing," Jase said indignantly, when Bren walked into his upstairs office. "Of all damned things for them to take."

"Galley," Bren said. And dropped into a chair. "I nabbed it."

Jase gave a shaky sigh. "I'll want it back."

"You're done in, Jase. Get some rest. Turn things over at least for two hours, while we analyze what we've got."

"I can't let the dowager take independent action."

"*You've* dissuaded her. Ship-aiji, she says. She accepts that notion. But in the way of things, if you have atevi allies, they're going to act where it seems logical. We have to face the possibility we won't get Sabin back. We *might* even have a worse scenario, that Sabin completely levels with the Guild and sells us out. The dowager wanted to know whether you can lead. I think she's satisfied."

Fatigue showed in the tremor of Jase's fingers as they ran over the desk surface. "I wish I was."

"Get some rest, Jase, dammit. Take a pill, if that's what it takes. I wouldn't like to predict our situation without a strong hand at the helm—so to speak, Jase. I truly wouldn't. And you're it."

"We know there's one alien ship out in the dark," Jase said. "For all we know—there could be another.

Or three or four. We know what we see. In my mind—and I don't wholly trust my mind at the moment—agreement with them isn't inconsequential here. Whether or not Sabin doublecrosses us, she doesn't need to tell the station what the aliens out there want—not if they've been holding a hostage. The hostage becomes a bargaining piece, right along with the fuel. And Banichi's talking about getting to him. Is that the deal?"

"About that, about the fuel."

"Our technicians aren't sure about that lock. They're studying the problem."

"So what are our options?"

Jase rocked back in his chair, thinking, it was clear. His eyes were red. His voice had gotten a ragged edge. "Our options are to sit here not fueling, not taking on passengers, and hoping the station's hostage keeps the situation stable, or to give the situation a shove."

"In what way?"

"Make life harder for the Guild. Put pressure on them to fuel this ship. Becker says the population's about seventeen thousand—more than we thought. I hope he's telling the truth. It'll be tight, but we can handle that number."

"Three things lend the Guild hope of holding out. Their control of the fuel. Us. And their hostage."

"Four things. Their absolute control of what the station population knows. If they didn't have the hostage, they'd have to fear the aliens. If they had to fear the aliens, they'd still have the fuel, and they'd have us—assuming we'd fight to protect them. They're sure of that. But if they lose their lock on information—that's serious. If they lose that, they lose the people."

"And the station goes catastrophic in a matter of hours. *With* the fuel."

"And the machinery to deliver it. If they lose control—things become a lot more dangerous. Everything becomes a lot more dangerous." A tremor of fatigue came into Jase's voice. "If we try to come in on station communications to tell the truth, their technicians can stop us cold. Anybody aboard who actually got the information, they'd tag before he spread it far." A little rock backward in the chair. "They've got tech on their side, in that regard. But I've been thinking. There's high tech, and there's low tech. And *your* on-board supplies include paper."

True. The ship didn't regularly use that precious downworld item. Reunion wouldn't. Atevi society, however—proper atevi society—ran on it. Paper. Wax. Seals, ribbons, everything proper as proper could be.

"Handbills," Bren said, catching the glimmer of Jase's idea.

"Handbills," Jase said.

"If we do that—they'll mob the accesses. And we can't tell honest stationers from Guild enforcers."

"They can't mob us. We're not hard-docked. Boarders will have to come up the tube, with all that means."

"No gravity and no heat. If we *don't* open fast, they'll die."

"They also can't come at us in huge numbers. They have to board by lift-loads, and go where our lift system delivers them: the tether-tube is linked to the number one airlock. Ten at a time's its limit, and we can override the internal lift buttons."

"So you're planning to do it."

"I'm considering it as an option. I'll write the handbills. I know the culture. I take it Banichi has an idea of his own."

"Somewhat down your path. Getting our hands on

this hostage. Knocking one pillar out from under their fantasy of safety. Safeguarding this individual before something happens to him."

Jase nodded slowly.

"How we're to do this," Bren said, "I don't know."

"I'll hear it when you do."

"Meanwhile—get some sleep. Hear me?"

"In your grand plan to get hands on the hostage," Jase said in a thread of a voice, "I take it you plan for atevi to execute this operation. And what happens when they're spotted? This station is armed and wired for alien intrusion. Your people will be in danger from the stationers. And you'll scare hell out of the people we want to talk into boarding the ship."

"Both are problems. Maybe your handbills ought to just tell the truth. How's that for a concept?"

"God. Truth. Where is truth in this mess? I'm not even sure I'm doing the right thing."

"Get some sleep. Get some *sleep,* Jase."

"The captain's missing. Banichi wants to take the station. How in God's name do I sleep?"

"Get a *pill* and lie flat. Do it, Jase, dammit! Let your staff rest. *Trust* your crew. Trust us, that we're not going to pull something outrageous without consulting. We're going to win this thing."

Jase looked at him. "Tell me how we convince near twenty thousand scared people to trust us when they come face to face with the atevi Assassins' Guild."

"You're on the ocean. Your boat goes down. You see a floating piece of wood. You swim for it. If your worst enemy spots it, too, you'll share that bit of wood. Instinct. Far as we are from the earth of humans, we'll do it. Atevi do it. It's one of those little items we have in common."

"You suppose those aliens out there have the same instinct?"

"May well. When the water rises and the world goes under, not just anybody, anything else *alive* becomes your ally."

"I'm not sure I trust your planet-born notions."

"Get some sleep," Bren said, and got up to leave.

"I want my picture back," Jase said.

"Cook has it. I'll get it myself."

"I'll send down for it," Jase said. "Get. Go. Do anything you can."

He left. Left a man who, on the whole, had rather be fishing, and wanted nothing more than that for himself for the rest of his life.

But fate, and Ramirez, and Tabini-aiji, had had other designs.

He walked the corridor behind the bridge, talking to his pocket comm, giving particular instructions, already making particular requests.

"Rani-ji, I shall need the paper stores. Jase will have a text for us to print, at least five hundred copies." He recalled, curiously, that five-deck had the only hard-print facility on the ship. Jase had known how to write longhand when he dropped onto the world, but nine-tenths of literate ship's crew had had to learn how to write coherent words on a tablet when they first saw pen and paper. Read, no problem: dictate well-constructed memos, yes. But they couldn't write; had never seen paper or written the alphabet by hand. Alpha and the crew had existed across that broad a gulf of experience—there was no shorthand explanation for the differences between Mospheirans and ship's crew.

And twenty-odd of the atevi Assassins' Guild were going to scare common sense out of the populace unless there was some immediate, visible reassurance to station that they were on the side of the angels. This was an orbiting nation that couldn't fly; that universally read and couldn't write; that knew gravity, but not a sunrise. That panicked at the flash of light and dark in the leaves of trees. Certain subtexts were unpredictibly lost when fear took over.

Someone had to make clear that atevi presence was there to help them. Someone had to demonstrate human cooperation with atevi. Seeing, in a very real sense, was believing.

And he had a clammy-cold notion where the paidhi's job had to lie in this one.

15

Jase, one hoped, was finally asleep, as Bren sat with his own bodyguard, his own staff, in the dining room, with his computer, with a pot of tea and a plate of wafers, and a number of pieces of printout littering the broad dining table.

"One has exhausted talk, nadiin-ji, where this Braddock-aiji is concerned. And that we have lost touch with Sabin seems no accident. Her departure left the ship with no skilled operatives, few that know anything of self-defense, this being a closely related clan, unused to internal threat. So Jase has no choice but appeal to five-deck."

"Does he then conclude," Banichi asked, "that Sabin-aiji is lost?"

"He is by no means sure." Bren had his own doubts of that situation, and accurate translation to an atevi hearer was by no means easy. Aijiin had no man'chi. It all flowed upward. And that a leader could desert her own followers was a very strange notion. "She may have acted on her own, against the Guild. Certainly she was aware that she was taking most of our protection with her—except atevi. And she took our one known traitor—if traitor he was, to her. Neither Jase nor I know whether she meant to protect Jase from Jenrette, or Jenrette from Jase."

"Perhaps," Jago ventured, "she may not have rushed

blindly into whatever trap they may have laid for her. She never seemed a fool. Perhaps she thought she took enough force to seize control of the station center; but why, then, take Jenrette?"

"That answer must be lost in the minds of shipfolk, nadiin-ji. A Mospheiran human utterly fails to understand it."

"Perhaps she did confide in Jase," Banichi suggested darkly.

"Even so, even with his strongest promise to keep such a secret—I can hardly believe he would keep it from me. And she would have known that, too." He thought on the matter of Sabin's intentions twice and three times and came to the same conclusion. "Either she betrayed us outright, in which case I would expect her to contact us, or she took Jenrette because she wanted his help, or his information. I think she may have intended some covert action of her own, yet to develop—perhaps something so simple as spreading information among the general populace; but more likely attempting to infiltrate critical systems."

"The fuel port," Banichi said, "and communications."

"Both likely."

"Asking no help from us," Jago said. "This seems likely, in Sabin-aiji."

"Risking failure," Banichi said. "We should take this station, Bren-ji. We need not run it, only evacuate it."

Bren's heart beat faster. And he couldn't say no to the outrageous notion.

"If we open our doors," Jago said, "we can evacuate it. But we lose our ability to maneuver this ship."

"Even so," Bren said. "And there remains the Archive, that we came here to remove."

"We can reach the command center through the

accesses," Banichi said, "and take that during the general confusion. We may find Sabin-aiji, if she should be inclined to be found. The ship, so I hear, can manage the fueling with its own personnel. Gin-aiji can pursue that. Take the command center, free this hostage this Guild retains, and pay our due to the foreign ship, all in one. The staff has every confidence the paidhi-aiji can negotiate, at that point, with all parties."

Dizzying prospect. On one level it was what he wanted to hear. He wanted to believe it was reasonable, and possible; and he hadn't prompted it. He had no doubt at all that Banichi had a clear vision how this could work, and how they could move quickly enough to assure they could refuel before a cascade of systems failures took the station down in an evacuation—if they were fast, if they supported key systems, Banichi clearly thought they could do it. And if they got to the command center and took Braddock, they could take everything at once.

Banichi could be right, and he knew he himself was notoriously wrong when it came to inserting his own plans in Banichi's area of expertise—but—

But—he had his doubts. Sane doubts. Doubts that had to be laid out.

"Yet, Banichi-ji," he said, "one fears taking on too much. If we should proceed too quickly, if we should fail to manage Central, being as few as we are—if this ship and its pilots should come under orders of this Braddock-aiji, or if the station should fall to that foreign ship—any of these events would lead to terrible outcomes: hostile action against that ship out there, wider provocations that might involve the world we came to protect." Damn, Banichi was always right. He had a most terrible foreboding about arguing with Banichi's advice, and more than anything, feared he erred by timidity. "If, on the other hand, nadiin-ji, we take this prisoner into our hands, before they realize that we can penetrate the station, then we take away their source of confidence that they can hold that foreign ship from attacking."

Banichi and Jago considered a breath or two. "Will this not unite them in resistence?" Jago asked.

"It will increase doubt toward Braddock." It was all soft-tissue estimation, the paidhi's word about human behavior, versus what atevi might do under similar circumstances; and it gave him no confidence at all that he could make no firm predictions. "I think it likely, at least."

"Will they not hold the fuel," Banichi said, "to counter our leaving with the hostage?"

"We *can* leave with the hostage, Banichi-ji. We can reach that ship in a small craft, if we have no other choice. And we can make it clear to the station population that we are here to take them to safety. We have not yet offered them boarding—not that we can rely on them having heard from Braddock."

"Shall we then tell them?" Jago asked.

"Jase has such a plan. Pamphlets."

"We pass out brochures?" Banichi asked, incredulous. "Like a holiday?"

Simply put, it sounded chancy. "Jase believes he can compose a compelling message."

Banichi leaned back from the table, simply contemplating the matter. Then: "So we take this prisoner. And distribute brochures. And perhaps we shall find Sabin-aiji and find out her intentions. There are very many pieces to this plan."

"And I shall go with you."

"*No,* Bren-ji."

"Absolutely necessary. I can walk up to humans and

wish them good day. *You* are far more conspicuous, nadiin-ji."

"He has a point," Jago said. "If these humans threaten us, we might hesitate to shoot them; but if Bren-ji is with us, we shall have no hesitation."

He had lived long enough among atevi that he had no difficulty following Jago's reasoning. There was a basic logic in it, instinctive protection of their household, with which he found no inclination to argue.

"So we shall have these brochures," Banichi said, "which we shall print, which will bring humans rushing to our doors. But will the Guild administration then arrive at our doors begging admittance, Bren-ji?"

"They will not. One believes they will hold out to the very last. *Then* we may need your plan to take Central, nadiin-ji."

"We should call Gin-aiji," Banichi said. Gin was their ultimate authority on systems.

"We shall need to inform Jase," Bren said.

"And Cenedi," Jago said.

So they sent the requisite messages, and informed Cenedi, who informed the dowager.

Whose reaction was far more moderate than one expected. "Shall we have television of it?" Cajeiri was reported to have asked.

In fact, there would be television, if they could manage it, but not for Cajeiri's delight.

Gin arrived, herself having caught a little precious sleep. The table was already paved with their own version of station plans and schematics, but Gin brought a schematic she and her engineers had marked up.

"There *are* access ports from the outside," Bren asked her. "Just as at Alpha."

"Damned inconvenient for repair crews if there

weren't," Gin said, and called up specifics of the area Becker and party had named to Jase.

The diagrams looked as innocuous and common as any other area of the station, which looked like Alpha: Bren knew, having translated a stultifying quantity of the technical manuals and the building plans.

"They may have modified this entire area for greater security," Banichi observed, pointing to a section door. "Here would be a likely control point, a minimum of fuss."

"Remembering, nadi," Bren said, "that they have had six years to fear that that ship might send a force in to rescue this person. Station may have laid traps."

"Not, however," Jago said, "greatly clever ones—if one may judge by Becker. But we should seek a means to distract attention."

Comforting thought.

"A good use for *roboti*," Banichi said.

"To draw fire with my robots?" Gin cried, when that found full translation.

"A small one," Banichi said. "A minor one. We can surely spare one to good use."

Gin considered, and a grim light was in her eye. "One," she said, holding up a finger like a merchant in a market. "One."

It ran like that. Gin laid her plans and went off to estimate how they could best annoy station security. Banichi and Jago and Cenedi went to estimate what items might be both portable and useful.

Therein the paidhi had no usefulness at all, having only the most rudimentary notion how to get into an electronic lock or how to defeat security closure on a section door . . . the paidhi only hoped to lie down in his own quarters, draw a few slow breaths, and perhaps to catch one of those hours of sleep he'd lost.

Prospect of a rash intrusion onto station and the

presence of station agents aboard, however inclined to change their views—that didn't make for restful thoughts. Banichi could sleep anywhere, on cue. He didn't have that skill.

And what if he dropped a stitch, and they ran into a trap?

What if they were killed attempting this, and the ship had to do without him, and explain matters to that alien craft—explain they'd tried, and explain to an angry and mistrustful set of strangers enough plausible excuses to gain the ship's release?

Sleep evaporated. He got up, found paper and pen in his desk, and began sketching, in their dot-pattern code, an explanation of their mission. Of—grim thought—mission failure. Of request for a meeting with ship's personnel. Jase would have to manage it, if it came to that, but Jase, of all others, understood. Gin halfway did. She would help. The dowager would help. It wasn't as if he was leaving Jase without resources.

More dot-patterns: the ship taking on passengers. The ship mining the area for fuel. The ship leaving the system. The ship conducting talks with the alien craft. The ship engaging in trade—a closeness they never sought, but might have to have.

Trying to imagine all the contingencies Jase might have to deal with, trying to reach across space and time to gather every stray possibility, was a curious enterprise. He tried to think of things. He tried to create a basic vocabulary of interactions: communicating the difference between coming and going to a foreigner who shared one's planet was hard enough. Communicating that useful distinction to a species that might only have a single word for movement or that might have a dozen more specific words—or, God help them, communicate in something other than nouns and verbs—was no walk on the beach. Go and come, give and get, infelicitous pairs of concepts that had distressed atevi at first glance, for no reason at all to human senses, and disturbing all sense of balance in atevi nerves. Fingernails on a blackboard, continual and unintended in all early efforts.

But civilized entities—if one had a right to expect any behavior out of a species that had gotten off its own planet—ought to have some concept that the universe was wide, that differences were likely, and that shooting as a first response would ultimately lead one to ruin.

Human and atevi together, he said in his dots. Human and atevi making agreements, taking this voyage, rescuing people from station. Human and atevi together meeting alien species in peace.

He tried.

He wrote a note to Tabini: *Aiji-ma, I am undertaking a mission aboard the station which involves risk, but which I have persuaded my bodyguard is necessary. Should this account cease, I have misjudged my abilities and apologize.*

To his brother: *Toby, the station has an alien prisoner we've got to pry out of there, and since the captain took all the security with her, atevi security is going to have to do this job, and they can't do it without someone to translate instructions. I'm the one that can do that. Jase would probably volunteer, but he's got to get this ship home, so there we are. If this letter ends here, it didn't work as well as I hoped. Love you, brother.*

To his staff, a paper note: *Thank you for the comfort you have provided. Should this mission fail, take all my effects to Jase, and then pursue your own man'chi.*

To Jase. Who would know where to bestow various letters, *Give the dowager a copy of everything, and a translation where appropriate. If you get this, my last*

*idea was a bad one. What more can I say? You're my
other brother. I'd say something to embarrass us both,
but I'm hoping like everything I get to erase this bit.*

He sent the dot-code up to Kaplan, by Jeladi and
one of Gin's engineers, with instructions not to wake
Jase, if Jase had gotten to sleep.

Then he undressed to sleep, that most elusive of
chances, feeling the sheets against his skin, watching
through slit eyes the living green curtain of Sandra
Johnson's plants—it always amazed him, how the
plants grew during their transits, as if they were mad
to live, mad to survive. Or took some benefit from
what reduced the wits of mobile creatures. He
watched the air from the duct stir the streamers and
the leaves, artificial wind in a steel world. Fluid moved
in their veins and simple light and nutrients let their
cells divide. A wondrous invention of planets.

So were they.

So was that other packet of life that met out here,
this far from other living cells. And they wanted to
shoot one another? Unacceptable. Entirely unacceptable. The lord of the heavens refused to take that
answer.

In that light, the whole universe seemed surreal, beyond easy belief, relative to those gently moving
fronds. One reality wasn't the other, and one found it
distractingly easy to slip into that green world. Here,
a stubborn set of human beings, and maybe some alien
hard-heads as well, had made a botch of what should
have been a simple situation—oh, hello. Anyone
home? Your estate? Do excuse me. I didn't realize
I'd crossed your boundary. And: Are you a neighbor
or a traveler? Do step in for tea.

Well, the dowager had done that, and half-killed
him. But he never believed that was an accident, and
the dowager knew, and he knew, and on that basis

they got along in ways that astonished the dowager's enemies, and his. God, he loved her.

Life itself. Dared one think that in this void where life was rare, life was bond enough, that a couple of reasonable entities might say they'd had their encounter, they both understood the limits, and could get along?

He actually slept. He realized that when he waked and felt Jago stir—he'd never felt her arrival. He'd slept so hard that getting his wits about him again required a few breaths, then a search for bits and pieces of the plan they'd made and what he had to do.

He had to call up and find out Jase's situation, and whether Jase approved. That was at the head of the list. But he hesitated to move, knowing he'd wake Jago at his stealthy best. So he lay there and rehearsed plans until she stirred.

"Good morning," he said—no endearments to confuse the issue. Jago would only brush them off with: We have business, Bren-ji.

So they did. And a light was blinking on the message center. He dragged his dressing-robe about him and punched the button for a recorded message.

"Bren." Jase's voice. "I understand your reasoning. All of you—if you need anything—ask. I've sent down the text for the fliers. I've sent down a key. My key. Note—I've searched the premises and can't turn up Sabin's or Ramirez's, and I did it with my key. So either I don't know where to look or Ramirez's key is with Sabin or with Ogun. I'm approving Gin's move and yours, and moving our own personnel into position for the duration. We're ready. Baji-naji, Bren-ji."

So it was. Fortune and chance. The wiggle-room in a rigid universe. And possession of the key to the ship, the station, anything humans out here would value. "Baji-naji," he muttered to himself, and took a quick shower, Jago having already departed, bent on what she would call business at hand.

And with staff's help, it was back into the blue sweater and plain trousers and jacket, hair in a plain, tight pigtail under the collar.

"Nandi." Bindanda quietly slipped Bren a simple card. "From Jase-aiji, which he avows is very important."

"It is, Danda-ji."

"And this, nandi," Narani said, offering his pistol, which he took, no question in this, intending no hesitation to use it. He tucked that into his right jacket pocket.

Then Jeladi gave him a cloth-wrapped bundle which proved to be quite heavy, and a glance proved the contents—*brochures,* Banichi had translated it, and brochures there were: *illustrated* brochures, beautifully printed, a sunset by the sea, the north shore of Mospheira—Mt. Adams and a ski resort, with Jase's— one assumed—description: Safe Haven; and text below, which gave details of their mission and instructions for boarding, with a photo of a representative cabin—Gin's, as happened. Below that, it said: Comfort and Safety. Captions, actually appropriate to the pictures, and Gin's hand somewhere in the mix.

"Three hundred more we have sent to the ship-aiji, nandi. One hopes they suffice."

"Very fine, very fine, nadi-ji." He found a place inside his jacket for a dozen brochures, and gave a little bow to the non-combatants of his staff. "Extraordinary accomplishment, nadiin-ji."

"Fortunately posed, one humbly hopes, nandi. One hopes the illustrations convey only desirable elements."

"Rani-ji, indeed, and my compliments."

He tucked the packet under his arm, bowed, and

went out into the corridor, where Jago and Banichi were in the last stages of preparation, black leather and non-reflective black plastics, and no few pieces of armament, besides breathing-masks and a black bag of gear.

"Gin-nandi is ready with her mission," Banichi reported. "Shall we carry the packet, nandi?"

He yielded it, and Jago put the brochures into the bag, while he patted his pocket to be absolutely sure of Jase's precious key.

"Cenedi," Banichi said, "will run the security station for the duration, paidhi-ji." Rare. They couldn't ask for better than that. "Jase-aiji has lent his key?"

"I have it."

"He has also lent a pilot. And Gin-aiji promises assistance. We shall go down to the life pods, Bren-ji, and cross to number 80 access, which is next to the section Becker-nadi indicated."

"Excellent." He hadn't tracked such operational details: he trusted Banichi for those, and any help they could get came welcome, in his opinion. They were trusting the word of a traitor; and if Banichi had been arranging pilots and plans, Jase had been the only translator awake—which said how much sleep Jase had gotten, and how much Banichi himself had gotten. The air felt colder and colder, a chill coming on, bringing him almost to the point of shivers, but Jago had zipped up the bag and slung it to her shoulder, and they were off down the corridor at what atevi called a brisk pace, and what humans called a hurry.

Going down to the pods. A pilot, not the starship sort, but qualified to run station-tenders and such. And Gin had to have one of her robots in action, or another pod. Details floated around him in a null-g soup of items and lists turned into substance full of surprises, details unreal to him. Their operations up to this point had been shaping pieces of a plan, a list of things that had to be cleared out of the way, not an inclusive list, but his staff had gathered up things he had had no skill to put together, and gotten Jase and Gin involved. Now they headed down the corridor with a bag of guns and brochures and cutting tools.

No begging off at this point. No changing directions. Haste was written all over the operation—haste, on little rest and less sleep, and people of unknown number and disposition on the station, and entities of uncertain patience expecting performance on promises. He recalled a dusty brown hillside near Malguri, smoke and, overhead, the pulse of an open-cockpit plane dropping bottle-bombs.

From there, to this, light-speed; and maybe things no more subtle than the bottle-bombs. Guns. Explosives. God, he hoped that key worked as advertised.

And minimal communications. Television, which would have delighted Cajeiri, was not possible. Transmissions of any kind became a liability, to be rationed out, used in case they had to report disaster and alert Cenedi to a cascading problem.

Three of the dowager's young men met them at the section end and simply fell in with them, young men carrying small bundles, equipped with guns and knives and spare ammunition in appalling quantity. Three of them and three of the dowager's, auspicious numbers; but they were now six, his nerves informed him—*six*, counting himself. Infelicitous six hit the pit of his stomach as they reached the end of the corridor. Six was an impossible number for the mission. It wasn't the end of the plan, he was instantly convinced of it; and as they passed the section door, out to the small area, indeed, one of Gin's staff met them—Barnhart, it was, with a packet under his arm and a com unit tacked to his jacket.

Fortunate seven, now: Gin's promised assistance took the form of one of her engineers in the party, to read the charts, if nothing else, to solve technical glitches having to do with human logic and human traps.

"Mr. Cameron." Barnhart gave a little bow at the lift, Mospheiran and having no trouble falling in with atevi habits. "Honored to be here."

"Mr. Barnhart. Welcome in."

They were a comforting number as they bundled themselves inside the lift—down, was the direction this time, relative down from the ship's metal heart, down where gravity grew uncertain and then left them prey to inertia of the car itself. Bren clutched the safety bar, running a last-minute check in his own mind of all the things he'd had to do, the notes he'd had to leave—had he missed any? Late to be adding anything. But it distracted him from utter panic.

Down to cold, ungravitied places—cold stung the skin, cold so bitter it felt like heat as the lift let them out facing a blank wall and a sign. *Emergency Evac 12*, it said, and *Lifepod*, with overlapping yellow arrows. Other signs saying *pressure hazard* and *volatiles present.*

They'd had their drills. He knew he was to follow the internal corridors to Lifepod 2, which this wasn't. This was somewhere down on the ship's cargo-carrying belly, where five-deck didn't go, in drills. And this pod might not have opened in the last three hundred years, since Taylor's age—it bore the patina of mechanical age, the cold surface other gloved fingers had recently touched, and left marks in the frost their breath recoated.

Now the pod hatch opened and *he* went through that portal, with five atevi and a Mospheiran engineer, into a dim, cold interior where atevi had to duck their heads. Metal walls seemed to drink in light and not give it up. Drifting plastic webs—he belatedly realized these were the evacuation pod's safety restraints for far more persons than their number. The hatch shut, and two ship's crewmen, shadowy and underlit in LEDs, moved beyond the webbing. Nine for the transit, he said to himself. Nine, fortunate as seven, thrice three. Jase's men. Jase's invisible, numbers-reckoning hand on this mission that they'd laid out: Jase wouldn't let atevi go out with eight.

Across a dark leap, not on the mast, but on the station cylinder itself, on the edge of the damaged section, was service port 80, a number one hoped to attribute to station administration and not to their effort.

Gin thought they could do it because, she said, there weren't many defenses on the inside of the station's curve and from that angle; and because, second point, lifepods had automated firesafe signals that were supposed to protect them from station trim jets and other hull-vicinity hazards—Gin swore that signal would protect them from anything more lethal the station defenses emitted on automated targeting. A lifepod was, in ship's and station's systems, always sacrosanct.

"Will they not think of this?" Jago had asked during their planning session with Gin. Depend on it, atevi security, if they were in charge of the station, would have had a list of security permissions and they would have consulted it and reviewed such weaknesses when their opposition changed from alien to virtually internal, moreover, likely armed with a builder's key . . . *would* station not have thought? Would they not have done something to counter?

They *would* do something sooner or later, which made the bearer of that key say, quietly, to his companions: "Nadiin-ji, Jase's key is in my right pocket."

In case he were lying on the floor unconscious or worse.

"One hears, Bren-ji," Jago said quietly.

Gin simultaneously would make a feint at the fuel port. And Jase's security meant simultaneously, and for real, to secure the personnel tube associated with the tether. To maintain that post, they would have to maintain hard-suited personnel constantly on duty from now on through general boarding; but one hoped it wouldn't be that long.

"We're ready any time, sir," the pilot said.

"They report themselves ready, nadiin," he said. Null-g was uncharacteristically making him sick. Or it was raw fear unsettling his stomach.

"Go," Banichi said in Mosphei'. Just that. *Go.* Banichi was de facto running this operation, which was the greatest comfort in the situation.

"Go," Bren confirmed for the pilot. While *Oh, my God,* was the whiteout thought that streamed through his head as switches flipped, lights blinked and grapples thumped loose. He hated shooting. He hated being shot at ever so much worse.

Oh, my God. As he seized a grip on the webbing and the light inside the pod went inauspicious red.

They didn't have a view, but they now had a definite floor—which, after a gentle shove and a deafening rumble like a train on a track, shifted again abruptly. A rail had indeed guided their release. Now they launched free, under full power.

He hadn't taken firm enough hold. He fought to keep his handhold on the bar, felt his gloved fingers losing his grip; but a strong atevi arm encircled his waist and held him. The floor rotated, began to be back *there*, the aft bulkhead, such as it was; but his guardian held him fast.

He wasn't heroic. He was a maker of dictionaries.

And he shivered in a cold far more than he'd bargained for. He daren't muster coherent conversation during this transit in which, baji-naji, his bodyguard had to have other things than inane chatter on their minds—their objective, and getting inside. Getting to that point was all up to Jase's two men, now, the skill to home this thing in on a moving station and the luck not to get them shot at or smash them to bits on some antenna or other ephemeral projection that might not be in the plans.

Gin swore there was a way in. Gin swore this pod could limpet itself to any kind of hatch and establish a secure seal—a seal which still had to be there when they got *back* from their mission with whatever prize they'd managed to lay hands on. The pod had to be there, or it was going to be embarrassing getting back to the ship—Excuse me, sir, can you point out a corridor which will lead us to the core? We seem to have lost our way . . .

"It's working very well, Bren-ji," Jago said: it was Jago holding him.

"One has every confidence." His teeth chattered from the cold. They didn't have suits. They couldn't use their equipment from suits and suits, even on humans, would say to anyone they met, *invader,* which wouldn't help at all. So they took their risk of vacuum, and glided in their pressurized bubble, weightless now, emitting only that pod signal, down into the heart of the damaged station's ring, and across. It seemed to take forever.

"Barnhart-nadi," Banichi said.

"Yes." Passable Ragi, that *yes*.

"Bren-nandi, say to Barnhart that if we come under fire, he will keep always to your left."

"Yes," Bren said, and relayed that vitally important instruction, which effort temporarily kept his teeth from chattering. If Barnhart was to his left, he noted, that put him to Jago's left—never on his security's right hand. Not in this.

Not since a certain hillside in Malguri's district, in the faraway east. Not since the day he'd learned what it was to get afoul of his own security. If he strayed out of order, his security would kill themselves trying to get to him. Their atevi instincts would send them toward him. All planning took that into account.

But the initial foray was his. All his.

The pod underwent an unplanned course correction, and his stomach tried to rise up his throat. Not auspicious, not auspicious, his brain insisted. He had to do better than this. He concentrated on that proposition, noting, by the glare of lights now green, that Barnhart was having no easier journey, while—God, did *nothing* bother atevi stomachs?

But whatever they had had to miss, they had missed. It was Jase's crew flying this thing. And somewhere— somewhere behind them—above them, relative to station—Jase was not idle. Jase would be talking to Guild authorities, pretending to negotiate the release of Becker and his men, keeping Guild officials as busy as he could. Meanwhile Gin did something involving a far smaller miner craft—while ship's crew attempted a simple descent to the mast, hard-suited and armed to the teeth in case station had thought it was going to take over that tube and control access to the ship.

It was more than guns that batch would have, however. It would be another batch of brochures, which were by now from Jase's office to that team's hands.

The brochures had said, among other things his eye had glossed past, in one desperate glance: *Reunion Station is disbanded by order of Captains' Council.*

All station citizens, administrative elements, and crew: boarding is imminent for Alpha Colony, where we have a longstanding, peaceful arrangement with natives of that planet. Expect mutual protection in an atmosphere of coöperation and economic prosperity.

Atevi were in there, buried in the fine print.

Baggage limit: 20 kilos per adult, 4 kilos per child, dimensions of standard duffle, exceptions granted for uncommon cause. Baggage must be yielded to security on arrival. Weapons must be declared and placed in ship's armory . . .

It went on into more specifics for evacuation of medical facilities, for children and elderly, and the use of the safety cable in the tube.

It offered people from deep space and curved metal horizons a sunset on the beach and a ski resort, and one had to recall how Jase, first landing, had had trouble looking at a flat horizon, and nearly lost his supper in a fast-moving vehicle. Among other details, the Council of Captains was locally down to one captain, if Sabin didn't turn up, and Alpha Colony hadn't existed for centuries as Alpha Colony, but it was the sort of thing the Reunioners would expect to hear.

The pod underwent more readjustments, then a sudden shove from the engines that taxed even Jago's strength to hold him. Bren clenched his teeth, trying not to think anything was wrong, trying to think of the brochure, not the arm cutting off his wind.

It went on, and on. *What are they doing up front?* he wanted to ask, if he had any air. *Are we in trouble?* But he'd long since learned not to chatter at people doing what they had to do, especially if it was going wrong. He clenched his teeth, breathed shallowly, and tried to keep his wits about him.

If somehow some armament didn't like the firesafe signal the pod emitted, and wanted to blow them to little agitated atoms . . .

Toby, he'd write, if he had the chance, *you won't*

believe where I'm going. You won't believe what we're doing. What we're hoping to do. We're absolutely crazy. There might have been a better plan than this . . .

Big bump. Jago nearly lost him from her grip.

Clang. Bang. Bump-scrape-clang. He gritted his teeth while the pod skidded over some surface it should be able to grab. God, they'd missed their grapple.

Thump-clang.

Jolt.

Whine.

"We're at the port," the pilot reported breathlessly. *Thank God, thank God, thank God.*

The whining kept up. And kept up. The whole pod seemed queasy in its attachment—but attached. Something had gone wrong, he was sure the pilots had improvised—but they had *weight.* His feet were on the floor again, which meant they'd reached a cylinder surface, and Jago let him go. She made a rapid check of her gear, as Banichi and Cenedi's men did, as Barnhart checked his pockets and his coat, and he took the cue himself: he had the gun still in his right pocket, despite the jolt, that, and the pocket com in his left. Brochures securely inside his coat.

The whining stopped. The pilot and co-pilot crawled out of their seats and began working at the forward port, pulled it back, and, dyed with blinking green light, showed them a metal wall, flame-blackened, a lot the worse for wear.

In the middle of that wall, a round port with a blinking green light in the middle of it, under lettering that said EPORT 81.

They'd missed number 80. They were at another access. How did *that* number match their numbers? Bren asked himself: was it up or down on the cylinder, and where were they?

The pilot and co-pilot opened the control cover, going for switches. There was a red handle. The co-pilot pulled it, and the whole surface of the door recessed rapidly.

White light came on, blinding, flooding their little pod.

Banichi and Jago went through, and Bren went, the rest of the mission behind them, through the open port, into a white-lit airlock.

"Good luck," the pilot wished the lot of them, and the door shut between. Banichi pushed a button and opened the door into Guild territory—a dimly lit engineering corridor that very happily had heat and light and air that didn't hurt. One could be ever so grateful for those basics. Bren personally was.

"This way," Barnhart said, and pointed with a gloved hand. They walked a considerable distance down that corridor, and the air by now didn't feel so warm.

But they reached a shut section door marked 80, which was where they were *supposed* to be, and an unfortified approach—far more luck than their skidding entry had forecast.

Bold as brass, Barnhart strolled in that direction, and Bren took a deep breath and got into the fore of the expedition as well, as far as a cross-corridor which was, to their vast relief, vacant. The pilot had stayed behind, keeping systems hot and waiting for them, but the co-pilot had tagged along with them. For a brief while they were to be infelicitous eight—disastrous eight, double infelicitous four. Only acquiring the prisoner could change those numbers to three of threes, the adventurously felicitous nine—God! The mind zigged and zagged in terror through superstition and operations—even his atevi bodyguard would call it nonsense, while their nerves twitched to it. At this point of the operation, felicitous numbers rested in accomplishing their mission. Jase's orders. Jase's sensitivity to atevi nerves. And now atevi lagged back and a handful of reasonable-looking humans, give or take the cold-area coats and gloves, had only to walk, calmly down the corridor, calmly, up to an ordinary lift, in the right section, the section they were supposed to be in.

Bren turned, gave a little nod and waited for atevi to join them and take up positions on either side of the door.

Then he stripped off the gloves, pocketed them, punched in a call—no need for the key—and waited for the lift.

The door opened. Empty. Not unexpectedly so. The lift system cycled people to sensible destinations, not detouring them through cold, dimly lit maintenance levels. People in cold, inconvenient spots had to wait while the lift system emptied a car.

"Nadiin," Bren said, first in, holding the door open, and Banichi, Jago, and the rest boarded and occupied the sides, atevi back against the walls, out of sight, humans to the center.

Barnhart input their destination. The lift rose. And rose. And rose.

And stopped.

The door opened. A single security officer faced them, not even yet expecting trouble as he walked in.

Bren grabbed his jacket and yanked him in. There was a yelp, the start of an outcry.

That stopped, if the struggle didn't. The car started up again.

They reached level four. And stopped. The door didn't open. The lift panel flashed a request for security clearance.

"Key," Barnhart said, and Bren put the keycard in.

The door opened tamely and without alarm. And while his key was in, Bren put the car into a maintenance hold, door open.

"Very poor," Jago said softly, "very poor provision." As they exited the lift.

They had one prisoner in the lift car, a slightly conscious and bruised prisoner. One of Cenedi's men remained with him. The rest of them moved out at a sedate pace, and without a word Bren took the lead, in a brightly lit, warm corridor, Barnhart beside him, the co-pilot close by. They were to make as soft an entry as they could into what their prisoners back on the ship told them was a detention area, creating as little fuss as possible.

Max security, Becker and his men had called it. Max security, as station understood the term. Jago thought it wouldn't be much. God, he hoped not.

Blind turn. And if they were getting close to occupied areas, it was the paidhi's turn to see, solo, what was down that hall. He gave a little tug at his slightly rumpled work jacket as he faced the corner. "Hang back," he said to Barnhart and the co-pilot, got a worried look back.

"Use great caution," Jago wished him, a whisper at his shoulder, "Bren-ji."

"One will do one's utmost, Jago-ji," he said. He pulled the com from his pocket, did a fast check of his shortrange communications, nothing so extensive as to reach the ship, and the answering flash said he had contact with his bodyguards.

He walked out, facing a sealed door, no guards in sight. Just very blank corridor on either hand, no designation on the door.

He used his key, locked the door open by means that gave as few signals to the system as possible, and walked ahead into an equally blank corridor, no doors, nothing but a left turn toward what his recollection of the diagrams said should be a main transverse corridor. He whistled tonelessly as he walked, not wishing to startle anyone around the next corner, and on inspiration, took one of the brochures from his jacket pocket—not that paper wouldn't be a phenomenon, but it posed its own puzzle to the eye, and distracted attention from the cut of his coat.

He walked around the bend, and saw a man at a desk, the image of men at desks in front of sealed doors everywhere in human civilization.

He walked up, whistling, preoccupied with his brochure.

"What's that?" the man at the desk asked him. And a second, closer look: "What department are you?"

"Technical." That explained almost anything, in Bren's experience. "You seen this thing?" Bren laid the brochure on his desk.

"Where did you get this?"

"Admin." That also answered everything.

The man handled the brochure cautiously, saw the pictures of beach and mountain. Opened it, gave it a scant glance, while Bren meditated simply hitting him on the head, but he was curious.

The man read, looked up, alarmed. "They're serious?"

"Very serious." He played it by ear. "Look, I'm supposed to estimate the prisoner's needs in this transfer."

"You have to talk to Madison. He's in charge. B corridor."

A name was helpful. But he couldn't leave this man unaccounted for. And he didn't know what to do with him. "Look," he said, improvising. "I've got to have a list."

"What list?"

"List, man. There's always a list, isn't there? Life requirements. That sort of thing. You're supposed to have one drawn up for me."

"I'm not supposed to have anything. That'll be Madison, that's what. I can call him."

Last thing he wanted. "Look, Madison's not in my instructions. *You* were supposed to have the list."

"I just sit at this door, man. I don't have any damned list!"

"Look, they swore up and down you were going to have it." He switched sides on the desk, drawing the man's eyes toward him, away from the corner where his staff waited. He put on a hangdog face. "Man, you're putting me in a hard place. *Shigai* said move on it."

There. Shigai wasn't a name. It was Ragi. And Banichi, and Jago arrived around the corner.

"Migod," Bren said, looking up.

The man turned his head. Fast. Bren pulled his own gun, as the man swung to look around—and made a dive for his intercom.

Bren grabbed his arm short of that button and held his gun right at eye level.

"No," Bren said. "Don't touch that button. I really wouldn't touch any button. They won't hurt you. I might."

Banichi and Jago arrived on the other side of the desk, and the man looked left and right, sweating.

"They're not from the same planet as the prisoner," Bren said. "They're from Alpha, matter of fact, same as I am. Same as he is." This, for Barnhart, who had stayed close to Banichi, along with the co-pilot. "And the brochure, let me tell you, is the truth. This station is being evacuated by order of the Captains' Council, and you've got a limited time to do it. Upper administration is being recalcitrant, not to the good of ordinary station folk. So we're seeing to the evacuation ourselves, trying to get all you good people onto the ship and lifted safely out of here before the attack comes."

"Attack."

"This station isn't going to exist in a few days. *We're* here to take you back to Alpha Colony, where it's safe, where there's an abundant, peaceful planet, and where you don't have an alien ship ready to come in here to get back this prisoner you claim to have. If we can have a little cooperation, here, I'll let you go. Then you and your family can go pack your belongings, advise your neighbors, and get yourselves off this station alive. That is, supposing we can get our ship fueled in time to get away from here. Which Mr. Braddock for some reason doesn't want us to do without following his regulations. Mr. Braddock has annoyed the aliens, lied to our senior captain, and otherwise made himself generally objectionable to us. Given the situation, and an irritated alien presence out there, we aren't in a patient mood. So decide what you're going to do."

It was not a pleasant sight, a truly scared man. But not a stupid man. He didn't move. He looked from him to Barnhart and the co-pilot, twice, and once, fearfully, at Banichi and company.

"Get up from the desk," Bren said. "You're quite safe. I'll send you where you'll *be* safe for the duration. I take it you have family who want to see you again. Just get up quietly. One of my associates will see you to safety."

"One of *them?* Who are *they?* What do they want?"

"The *legitimate* inhabitants at Alpha. As for what they want—after several hundred years of careful negotiation, they're our hosts, our allies, and on our side. Nadi-ji, escort this good gentleman to the lift car."

One of Cenedi's men, behind Banichi and Jago, took that request. "Kindly comply," that one said in Mosphei', certainly a surprise coming from the dowager's staff, and a greater surprise to their detainee, who had broken into a sweat.

"And *where* is this prisoner?" Bren asked.

The man looked at him as if he had the only life preserver.

"You're safe with him. Worry about *me,* and be very accurate. Where is the prisoner?"

"B," the man said. "B17." And helpfully pointed the direction B was supposed to be. "There's a restricted section. Three guards."

The Guild didn't seem to command the highest loyalty among the populace.

"And *who* is this Madison?"

"In charge of the prisoner. In charge of the section."

"This person says the prisoner resides in B17, and we may expect three more guards there." Bren gave a dismissive wave of his hand, quite calmly so—the dowager's gesture, he was disturbed to realize—but the mind was busy.

Cenedi's man took their anxious detainee back down the corridor toward the lift, there to join the unfortunate from the lower deck . . . a collection that might grow further, Bren thought desperately, and none of them the ones they wanted, while they were keeping a lift car out of the system longer and longer, which might soon raise questions from maintenance.

He gave a cursory glance to the man's abandoned console, read the story implicit in key wear, and looked down the corridor, reading signs like scuff on the floor tiles and the invisible signs of human handedness that confirmed to him that, yes, traffic did go through here, and key wear could almost tell him which keys the man used when people had valid authorizations.

No labels here. *That* ship-habit the station definitely had. But security was all soft.

He walked further, toward the door in question, and exchanged his gun for his keycard, trusting it more than the console. He was about to open it when he became aware of his bodyguard still in view, close to him.

"We may take the lead from here, nadi-ji," Banichi said.

"Not without casualties, nadi-ji. I insist. Stay back. Let me attempt this."

His security was not happy to wait. They had other armament ready. They were far enough in, and prepared to finesse it, as Banichi would say, from here on. But Banichi motioned his contingent back against the wall, into what concealment the section door frame offered, while he keyed the door open and locked it into position.

He and Barnhart and the co-pilot walked into a corridor that could be any stretch of small offices, no windows, nothing to indicate who was where, or that this was a high-security area. He counted doors. Ten.

First intersection of corridors. The habitual scuff marks in the corridor took a turn. Bren pulled a brochure out, sole precaution. And around that corner they faced a uniformed guard.

"Banichi," Bren said under his breath, to his electronics, "one armed man at a desk and a shut door." He kept walking, himself and Barnhart and the co-pilot, as if the guard himself, not the closed double door beyond, was their objective.

"Who are *you*?" the guard asked.

"Looking for Madison," Bren said, and laid the brochure on the desk. "Have you seen these things?"

The man took a split second to read the title and

look at the pictures. And looked up into a gun-muzzle—a weapon in the hands of a very scared paidhi-aiji who really, truly hoped his security would hurry so he and his two non-combatant allies wouldn't have to defend themselves. "Don't touch anything. Don't make a move."

The man considered carefully what to do with his hands. He was indeed wearing a gun.

"Read the paper," Barnhart suggested. "It explains what's important."

The guard looked down, opened it as if it had been a bomb. And looked up, alarmed at what he read—twice alarmed, as Banichi and Jago turned up silently.

The guard looked from Bren to them and very carefully didn't move a muscle.

"We're from Alpha," Bren said calmly, "and these are our neighbors, no relation to the people who blew a hole in your station. This station is in imminent danger, we're here to get the prisoner and evacuate the station as quickly and quietly as we can. Stay very still. We're going to remove the gun. You don't want to use it, anyway."

"Damn you!"

"Mind your tone. They don't speak much of our language. Be polite and smile at them."

"The hell!" The man moved to prevent Jago lifting the gun from his holster. Mistake. Jago took the arm instead, yanked him up straight out of his chair, and Banichi took the gun in a wink.

"Be still, sir," Banichi said in Mosphei', and the guard said not another word.

Bren moved on and inserted the keycard at the next door: *the* door, the hallway in the other direction showing an office-like door at the end.

The door didn't open. The builder's code didn't work. That wasn't supposed to happen.

"Code's not working," he said. "It must be a jury rig. Not on the system."

"Finesse will not suffice here," Banichi said in Ragi, and took a fistful of the guard's jacket. "Open the door."

The guard commendably refused.

Just as someone, an administrative sort, opened a side office door and blithely walked out into the situation.

Blinked, open-mouthed.

And ducked back. Other doors stayed shut. Jago walked down the short corridor, dragging the unhappy clerk with her, shoving small clear wedges into the small gap between door and mounting—assuring someone from the outside was going to have to release the occupant; but the alarm by now would go to Central.

"Gas," Banichi said, gun in hand, and Bren tugged the mask out from under his collar as the others did the same.

Banichi ripped the panel off the double door, clipped a line and attached a small switch, which quietly opened the door on a wide open area that suddenly, in Bren's recollection, matched their charts—he was thinking that and thinking he had better get himself to the fore, when Banichi tossed a grenade that went rolling down the hall.

A guard ran to grab it, and it blew out a cloud of gas and went on spewing, while the guard, a shadow among other shadows in the gas, doubled over. Jago and Banichi charged in. Bren ran. Man'chi, whatever impelled a sane human—he went in, gun in hand, desperate—skidded to a stop as Jago pitched another grenade, this one percussive, with a great deal of smoke, a shock that deafened human ears. Two human senses were impaired.

Sirens started. Red lights dyed the gas. They'd gone in as civilized individuals. They'd become invading, masked monsters. Guards, whose defenses hadn't included gas masks, were down and choking in front of a clear-walled enclosure that itself was filling with gas; and the yellow-clad figure caught inside that cube of slowly obscuring air, white-lit in the general haze of red, could have been a very stout, brownish-gray human in a baggy yellow coverall.

The occupant of that glass cage applied stocky dark-gray palms to the glass wall, pressed close, trying to discern the nature of the invaders. It had a broad, large-eyed face, heavy-jowled, heavy-browed. All of that, Bren saw at first blink, before Jago blew the clear plastic door in, and the yellow-clad alien turned away to face intrusion.

Then the alien turned full circle, as if seeking some other route of escape—or expecting to die by the hands of some oddly composed lynch mob.

Banichi invaded the cell, seized the alien's massive arms and hauled the alien toward the shattered wall. Banichi had brought a spare mask. He whipped it out of his jacket and pressed it over the alien's mouth, and at that point the alien stopped fighting, held the mask in place with his own hands and, perhaps conceiving of safety, cooperated in the rescue, accompanying Banichi, trying to keep up with a wider stride.

Jago stood with rifle ready to provide covering fire, and as they brought the alien past, Jago folded their expedition inward and began a fast retreat. Bren tried to observe that plan, grabbed Barnhart by the arm as they reached their rear guard, accounting for the co-pilot: he meant to get to the fore again, but Jago took the lead and Banichi dragged the rescuee along with them.

Cenedi's man stayed rear guard. Bren didn't look

back, except to be sure that all their company was retreating with them, a rush back toward clear air, back past rows of—thank God—closed office doors, where people were likely phoning for help, but nothing but another builder's key could close a door a builder's key had locked, so Gin swore, and so far things were working.

Someone, maybe the guard, rushed at them at the corner: mistake. Jago flattened the man with an elbow and light-footed it ahead, pausing for corners and doorways. They reached clear air at the corner by the desk, and pulled the masks down in favor of unobstructed breathing and vision. The prisoner, seeing others give up the breathing masks, removed his own—then looked wildly about at a thunderous rush behind them.

Men came running behind them; and all of a sudden Jago heaved another grenade down the corridor, and running attackers skidded to a stop and tried to get back.

It blew in a cloud of gas. And Cenedi's man blasted the overhead light panels, a neat, one-after-the-other chain that darkened the corridor and drove their pursuers in retreat.

They ran, then, Banichi dragging the stocky alien, as fast as he could; and Bren had his gun in hand, keeping an eye to pursuit behind them, not wanting to shoot any hapless guard. The doors had stayed open; and he found the presence of mind to shut one and lock it with his key.

Then he ran to catch up, almost hindmost, around the last turn. He passed Barnhart, passed Banichi, caught up with Jago just as she reached the lift.

Cenedi's men had trussed their terrified detainees and kept them flat on the floor; and now they all

jammed themselves into the lift, straddling their detainees, dragging along a frightened, sweating alien
who smelled like overheated pavement and bulked
like a small truck. Bren shoved his key in the slot
and Barnhart punched in their destination before he
extracted the key and pocketed it.

"We'll let you go at the bottom," Bren said then to
the two white-faced, absolutely terrified humans
crouched at their feet. He reached down and assisted
up the man he'd dealt with. "Come to the ship when
you're ready. The paper isn't a lie. Believe it!" He
remembered the rest of the fliers, took the sheaf of
them from inside his jacket and shoved them inside
the man's jacket. "Here, have some brochures."

"Yes, sir," the man muttered. The other, still on the
floor, seemed beyond speech, as Jago extracted the
whole packet of brochures from their kit and set them
in his lap.

"Safe," she said to him, encouragingly.

"My bodyguard says this is your ticket aboard,"
Bren said shamelessly. "Pass them out. Brochures get
first boarding. The access is open now. We have a
handful of days to get everyone aboard."

Down and down the levels, all the way to the bowels
of the station's maintenance, down to the service-port
and the dim, cold depths. Banichi was on the comm
the moment the doors opened, and they freed their
two Reunioners, then shoved their rescuee out into
this place that, whatever thoughts might be going
through the alien's mind, certainly wasn't the prosperous end of the station.

They ran, then, dragging the alien with them. Cold
hit like a wall, burned the lungs as they tried to make
time, down dim corridors, into section 81.

There escape in fact loomed in front of them: the

co-pilot had opened the emergency hatch from his side, the only way it *would* open, and with a broad inclusive wave, beckoned them in.

Safe, now. Two frightened humans trying to raise an alarm upstairs might only tell where they *had* been, in a very few moments, but if they were the least bit worried, Bren thought, those two might keep quiet, believing those brochures were a precious thing, to be passed out quickly among reliable friends.

Meanwhile their assorted party crammed themselves inside the airlock, within the webbing. The alien looked about him, large, dark eyes glittering in the dim light, a liquid glance passing jerkily over strange sights and strange faces—thinking of escape or murder, more than likely, but if they knew one thing about this person by now, they knew this was by no means a fool. Cooperation remained the moment-to-moment rule, compliance as the pilot and co-pilot got the pod door shut—no fuss, no argument. They were leaving the place that had held him and that suited the alien fine.

Haste and distance was their collective intention: haste in reaching the cover of the ship itself was all they could do to protect themselves from the station. And if the pod had been close quarters going out, now, with the door shut, they jammed themselves up closer and tighter, human, atevi, and shivering, strange-smelling unidentified.

Thump! Clang! They were free, rotating alarmingly at first. Then a steady hard push of propulsion cut in, compressing the whole untidy mass of them toward the aft bulkhead, a painful tangle of muscular flesh punctuated with other people's knees and elbows.

"We did it," Barnhart panted at Bren's ear, breathless and astonished, and Bren only thought, enduring a hard atevi elbow between his shoulder blades, and air too dry and thin for comfort, *For God's sake, man, don't jinx us.*

Then the alien they were transporting began struggling—huge arms, legs like tree trunks and a swing, if they hadn't all been pressed together like a sandwich, that could have cracked skulls. Banichi grabbed one arm and pinned it. The alien's eyes showed wild, broad nostrils flared and the mouth—omnivore, Bren decided, just like humans—opened in frantic gasps.

"Air pressure!" Bren shouted against the weight compressing his rib cage. "Take the air ship-normal! Fast!"

Fast still wasn't an instantaneous process. They were in freefall and the pilots had their hands full, what with the possibility that the station might at any moment find something capable of taking a shot at them, either inside the ring or once they started up the mast toward the ship. Bren personally didn't want to distract them—but they had an alien laboring for breath, close to passing out after his wild exertion: he must have stood it as long as he could, and gotten desperate.

"Short distance to our ship," Bren yelled into the alien's face. Touching him could be reassuring. It could equally well be deadly insult. He opted for hands-off. "We want to help you. Be still. All right?"

He didn't know whether the alien heard or understood. Banichi's grip held the alien fast against a new burst of resistance, and now one of Cenedi's men began to wind self-adhesive restraint about him, which didn't calm the situation or likely help his breathing at all.

"Caution, Bren-ji," Banichi said, struggling to hold the massive arms out of action, and if Banichi was having trouble keeping his grip on those arms, Bren found no chance. He wriggled to back up as far as he could, acceleration pressing them together. Then Jago added her efforts, inserting an arm and struggling past him to get the binding wrapped.

But it all became easier as the alien stopped fighting and let his head loll, close to passing out.

"Easy, easy, easy," Bren said, and took a chance. "Oxygen. Can we get the emergency oxygen, Jago-ji?"

Jago reached a long arm to an emergency panel. In a moment more they had an oxygen mask roughly over the alien's broad, flat face, and the last fighting eased as their passenger gasped for breath.

Not a crazy person. One trying to breathe.

Then acceleration stopped, all in one stomach-wrenching moment, and the axis spun over. They began, despite the testimony of senses, to slow down, trying not, Bren said to himself, to impact the ship and smear their little mission all over their ship's travel-scarred hull.

Slowing down. Slowing down. The pilot and co-pilot were talking to someone with an incredible and reassuring calm. Bren found himself breathing as if oxygen for all of them had grown far too short and he wished there were a mask for him.

But the pilots worked calmly just as if they were coming in at Alpha station, a precise set of communications and maneuvers.

Their alien's eyes opened slightly. He was no longer fighting them. He might not know another word of who they were, but air was potent, the most basic requirement. They had satisfied that urgent need, and they had taken him out of that clear-walled cell, and they weren't where he had spent the last six years— they had that to recommend them.

"We're coming to our ship," Bren said to their alien, in the hope that those years in human hands had taught him some few words. "My name is Bren. This is Banichi. We're from the ship. We want to help you. Do you understand me at all?"

The alien gave no response, only a slow, blinking stare.

"We're coming in," the copilot said. "Brace, all."

Thank God. In. Safe. *They* had the station's precious hostage, and—now that the station knew they'd been robbed of that asset, now that the station had the ship's offer of rescue coursing the halls and soon being gossiped in the restaurants—maybe the station would just give up quietly, turn Sabin loose, and let them have the fuel.

Maybe rainbows would shine in deep space.

But, he thought, up against this strange creature who smelled like pavement, they did have a major asset in their hands, they'd told the truth to a handful of people. And they hadn't killed anyone during their mission.

Let the Guild recalculate its assets now.

Thump-clang. Rattle and stop. *Blessed* stop.

They were in. They were safe.

"Mr. Cameron," the co-pilot said, "captain's compliments, and will you get up to his office at the earliest after dock?"

Urgently, never mind they'd just worked a miracle and he had an alien he had to talk to—get upstairs.

Something wasn't according to plan.

16

Come up, Jase had said, and to the bridge Bren went immediately, gun in pocket, jacket torn and rumpled, sweat and the lingering stink of noxious chemicals about him. It made his eyes water. Narani would be scandalized, Bren thought, aware he was light-headed at the moment. He needed to be down below to supervise their alien guest.

But Jase needed him topside, fast.

The lift door let him out. He spared only a quick leftward glance to be sure Jase wasn't on the bridge. Crew there was busier than it had been, which said something on its own.

And—God!—a blood trail snaked down the corridor from the lift, a set of dots leading down to the executive offices.

Jase's was the second door. Where the dots entered. There was no bodyguard outside.

He buzzed it and opened the door almost in one motion, hand on the gun in his pocket.

Jase was at his desk.

Jenrette sat opposite, Jenrette, who'd gone aboard the station with Sabin. And Jenrette's right arm was wrapped, sleeve and all, in bloody bandage.

Kaplan was there, too, Kaplan with blood all over

his sleeve, likely Jenrette's, and Polano stood in the other corner, neither looking happy.

"You got him," Jase said. Meaning their alien, Bren judged. "He's alive."

"Yes. In good shape." He was a little set aback, that Jase would talk other business in front of this man, but there was nothing he needed to conceal. "Can't speak to his mood, but no physical damage. He cooperated, in fact."

"Good."

"Mr. Jenrette." He gave a nod to the man leaking blood onto the chair arm and directed his primary question to Jase, all the same. "I take it there's a problem in other areas."

"One of the robots blown to hell," Jase said, "Guild agents in the mast, but *not* in the tube at this moment: Hendrix and Pressman are holding that. In the confusion that broke out after the fuel port event, Mr. Jenrette got himself to the tube and reached our team inside, to give us Captain Sabin's instruction—which was to be careful and don't create a problem."

Bren sat down. "Well, *that* came a little too late."

"Notably," Jase said. And hadn't at any point spoken in Ragi. Or evidenced any distrust of Jenrette. Both circumstances told a tale, to a man who'd shared quarters with Jase in Shejidan. Jase, however, was cool and calm. "Explain, Mr. Jenrette. Our atevi allies need to know."

"Hiding in the vicinity," Jenrette said, clearly in pain, teeth chattering. "Freezing. They've set a guard down there, near the tube access. Or they had one. But when the robot blew at the fuel port, I suppose, or when your team moved in, the guard moved away. Alarms were going. They went to the lift, maybe to get secure-line communications, and I made a break for it. They spotted me and started shooting. Our force started firing back and I got inside."

Gin's mission had upended the figurative teakettle. So it seemed.

"Mr. Jenrette says he doesn't know what's happened to the captain, except she didn't like the way things were going. She sent Mr. Jenrette back to report to us and the Guild took exception to him leaving. Whether she's been arrested or whether she's trying to reason with them, we have no idea. Meanwhile, by Mr. Jenrette's evidence, they were shooting at her bodyguard."

Jenrette was the last member of her bodyguard Sabin would send on a mission to report to Jase—no. Jase didn't believe it either.

"I got to the mast. I hoped I could get past the guard and get to the tube. I didn't know whether you could get anyone to cover me, sir, and I was afraid they'd tag me if I called. But it was getting to where I'd freeze to death if I didn't. Then the alarm happened."

"Sabin won't be using ship-com, I take it," Jase said, "for the same reason."

"There's a contact in the Security offices. Coursin is his name. Amin Coursin." Jenrette moved his arm and winced. "Soon as I get this arm seen to, I'm to deliver what I've told you and get back to that meeting point. I'll carry anything you want to tell her."

"In Shejidan," Jase said, "I learned one thing, Mr. Jenrette: if the person who told you to rendezvous is *missing—don't* use their contacts. That wouldn't be wise of you, to go there. And you *are* experienced security."

"I'm experienced security, and with all respect, captain, I'm not under your command. I'm under hers. I've delivered my message, for what little good it does now, and, again with all due respect, sir, I'm going back to her command, with or without medical treatment."

"Settle in. You're not going anywhere."

"I beg to differ, sir."

"I said settle down. Your fight is over, Mr. Jenrette. You may be Guild—"

"No, sir!"

"Aren't you? For that matter, isn't the senior captain, herself? Damned brave of you—taking a hit for verisimilitude. But while we're not trusting suspect contacts, Mr. Jenrette, you have to be at the top of that list."

"Sir!" Jenrette started out of his chair.

Polano moved. So did Bren. And, on his feet, he held an atevi-made pistol aimed at Jenrette's middle, where even a non-professional couldn't miss. "Sit down."

Jenrette subsided back into his chair and sat there like a statue. Bren kept standing, glad Polano was there and armed.

"So we're at odds," Jase said. "But I think we've been operating at cross-purposes, Mr. Jenrette. I have my own theory about what's gone on to bring us to this situation. I think the Old Man was going back to *take* Alpha, at least that those were the orders the Guild gave him. So the Guild wasn't totally surprised the ship was gone a while, was it? Our long absence only indicated to them that there'd had to be a change of administration at Alpha Station, possibly a messy change of administration."

To *take* Alpha Station, *their* station, Bren thought, certainly hadn't turned out to be a simple matter of sailing up and taking control. In the end, there'd been anything but Guild loyalty dominating the Captains' Council.

And increasingly one suspected Ramirez had worked at counter-purposes with the Guild, start to finish, and hadn't taken his orders from the Guild as any use to him.

"Was *that* what Tamun found out about, Mr. Jenrette?" Jase asked. "Guild orders?"

"Nonsense," Jenrette said.

"Your old partners on Ramirez's security team all died. Tamun shot them. People you'd shared duty with for twenty years. Does that mean anything to you? Not a shred of personal regret for your partners?"

"Tamun was a bastard," Jenrette said, jaw clenched. "No regrets at all *he's* dead. And he's irrelevant to the case at hand."

"Regrets for Ramirez?"

"Regrets for Ramirez," Jenrette said somberly. "He was the Old Man."

"But he wasn't Guild, was he? He didn't take the Guild's orders. He didn't take their orders when it came to poking about in other people's solar systems. The Guild wanted resources. But he was constantly looking for an alterative, not so much for Reunion as for the Guild's leadership. I rather think you went along with that for a number of years. But he was getting older and no stronger, and when the business blew up and Reunion got hit, then you were going to see to it he carried out Guild orders, if you had to shift the balance of power on the Council. You were going to stop him from his old-age ambition to settle this mess, because you thought he'd become a fool."

"That's not so."

"You'd spied on him all his life. You'd told the Guild as much as kept the Guild happy. And when Ramirez began to look weak, you jumped over to the Guild's side."

"Ramirez was, longterm, looking for alternatives to

the Guild," Bren interjected. "Looking at every likely star in reach. And he finally found his answer at Alpha—a whole planetful of alternatives. And not all human. And that's when he made a choice. And I think that's when you did, Mr. Jenrette."

"He was the Old Man," Jenrette said. "I was with him."

"And when he made an agreement with the atevi," Jase said, "and kept it—did you try to save him from himself, too, Mr. Jenrette? When he was dying, were you the one who let the rumor out, about survivors at Reunion? You knew the truth. You'd known it from the time you went into Reunion."

Hesitation. Hesitation, as if somewhere in the whole equation, there was still a fragment of real loyalty in the man, a desire to justify himself to himself.

"You double-crossed Ramirez when he was dying," Jase said. "Damn you. And you double-crossed Sabin out there. You didn't bring us her orders. You brought us theirs."

"No."

"The Guild's orders, Mr. Jenrette. You're working for the Guild, and you have been since your visit here. I'd like to have known what went on after the record ended. I'd like to know what they said, or did, to turn you so thoroughly to their side."

"There never was a side," Jenrette said. "I didn't double-cross the Old Man, and I didn't double-cross the Old Lady. I want her back safe. But safe isn't going against the Guild, safe *isn't* letting atevi run the ship or taking your orders from *him*, sir."

Meaning the paidhi-aiji, quite clearly.

"A bloody great hole in the station is safe?" Jase retorted. "A mess with an alien ship out there is safe? You'd better stop and look around you, Mr. Jenrette. You want to say what you think? I'm a jumped-up theoretician? I'm too friendly with the atevi? I'm not really qualified and you're going to save the ship by steering another batch of us into a Guild trap, when they set the captains against them, when they've kept their own population at risk instead of shipping the majority of them out of there? You *have* double-crossed Captain Sabin, Mr. Jenrette, in your mistaken conviction that a handful of deskbound fools have any clue how to assure human beings survive in this universe *with* our culture and our common sense. Rethink, mister. Rethink and tell me I don't have the real picture. *They've* got a theory. *We've* been there and back again. We've dealt with aliens and we're still human, last I looked in a mirror. Not human enough for you, maybe, but that's the reality, and theirs dead-ends. It's going to dead-end completely in not so very long, because we're pulling the population out of here. So where have you ended up, Mr. Jenrette? Doing anything good? I don't think so."

Long silence. Jenrette shook. He outright trembled, in the shock of a real injury, but Bren didn't find himself in the least sorry for the man who'd been a long-term traitor to three captains, his own comrades, and the ship's whole crew.

"Well," Jase said, "so what you wanted, Mr. Jenrette, isn't happening. We're undertaking the steps to let us board passengers. We're shutting Reunion down. And if you want to find a way out of your situation, you'd better start trying. Mr. Cameron, do you have any questions for him?"

Bren had not the remotest idea what questions Jase wanted asked of the man, but Jase, sitting on his well-known temper, probably didn't trust himself to find all the requisite threads at the moment. He didn't have specifics, but he had keys; and if he could only open a door to information, he hoped Jase might find a wedge to keep it flowing.

"Mr. Jenrette," Bren said quietly. "Mr. Jenrette, I'm relatively sure you're quite adept at leaking information. Maybe you dropped just enough hints to provoke Tamun to turn on Ramirez; and Tamun killed your partners, which was why you swerved about and turned on Tamun. I've no doubt you were at Ramirez's ear for years. I'm relatively sure if anything aboard this ship for the last twenty years has skewed off course, your fingers are somewhere in it. All these things I believe are the truth, but they're all past. What is important is that we're going to get the fuel we need, we're going to get everyone off the station that we can persuade aboard, and then we're going to have to blow up the station with everyone that's left aboard—your Guild, foremost. Probably our senior captain and your latest colleagues in her bodyguard, but she knew the risk she ran, and I'm sure you did. After we blow it up, we're going to take our alien guest over to his people, and take what agreement we can get and go back where we came from. That's what we're going to do, Mr. Jenrette. But you know what we came here to do. And I'm sure you've told the Guild. Why of all things did you think you could walk back in here and be believed, with me, and with Captain Graham? Or was that the job Guild leadership gave you? You'd lost your usefulness with Sabin: she was onto you. So they just made a last-ditch try and sent you here—because if you've hired a traitor, you don't go on using him. You find someplace to send him where he'll be taken care of. Unhappily, we're the only other place there is. You're supposed to do some sabotage. Use your skills on their side. Never mind what you contain. What you know. You'll be a good follower, and die trying. Then Braddock won't have to meet you again."

Jenrette stared him, jaw set, full of anger, and said not a word.

"If you'd stuck with Sabin," Bren said, "you'd have had her ear. But you've thrown away your influence. Sabin did have reservations, exactly as you do. The dowager respects the senior captain: *atevi* would have listened to her as a strong voice for her point of view. But you've silenced her. You've silenced *all* the voices of human dissent. Thanks to their own mismanagement, the Guild likely will fall; Ramirez is dead, and Sabin may not survive. Tamun, in his rebellion—he didn't do what you wanted. He decided Ramirez was lying, when most of the lies were yours. Between you, you and Sabin and Tamun, I suspect you kept Ramirez from ever trusting us with the whole truth. How am I doing?"

"Go to hell."

"Pretty well, I'll imagine."

"Listen to me," Jenrette said. "Listen to me! All we have to do to get out of here is for *him* to answer Guild rules. Then we're *all* away free, with no trouble."

For Jase—to surrender *Phoenix* and come under Guild command.

"Meaning Sabin's also refused the Guild's orders," Jase said. "Interesting."

"It's your choice." Jenrette swung round toward Jase. "In a post you don't remotely qualify for. You're no captain of this ship. You have no right."

Jase shook his head with amazing patience. "The stakes are too high, Mr. Jenrette. And trust me, your hand isn't nearly high enough. Sabin tried to help you—maybe knowing all the while you're a Guild agent. And look what she got for her trouble. It's damned lonely being your friend, Mr. Jenrette."

"Shut up."

"You know, Braddock himself may have figured you're always on your own agenda, and that's not a wholly useful agent: Bren nailed that, didn't he? You're a total fool, but you always know better than your captains, than the Guildmaster, than everybody. Consequently you're no use to anyone. So Braddock sent you here. Best use for you."

"Taylor's bastard," Jenrette spat. "You don't have the answers. You weren't born with any answers. You aren't God. Just existing doesn't make you *anybody*, Graham. Not anybody!"

"Take your pick," Jase said. "I'm sure, if your devotion to the Guild is that strong, Mr. Jenrette, we'll let you go join Mr. Braddock. He may even remember your name, and he might even keep his promises to you—even if he hasn't kept them with his own station population."

"On the other hand," Bren said, "if your convictions aren't strong enough to die with the Guild— maybe you aren't so convinced that's the best course."

Jenrette wouldn't look at him. Not at either of them.

"Make your decision," Jase said.

"What kind of deal?" Jenrette asked. Not, one noted: I see the light. I change my ways; but: What kind of deal? It was possibly a glimmer of truth.

"You want a pardon?" Jase said.

Jenrette looked at Jase—interested for about a quarter of a heartbeat; then very, very wary. That face he saw wasn't genial Jase Graham, usually silent second to Sabin. It was Jase Graham who'd stood in the aiji's court and held his own with the lords of the Association.

"I'm putting you outside," Jase said quietly. "And there's only one way you'll get back aboard. And that's if you bring the senior captain, alive and well, with every one of her escort."

"I can't do that," Jenrette said.

"Because she's dead?"

"No. I don't think she's dead. But look at this." Jenrette demonstrated his wounded arm. "You're sending me out there to get me killed."

"Mr. Jenrette, I'm not sending a station shopkeeper to do this job. I'm sending a covert professional, who's managed throughout his life to be secretive. You'll find a chance to get to her. You'll have a wider chance as the panic spreads and as the station loses its personnel—wider still, as Braddock's trusted people get the notion their only hope is this ship. And let me make it very clear. I will let Mr. Braddock aboard. I will *not* let you aboard unless you satisfy my condition. If we don't get Sabin, you'll stay on this station. You'll be on it, all alone, in the dark, when we blow the remnant of this station to cold space." Jase had leaned on a chair back nearest Jenrette. Now he stood back. "Mr. Polano."

"Sir."

"Are your reinforcements outside?"

Polano cross-checked on his com-set. "Yes, sir, they are."

"Then take him out of here. Get the arm treated. Then put him out into the mast where you found him."

"Free, sir?"

"He doesn't come back aboard unless he's in Captain Sabin's company."

"Yes, sir," Polano said with satisfaction. "Yes, *sir*."

"Mr. Jenrette," Jase said nicely, with a little wave of his hand. "Go with Mr. Polano and company. Goodbye and good luck."

"Damn you," Jenrette said, and got to his feet. And clearly thought about a move.

Polano showed him the door. And after a self-preserving second thought, Jenrette turned and walked to the door.

There were half a dozen men outside, ordinary crew, armed, and backing up Polano.

The door stayed open a second or two after Polano and Jenrette left, and shut.

"He may do one thing," Bren said, "or the other. Fifty-fifty he reports to Braddock."

"I put it sixty-forty against," Jase said. "Jenrette's not atevi. He's a survivor. And I think he's not found the chaos he hoped to find aboard. He doesn't like what he'd have to tell Braddock. Eighty-twenty he'll lie to Braddock. Question is, can he make Sabin believe him?"

"You're lucky Sabin took him out of here. God knows what he'd have done."

"I don't think luck had anything to do with it. I think she knew what he was. I don't think she knew how far he'd misinformed Tamun. But she didn't trust me, with him aboard, to keep this ship out of Guild hands. I think she thought I'd let my guard down."

"And if he comes back?"

"If he comes back with Sabin—he'll have his chance to convince her he's a hero."

They were committed to the hilt.

And Bren shakily pocketed the gun.

"Our alien's alive and well?" Jase re-asked him.

"In good condition. Tolerates our air, clearly hasn't died of our food in six years—a lot of problems short-cut by those two items . . ."

"Shortcut by the plain fact the Old Man was poking around among planets with our life requirements," Jase said. "So the Guild had an alien hostage. And they don't, now. We do. We've got Jenrette. We're short a robot, but the word is out. We've papered the mast with our fliers. They'll have hell's own time rounding those up."

"We dispersed others on the far side of the station."

"Any shooting?"

"We made a fair amount of racket—Jago tossed a few grenades, but nobody got killed, nobody hurt on our side. About the brochures—I confess I told certain people they were first-boarding tickets."

Not much had struck Jase as funny in the last number of hours. The laugh was startled, quickly gone. "We urgently need to talk to this alien. Any possibility?"

"Six years in confinement . . . if he hasn't learned at least *yes, no*, and *go to hell* I'll be surprised."

"But that's not guaranteed by anything you've heard."

"No. It's not guaranteed. I've sent him to five-deck. Furniture that fits his size. Personnel with the physical strength to hold him. He's large. He's far too strong for human guards. He's almost too strong for Banichi."

"I trust you know what you're doing." Jase tapped a stylus on his desk. "We've made a fair stir here. Observers on that ship out there are going to start wondering. I don't want to back this ship out and take them the hostage, for several reasons. I don't want to panic the station. And I don't want to get involved in negotiations with the aliens out there before we board our people. I want it a fait accompli. But if we take all that mass on, we've got to chase the fuel situation to a conclusion, next number one priority. We lost a robot. We did get some pictures. And we know where the guns are."

Risky venture. But so was everything.

"If we could get a long-distance understanding with that ship out there," Bren said, "if we knew we could gain time . . ."

"That would be very useful, if we knew that for certain," Jase said. "I'd really like that—if you can figure how."

"I'll find a way," he said to Jase. "I don't know yet what our guest may know. Hold off on attempting the fuel for at least six hours. I'll see if I can learn anything."

"Six hours," Jase said. "Six hours, if nothing else happens. Don't bet too heavily it won't. The stationers you met have seen atevi—not to mention Jenrette's almost certainly told what he knows. So that secret's out. Becker's out and away, armed with more of your travel brochures. He and his men say they're going to get their families and relatives packed and ready—or they could could to run straight to the Guild, if any one of them thinks what they've learned is that valuable to Braddock."

"You can judge their intentions better than I can."

"I don't know," Jase said. "Likely they themselves didn't know what they were going to do when they left. In their line of work, they're cautious. They don't trust things. They'll try to verify what's been going on before they make any decision. And my bet is they'll go immediately to their closest contacts. They'll take a look at their wives and their kids. I think they'll come back. The way I halfway figure Jenrette is adding up the odds and thinking how to get Sabin back here in one piece."

"One hopes so," Bren murmured in Ragi, and reached in his pocket and handed Jase the builder's key. "This was useful, nadi-ji."

"So nothing's changed."

"One new door not on the system. That was all we found that failed to answer it."

Jase pocketed the key himself. "Useful to know. I'll advise Gin of that."

"I'm going," Bren said, switching languages without thinking. "I'll call when I know something."

Scary business. A change of clothing was in order, at very least, a change of clothing, a quick wash, a change of direction, a change of mind and mental state away from fight-flight and panic, and toward orderly problem-solving.

Among first things, the gun went back into storage. He was as glad to shed that as he had been to turn the key back to Jase's keeping.

"One is grateful, Rani-ji. It was extremely useful."

"Nandi." Narani absorbed the compliment as graciously as Bindanda would accept praise for a fine dinner. The gun had not been fired—a condition that pleased them both.

"One wishes also," Bren said, "Rani-ji, a change of clothing for our guest, somehow. One observes a very great girth."

"One has already provided him an adequate bathrobe and estimated his measurements, nandi. One hopes this was proper."

"Indeed. Thank you, Rani-ji. And food and drink?" Without knowing his preferences, one might think bland food close to its natural state might be a safe choice; but there were hazards in atevi cuisine, a fondness for alkaloids humans had found quite distressing. Even fruits were not without difficulties, for some individuals. "Bland fruit juice. *Abi*, I think, and cold water. Unleavened breads."

"At once, nandi. We have only awaited your order."

"Perhaps sweets as well." Food must be one of those very basic things to species which didn't live on moonbeams, sugars were fairly simple, as best he could recall, and a cool drink, a meal, and a change to comfortable clothing improved any disposition.

Narani accordingly went off to inform Bindanda, and he went for a shower that might relieve the stinging in his eyes—a discomfort worsened since he had rubbed them on the way down. Red-eyed, he was sure. Slightly smoky. But generally undamaged, except for seeing that clerk's frightened face every time he shut his eyes . . . God, he was not cut out for Banichi's and Jago's line of work.

He scrubbed. Furiously. And began to shift mental gears, began to trust his surroundings and get the shivers out of his system.

He hoped their guest had taken their intervention in his situation as a rescue, not a dive from frying pan to fire. He had no idea what they were dealing with, beyond that—whether they were dealing with an ordinary soldier, a ship's crewman, a belligerent warlord bent on conquest or perhaps some hapless scientist or maker of dictionaries who'd come in to learn what they were dealing with.

Who, among aliens, *would* logically comprise a team sent aboard an apparently war-wrecked station, their own handiwork? Someone like himself would be most logical . . . to human beings of a certain era of humanity. But that certainly wasn't a given, here. For all they could know, it was a priest come to bless the event, a political activist who'd run aboard to stage a protest. Civilizations of advanced sort could be amazingly baroque.

And what would an individual of whatever original intent have been planning for six years of captivity in a glass cage?

In their guest's position, Bren thought, he'd try to
learn something, he'd try to escape with what he
knew; and being unregenerate terrestrial primate—
he'd try to stay alive to get revenge, if nothing else.
What would Banichi or Jago do? Attempt to return
to their aiji, to their association, working mayhem only
on what frustrated that aim, bearing personal resentment not at all, except as someone got in their way.
Humans had jails. Atevi had the Assassins' Guild. Neither side could understand the others' problem-
solving.

And what was their guest thinking now? What frustrated instincts were they dealing with?

He got out of the shower and Jeladi helped him
into his dressing-robe. His clothing was laid out on
the bed, dignified, but not fussy. He approved Jeladi's
choice: he had yet to report to the dowager, among
other pressing matters. His good blue coat was an excellent choice, a soothing color.

Jago came in while he was dressing, Jago with not
a hair out of place—nor ever had had, that he had
detected, not even while wrestling with their rescuee
in the pod. She had changed uniforms for one that
didn't reek of fumes.

"No scratches or scrapes, one hopes, Jago-ji. How
is our guest?"

"Well enough," she said. "One should add, however, Bren-ji, this person has formidable teeth. He did
attempt to use them, so Banichi advises us."

"He was bitten?"

"Not successfully," Jago said.

"Well, one is certainly warned," Bren said, tugging
at a cuff, arranging the lace—in his experience, high
civilization discouraged biting. Which might only say
how stressed and desperate their guest had become.
"One hopes an intelligent species has no natural

venom, and that his native bacteria are not something either atevi nor humans may easily share." He had spent the voyage reading biological speculations, among other things, which now only made him nervous. "The difficulty with the air, nadi-ji. Have we resolved that to his comfort?"

"As best one can," Jago said. "He seems to tolerate shipboard conditions well enough, and evidences no current discomfort. We have shown him the thermostat, the shower, the accommodation. Narani has provided his own cabin—he has hesitated to provide blankets, for security reasons, but our guest has not adjusted the temperature. He has exchanged the station garments for one of Bindanda's robes, which was of sufficient size, and seems better pleased with that."

Temperature preference satisfied. Gift accepted. He absorbed the information, comforted, after all that had gone on, simply to hear the lilt of Jago's voice. Humanly glad, perhaps, in ways that didn't address man'chi and the sensible feelings that mattered to any ateva—though he doggedly thought his bodyguard was more than pleased to have gotten him back again: that somewhere in their impulse toward man'chi, they must be equally warm and happy inside. He could scarcely think about the dire outcomes possible in their raid into Guild territory, but now that they were all safely through and back again, he began to have flashbacks of smoke and fire.

And belated panic.

"Gin-aiji is safe in her office," Jago said smoothly. "But, as the paidhi-aiji may be aware, with less success. A robot is lost. We have, however established the location of guns guarding the fuel port."

"And now we have Jenrette as well. And will release him. You followed that."

"Yes," Jago said. "Jase-aiji has him in the medical facility now; and will not trust him. Wise."

His staff knew exactly what transpired on two-deck. He was occasionally astonished.

"I think his plan might even work," he agreed. "If Sabin-aiji isn't in Guild hands—or even if she is—Jenrette might act to save himself."

"Sigaiji," Jago said—an untranslatable word. An aiji no one would follow—born with the emotional makeup to lead, but not able to persuade followers to join him. *Rogue* leader was tolerably descriptive.

"I think he is," Bren said. "I think in his case, that's very apt."

"Does he think Sabin is higher than he?"

In atevi minds, a very telling question. They had asked a man who might think his own beliefs the highest law—to rescue someone who claimed authority over him. In that thought, he was even less hopeful of Jenrette than he had been.

"One believes he can accept it, nadi," he said to Jago, "unless he knows he has gone much too far to regain her trust. Then he has to consider whether he believes he can die, and what that life may be worth to him."

"One would not like to be Jenrette."

"One would not, Jago-ji."

"Even if he performs," Jago said, "he is what he is. Not a person to rely on."

"One agrees," he said, and knew that that item was decisive in Jago's mental files . . . decisive and a switch completely ticked over to *foreigner.* Not of our association.

"So Braddock-aiji has moved against Sabin; we have moved against Braddock; Braddock sends this person before he knew we were taking one of his assets away. Gin-aiji has lost a robot, but she urges another attempt, as soon as she can analyze what they saw. There are pictures."

"Very good news."

"One assumes that Braddock-aiji is taking other measures."

"One hardly knows how to predict the Guild," he said. "Their security has lost it one of its two prime assets. They would reassess, if they were wise. But if they follow true to form, certain subordinates will exert their energies to mislead the Guildmaster about their deficiencies."

"One has known lords of the Association to do the same," Jago said dryly.

"One has known lords of the Association to be completely paralyzed in such debates." Recalling the Transportation Committee, of, God! such tame, quiet days. "One wishes they would remain paralyzed, but one fears Braddock-aiji will not act like the Presidenta of Mospheira—more like one of the ship-aijiin, without consultation. If he lets passengers board us, he will attempt to infiltrate his agents among them. I expect that, next. But the ship has foreseen unruly passengers, and installed precautions. So that becomes a smaller worry." Crew had spent their voyage reorganizing systems and isolating those decks: granted anything less than a nuclear device, what happened on those decks should be limited to those decks. Switches governing air circulation, light, and temperature were all governed from the ship's bridge. "One hardly knows, Jago-ji, what Braddock-aiji will do. Or what that ship out there will do." He adjusted his cuffs. He had one of the most essential jobs of his life before him. "One assumes the dowager expects a report before I get to work."

"She says: Visit when you have ascertained the nature and quality of this foreigner. Her own bodyguard has reported to her."

Common sense and her own channels. Thank God.

The dowager was a veteran of fast maneuvering and practical necessity.

"Shall we go with you to deal with this foreigner, Bren-ji? We both *strongly* urge it."

"I entertain no other thought, Jago-ji," he murmured. His initial session with their guest might be lengthy and tedious, and he wished his staff might snatch a little rest; but they were, themselves, skilled observers, and they had the strength and size and foreignness to keep their guest focused on communication, not thinking he could overwhelm a small individual of the same species that had kept him caged for six years.

So, yes, he decided his staff's help might be a good thing.

Banichi joined them on their way down the corridor, Banichi and Jago neither one having yet found time to change to less businesslike kit, except to put away the heavier weapons and the heavy jackets. *They* had likely gone straight to a debriefing with Cenedi, which might already have involved the dowager—he rather bet that it had.

"One can observe our guest by way of the security station," Banichi informed him, "should you wish to do that unnoticed, Bren-ji."

"Excellent," he said. Surprised that his staff had arranged surveillance? Not in the least. Narani's cabin, so graciously tendered, had given their guest adequately sized furniture, an atevi-scale bed—and by fairly fast and discreet work, had given them direct surveillance on a monitor in the security station, where Asicho kept faithful watch.

"He has paced out the room, nandi," Asicho reported when they stopped there to observe. "He has investigated the switches, tested the mattress, the chair and the cabinets, which are emptied, nothing damaged. He has bathed and dressed in one of Bindanda's robes and nightshirts." Tape accompanied this report, a quick skip through key actions, and a sequence of their guest in the bath, gray-skinned, with heavy folds that might indicate, unlikely as it seemed, given such a bulk, emaciation. Embarrassing, perhaps, to observe an individual in such a state, but necessary for their collective well-being.

"One fears they didn't feed him near enough, nadiin-ji," Bren murmured. "Or perhaps the station food disagrees with his stomach. We shall endeavor to better that. Advise Bindanda."

"Yes," Asicho said smartly, and did that.

In subsequent scenes their robe-clad guest drank multiple cups of water, five cups, as Asicho commented, before testing the bed gingerly and lying down.

Evolved in conditions of more water, rather than less. More vegetation rather than minimal, one might then guess. High water need. Heavy skin, the evolutionary value of which eluded his meager study. He wished he'd borne down just a little more on the theoretical end of his biology classes, back in his monofocussed youth. If a fact hadn't applied to atevi, in his youthful arrogance, he hadn't been interested. Now he was extremely sorry.

"Narani-nadi has discreetly estimated his size for better tailoring, nandi," Asicho said sotto voce. "Bindanda is attempting to construct suitable clothing as quickly as possible."

"A very good idea," Bren said, with a mental image of their guest in atevi court attire. But who knew? Being dressed like his hosts would surely be a psychological improvement over the prison garb, an evidence of better fortunes.

"He seems in many points like us, nandi."

"That he does," Bren said. Four limbs, a similar musculature to move them, an upright stance and the spinal curve and gait that kept a bipedal creature from falling over. A not exclusively vegetarian dentition, Banichi informed him: meat was likely, then, on his menu.

And jaw curvature and fine control of tongue and throat for articulate speech? In that broad face, yes, likely so. In that large head and that ship waiting out there for six years, definitely a brain and a sense of purpose, however he communicated.

Eyes, two. Nose, useful to any species, short, broad, positioned above, not below, the mouth, a sensible design, in a human's estimation.

A bullet head that sat down onto huge shoulders. Broad grasping hands, flat, broad feet that certainly weren't going to fit into any boots they owned—nature of the toes wasn't clear.

Huge rib cage. One assumed it protected the breathing apparatus and that digestion fit rather lower into the frame, the finish of that process as far from the intake as anatomy could manage, simply to give chemistry as much time to work as feasible . . . again, a reasonable arrangement, as seemed.

Sex indeterminate in folds of skin, if the location of the distinction was involved neither with respiration nor digestion, and the young, connected with that process, had to get out of the body somehow: again, design seemed to follow gravity. *He* as a pronoun was a convenience, not a firm conviction.

And while gravity and the need for locomotion, perception, and manipulation of the environment (wasn't that what his professors had said?) might make biological entities look rather more alike than not—gravity had nothing in particular to do with the mind, the language, or the attitudes of a long cultural history, which could be damnably soft, mutable, and difficult to predict.

His professors would be highly useful right now. He wished he had the whole resources of the University on Mospheira, and their labs and their committees, to back him up.

He wished they were safely back in orbit around their own planet and he could take years doing this.

But they weren't, and he couldn't. He gathered himself up with a deep breath. "Do not hesitate to notify us, Asi-ji," he said to Asicho, "if there should be any word from Jase or the dowager on any account."

"One will be closely attentive, nandi," Asicho assured him softly.

He left, Banichi and Jago close on his heels . . .

And outside, he discovered Cenedi. So the dowager *was* interested, and not entirely patient.

And with Cenedi and his two men came a very unofficial presence, Cajeiri, tagging the dowager's men at a safe distance, looking as inconspicuous as possible. And—one should note, who hoped for quiet and sanity—Cajeiri stood eavesdropping, toy car in hand.

"The dowager inquires," Cenedi said.

"I am proceeding immediately," Bren said.

Cajeiri noted that look. "Might one just *see* this foreigner, nand' Bren?"

Cenedi bent a stern look aside and down.

But, it flashed across Bren's mind—in the naivete of that question: in the extreme pressure of time, to convince another species that one was not a warlike, ravening enemy—dared one think?

Dared one remotely think a child might be useful?

"Perhaps the dowager might permit him, Cenedi-nadi. What if we were to work on this foreigner what we worked upon Becker-nadi? What if this foreigner were to see we have young children and elder statesmen aboard?"

His own staff looked at him, appalled. Cenedi looked decidedly uneasy. "Hurrah!" Cajeiri cried.

Yet was it not the case, the paidhi asked himself? The fragile, troublesome side of every intelligent species must be its young—young in an intelligent species requiring a prolonged learning phase. Young who were apt to do any damned thing. Young who routinely made naturally forgivable mistakes.

How best, without words, to demonstrate one's pacific intent, than to show one's softer side? The dowager had rarely come under *that* description. But she could manage a grand graciousness. The ship's crew venerated her.

"Perhaps, Cenedi-nadi, we shall invite our guest to the dining hall for refreshments—tired though our guest may be, he would surely like to know his situation, and perhaps we can demonstrate our hospitality. Perhaps the young aiji might indeed come and bring his toy. Though it is a *very* adult business, and the young aiji must bear extreme tedium with extraordinary patience. Perhaps the dowager herself would come and observe."

Cenedi looked worried. "One will certainly relay this invitation, nandi."

An invitation unwritten, testing the limits of atevi courtesy: but Cenedi clearly had no doubt the dowager would be amenable, and laying her own schemes on her next breath.

"Shall we speak to this foreigner, nadiin-ji?" Cajeiri asked.

"Perhaps," Bren said, "we may convince him even our youngest are civilized and polite."

"A subterfuge," Cajeiri said with restrained excitement. "A subterfuge, Cenedi-nadi!"

"His new word," Cenedi said, and to the offspring: "If *mani* agrees, you may be present and you may speak, young lord, but *judiciously,* and one does not believe the paidhi-aiji intends civility as a hollow subterfuge."

"Yes, Cenedi-nadi!"

"We shall ask your great-grandmother," Cenedi said—indeed, ask the dowager, who thought a headlong ride down a rocky mountain was sport, at her age. Cajeiri worshipfully tagged Cenedi down the corridor toward the dowager's door.

Bren looked at Banichi and Jago, knowing—*knowing* that he was about to test the limits of reasonable risk and his staff's resources. He would assuredly have his own fragile neck at risk, and if he showed a potential enemy their softer side, he also showed that enemy a softer target—not even figuring it might go all wrong and he might offend or disgust the individual they had to reach. There were no certainties. The fact was, there *were* no facts to work on: they had the what, but not a shred of the why.

"Safeguard the dowager and the heir at utmost priority. I insist, nadiin-ji. *They* would be the soft target, if I make any mistake. You will give me an opportunity to retreat. And I assure you, I promise you, I promise twice and three times—I shall run."

"One agrees," Banichi said—viscerally as hard for his own bodyguard, that promise to abandon him, as a leap off a cliff. All instincts warred against leaving him. But they were not slaves to those instincts. They understood him. "Yes," Jago said flatly.

"Nadi-ji." A little bow. He trusted word was already passing, from them to Asicho, from Asicho to both staffs. Information flowed, swirled about them, a constant bath of attention and preparation.

And he walked calmly toward that other door, bent on testing the waters before he committed their more fragile elements. He rang for admission, as if their guest had any control over his own door, before Banichi reached out to the button and unceremoniously opened it.

Their guest, dressed in Bindanda's blue bathrobe, met them on his feet, apprehensive, to judge by the rapid pace of the nostril slits. The room smelled of hot pavement.

"Good afternoon," Bren said in Mosphei', showing empty hands and making a small bow—aversion of the gaze was a fairly reasonable, though not universal, indication of quiet intent. He laid a hand on his own chest, avoiding a rude stare in this formal meeting, experimenting shyly with eye contact. A glance seemed accepted, maybe expected, though met with a stony stare in a face that held little emotion.

"Bren. Bren is my name." A flourish of a lace-cuffed hand toward his staff. "Banichi. Jago." An expectant, hopeful flourish toward their guest.

Who simply turned his back.

Well. *There* was a communicative gesture.

"Be respectful," Banichi said in a low voice, in Ragi; but Bren made a quiet, forbidding gesture.

"Have patience, nadiin-ji. His treatment by humans was hardly courteous. It's a very small defiance. Perhaps even a respectful dispute, in his own terms. Let me see." He walked over to the corner of the room, gaining at least a view of their guest's profile, a precarious proximity, though he had Banichi and Jago looming at his left.

"We would like to take you to your ship," he said quietly, soothingly, to that averted shoulder. "We wish to take the occupants of the station onto this ship and leave this station. We are here to help, not hurt."

It was a lengthy speech, in Ragi, certainly pure babble to alien ears. But it won a direct gaze, sidelong and, dared one think, perhaps reckoning that that was *not* the language, and therefore not the culture, he had met before.

"We hope you will be comfortable aboard until we can arrange your return to your ship," Bren said in a low, talking-to-children tone, still in Ragi. "Narani, the senior director of my staff, has disarranged himself to provide you this comfort, giving you his own bed. *Do* treat his cabin with respect. He's a very fine gentleman, and offers you the use of objects which he greatly values."

A profile, now. A mouth like a vise, a brow that lowered over large eyes to shadow them—not actually an unpleasant face, once one tried earnestly to see the symmetry of it. But Jago had warned him there were very good teeth, and he could see for himself the huge hands, a grasp which had challenged even Banichi's strength.

"We talked to your ship," Bren said, this time in ship-speak. He kept the vocabulary small and repetitive and the syntax very basic. "They showed us pictures, how station took you. Your ship says bring you back. We say yes. We leave this station. We take all the people out of this station and go. We want peace with you and this ship."

Now the full face, as their guest turned to face him— a scowl, was it, or a friendly face in sullen repose? And did turning toward him and meeting his eyes express courteous attention, or defiant insult?

Massive hand went to massive chest. "Prakuyo."

"Prakuyo. —Bren." He made a bow: one didn't hold out an intrusive hand, not with atevi, at first meeting, and not to any foreigner, in his opinion, without knowing the other party's concept of body space and invasion. On the contrary, he kept his hands to himself and dropped his eyes for a moment, primate respect, before looking up. "Do you understand, Prakuyo? We take you to your ship."

The jaw remained clenched.

But the eyes darted aside in alarm as a disturbance reached the open door.

A very junior disturbance, as might be, who brought up short and wide-eyed, and who for a moment distracted him, distracted their guest—*not*, however, Banichi, as Jago alone gave a measured look at the doorway.

One hardly needed guess Cajeiri had escaped the dowager's party.

"This is the foreigner," Cajeiri surmised.

"Young lord," Bren said, now that his pulse rate had slowed, "kindly go back to Cenedi. Immediately."

"He's as large as we are," Cajeiri said, marveling. The heir, highly overstimulated by the situation and long bored, was being a seven-year-old brat.

"Go," Jago said, just that, and the boy ducked back out of sight.

"Pardon. He's a child," Bren said calmly, as their guest continued to gaze at the vacant doorway—as if, next, fairies and unicorns could manifest. Interesting, Bren thought. Even encouraging. "This room is in our ship. We live here. This is not a prison."

Prakuyo, if that was his name, turned a burning look his way.

"Do you understand?" Bren asked him. "Six years on the station—I think you might have learned *good morning, hello, goodbye.*"

"Damn dumb shit," Prakuyo muttered, in a voice that sounded like rocks hitting together.

Had he just heard that? *Damn dumb shit.*

Yes, he had heard that. So much for good morning, good afternoon and other station attempts to establish communication.

"*Thank* you," Bren said all the same, and made a bow. "Go *home.* Does that make sense?"

"Madison." It wasn't a particularly happy tone.

"Do you *want* Madison?" Bren asked. That was the person who'd been in charge in that prison. He laid a hand on his own chest. "Bren, *not* Madison. I don't know Madison. *I* make the law here. Do you want Madison?"

"Madison." Prakuyo hit fist into palm, not a good indicator for Madison.

"Bren," he said, laying a hand on his chest. "Thank you." Another bow. And the paidhi-aiji, in a sense of timing that had served well enough among atevi, made a wide decision—that even a small advance in communication had to be rewarded, that body language and cooperation indicated they dared run the risk of a boy not being where he was supposed to turn up. He recklessly indicated the door and trusted his staff together could flatten their guest, if they had to. "Come, Prakuyo. Walk with me. Outside."

That upset their guest's sense of the universe. Nostrils worked hard. Need for more oxygen was a basic biological preface to high action, one could take that for a fair guess; but it could also accompany decision. Bren walked easily, cheerfully, to the door, bowed his courtly best and made a clear gesture of invitation outward—spying, in the process, a clear corridor.

Their guest advanced to the door. And ventured out. Bren showed him the way down the corridor, walking with him, Banichi and Jago a little behind.

"We live in these rooms," Bren said, gesturing left and right, prattling on mostly to keep the tone easy as they walked. "My companions are atevi. I'm human. Not station-human. I live on this ship. What are you, Prakuyo?"

He got no answer to that attempt, not the dimmest hint of understanding. Prakuyo lumbered slowly forward, with heavy swings of his head and shifts of dark, large eyes, taking in every detail of a corridor Narani had done his best to render *kabiu* and harmonious. Certainly it had to be better to alien eyes than the sterile prison section: a little table, a few hangings . . . one hanging, to be sure, harmonizing the troublesome dent.

"Come in," Bren said, showing their guest through the door into their dining hall.

Again, not ship-bland. Atevi-scale chairs sat around a large table. A tapestry runner relieved the sterile modernity of the arrangement. Wall hangings provided a sense of space and harmony. A graceful vase sat in the center of the table—a moveable object, Bren noted. It held lush greenery, from Sandra Johnson's now wide-spread cuttings.

Prakuyo stood stock still.

Bren laid claim to Banichi's ordinary chair on the doorward side—his security had hammered home such points with him; Banichi and Jago stood, not inclined to sit down, but their looming over the table intimated a threat that scarcely helped.

"Do sit, nadiin-ji," Bren said quietly. Their guest picked a central chair on the opposite side and sat down . . . whether that was his preferred posture or not: the chairs here were at least of a scale that would bear his weight.

Prakuyo was cooperating, at least . . . cooperating, possibly, to learn what he could before making a break for the vase as a weapon. But they couldn't act as if they expected that. Prakuyo's momentary attention was for the vase—or the greenery, that anomaly in this steel world. His eyes showed numerous frown lines, a clue, at least, that the general lighting might be too bright.

"Jago-ji, dim the light a little."

Jago rose and did that, and Prakuyo looked up, the frown lines relaxing.

The lights might be too bright, the air pressure was probably a little lower than their guest truly liked, but the cooler temperatures seemed not to bother him. He'd had all the water he wanted, on the whole, surely that brought an improvement in his mood.

"The station was not good to you," Bren said, deliberately rattling on, to see if the vocabulary provoked a reaction—or whether their guest's comprehension went beyond single words, to syntax. "Station did bad. Were you angry with them?"

Silence.

"Or were you angry at the ship?" Bren asked. "Did the ship go somewhere they shouldn't have gone? Did they do something that offended you? Something that *scared* you?"

Silence still.

"Can I ask him what his name is?" Cajeiri turned up at the door. Another skip of the heart.

"One believes you have just done so, young sir. And his name seems to be Prakuyo. But if he doesn't understand my language, I very much doubt he understands yours. Have you brought your car?"

Cajeiri brought it from behind him. Their guest looked alarmed.

"Run it end to end of the table," Bren said.

"Shall I use the remote, nandi?"

Bright lad.

"You can. Just run it very slowly down the table."

Down the sacred dining table. That was a daring

enterprise. Cajeiri took the remote from his pocket, which Prakuyo watched apprehensively, and operated his car very slowly, quite circumspectly.

Bren paid all considerate attention to the toy, which made its way at a jerky pace past the antique vase of greenery and into his hands.

"Now call it back."

Cajeiri did that. Grind and whir. Wobble and correct. The car did far better with grand movements, and one so hoped the young fingers would keep the rate steady and not zip it into their guest's lap. By now Cenedi's men were in the doorway, watching this performance.

Their guest, Bren marked in his peripheral vision, had looked ready to bolt at the first manifestation of the car, and at the remote control, and now just stared as the toy zigged and zagged and trundled safely back down the table.

"And back again," Bren said. While the fate of worlds trembled in the balance, while armed security outnumbered the civilians. And while a traumatized foreigner watched a child's toy wobble down a table top.

"Does he want to try it?" Cajeiri wanted to know.

"One hopes not to offend our guest's dignity," Bren said. "But our guest should know we do other things less terrible than shoot at those who don't look like us, should he not?" He smiled. Deliberately. "Are we having fun, young lord?"

"Shall I make it go fast now?"

"Slowly," Banichi said in his low tones. "Slowly."

Surely if Cajeiri were demonstrating the car for another boy, *fast* would have been very impressive. But Cajeiri, despite one accidental spurt, dutifully concentrated on keeping the movement slow. And at that

moment Bindanda excused his way past Cenedi's two
men, bearing a tray with a sizeable pitcher of ice
water, and fine crystal cups, and a pile of white sugar
cakes that smelled of fresh icing and recent baking.

"Excellent," Bren said. *Whirr* went the car, rapidly
back to Cajeiri. But the car was forgotten. Their
guest's attention was on those cakes.

"Danda-ji. Thank you."

Their guest duly accepted a crystal cup of water,
formally served, sipped it with restraint, accepted an
atevi-sized tea cake, eyes sparkling with animation
and excitement.

Dared one think that tea cakes had *not* regularly
been on the station's menu, for their prisoner? That
for most of ten years, the fare had been ship-fare,
bland yeasts and synth?

Cajeiri wanted his tea cake, too, but waited, hushed,
toy car tucked out of the way, waiting his turn as
Bindanda served all round, served Banichi and Jago
as well, and deftly replenished Prakuyo's cup with
ice water.

"A welcome to our guest," Bren said then, lifting
his cup in salute. *"Welcome,* Prakuyo-nadi."

"Welcome," Cajeiri said in great enthusiasm, and
likewise lifted his cup.

Could such an immensely strong hand tremble? It
did, and spilled water over the rim of the cup. Prakuyo
drained another icewater, crunched the ice in, yes,
very healthy grinding teeth behind those incisors—
definitely an omnivore—and followed it with the cake.
Bindanda poured yet another water, and with a re-
offer of the plate, indicated Prakuyo should take more
tea cakes, until he had fortunate three—in such arcane
ways culture manifested itself.

Then their guest looked doubtfully at Bren, perhaps

realizing he had just forgotten that cardinal precaution appropriate in prisoners—that he had just ingested doubtful cakes and suspicious ice water.

Greenery. Cakes with natural sweetness. Greatly appreciated: Prakuyo, or at least his culture, was not that long divorced from blue sky.

"It's safe," Bren said, lifted his cup and drank, and took a bite of cake. "*Tea cake*. Safe. Eat."

Prakuyo ate another, no question. The cakes disappeared, each almost at a bite.

"More tea cake?" Bren asked. "Danda-ji, perhaps an assortment of breads and cheese as well. A small offering of meat. One can't know his customs. Provide a picture of the game offering, so he may know what it is."

"Nandi." Bindanda bowed and took the service and tray away for a refill.

Prakuyo's gaze traveled after him, dared one say, with longing and deep thought centered on those tea cakes—perhaps telling himself that these tall black ones were very different from little varigated humans, offering much better cuisine.

"He'll bring more food," Bren said. Certain needs were, if not wholly satisfied with mother's cooking and a sight of home, at least assuaged. Their guest's facade of glum indifference had given way. That was a success. They had a few words, reinforced with food—dared they say their guest knew a Ragi word now, for tea cake? The situation with Gin and the fuel remained unresolved. God only knew what the Guildmaster and Jase were were doing with each other. But the paidhi's universe shrank necessarily to this deck, this room, this table, and he carefully, slowly, drew out of his inner coat pocket a few folded sheets of precious paper, and out of his outer right pocket a writing kit.

In fair sketch, on a blank sheet of paper, he drew a burning sun, a planet, a station, a ship tied to the station with an umbilical, just exactly their situation.

"The world and the sun," Cajeiri said helpfully in Ragi, leaning, elbows on table, past Jago. Then: "Is it our ship, or his ship?"

"Shall we see?" In Ragi. Then in ship-speak. "Ship," Bren said. "Sun. Planet. Ship. Station. Here." He tapped the table, waved a hand about the room. "Ship."

"Ship," Prakuyo said suddenly, explosive on the *p,* which alone distinguished that word from his other notable ship-speak phrase. "Bren ship."

"Human *and* atevi ship. Human station." Bren drew another ship, far distant, off to the edge of the paper. "Prakuyo ship."

Prakuyo paid burning, deep attention to that.

"Shall you not ask him where he lives, nandi?"

Surely when the legendary paidhiin of the past had done their work, they'd done it without an inquisitive boy at hand.

But the toy, at least, was useful. "Car," he said, in ship-speak, and indicated the car in Cajeiri's possession. "Kindly make it run again, young lord, slowly." Cajeiri ran it. "The car goes." All the way to the end of the table. "The car turns. The car comes back."

Not a helpful word out of their subject, but Prakuyo watched intently.

"Station." This was the vase. And the drawing. "Ship." This was the car. One hoped the capacity for abstraction existed in Prakuyo's kind. One rather expected that basic gift in spacefarers. "Send the car to the end of the table, young lord. Just so." In ship-speak: "The ship goes." In Ragi: "Now to the vase, young lord, if you please." In ship-speak. "Bren's ship goes *to* the station."

"Bren's ship goes," Prakuyo said obligingly, fighting a valiant battle with the consonants. "To the station."

Bren drew hasty tall stick figures on the paper. Numerous. With a loop that made a station. "Human. Human go human ship." Never mind grammar. Finesse came later. He had Prakuyo's attention. "Prakuyo go Prakuyo's ship."

Long concentration. Tension, Bren much feared. Worlds hung in the balance.

The car whirred. Jerked forward on the table. Cajeiri grabbed it. Hugged it close, wide-eyed. Banichi's attention and Jago's was immaculately for Prakuyo.

"One is very sorry, nandi." This from Cajeiri, with the offending car hugged tight.

And just about that moment there was quiet noise outside—Bindanda, Bren thought at first, and their second snack. But the approaching tap of a cane foretold a more notable intrusion. He rose, and Banichi and Jago did, Cajeiri, too, and bowed, as, sure enough, Ilisidi arrived, with Cenedi. The dowager bent a forbidding look at her great-grandson, then a benign and gracious one toward their guest, who slowly got to his feet and gave a little bow himself.

"Well, well," Ilisidi said, clearly pleased, leaning on her cane, surveying the room. "Present this person, nandi."

"This is Prakuyo, nand' dowager. One fears communication is at a minimum."

"Nonsense." Ilisidi said cheerfully, and moved to take the seat at the head of the table, Cenedi assisting her with the chair. "He has a sense of courtesy; we shall manage. Sit. Sit, Cenedi. Make us a fortunate number. My great-grandson with his foolish toy will have us at war before we achieve understanding. *Say* to this individual that we consider war is foolish. That we offer alternatives. Let us get to the point, nand' paidhi. Let us get this individual to his ship and get your troublesome relations to fuel us and get themselves aboard, shall we not?"

"Nandi." Bren gave a little bow, then sank into his chair as others did, feeling overwhelmed.

And yet—weren't they well on their way? Wasn't it, after all, the ability to wish one another well— civilized and peaceful?

"One very much regrets the car, mani-ma." This from a great-grandson whose whole universe still revolved around his own mistakes, his own necessities.

"We are quite sure," Ilisidi said with a wave of her hand.

And in the next moment Bindanda hastened through the door with tea cakes and offerings of bread, seasoned curd and meat. With an illustration of the fish involved . . . wise choice. In no wise an intelligent-looking fish.

Narani too arrived, hard on Bindanda's heels, with a tea service, tea, and a pitcher of bland fruit juice.

A meal had arrived.

"Serve, nadiin," Ilisidi said, and they served with ceremony, settling a respectful hush upon the room, a proper appreciation of the chef's efforts and the sacrifice of edible creatures and plants. Plates were laid out. Tea cups were filled. Each item was doled out with grace and intent. The illustration was presented to Prakuyo, demonstrating the meat dish.

Prakuyo observed, and by no means refused the fish. He attempted the eating-sticks, but his large, blunt digits—he had three, and a medial opposing one, like a thumb, but not quite—made it very clumsy.

"Prakuyo," Bren said, requesting attention. He made a sandwich of bread and curd and meat. And offered it across the table on a saucer.

Prakuyo took the offering cautiously, carefully. And

set it down next his own plate. And then a very curious vibration hit the air, deep enough to make the table quiver. Prakuyo simply sat there with head bowed, and it was clear this vibration came from his chest.

Then he got up from the table—security watched, poised, at this breach of custom; but Prakuyo turned his back and continued this strange humming that made tea dance in the cups.

"Is that the ship or is it him?" Cajeiri asked, alarmed. "Is he unhappy?"

One remembered this creature had been confined for most of a decade, and that it might not be sane. Or might be ill, for all they knew. One desperately hoped they hadn't poisoned him.

At length Prakuyo turned to face the table. The dowager had graciously paused, having done away with a sandwich of her own. But now Prakuyo joined his hands together and carried them to his middle.

"Prakuyo An Tep," Prakuyo said in a voice deep and still quivering with that strange sound, and laid a hand on his chest. "What want?"

Well, Bren thought, heart beating fast. Prakuyo *hadn't* wasted six years of his sojourn among humans. *Damn dumb shit* wasn't quite the limit of his understanding.

Bren rose, quietly, and with a gesture, invited Prakuyo back to his chair. "Sit. Eat. Good. We take Prakuyo to Prakuyo's ship."

Face contracted in some emotion, Prakuyo made a gesture to him, to the rest of the company. "We!"

"We." Bren was, at first blink, puzzled, then saw, indeed, they did comprise a different sort of *we*, for someone whose universe had been, for six years, a very limited set of humans. Admittedly, they formed an odd sort of *we* under any less exotic circumstances . . . short and tall, strong and weak, young and old, different colors, different manners, different languages—all at one table and constantly changing back and forth between Ragi and ship-speak.

Was there not a step for beings, beyond just— civilized—or rationally adult?

"Not station *we*," Prakuyo said.

"No. Not station *we*. Ship *we*." Bren made his oddly assorted group inclusive with a gesture, and Prakuyo all but trembled. The sound vibration shook cups on the table.

"We wish to go home," Ilisidi said. "He wishes the same. Is this not the heart of matters?"

"One agrees, aiji-ma." Of all civilized ideas at least among atevi and humans, a very potent one. Home.

"*We* once regarded a foreign star in our skies with intense suspicion. Our associations were confused. Our order was overthrown. From such troubled waters rose the *aishi'ditat*. Was it to the good? No matter asking. It *is*. What *is* must be accounted, and only when it is accounted, what is *kabiu* will suggest itself."

Play it by ear. Adapt. Abandon the plan. Look for the new pattern in events as they fell. It was not the human view of crisis management. But it was profoundly atevi, profoundly valid. Had not such thinking even become Mospheiran, over the centuries? Had not the paidhiin worked and fought within the university and the government to get that flexibility with their neighbors installed in place of a more rigid, history-conscious policy?

"Ilisidi, who is very wise, Prakuyo, reminds me that atevi once saw a new star appear in atevi space. Humans came down to the atevi. She says it's not good, not bad. It is. *We* simply live together. Humans have a station. Atevi live on the station. *We* sit at one table. *Prakuyo* can sit at this table."

Did Prakuyo pick out even a dozen significant words—and put them together in any sane way?

Intense humming. Prakuyo sought his chair back and leaned on it as if he were reaching his physical or emotional limits.

"These are very excellent cakes," Ilisidi said, waving a hand at the nearest plate. And in Mosphei: "*Sit* with us, Prakuyo An Tep."

Bren had to take a breath of his own. A full sentence, in Mosphei'.

Prakuyo said something deep and sonorous, a modulation of quivering sound. And abruptly he sat down again at table.

"I have books full of pictures," Cajeiri piped up. "*I* can show him words. Will he like to see those, nandiin?"

Clever boy. Precocious boy. Not even a bad idea— if those picture books told a little less about the atevi homeworld. But the very flavors that won Prakuyo's interest admitted a planet. Stations anchored to planets. People occupying stations came from planets, and that ship out there would have tracked their entry, from what direction, and might easily find the world involved. The things he had once thought they might conceal seemed apparent now. They were in this game to the hilt, everything admitted. A visit to atevi space seemed likely. It was up to them, here, to see it was peaceful.

"Perhaps," Bren said, and Ilisidi waved a negligent hand—which sent Cajeiri running (pursued by a sharp stare from his great-grandmother) out the door.

"Tea?" Narani asked, and offered a cup, which Prakuyo took in both hands. Prakuyo sipped it, seemed at first to find it strange, and then to savor it greatly, dumping in a considerable lot of sugar.

The food on Prakuyo's plate disappeared as rapidly

as that on Ilisidi's—for that matter, on Cenedi's and Banichi's and Jago's, long after Bren had reached his limit on tea cakes. He sat there waiting for a seven-year-old's picture books, trying to think of the verbal routes he might use to reach some sort of abstract understanding. *Friend* hadn't even crossed the boundary between what was atevi and what was human. *Friendship* equated with atevi *association*. But intimate, heart-deep divergence of how person connected to person remained elusive to this day. The constellation of emotionally mediated, non-rational, instinct-driven connections escaped them: one side simply did not perceive as the other did.

The one thing they had worked out was that truth was best and that politely pretending to understand was a lethal trap. Nearly impossible to straighten out a transspecies perception of betrayal or, worse, a real nest of lies. There was danger in every direction. But trust . . . a foregone conclusion of benign intent—could tip the balance at least toward a presumption of good behavior.

Banichi touched his arm—rare; but Banichi wanted his quiet attention.

"Jase-aiji informs us the foreign ship has begun moving toward us. He asks your presence."

Damn.

But not nearly as heartfelt a *damn!* as might be if they weren't sitting at table with a critical condition satisfied—even satiated on tea cakes.

Jase needed to know that. Jase urgently needed to know there was progress.

"Dowager-ji," Bren said. "Prakuyo-ji." Two bows. "Forgive me. Jase needs me urgently. Prakuyo, ship wants me. I come back. Eat. Eat. Lot of food." He bowed again to one and to the other, and ducked outside, Jago in attendance, Banichi having remained with Cenedi, security being stretched perilously thin in that room with a table dividing a very strong guest from two very fragile persons. "Jago, I need to go. I shall not be long. Stay here. Assist. If Jase must speak to that ship, I should be there."

"Yes," Jago said with economy, and Bren hurried down the corridor, already thumbing buttons on his pocket com to reach C1.

"This is Bren Cameron. I'm on my way up there. Tell the captain."

17

He was approaching the end of the corridor as C1 answered him. *"Mr. Cameron, sir, the alien craft is moving at a cautious pace; it will have been moving for some time. Indications are it moved shortly after the visible flash when we lost the robot."*

Reasonable. The question was what it intended or what it thought was going on. It was a short list, and one hoped it had simply observed that flash and gotten worried. "Has station noticed this movement?"

"Captain Graham is talking to station administration now, advising them not to take any hostile action."

"As they value our collective lives, C1. I suggest you run the initial contact pattern for the alien. Send it and try to establish contact. Let them know we're still alive and keeping our agreements."

"Captain Graham has already given that order. We are currently transmitting and repeating."

Jase was no fool.

Neither was he. He punched the alternate channel on his com unit as he reached the section door, passing Ilisidi's guards, passing the door. "Isolate photographs of our guest, nadi," he asked of Asicho. "Produce a good still image of him and reduce it to black and white, no grays. Send that image to the bridge. A picture that looks happy or serene, if possible to judge."

"Yes, nand' paidhi."

He reached the lift, punched the call button, and changed com channels. "C1, Cameron here. Five-deck is sending you an image in a moment. Prepare it for transmission to the alien ship. I'm on my way up there in two seconds." The lift car door opened. He stepped in, input his destination.

"Bren?" Jase's voice, as the car started moving.

"We're doing fine down here," he reported to Jase. "His name seems to be Prakuyo, he speaks a handful of understandable words, and he's currently stuffing himself on tea cakes and tea at the dowager's table."

Small silence. Then: "Get up here. Bren, *get up here.*"

The lift car didn't move fast enough: it seemed forever until it let him out at the back of the bridge, and he headed straight for his first glimpse of Jase leaning over C1's console.

Jase was talking with someone on com, angrily so, something about risk and responsibility and innocence. Then:

"Let us handle it, Mr. Braddock. I advise you, let us handle this ship and everything to do with it. You've got one hole in your station as is, and if you start shooting first, we won't lift a finger to help you. I'm very serious about that." Jase made a motion to C1, reached past the man and opened a small compartment in the console, extracting one of the communications earpieces. He handed it to Bren. Bren switched it on and stuck it quickly into his ear.

". . . reject your credentials for this or any other such operation. You have no authority to contact that ship on your own behalf or ours."

Patience ended. Ice entered Jase's tone. "You *had* an alien hostage. Now we have him. You say let you manage communications between that ship and us; but if they contact us, we have no way to explain to them they're supposed to talk to you, since in six years you don't seem to have established any relations beyond a hostage situation. We've produced a set of communication files, we are using them at the moment, and you can see it's not shooting. More, your population knows by now why we're here, they know your hostage is in our hands, and we offer an alternative. Take our offer, sir. Come on board. Let's shake hands and not even discuss old history."

Jase wasn't doing badly on his own.

"Captain Graham, you are ordered to desist all independent operations, dock, and open your doors."

The one that could use a negotiator's help was Braddock. Unfortunately he wasn't inclined to take help when it was offered.

"Mr. Braddock," Jase said quietly, "we're providing you and your family a comfortable place in our colonial residency, where you can settle in far more comfort and safety than this station can ever offer. We've established contact with the alien ship and we have some confidence it won't shoot unless provoked, but the point is, Mr. Braddock, it's *alien,* it's *foreign,* it's *not* subject to either of us, and it's apt to do any damned thing, which means we have to deal with it moment by moment. Negotiations are ongoing. If they break down, you can't defend yourself; we can't defend you; and we're going to need fuel to get you and your station population to safety. Open the fuel port and allow an orderly boarding, for your own protection. The alternative is unthinkable."

"Captain Graham." Different voice. God, it was *Sabin's* voice.

"I'm here," Jase said.

"Captain Graham, relax. The Guildmaster and I are close to an agreement on the fuel and on the boarding. I have every confidence we can do everything we came

*to do. In the meanwhile, let's get the preliminaries done.
Hard dock. Then we'll arrange for fueling and and
orderly boarding."*

Jase listened. And frowned darkly. "Captain. Good
to hear from you. Why the silence?"

*"Station security precaution. We've reached an un-
derstanding. Bring the ship in."*

"Shall I move to the fuel port, captain?"

"Negative. Bring her into personnel."

"We took a ping off that explosion. We're testing
systems at the moment."

*"You can test at hard dock, Captain Graham.
Proceed."*

"Good try," Jase said. "But nothing's changed,
Guildmaster. You don't convince me, and pretense is
only going to get us in trouble."

Silence. The contact broke off on the other side.

"Synthesized," Jase said. There was a look from C1,
a deep breath. Bren heaved a deep breath of his own
and put his hands in his pockets, chagrined—silly lad
from the island, *he'd* believed the voice halfway
through that performance. He understood that a computer could in theory reproduce a face as well as a
voice, but he'd never heard one do it, and it was an
astonishingly good rendition. But linguistically—even
computer-assisted—he'd heard definitively non-Sabin
word-choices.

"Doesn't encourage optimism about a solution,"
Bren said.

"No. It doesn't. I'm afraid she's in a very great deal
of trouble." Crew overheard that, and Jase made no
attempt to conceal the facts of the situation, even
looked at certain of the crew as he said it. "Her orders
took that into account. We hope she's alive. But we
can't help her by giving in to the Guildmaster, and

we can't help her by putting the ship in reach of an armed takeover."

"Jenrette knows," Bren said. "Jenrette knows at least how and where he left her."

"It doesn't look good. But I have my orders. And just as urgently, we've got that ship moving in on us."

"C1," Bren asked the chief com post, "have you received the image from five-deck?"

"Yes, sir." C1 pushed buttons. Prakuyo's face, stark black and white, with drink in hand, lit a display. Happy? Their guest looked positively beatific.

An advanced technology might fake the celebratory pose—to judge by quasi-Sabin's appearance—but the camera had to have Prakuyo's living image to get that face and manner.

"I'd like to transmit that to his ship," Bren said to Jase.

"Do it," Jase said; C1 moved, and a reply window began ticking on the display.

"Brilliant," Jase said with a deep breath, then asked, sotto voce: "Is he really that cheerful?"

"He's enjoying the dowager's company."

Jase shot him a properly apprehensive look.

"Sir." C1 suddenly called for the captain's attention. "Mr. Braddock again."

"Let him stew," Jase said. "I'm not available."

"He's making threats, sir. About voiding the fuel."

"He's made them before."

"Yes, sir.—The captain's not available, sir. Sorry."

"C2, do we still have contact with Mr. Becker?" Jase asked.

"Yes, sir," C2 said. "He made it to the commercial zone half an hour ago, no problems."

"We're going to see action reasonably soon, I think," Jase said. Meanwhile the lift had cycled, and opened. "We're still short of experienced personnel, Bren. I don't want to ask this—but we've just seen what hope there is of Mr. Braddock taking a reasonable view. We've got to lay plans to get into Central—maybe with local help. Maybe not. Our alternative's pretty grim."

Blowing the station up with people in it—even if one was Braddock—wasn't palatable.

"Small-scale demolition? Take out the archive?"

"The way we were going to do it if we got cooperation. We do it without. We're going to have to call on five-deck again to do this. Can Banichi and Jago do it?"

"If I go." It was the last job he wanted, but he'd been helpful in the last try, and he was prepared to be stubborn. He saw refusal shaping Jase's next word and he was faster. "If I go, Jase. What do you want, the whole mission stalled out because some scared stationer with a gun wants to fight my bodyguard, when if I was there it wouldn't happen? We've got our routine down pat. We can do this."

"You're essential with the hostage."

"What's essential is to get him, alive, back to his ship. That's already set up. He's stuffed on tea cakes, happy as a freshman on break, and if I'm delayed, you can take over communicating with him—in your spare time."

"The hell."

"You ask for Banichi and Jago, you get *me*."

"*They* wouldn't understand that."

"I do. And you do. That's enough."

A deep, frustrated sigh. "Plan it," Jase said.

"They already have, I'm relatively sure. We'll review it, in light of what we know now." He cast a look at the ticking reply window. Expected that reply any second. But the other side had to get organized to answer, and decide how it was going to answer . . .

Not that great a delay, however. Almost as the reply clock went negative, lines began to appear and assemble on that monitor, at C1's station, mesmerizing process, line by line development of an image. Bren couldn't make out what it was yet, and meanwhile something had begun nagging him. "Sabin *took* most every security-trained crew member we had, except your bodyguard. If Braddock had to try to counterfeit her orders, she's clearly not cooperating. Her com went silent—but I think we should take into account the possibility she's not dead and not confined." Sabin was a direct thinker, set a goal and go for it, no diversions. "She *may* have made a try at the fuel port. Or some target she thought she could get to with twenty men."

Jase's eyes, distracted by the com panel, shifted to him, flickering in rapid thought. "Jenrette."

There was a man who'd gone initially to Braddock. Bet on it. Maybe sent to him—but certainly working for him. He'd betrayed Sabin and his shipmates. Or they couldn't read character.

"She's capable of *sending* Jenrette to Braddock," Jase said, "to see how Braddock received him, and maybe what Jenrette would do next. Then Braddock sends him to us."

"Or maybe she sent him precisely to disinform Braddock. She sends Jenrette to tell him one thing and she does something else, and *doesn't* turn up in station offices."

On the screen lines marched on, making a shape. Two beings facing one another, empty hands uplifted, one human, one Prakuyo's kind.

"Echo it to them," Bren said. Message received. "It's good. I think it's good."

There was an uncharacteristic stir on the bridge, an infinitestimal head-turning, a collective deep breath.

"A good guess where the senior captain might have gone if she's able," Jase said calmly. "Either the fuel—or Braddock."

"Captain." C1. "Lt. Kaplan."

"Go," Jase said, and a man in a cold-suit appeared on monitor 3.

"Captain?" Kaplan said. "Captain, there's action going on. There's ten, fifteen people and God-knows all sort of baggage coming out the section doors, and we shot a safety line over there, and it took, but this doesn't look orderly, not half."

"Two at a time, Kaplan, no baggage, no hand baggage," Jase said. "C1, get the cargo chief down there. Everything and everyone scanned through." Deep breath. "It's started—*if* this isn't one of Braddock's gifts."

It wasn't good. It wasn't when they'd have chosen to have it happen.

"All we can do," Bren said.

"Kaplan," Jase said. "Kaplan, cargo team's coming. Keep it slow and calm. Route the cars to three-deck, no detours. If anybody needs medical, we'll send medical to them—no way any stationer gets loose off three- and four-decks."

"Understood, captain. There's *kids* in this lot. There's an old man. They don't look hostile. The old man's got one of our fliers. But there's more coming."

"Boarding pass," Bren said under his breath. "I told them it was a boarding pass."

"Calm and easy," Jase said. "Calm and easy, Kaplan. Be gracious."

"Yes, sir," came back, and in the background of that picture another suited figure, Pressman, most likely, was looking out the open lock.

"Shift to C2 and monitor," Jase said to C1, and shot a glance at Bren. "A conspicuous gold-plated disaster is what they want, create a mess for us. They've taken our warnings and devised their *own* solution. And after the old man and the kids—bet their operatives will be in there."

"Or a handful of security guards bent on getting their relatives out. Where I dropped those brochures—God knows which; and damn the timing." He'd have wanted his own team out and clear; and they wouldn't be. "We'll have to go through them to get into the station. No question. We'll have to lock the doors open to get back."

"Can't be helped," Jase said. Something about the captaincy settled a look on the wielder, and Jase had gotten to have it—a furious, measuring glance, the distracted habit of a man tracking a dozen emergencies at once. While the image on the monitor took shape: *Ship. Station.*

Meanwhile the lift had arrived, crew coming up, Bren thought. But brisk steps presented Gin Kroger, in cold-boots and parka, still frosted from working God-knew-where.

"Heard there was a meeting up here," Gin said. "Heard you were involved." With a glance at Bren. "I'll guess we're going to do something."

"We're going to do something," Bren said.

"We're going in," Jase said, "And we've got passengers coming on."

Gin held up a disk. "Image. Fuel lock. Enhanced photo. Give me a suit and we can drill it."

"Disable it?" Jase asked.

"Maybe," Gin said. "*Maybe.* I want a suit. I can stealth it with a spray can."

"No," Jase said.

"We can spend ten hours re-rigging a robot to reach

into that angle while people are hammering at our doors or I can sneak out there with a hand-drill and do the job in half an hour."

"A hand-drill."

"This goings-on is the best cover we're going to have," Gin said, "right now, in the ship's shadow, while the Guild's busy with people trying to get to us. I can get in there, myself—"

"No way in hell, Gin!"

"Look, there's a reason I've got the doctorate, captain, sir. They're not going to blow that tank up. It'd take out the mast, which would take out the whole station. If the contact trigger's tripped, the only kind of explosion they'll want is to crank up the pressure and blow the explosive bolts: the tank's already got provision to blow out if there's a serious pressure anomaly, precisely to protect the mast integrity. The whole sensor system that runs it is just a limited kind of robot: that's what they've rigged into. I know what I'm looking at in our remote images, and I've been talking to the atevi, who are very good at this sort of thing. They say the same. It all depends on power to that system, which I can take out."

"We've got too many people in motion," Bren protested. "Too many operations. We can't rush one, Gin. Just wait. We may be able to get at this from inside."

"If you're threatening them, they're going to threaten back, won't they, to push the button and dump our fuel? I'm not a risk out there, I'm a precaution. I'll kill the pump that could let them retaliate and save us a year mopping it up. We can patch the system back, no problem."

"Do it," Jase said. "Take a suit."

"Got it," Gin said, and turned and headed off at high speed.

"Damn," Bren said.

"She's at risk," Jase said. "We're all at risk. No one's is more acute than anyone else's if we let the Guild deal with that ship out there. I want them busy, Bren."

"If we can get into Central we can get past that lock ourselves, with no loss of lives."

"With your neck at risk."

Different. He controlled that. Expressed one thought in Ragi, a cipher to the bridge crew. "We are doing all we can to gain our guest's good will. But one missile from the station could undo all that."

"We have to prevent it," Jase said in shipspeak, "Becker's loose in there, Sabin may be in there, the ship's scaring hell out of Central, and we just let two people go on the station with a handful of travel brochures. C2, get Mr. Cameron a handheld, C1's channels and output. Fast."

"Sir." C2 pulled a module right off his console, keyed it in half a dozen rapid motions, and offered it to Bren. "Just say *image* and you can key through images, say *voice* and you can talk to C1: don't say *console*, sir: that's straight to the keyboards. You won't want that. Won't want to carry that off the ship."

"I have it," Bren said, and tucked it into his coat pocket. His court finery.

"Add one thing to your plan. I want those accesses to the mast open. I don't want Guild able to lock them against us. And come *back* if you can't get through."

Coming in the way they had before—taking a vulnerable pod-ride across that gap with the Guild paying full attention to them—he hoped not to do that again. Going in by the mast seemed highly attractive. With the bonus of having that key and those doors open, to let population into the mast.

"I'll ask Banichi," he said. "We'll see what we can do with that idea."

Jase reached into his jacket pocket and handed the key to him. "Take care," Jase said, clapping him on the arm. "Take *care* of yourself, Bren."

"That's a high priority," he said, and hied himself off at Gin's speed, resisting any temptation to cast a look back as if it was a last look. He made up his mind it wouldn't be. He left the bridge and went to the lift, pockets full of electronic connections, the key, all manner of responsibility he'd rather not have, but had, and a mission now diverted from the one he knew how to do, onto an operation that didn't involve sitting at a dining table.

"Asa-ji," he said to Asicho on his way down in the lift, "how is our guest?"

"He seems well, nandi."

"Advise Banichi and Jago they may leave our guest to Narani's and the dowager's judgement and meet me in security. By no means alarm our guest, but the foreign ship is moving toward us and the station has offended Jase-aiji. We are being threatened."

"Yes, nandi," Asicho said; and, depend on it, that was done.

He checked the bridge remote, and saw the current displays as the lift reached five-deck—no change in that situation. The alien ship was still moving; the flow of images was under Jase's management—their own latest output redemonstrating their desire to board passengers and refuel. And at very worst—at very worst, Jase could put Prakuyo on mike and tell him talk to the foreign ship, and just hope for the best—

Hope that, meanwhile, station hadn't taken a rash potshot at the advancing ship. One recalled that slagged station surface. A, one didn't want to destroy an alien craft and have *that* to explain to the next ship that came asking, and, B, one didn't want to damage that alien craft and have them retaliate at everything in their gunsights. Which meant getting present decision-makers away from the fire button in station Central, and hoping nothing they did put innocent people into an area that ended up vacuum.

He had an argument coming with Banichi and Jago, and he hated to dispute them—but assuredly he would. He was going with them. He had to. Couldn't see them forced to shoot it out with scared, mostly innocent stationers . . . having to mow them down in rows to get at the guilty.

He entered the atevi section. "The dowager, nandi, is still with the foreigner," Ilisidi's guard at that post advised him.

"Thank you, nadi," he answered, hardly pausing, all the while trying to figure how, in addition to other troubles, he was going to explain the situation to Prakuyo . . . or *if* he should explain, at all. Leave matters as they were, he thought on his way to the security post. Explain nothing. *Hope* that all explanation in Prakuyo's case became extremely simple: *The station is cooperating. We have fuel. We shall take you to your ship. Let us leave now. Goodbye. Good luck.*

God, if *only* it could be that easy.

He reached the security post. Asicho shared the boards with one of Ilisidi's men. Banichi and Jago were there waiting for him. With their fighting gear and their black bag. That fast.

"We have understood," Banichi said, "Bren-ji."

"Gin-aiji will send Barnhart," Jago said. "We are ready. The aiji-dowager will see to matters here. Staff will attend our guest."

A negotiator braced for argument hardly knew what to do at that point.

"I have to change coats," he said.

*   *   *

A quick change, down to the skin, and back to station-style clothes. He was wearing out his wardrobe in a day.

He added the gas-mask, a rolled collar about his neck. Back came his gun, too: "One hopes not to need it, nandi."

"One heartily agrees, Rani-ji." He had the precious key in hand, and transferred it carefully to a zippered pocket, to be doubly sure. He made a fast check of the handheld unit Jase had lent him and saw the slow-moving dialogue of yes-no, black-white, off-on images proceeding, while communication with the station—God only knew. He had his pocket com. He didn't want to attempt using the unfamiliar handheld for voice communication. "Bren Cameron, for Captain Graham," he said to C1, and immediately had Jase on.

"Change of coats and we're ready to move," he reported to Jase. "Our plan is set. Banichi and Jago will brief me on the map in a few minutes. How is Gin?"

"*Says she's prepping the suit. We want to do this about simultaneously. You're going to have to hold up and wait for her.*"

"That's all right. I'm not eager for this. Our guest, by the way, is enjoying dessert. He can out-consume Banichi. They hadn't fed him enough. Or the right things."

"*Ship cuisine benefited greatly from Bindanda's influence,*" Jase said quietly, and said something aside from the com, then: "*If things get dicey, I'm thinking of putting our guest on com, let him talk to that ship. Good idea or bad?*"

"Could be a good idea. We don't know what he might promise them or encourage them to do, that's the situation. Not a good idea they move into line of the station's guns. He speaks a few words, Jase. Not

many, but at least a few. Maybe you could get him to
follow a diagram, maybe you could show him where
the guns are and let him explain the situation."

*"God knows what they'd understand the situation is
between us and station,"* Jase said. *"I'd like to control
communications better than that. We don't know but
what he'd say come in and get me."*

"You're probably right," Bren said. "Listen, I'll
handle it when I get back. See you." Gallows bravado,
as he clicked off. It was increasingly dawning on him
that this was the craziest thing he'd ever done—fueled
by the optimism of a little dive into the lightly watched
perimeter of the station, where, in a uniform society,
nobody was expecting a security breach. Now they
were expecting it—well, they'd be expecting it by the
time they noticed their doors weren't locking. This
was the high stakes move. The very high stakes. Control of the whole station. Most important, *stopping* the
station from taking a shot at that ship.

And, along with that, right at the top of their list:
blowing the Archive. Preventing the whole cultural
works of the human species from becoming a prize
of war.

"Our guest is enjoying another dessert," Narani informed him, "and greatly appreciates the fruit pie."

"Excellent. One has great confidence in the staff.
And in your resourcefulness, Rani-ji." The whole rest
of the staff was hovering about the dining hall, being
sure nothing untoward happened—their collective
strength surely enough to subdue their guest and rescue the dowager and Cajeiri, if needed.

Fruit pie hardly sounded like discontent or dispute,
except the sugar high of all those tea cakes.

He patted the gun and the key a second time, then
gave a little bow. "One hopes to be home for
breakfast."

"Nandi," Narani said with a little bow of his own, and let him out the door, down to security where Banichi and Jago were in preparations, giving last-moment information. Barnhart was there, hands in coat pockets, heavy cold-boots on his feet, gas mask tucked down at his collar—certainly not the sort of gear one wore in one's office.

"Thanks for coming," Bren said, and held out a hand, Mospheiran-style handshake. "We're on a rush move here. I trust you know about the ship moving in. I appreciate the backup."

"No question," Barnhart said.

They were ready.

18

The lift had begun to work overtime, cars rigidly locked on their task, shuttling back and around from the forward airlock to the decks above—specifically to three-and four-deck, where common crew by now must have spread out in sections to assign cabins and see that station-born residents obeyed stowage, that they understood the movement rules, the alarms, and the plumbing and the area restrictions—crew that made themselves living rule-books, because human beings under stress didn't reliably absorb labels and lists. The ship had laid out and rehearsed all the plans during their voyage. They'd held weekly drills, such that Bren had a very clear inner vision of those corridors, rows of doors like every other, but now with real live people inbound with their kids, their small bundles of baggage. They came thanks to Narani's brochures, thanks, perhaps, to his handing out sheets of printed paper in a remote region of the station where station security didn't expect contraband and hadn't been prepared to defend the station's version of truth against a simple handful of printed papers.

Their clerk might have run to his office, called his wife and said, simply, Pack; the ship will take us to Alpha; and a wife might have called a mother who called a father, who called his second daughter at work, and that daughter called her husband, who called his sister and her teen-aged kids: human relations went like that, and if people really believed his promise that the brochures were a boarding pass—then God save them, he thought. They were naive, they were innocent of Braddock's policies, and they deserved rescue, if the ship could get nobody in adminstration out alive.

This time there might be shooting. There was likely to be.

He clung barehanded to the safety rail in the car, next to Banichi and Jago. Barnhart was behind him with Desabi, Anaro and Kasari, three of the dowager's young men: fortunate seven. They were off to take a space station that could, undamaged, have housed a city full of humans.

The illusion of gravity, supplied now only by the car's jerks and turns and final stop, ceased altogether. The doors shot back with a sigh and showed them a safety web in dim lighting and a clutter of stationers and small baggage every which way—stationers that caught sight of Banichi and Jago and stared, wide-eyed. There were startled outcries.

"Allies!" Bren shouted. "Friends! You're perfectly safe! Keep moving!"

A good sign, he thought, that the refugees were more concerned about getting into the car they'd just vacated, and two of the ship's own crew were there to get them on in good order.

"No crowding!" one shouted as they left that problem behind and forged ahead, past the round tube entry where Kaplan and Polano were in charge of a handful of crew, armed and hard-suited against the unthinkable, that they would have to slow down a panic rush or a takeover attempt. Beyond them was utter dark.

"Outbound!" Bren yelled at the pair.

"Mr. Cameron, sir," Kaplan said. "You take care!"

"Intend to," he answered. Meanwhile a lighted gold ribbon of a conveyor line delivered more would-be passengers up and, past its sprocket, headed down into infinity. Banichi grabbed it, Jago did, and Bren tailed on, yanked authoritatively down past ascending passengers.

"Allies!" Bren shouted at those frightened looks in the dark, underlit by the conveyor line itself. "Hang tight! Warm space coming!"

Cold was all here—air in the tube stung the nose and burned the lungs, and dim light made them all shadows, except the light from the conveyor line, a golden glow that touched hands, underlit faces and edges of coats, bundles—they were ordinary folk, might-be shopkeepers and schoolchildren, workmen and businessfolk attached to this ribbon of light, grandmothers shepherded by younger folk, women carrying bundled children in one arm, one-handing their way up the conveyor, all packed tight for a space. That made about a lift car-load or two. Then there came a vacant space on the line, where crew below must be parceling out the refugees, lumping them into groups, sending them out a long, long ride in the absolute dark of the pressurized mast where the station itself hadn't deigned to turn the lights on.

Their own party was the only one downbound, and Banichi and Jago wisely kept upper bodies turned slightly away, where atevi eyes wouldn't catch the indirect light of the conveyor line. Down and down they went, past another clot of refugees, then into the spotlight glare of the tube entry, where a few bright lights overpowered the dark beyond.

No lights in the mast. No power, or no cooperation from Central for their own people voting, so to speak, with their departure. But no lights suited invaders very well. Invaders found a safe concealment.

Maybe he should have sent Prakuyo back to confinement before he left. Certainly leaving him in the dining hall with Ilisidi and the boy was worth a cold second thought. But it was far out of his hands now.

Long, long ride to think about that. And not a thing in the world he could do. No com. No information, either direction.

Then bottom. End of the line, down in the spotlights that shone on desperate refugee faces, a parka-coated crewman.

"Friends!" Bren said as they met and passed one another on the lines, and an alarmed outcry was swallowed up in dark and cold.

They were at a lift station, where the glowing dot of a button said a car was coming, doubtless with more people.

It arrived, brightly lit as the door opened, tightly packed with refugees who in their haste to get off and find their way, never noticed some of the people waiting in the dark for a lift were taller and broader than ordinary. The passengers cheered with relief to see the conveyor lines, to realize they'd met ship's crew; they came burdened with children and bundles, and wanted through this ordeal of cold and dark as fast as possible. They wanted safety, and reassurance.

Bren got in, held the door for Banichi and Jago in the warmth and light: Barnhart and the dowager's men entered, all of them, pressed close to the walls.

Time for the precious key. Bren pulled it out, fighting cold-stung tears that froze his lashes together and obscured his vision. He stuck it in the slot, input the builder's code, A1, which was as close to the operational heart as a car could get.

Doors shut. The car banged into motion. Feet hit

the floor and Bren tucked away the key and zipped the pocket, fingers so numb he had to look to be sure he had the zip secure.

Perfectly ordinary lift car. It could have been on their home station—give or take the level of weaponry around him. It rose, it clicked through ordinary operations. He watched Banichi and Jago take out sidearms and asked himself whether he should draw his gun and prepare to threaten the opposition, shoot without warning—or attempt the civilized approach he had envisioned when he insisted on coming.

"Let me attempt to talk to whatever individuals we meet," he requested of them. "Barnhart, the atevi have body armor. Keep to the rear; we don't want to lose our hands-on person."

"Enough said," Barnhart answered him.

The car slowed. The indicator didn't say first level. *Someone* had a priority code.

"To the sides," he said in Ragi—*foolish* of him to attempt to direct the operation, but they understood him and got to the protected sides.

The car stopped. A man in a suit, communications to his ear, simply got on, and didn't seem to register there was anything particularly unusual until the dowager's men flattened him and took his handheld away. An item sailed out of the car, far down the corridor— the handheld, Bren thought in one heartbeat, before a siren started up, where that object landed.

"Evacuate immediately," that object screamed, deafening in volume . . . in Gin's voice. *"Instability warning. Evacuate to the mast. Prepare for cold. Evacuate immediately . . ."*

Conspiracy between Gin and his staff. *His* heart thumped as he shoved his key back into the slot— deciding this time not only to punch the button, but to hold it—he'd seen maintenance do that. It might work.

The car got underway. Not a sound from the man in the suit, and a glance back didn't even show his presence, only Ilisidi's three guards in the corner.

Level 3. Section 2.

They were getting into the critical area. Holding the key in and the button down was working or they'd met a run of luck not too surprising in a station bleeding occupants toward the ship. Jago had gotten a small gray box out of their bag, and had that in hand. A grenade? Another noisemaker? He hoped not to meet resistence. And was sure he wouldn't get his wish.

He squeezed his eyes shut, trying to get the sweat out. Wiped them clear, trying not to hyperventilate. Banichi and Jago were right with him.

Level 2. Section 1. They were nearly there. Nearly there. Atevi had guns at the ready. Barnhart had wedged himself in the back somewhere. Question was, when they'd built the station, A-1 had been the building center, the core of original construction. It was *near* the control center. It wasn't necessarily *inside* the control center.

Level 1. Section 1.

The car stopped. "I shall have a look, nadiin-ji," Bren said, snatching the key back as the doors opened. He stepped out into an ordinary corridor, typically without numbers or signs; but with a single clerk in rapid motion; and he could see the secured doors of what was surely Central just to his left.

"Alarm on four!" he called out, which happened to be the truth. "Alarm on four! They're evacuating."

The clerk looked at him in shock.

"Get out of here!" Bren said; and about that time his company exited the lift car. The clerk pasted himself to the wall.

"Grenade!" Jago said, and Bren translated it: "Grenade! Run! Ship's boarding!"

As another noisemaker hit the corridor, siren shrieking, Gin's voice saying over and over, *"Evacuate!"*

Banichi and Jago ran for those doors; and Bren ran, Barnhart ran, and two of Ilisidi's men ran with them. Down went the black bag, Banichi opened the flap, and handed Jago a small object and a sticky wad which Jago pressed together into the door seam— Bren was watching that as Banichi, black bag in hand, jerked him back and pressed him against the wall, Banichi and Jago on either side of him. The stuff exploded with a shock that came up through the decking. Alarms screamed and machinery operated down the hall. Doors shut.

Central knew they were here, no question. Sirens warred, out of sync, theirs and the station's, as Banichi and one of Ilisidi's men seized the pair of damaged doors, wrestled something like a truck jack into the bottom.

Fire from inside the room pasted back, close to Banichi. Bren drew his gun, sole comfort in a situation that hadn't turned out in the least diplomatic. Barnhart proved to have his own gun; but the human contingent could only watch as the second of Ilisidi's guards added his strength to the jammed doors, as machinery and atevi muscle warred. More pellet-fire streaked out of that room, burning two streaks in Banichi's sleeve, making him wince.

An office door opened halfway down the corridor, and fire came from the lift car: their own guns keeping whoever was in that new doorway pinned down and out of action; Bren tried to see the target and couldn't.

Their own doors widened, jostled aside. Jago dropped down to the deck in the doorway, rifle braced at ankle level, and fired into the room.

Pellet fire came out, over her head.

Banichi pulled a grenade out of his jacket and tossed it in. Jago rolled over, out of the way, shielded by the ruined doors.

Percussion grenade. Flash-bang. It no sooner went off than Banichi and Ilisidi's men charged over Jago's position and dived to either side within the room.

Jago scrambled up and in.

And damn if he was any use back here. "Watch the hall!" he shouted to Barnhart, and dived low inside the jimmied doors, skinned through the gap on his belly, facing a console base of some kind, only to feel a powerful hand seize the coat in the middle of his back and drag him aside and back against the wall.

Not so much use here, either. Jago had him, hugged him close in the process of wedging him further back into the corner, where her armor protected him. A pall of smoke hung over the place, reddened by the lights blinking on consoles, and sirens were still going off.

Banichi and Ilsidi's men inched toward wider positions.

And people were going to die.

If he didn't think of something.

"I'm Bren Cameron from Alpha," he shouted, "here with local allies from Alpha. Cease fire and get rid of the weapons. We're a rescue mission! Just don't fire and you'll all get out of this alive!"

Fire answered that offer, pellets richocheting everywhere, doing no good for the consoles, which began beeping protests.

"One doubts they will surrender," Jago said, incredibly patient.

"One regrets the attention, Jago-ji." Pellets richocheted all about them. "Barnhart is out there watching the hall."

"Excellent, Bren-ji." Jago moved a little. "Stay here. Cover your ears."

Banichi and Ilisidi's men had just that instant passed out of sight behind a console, and now Jago moved—he *hoped* he hadn't thrown their timing off. He crouched low, trying to become invisible.

Bang. A pop-grenade, a distraction. A man broke cover into his aisle, low as he was, and Bren braced his back in the corner and braced his pistol against his knees, affording that security guard a view down the gun-barrel.

"Stand up," he said. "Stand up. Hands up. You'll survive only if you do as you're told. Where's Braddock?"

"Office."

"Stand *up!*" he snapped; but about that time pellets flew all about and the man, starting to stand up, ducked down, covering head and ears.

"I can't!"

Another grenade explosion went off. What light panels hadn't fallen, came rattling down everywhere, and Jago appeared on her knees behind his prisoner, snatched him by the foot and flattened him with an elbow and an open-handed blow that sprawled the man flat on the deck.

"One apologizes," Bren whispered, too deaf to hear his own voice, and Jago scuttled toward him, seized him by the arm and dragged him off to another aisle of consoles where a handful of harmless, non-combatant station techs, caught between invasion and security forces, had taken cover and lay in heaps, covering heads and necks and each other.

A door was down that aisle. A windowed office.

"He said Braddock is in the office, Jago-ji."

"Tell these persons to move."

"Crawl out of here," Bren said. "Clear this aisle. You're safer outside: just stay down and don't act hostile. Move, and you'll survive!"

Most of a dozen techs and clerks mobilized themselves, scrambling out of the aisle, down into another row, an aisle that led potentially to the door; and Jago eeled forward, low, up against the door in question—stuck a device to it and got out of the way, as pellet-fire erupted from another aisle.

The limpet went off—blew a hole where the door edge met the wall; and fire-suppression went off, clouds of vapor coming down.

"Gas!" Jago yelled, and Bren dragged up his own mask, while the air grew thick with fog.

Jago, meanwhile, got a hand on the door-edge and pulled, and pellet-fire came out at them.

Didn't stop Jago. She charged in and there was a heavy thump.

Bren scrambled to the door on elbows and knees, saw Jago on her feet, dragging no less than Braddock himself, who was swearing and flailing.

Jago's patience ran out. She swung the man around in a restraining grip and shoved him onto the floor, under her foot.

"Bren Cameron, Mr. Braddock," Bren said, ducked as low, at least, as the window-edge, bulletproof as it might be. "I'd advise you give up and get your people aboard."

"Traitor to your own species!"

Name-calling. A disappointing lack of common sense.

"I did my best for you," Bren said. "You're on your own, Mr. Braddock. I just hope to prevent most of your people getting killed, because we're taking this station down."

"The hell!" Braddock yelled, and broke out in coughing and shortness of breath.

Jago simply flattened him.

"Banichi?" she called out. "We have the station-aiji."

"We have the main area," Banichi said, outside, not far distant, and appeared in the haze, standing up, leaning with a casual air against the ravaged door. "It was hardly a well-thought defense, particularly the firefighting system."

Jago gathered Braddock up, half-conscious as he was. Bren thought it finally safe to stand up; and he could see, in the thicker fog outside, Ilisidi's men moving about in the aisles.

"They'll die," he said, concerned for the techs and even for Braddock, but as he came outside he saw Ilisidi's men were clearing the aisles of downed workers, simply dragging them out into the corridor, one and two at a time. Jago took Braddock himself to the wrecked doorway and the clearer air.

And Barnhart had come in, masked, walking over fallen light panels to get to the main console.

Station systems. Barnhart knew those, having built them. He started flipping switches. And took up a microphone. "This is station Central announcing a general boarding. Take only essential items and medications. Essential personnel, remain at posts during boarding. You are assured time to reach the mast in an orderly evacuation. We have reached an understanding with the alien craft. Fuel operations techs, report to ship's officers stat."

"Can you lock the board, Bren-ji?" Jago asked, and Bren shook off the spell of Barnhart's general announcement echoing from the hall outside, fished out the precious key and looked for a key-slot. Any key-slot, his being universal.

Barnhart pointed. He slid it in and Barnhart punched buttons.

"They can't lock the board down," Barnhart said, and flipped more switches. "Data's all over this system. But main storage is over there."

"Banichi," Bren said, and translated: "That is the Archive."

Banichi got into the bag and took out an alarmingly large limpet. And stuck it on.

"We should leave now, Bren-ji," Banichi said, and said in Mosphei', "Run. Now."

Sabin, Bren thought, realizing the finality of the next explosion. They had no idea where Sabin was. But Jago shoved him and Barnhart at the door and through it, Banichi and Ilisidi's men following, out into a hall where the third of Ilisidi's guards maintained one foot in the lift and held under threat of his rifle all the coughing, terrified technicians sitting on the floor. And he didn't see Braddock.

"We should go support Gin-aiji," Banichi said, and waved an arm, beckoning the frightened civilians. "Run! Go to the lift!"

The techs scrambled up and ran. Ilisidi's man stepped out, and Bren stood in the lift door and beckoned the techs. "Come on in with us. We'll get you to safety. Hurry!"

A handful hesitated, then rushed into the car; the rest scattered.

"Don't go back into Control!" Barnhart yelled at those that stayed, and about that time the charge blew. One of Ilisidi's men yanked Barnhart back into the lift and Jago shut the door.

Key. Bren shoved it in. The humans with them jammed themselves into one corner of the car, scared beyond speech and probably now asking themselves if they'd made the right choice.

"Anybody know fuel systems?" Barnhart asked, and in a silence aside from heavy breathing and the thumps of the moving car: "If we can't move the ship, we're all in a mess. *Is* there fuel?"

"There is," a smallish man said, coughing. "There ought to be."

"G-10, by the charts," Barnhart said, and Bren punched that in.

Bang-thump. The car started to move. Bren's heartbeat ticked up in time with the thumps and jolts the car made.

"All the rest of you," Bren said, keeping his voice calm, at least, "all of you just stay in that corner and don't do anything when we get down there. Chairman Braddock claimed you've rigged the fuel to explode. We're going to try to get past that lock to refuel the ship that's going to get you out of here and back to Alpha. When we get that done, you'll be free to do whatever you want—get your families aboard, gather the family heirlooms, or run hide in a closet on the station, which we don't advise. That alien ship is moving in to get its next of kin back, which Braddock has been holding prisoner for most of ten years. Now we've got him, and we're going to give him back and get the ship out of here. Join us if you like."

Banichi reached into his coat and pulled out, quite solemnly, several of the color brochures, which he offered to the stationers. "Baggage rules," he said.

The stationers took the papers very, very gingerly. Banichi *smiled* down at them.

The car slowed. Bren hit *lock*, then pocketed his key: no car was coming in—this one wasn't getting out. "I've locked it," he said to the workers. "Safest, to stay inside until the dust settles. One of my associates will stay with you. *Don't* put your heads out if you hear gunfire." He straightened his coat, glanced at Banichi and Jago, drew a deep breath, and looked out into the corridor.

Deserted. But fire-scorched along the wall panels. Ceiling panels down, showing structural elements that themselves were potential sites of ambush. It looked as if, please God, everyone had deserted the place.

"Hello?" he called out, playing tourist on holiday, looking, he hoped, not like a foreigner. "Hello?"

Heads popped out of a room down the hall. Projectile fire went past him, and he hit the floor, flat on his face, playing corpse. Pellet-fire came from the room down the hall and projectile-fire came back from at least two sources.

"Bren-ji?" Jago's voice, from the lift car behind him.

"Cameron?" a hoarse yell from behind him, from a corridor past the lift. Clearly someone knew him. He didn't quite peg it. "Cameron, get back!"

"Cameron, dammit! *Keep down!*" God, he knew *that* voice. *Sabin.* That came from still farther back down the corridor.

"I'm lying very flat," he called out to his own team, beginning to creep sideways, over against the same wall as the lift.

Heads popped out of the doorway up the corridor. The occupants fired. Banichi and Jago fired, Sabin's position far behind him fired, all over his head, and he scrambled backward along the wall, pushing with his palms and knees.

Then a curious object whined along the decking, past his head—one of Cajeiri's toy cars, with something taped to the top. He was completely mesmerized for the moment, at ground level, watching it zip ahead down the corridor. It finessed a sharp turn, right into the appropriate room—Banichi had to have his head exposed, steering it: that was Bren's immediate thought.

The car went off in a white flash of brilliant light. A cloud of gas rolled out of that room.

Ilisidi's men raced past his prone body, as a strong atevi hand grabbed him by the scruff and hauled him up—that was Banichi—and another, lighter footstep came up beside him.

Jenrette. A white-faced, anxious Jenrette, gun in hand. Damned right he'd known that first voice.

If Jenrette intended trouble—he had to admit—Jenrette could have shot him.

"Trying to follow Graham's orders," Jenrette said. "I knew she'd come here, if anywhere. Tell her that."

Vouch for a many-times traitor, at this critical point, whose reason for not shooting him was far from altruistic? *Sabin* was farther down that corridor, down by the intersection, still under cover, not coming out into the clear.

Banichi, meanwhile, had joined Ilisidi's men. Jago had possession of the corridor, rifle in hand, and waited for them. For *him.* For the *key,* which he had, dammit and bloody hell!

"Stay down by the lift," he snapped at Jenrette. Barnhart had run ahead of him, halfway to Banichi. Bren caught a shallow breath and ran, too, on legs that wanted to wobble as if the emergency were already over.

Which it wasn't by a mile. The rules had changed, but the machinery in that room was still operating. If any of the techs inside had vented the fuel or set something ticking in that gas-filled room, they had a problem.

Next was an intersection of corridors, ambush possible. Banichi and Jago, masks up, entered the room,

Ilisidi's men went to the T of the hall; and there ensued bangs and thumps from inside the gas-clouded
room, bodies hitting consoles, God only knew. Bren
reached the door beside Barnhart, pulled his gas mask
up, already feeling the sting of the gas. His limited
view made out Banichi and Jago on their feet, and
two lighted consoles in this moderate-sized room, two
monitors lit—the techs who should be watching those
monitors were on the floor, at the moment, coughing
and struggling, and Banichi and Jago were kindly
dragging them out.

The mercy mission exited. Barnhart headed in. Bren
did. His hazed view of the monitors shaped a camera
view of machinery on one screen in the middle of the
consoles, graphs and figures on the other, the rest dark
and unused. This place handled refueling. Controlled
the pumps, the valves, the lines, the booms, and none
of that was going on; but that monitor—that one monitor had what looked like a camera-shot of the fuel
port; and that, more than the switches, was where
Bren directed his attention.

If Gin was out there, he had no idea where; but if
she'd gotten there, trying to take the power out—she
was still at risk from anything wired in, independent
of station power, and they couldn't communicate
with her.

"We don't know where Gin is," Bren said, muffled
in the mask. "Hang on, hang on before we start pushing any buttons." He had his own communications, in
the pocket com, in the handheld, and took it out
uncertainly.

"That won't reach the ship," Barnhart said.

"Lights. Gin'd see that. Can we get an on-off? Let
her know we're here."

Barnhart moved his hand over one board, looking
for a switch in the haze, then reached across the board

and flipped one. Camera view dimmed. Brightened. The spotlight on that port went off. On. Off. On.

That had to tell Gin she had help inside. That risking her neck had suddenly gone to a lesser priority, and she had time.

And they, meanwhile, were faced with an array of buttons none of which was going to be labeled *blow the damn fuel*.

"I don't think we should touch it, yet," he said to Barnhart, extending a cautionary hand. "Just guard it and get some of the ship personnel up—"

Shots rang out from the left hand of the door. That intersecting T-corridor—he could see it in his mind. Ilisidi's men. They *weren't* safe here. They were far separated from safe territory.

Shots became a volley. A firefight. And Banichi vanished from the doorway, headed leftward, leaving Jago alone to hold the door. As fire broke out from the other direction. Jago pasted a shot in that direction, and crouched down, delving into Banichi's black bag.

Bren left the consoles to Barnhart and joined Jago, hand on the gun in his pocket. "I can lock these consoles down, Jago-ji," he said. "We can make a run for it. Can we tell Banichi that?"

A sudden fire was going at either side, and there wasn't a safe place for anyone in the corridor, where they'd dumped the hapless ops center technicians. Banichi and Ilisidi's men stood their ground at the corner; while fire down the corridor was coming from midway and far down, and the technicians, crawling, attempted to go in that direction.

Jago was assembling another of Cajeiri's little cars with tape and a black box, and with a fast wrap of tape, she set it loose, steered it left, down the corridor toward Banichi's position and right around the corner.

"Twenty farther!" Banichi yelled out, and fired

around the corner. "Farther, farther. Right turn—
now!"

Boom!

Banichi and Ilisidi's men dived around the corner,
not a second's hesitation, one covering their rear in
the T, a thunder of booted feet on the deck and a
second explosion. Jago squatted, assembling bits again,
this one a knob on a stick.

"I think I know the right switch," Barnhart reported
from behind them.

"Not yet!" Bren said. His full attention was for the
way he could watch, while Jago was on one knee,
delving into the black bag while snatching looks down
the corridor the way they'd come. The technicians
they'd evicted had made it halfway to the lift, crawling
the distance, coughing and half-blind. Beyond the lift,
where the third of Ilisidi's men maintained position
with, presumably, Jenrette, and a handful of stationers, Sabin was still down there under cover—about,
he thought, at the next T-intersection. Whoever was
firing up the hall was farther off than that, bad for aim,
but not comfortable for them getting back to the lift.

Jago made a ripping move, stepped full into the
corridor and made a throw with all the considerable
strength of her arm. She ducked back as fire came at
her, as the grenade hit the decking and exploded in a
cascade of ceiling and wall panels.

A section door went shut down there, likely automatic at the explosion, possibly sealing off someone's retreat.

"It's sealed that direction," he said; and about that
time another door opened and fire came out toward
them. "Damn!"

Jago was on the pocket com, advising Banichi: the
things operated independently on short range and

searched for signal. "The section sealed in our direction, but we have another site two doors off the lift, nadi, do you hear?"

"One hears," Banichi seemed to say, difficult to understand. "We have cleared this corridor. It would be wise to close our section door."

That took a key.

"I'm coming," Bren said, springing up. "Tell him I'm coming."

"Nadi!" Jago protested; but he wasn't the shot she was, and *she* protected the fuel supply. Momentarily expendable, he ran, hung a tight right at the intersection, almost into one of Ilisidi's men, and down the hall where Banichi waited.

Banichi hadn't wanted *him,* he was sure of that as he shoved his key into section control and got the control panel open. "One is long out of practice, nadi, with the gun." *Section door close* was a two-fingered operation, and he did it, fast. That door cut off anyone coming from that direction. "Better Jago holds that door." Another breath. He had a stitch in his side from the sprint he'd done. "One or more enemies with a pellet rifle at the end of the corridor; Jago has thrown a grenade down there. Jenrette should be in the lift and I think Sabin is somewhere between us and our enemies. We have tried to signal Gin-aiji. *Everyone* is here."

"For the fuel," Banichi said, sensibly, and pushed him along, back down the corridor toward the intersection. "For control of that commodity. Which we desperately need. All sides will come here. But one takes it there is fuel to defend." They reached the corner, where Ilisidi's two men stood on opposite arms of the T. "So we have it, and we shall hold it."

"Sabin's got ship's security with her." Out of breath,

thoughts jarred loose in his brain. "Jenrette knew Sabin-aiji would come here. She never went to Central."

"She cannot have been here long."

"We made a great deal of noise upstairs. There may have been a standoff, if only in the last hour. But that Jenrette is here, too—one cannot trust him, Banichi-ji. We cannot trust him, and I sent him to the lift!"

Banichi took out his pocket com. "Kasari-ji, disarm the ship-human immediately."

Banichi had the com close to his ear. Bren strained to hear, glad there was a reply—not glad that a frown touched Banichi's face.

"Jenrette never went to the lift," Banichi reported, and said, via com: "If he arrives, disarm him."

"He must have moved toward Sabin's position," Bren said. "Jase has banned him from the ship unless he comes with her, but I by no means rely on his man'chi."

"This relies on human thinking," Banichi said to him, "which is notoriously convolute."

"Simple, in this case, nadi-ji. His man'chi may lie with Braddock. Kill Sabin, kill all the ship's senior security, and board with Braddock, trying to take equal power with Jase-aiji during negotiations with the alien ship. Or ally with her, and Braddock. Get aboard. And strike at Jase and the dowager by treachery in the homeward voyage—perhaps taking possession of Tabini's heir, to strike at Shejidan. This thing might have either of two paths, but one destination."

One might expect Banichi to be appalled: but Banichi, reloading his gun, shrugged. "Greatly discounting Cenedi."

"I would never discount Cenedi."

"Nor would I." Banichi employed his pocket com

a second time. "Nadiin-ji, Bren marks Jenrette as dangerous."

It was a death sentence. I would never, he wanted to say. Civilized Mospheirans had process of law, of courts, of appeals and debates.

In the aiji's court—there was Banichi's Guild. And here was no place to file Intent. Only to move on targets until there was leisure for consideration.

Click. Banichi reloaded his second gun.

"Go to Jago," Banichi said. "*We* will find Jenrette."

"No, nadi. He will have appealed to Sabin with a lie. I can deny that." He took out his own gun, that long-ago gift, not sure he could hit the opposing wall after years of no practice, but it posed at least a visible threat. "My presence is absolutely necessary."

"Movement," Anaro reported, Ilisidi's man, next to them, never having taken his eyes off the intersecting corridor.

Bren looked. At that farthest intersection before the closed door, dim with smoke-haze and Jago's having blown the lighting down there, a handful of humans had come out of hiding, headed up the corridor toward the lift. Sabin. He could make out the silver hair. A dozen or so of her security. He didn't see Jenrette, and that was worrisome. If Jenrette had communications, and was in touch with Braddock—

"Sabin!" Bren yelled. "Look out!"

Fastest he could think, and the desired result: her security moved to protect *her*, bodies between her and any conceivable threat, and up against the wall, trying to get to the lift.

"Sabin, we're in the lift! That's safe!"

Fire broke out from the place Jenrette had occupied before, the intersecting hall a little down from the lift. Two of Sabin's party went down, a third hit.

Banichi ran; Bren dived after him, a hard sprint down the corridor toward what had become a firefight. They passed Jago's position; passed the lift, where Kasari held the doorway, no one in position to get the sniper that was taking down Sabin's guard.

The sniper put his head and his sidearm around the corner.

Banichi braked so fast Bren nearly hit him; braked, and fired, and the sniper vanished backward, leaving an appalling spatter against the opposing wall.

Fire had stopped from Sabin's party; Banichi flattened himself against the wall and whipped around that corner, but the immediate relaxation told the tale, and Bren didn't think he wanted to see the damage that had left its evidence on that other wall.

Banichi wasn't so fastidious. He squatted down, collected items from Jenrette's pockets, a sidearm, a pocket com and a handheld, on each of which he killed the power with a press of his thumb.

Those were worth later investigation.

Sabin arrived, her guard battered and bloody, herself with a bloody forearm and a ripped sleeve.

"Mr. Cameron?"

"Yes, ma'am."

"Is that Mr. Jenrette?"

"Yes, ma'am." They didn't have time for question and answer. There was that ship moving in. "Dr. Kroger's out there trying to defuse whatever-it-is, we've got the station up there, we dislodged Braddock from Central and blew the Archive. Captain Graham's boarding civilians fast as he can. We took the alien hostage Braddock was holding, we're trying to get communication with him, and last I heard, his ship's moving in, but we're talking to it."

Several blinks. "Not half bad for a day's work."

He was numb. He had a dead man at his feet. And

a captain who'd tried her best to take the station from inside, with the force she had. And not done a bad job of it, counting she'd ended up at the right place to secure the fuel, the high card *she'd* known the station held. "Captain Graham will want you aboard soon as possible."

"Possible, once we get the fuel flowing." Sabin gave a glance aside as Banichi stood up; and up. *"Hato,"* she said. Ragi, for *good*. It applied to food and drink, not quite apt.

But Banichi understood.

And called Jago. "Jago. Jenrette is dead. Sabin-aiji is safe."

Jago said something that made Banichi smile.

"Barnhart has found Gin-aiji," Banichi reported. "She has swum up to the camera and made encouraging signals. One believes she is in direct communication with Jase."

"Get my wounded aboard," Sabin said. "I'll handle the fuel."

"Get them into the lift," Bren said. "We'll manage. Fast as we can. —Banichi-ji. We are requested to take the wounded back as quickly as we can. Sabin-aiji will manage here."

"Yes," Banichi said, and relayed orders to his associates in three positions.

They'd done it. His knees felt weak. They'd actually done it. It didn't *feel* done. They'd been attacked from two fronts and the middle, and the way down wasn't guaranteed safe—particularly sneaking a handful of very tall atevi back on board; but they did what they could.

"I have Jase's key," he confessed to Sabin. "I need it to get them back." Meaning the wounded, and the handful of techs in their keeping.

"You're just full of tricks," Sabin said. "Go lock

those section doors with that key, Mr. Cameron—I trust you know how to do that—and then get that thing back aboard the ship. Fast."

The lord of the heavens had his bailiwick and his arena of understanding; it didn't include ship's operations, or that fueling station; and when Sabin suggested locking the critical doors with an unbreachable lock, barring all station access to this place, it seemed a good idea to do exactly that, and fast.

19

"Go," Bren said to their detainees, once the lift
car reached the mast entry level—one expected that to be the most desolate area of the station;
but it was jammed with refugees, men, women, children carrying other children and parents carrying
baggage—and their detainees vanished into jammed
lines of refugees. Terror rippled the lines as unprepared stationers saw atevi exit the car, but they were
locked in that essential fact of station life, the line,
the line that gave precedence, the line in which all
things were done and solved, the line which meant
entitlement—in this case, to ship-boarding; and the
line buckled.

"They're from Alpha!" Bren shouted. "They are,
and I am! Pass it on! We have injured people here—
excuse us. We need through to medical immediately,
please!"

They didn't have access to station communications;
but word of mouth rippled both ways in the moving
lines—lines ultimately diced and packeted by the lift.

They had one of ship's security, walking wounded:
Barnhart had an arm around him, helping him along.
There were three who couldn't walk, one in bad condition, and Ilisidi's men carried them like children,
gear and all—atevi protocols: Banichi and Jago had
their lord present, and guarded *him*, and that was the

way of things. So he went, scaring evacuees—until humans saw a bona fide mission of mercy, and blood, and atevi carrying human wounded toward the ship. Then stares attended them, and confusion swayed the line, but no panic ensued.

"Excuse us," Bren said, all the lengthy way up the line to the lift. "Excuse us. We have to get to medical. Urgent. Excuse us."

He was breathing hard, despite the lightest of station gravity. They reached the lift, and stationers there, next in line for salvation, clearly didn't want to wait—"We have children," the head of the line objected.

"We have a man critical," Bren said, in this contest of crises. "Ship's officer. We can take the children through with us, if you want. Rest a minute. Protect those kids' faces. It's a long cold on the other side."

The man didn't half know. Frustration, fear and resentment of alien presence were all in that expression; but he was willing to argue with ship personnel and half a dozen towering aliens to get to a safety that— he hadn't thought it through—likely had more such aliens in charge; and Bren didn't altogether blame him for his confusion. If a station was going into critical failure, as these people began to realize, it was a very thin bubble in a very big dark, and anywhere with air, light, and power was life itself.

The lift car arrived. Bren crowded his own party in and punched the button, no key. The car shot off, express for the mast; and they were alone for the moment, hoping that Sabin, upstairs, was managing the fueling station without interference.

But the more that line of refugees grew, the more people would begin to realize the station was in trouble; and when neighbors started leaving, people started calling those they cared about. By now, anyone calling Central might not get through. And a failure of communications meant a spread of rumor, in a station already half-dead, already having lost one essential asset, and all protection from alien incursion. Families were taking the ship's offer. Individuals with non-critical jobs were. Probably a few *with* critical jobs had begun to weigh staying and going, and if one bolted—more would.

Faster and faster. More and more desperate. They'd gotten through a line reasonably well-ordered and willing to reason, in this early stage of the evacuation. Later—as systems started failing—panic was going to pack more and more people into that line.

"We still cannot reach Asicho, nandi," Jago said.

"Soon, at least, Jago-ji," he said. "One believes Gin has relayed reassurances to Jase. And perhaps Sabin-aiji has gotten through."

Warning lights flashed red. The car began deceleration and the comfortable illusion of up and down shifted, an assault on a stomach already uncertain—he didn't like this, didn't like it, stared at the indicators for proof of their location in time and space, reassurance of destination imminent.

The car stopped. They were weightless. And a startled *Phoenix* crew member met them.

"If you've got com," Bren said, "advise Captain Graham we're coming, with injured crew."

"Yes, sir," the crewwoman said.

The lighted conveyor ran past them. Bren grabbed it one-handed, felt it take the mass of Banichi and Jago behind him and then, presumably, Barnhart and one crewman; and Ilisidi's men, with two of Sabin's, as best they could.

There was little stress on the arm, enough to prove they were moving, while all he could see was the glowing ribbon winding through a vast, numbing-cold dark:

an illusion of infinity, that ribbon interrupted by silhouettes. In the far distance, dots that were families
interrupted the glow, refugees, holding together, half-
frozen and caught in nothing, in nowhere—thank God,
Bren thought, that the lighted ribbon did move, and
moved with a fair dispatch, because if ever some one
of the refugees let go and became lost off the ribbon,
they might lodge up in the unseen recesses, helpless,
to freeze before rescue could find them. The conveyor
was designed for the able-bodied.

Clips, he thought. They ought to find clips somewhere.

The ribbon had an end. Or a returning-point, where
it doubled back. And there *were* a few clips floating
past, attached. Someone was using his imagination.

There were crewmen at that end-point. Safety. And
nothing would hurry this line. Bren watched the crew
help one after another clumps of people into the tube,
and onto the next conveyor line.

Their turn came. Crew had seen them coming.

"We've got wounded," Bren said. "For two-deck."
And the masked, parka-clad crewmen delayed them
not at all, only sent them up the umbilical connection
to the ship itself.

Faster trip, this.

"Mr. Cameron, sir." Welcome voice, behind that
mask: Kaplan met them on two-deck; Kaplan and Polano; and medics, instantly taking charge of the
wounded.

"Sabin's alive. At the fuel station," Bren said.
Kaplan deserved that information. "Need to see the
captain."

"Go right on up, sir." Kaplan held the lift door for
him and his, and let the door shut once they were
inside.

Light. Glorious, brilliant light, and warmth. Air that

didn't feel like the same substance as that burning chill outside. A solid feel to the deck under his feet. It was like emerging from near drowning. Everything was sharp-edged. Every familiar sight was new.

And the handheld worked, if numb fingers could get it out of his pocket and hold on to it. It gave him a series of images his watering eyes couldn't quite bring into focus; one dark. One was an animation. They were talking to the alien ship. One—one was a suited figure in a lot of dark, beside machinery. Gin. He didn't know how to bring in the audio, and lost the image.

"Damn!" he said, then, conscious of his companions, and then of the fact their personal electronics were in contact again, and that Asicho, belowdecks, was likewise receiving: "Asa-ji, we are all well." And to his immediate company. "My fingers are numb. But they seem to be talking to the foreign ship and Gin-aiji seems still at work outside. Perhaps Jase-aiji wishes now to move the ship closer to take on fuel, but with people coming aboard in bitter cold, impossible to hold them off."

"This ship cannot in any wise maneuver," Jago observed.

"One believes," he began to say, but the lift reached its destination and let them out on the bridge: him, his bodyguard, Barnhart, and the dowager's men, all of them, he suddenly realized, in the pristine cleanliness of the bridge, bloody and sweaty and reeking of fumes as their clothes thawed, their whole party laden down with all sorts of battle-gear.

Jase met them the moment they cleared the short partition, met him and seized him by the shoulder. "Bren. What's the story over there?"

"Sabin's at fueling ops, the archive's blown, Central's out, and we left word on several levels to evacuate—which people seem to be doing, fast as they can. What's this side?"

"We're running out of pictures to send, that ship's still moving in, and Gin's out there in short-range communication. We've got fuel if we could move to get it. If the station doesn't go unstable before we can get the fuel off. That's our problem. Yours is down on five-deck. We need our houseguest to talk to that ship out there. We need time, Bren. We've got to get an emergency crew onto the station to keep it stable and keep it running."

"It's not secure over there. Braddock's still alive. Jenrette isn't. But Sabin's got the section doors locked on the fuel center. There were several tries at us while we were taking it."

"Station's getting shorter-handed by the hour, and we can talk to *them.*" Jase gave a shake at his shoulders. "We can talk to station. You can talk to the other side of this situation. Get us some time and everything's a lot better."

"Understood," Bren said. He was shivering from recent bone-chill, at that floating-feeling stage of exhaustion, but Jase was right, no question. "I'll handle it. Key." He remembered it, and took it from his pocket and gave it back.

"One is grateful, nadiin-ji: one is extremely grateful." With a small bow to the atevi in general. "Barnhart." A nod, a warm handshake. "Get a rest."

"Rest isn't likely," Barnhart said. "But I'll get on it."

"Nadiin," Bren said, gathering his company, and went straight back to the lift. Bath, he was thinking, warm bath, warm up the surface, get the brain working, maybe one of Bindanda's tea cakes and a hot drink: he had to shift gears, get his thoughts out of fight and on to the delicate business of communication. Fast.

He shoved the handheld and its problems into his pocket on the way to the lift—got in, and started to give a surreptitious sniff at his hand, wondering whether fumes had adhered to his skin as well as his clothes and whether he could forego the bath; and saw it spattered with dried blood.

Bath, he thought. There were certain things one didn't want to explain. God knew what evidence his face had. Barnhart's coat was bloody. Atevi uniforms were no better off, and Banichi—

The blood seeping down Banichi's fingers wasn't old, and Banichi hadn't been helping the wounded.

"Banichi. How bad? How long?"

"Minor," Banichi said. "Minor, Bren-ji. Not long."

"Jago-ji, be sure of it."

"Yes," Jago said, and sternly, when Banichi only looked as if he might object, "*yes,* nadi."

"Yes," Banichi said, which took one crisis off the paidhi's mind.

"One will be grateful if you take it as a first priority," he said, as the lift reached five-deck and the door opened. "Barnhart. Owe you a drink."

"I'll collect," Barnhart said, and went off his direction, toward the Mospheiran domain; Bren and his bloodstained band went straight on, to request entry—which came before they could so much as signal: thank Asicho for that.

"Nandi." Respects, from Ilisidi's guards.

He acknowledged the courtesy and kept walking briskly, intending to deliver most of his company to the dowager's staff, to the dowager's staff medic, intending to have that bath, too, before he thought about the problems of the alien ship.

A brief stop at the security station, where Asicho, one of Gin's men and one of Ilisidi's all sat duty: "Nadiin-ji, we are all back aboard, mission accomplished." They would have heard everything he said to Jase. "We shall want the doctor as soon as possible. Kindly tell the staff not to divert itself from care of our guest."

"Yes," Asicho said; and he kept walking, trying to hammer his wits into an utterly different mode of operation.

He hoped not to be noticed as he passed the dining hall. He wanted no explanations until he was clean again, and until he and the rest of his staff could shed the firearms and the bag of explosives and such.

But as he passed, he saw the dining hall ominously dimmed, and heard—

Heard vigorous applause, and muted cheers, and lively music.

He slipped in the door, appalled to find a ring of atevi, including the dowager's security, and his staff, Cajeiri—that was no surprise—and their guest—and the dowager herself. On the screen, in black and white, a cartoon mouse eluded a cartoon cat.

A fishbowl tottered, sloshed, and Cajeiri shouted a warning, pointing out the obvious danger to cartoon protagonists, as cat and mouse darted this way and that in an elemental antagonism innocent of association.

Now . . . with their lives hanging in the balance . . .

A chair went over. Draperies went down. To the dowager's evident misgiving and Cajeiri's and Prakuyo's collective delight.

But by now staff had seen him or heard him, prompting uneasy glances back.

Staff stood up. The dowager looked at him expectantly. And Narani brought up the lights.

Solemn faces, concern. Prakuyo stood up. So did Cajeiri. Only the dowager stayed seated, hands clasped on her staff.

Bren gave a solemn bow. "Nand' dowager, nandi—" A bow for Prakuyo. None for boys. "Success aboard the station. We are now bring the people aboard. The security staff is intact, except a minor injury. Prakuyo-nadi—" Change of languages, and a second bow. "Your ship speaks to us. It is coming."

"Ship. Prakuyo ship. Coming." Anxiety was evident, in every line of Prakuyo's stance.

A bow. Agreement. "Yes." A hand-motion. "Coming to us. I go wash."

"Wash, yes." Perhaps it was a mad notion. But Prakuyo bowed, apparently in complete agreement with such a crazed proposition. Or he smelled that bad.

He bowed a third time, shaky in the knees. "Dowager-ji, one is grateful for your staff and your assistance." On which, at a little nod from Ilisidi, he walked out into the corridor, wondering if the knees were going to hold out as far as his own quarters.

He was pursued, however: Narani and Bindanda arrived on his heels, and saw him into his quarters, and began at once fussing with his jacket, and the shirt, and the boots, and the sweaty pigtail.

He shed the rest and showered, a quick, steam-filled warmth that began to warm him from the outside in; that soaked his hair, and took the stench of gas out of his nose, and soothed a throat he'd been too numb to realize was sore. He coughed, and blew water, and came out before the dry-cycle had had half enough time, but Bindanda met him with a towel, and rubbed life into him, and threw a robe about him—

He had communication. Thanks to the other residents of five-deck, he seemed to have Prakuyo's good will—an understanding, at least, of benevolent intent.

He *didn't* take for granted that would override cultural or biological imperatives or save their collective necks from political policy.

And the dawn of reasonable worry told him that hot water had brought the brain online.

One more change of clothing, as freshly pressed as any morning in Shejidan, court casual, as he thought of it—not good enough for high meetings, but perfectly adequate for bureaucrats and offices.

It brought shoulders back and head up, or one cut one's throat on the lace.

"How is Banichi, Rani-ji?" That worry was with him, too, and he was sure word had flowed through the staff, what they had done, who was where, what was going on outside: he was sure, despite the scene he had met in the dining hall, that no one on five-deck but Cajeiri and Prakuyo had done anything but follow every word Asicho could gather.

"He is with the dowager's physician at the moment, nandi. So is Jago."

"Is she hurt?"

"A minor injury, nandi. So with two of the dowager's bodyguard. But none life-threatening."

Damn, he thought, with a heavy heartbeat and a sting behind the eyes. *Damn!* that, he hadn't seen. They'd fooled him all the way back to the ship. And he couldn't take them all off duty and stand over them until they mended.

He pinched the bridge of his nose until the stinging stopped and tried to get his wits about him—back to work, back to work, fast. They weren't safe. They wouldn't be safe until they'd put Prakuyo where he belonged and this solar system behind them.

And meanwhile the sound one expected when traveling about the ship had never stopped, the lift system whining and opening and closing doors, cycling cars back and forth, back and forth, with the wholesale energy of a factory.

Four-deck was coming to life as if there had never been a glitch in their plans. Crew, variously occupied through the voyage, was in high gear, settling in newcomers, instructing them *not* to leave objects loose, *not* to take a leaky tap for granted, and how to read the various sirens and bells that advised crew about the ship's behavior.

As if they had their fuel and were ready to leave.

He thanked his staff and went back to the dining hall, where the lights were up; where—strangely or not—he heard the whirr of small wheels before he darkened the door.

Not all Cajeiri's cars had met an untimely end.

His security sat at one side of the room with their guest, the dowager sat at the other with Cenedi and one of his men, and Cajeiri—Cajeiri entertained the company with his toy.

Prakuyo, however, paced the room, a lumbering slow pace, but a pace . . . anxious. Knowing there was news.

"Prakuyo-ji," Bren said with a little bow. The car stopped.

"Well?" Ilisidi asked him. "Are we making progress?"

Bren bowed. "Indeed, nand' dowager. We are. Fuel is on the horizon. Gin-nadi is investigating that."

"One prefers it in this ship," Ilisidi said sharply, and waved her hand. "This person has been inconvenienced. So have we all, by this *Braddock-aiji*."

"Gone, aiji-ma. At least in retreat. And far less of an inconvenience."

"Jenrette is dead."

"Yes, aiji-ma." A second bow, to Prakuyo, who waited anxiously. "Prakuyo-nadi. One is very glad to see you at your ease."

The Ragi might have been ancient Greek. But Prakuyo rocked forward, a sort of a bow of his own, carefully imitated. "Bren-ji."

"One is amazed," Bren said, not without a glance at the dowager, who sat smugly in possession of all news on five-deck.

"The children's language," the dowager said, rising, leaning on her cane, "seems particularly useful, lacking numerical precision. And he is very quick."

"Association," Prakuyo said energetically in Ragi, and indicated Cajeiri and the dowager and Cenedi, and him. "Association. Associates. Associates. You, you, you."

"Indeed, nadi," Bren said—again with a bow, with a very inclusive sweep of his arm. "Associates. All associates."

"Atevi. Human. *Associates.*"

"Yes," Bren said. *Associates.* Had no human being in most of ten years of holding this person never tried *friend*, or tried to speak to this person about ordinary things?

Or was *friend* somehow too chancy a word to get across to a different species at gunpoint? *Associate*, among the visibly dissimilar species of five-deck, might hold out a peculiar hope to their guest—the presence of the young, the silliness of toys, the *aishi*, the easy association that to any casual eye, certainly included more than one species involved in a fair degree of shared trust and authority.

Dared one, for half a breath, feel a little chagrin about the situation—that the paidhi, neutral and noncombatant, had been off aiding the Assassins' Guild in the overthrow of a government and the aiji-dowager, potent and intensely political, had been sitting here with a seven-year-old and an alien, making a breakthrough he hadn't.

Their guest made a sweeping gesture. "Prakuyo, Bren, Ilisidi, Cajeiri—associates."

He bowed. Prakuyo bowed. The dowager, who did not bow, gave a nod of her head.

"Good," Prakuyo said. "Good. Ship?" Gesture of uplifted hand and distracted stare, a where-is-it apparent past any barrier.

Measure between fingers. "Close."

"This person should speak to his associates," Ilisidi said.

"Dowager-ji," Bren said. "There are unresolved issues."

"What issues?" Ilisidi asked. "What issues can there be, that we have undertaken to return this individual to his association? This seems relatively simple, and need not observe all the prolonged fuss of ship-folk arguments."

"We have no promise from them."

"How shall we reasonably expect one, with nothing given in earnest? We sit in ignominious danger so long as this foreign ship remains in doubt of our honest intentions. This is not acceptable. This is a sensible person who shows every capability of rational dealing with the *aishidi'tat*. Call this foreign ship, allow Prakuyo-nandi to say that we have reached a civilized understanding, and let us borrow fuel from *them,* if we reach further impasse with these station-humans. These ingrates have shot at my staff and injured our associates. One is entirely out of patience with them, and after six years, one believes this foreign gentleman is thoroughly out of patience, too."

One truly did. And he had dealt with Ilisidi long enough to know that, whatever else, this was not an opinion that arrived on the spur of the moment, or without Ilisidi's very excellent perspective on politics. It did contain a certain nonhuman basic sense: that the very worst thing they could do was demonstrate themselves so closely allied to their badly-behaved station that Prakuyo's people couldn't insert a tissue of conjecture between them.

Ilisidi tossed him a live fish, as the proverb ran; and he could improvise. He could very well improvise.

"Associate," he said fervently, and bowed deeply. "The aiji-dowager wishes Prakuyo call Prakuyo's ship. You, she, I, associates."

"Bren," Prakuyo said. "Nand' Bren." A hand extended. "Bren. Come ship."

Oh, he didn't like that. He pointed at the deck under his own feet, hoping he hadn't understood.

"Bren ship."

"Bren come Prakuyo ship. Make—" Clearly a word was missing, frustrating communication. "Associate."

One truly hoped *associate* hadn't been mistaken in meaning.

And he knew what Banichi and Jago would say, but Banichi was off getting his arm sewed up, and they had fuel to get, and an alien craft still moving toward them.

He touched his heart. "Yes. Bren go Prakuyo ship."

Done deal. Civilized understanding. It pleased Prakuyo, not deliriously—dared one imagine just a little worry on that strange face?

"Bren go. Ilisidi, Cajeiri go."

God, no. He saw Cenedi's face.

"Shall we truly, mani-ma?" Cajeiri asked.

"We shall see this ship," Ilisidi proclaimed, in Cenedi's pained silence. "Prakuyo will make a civilized call, we shall arrange a visit, and we shall have our understanding with this foreign association."

He was aware of Cenedi. He daren't look at him.

One dared not start an argument involving a dangerous guest with whom he could by no means argue fine points. One smiled, one made the absolute best of the situation—one only imagined how one was going to explain it to Jase—but the very next thing to do was to patch Prakuyo through C1 and get voice and visual contact, before something else went wrong—assuming those who knew such things could figure out how to make the equipment talk.

"Come, Prakuyo-ji," he said, in that language free of all unhappy precedent. He gestured toward the door, and Prakuyo strolled solemnly forward, a short walk down the corridor toward the security station—ordinarily *not* a place five-deck entertained outsiders.

But the dowager had notions of her own—and the foreign paidhi—whose grasp of Ragi was decidedly from scratch, and impressive—was cooperative. Tell Jase? They had to tell Jase, never mind dealing with Sabin. He had to explain matters and get Prakuyo that requested clearance.

Asicho and Ilisidi's man on watch knew they were coming, and cleared chairs for them.

"A contact with C1," Asicho said quietly, "nandi."

"Excellent," Bren said, though he could have made it on either piece of equipment in his pocket: he chose to do it on the console mike, and chose to make the argument in Ragi, which Prakuyo might understand as a good faith gesture.

"Captain Graham," he asked of C1, and when he heard Jase's voice answer:

"Mr. Cameron?"

"Prakuyo-nadi has made strides not in Mosphei', Jase-nandi—although I think he may indeed understand more Mosphei' than he admits—but in Ragi."

"In Ragi." For a human, speaking Mosphei' or its like, Ragi was a vast linguistic jump.

"His native language may find that a simpler transition than that to Mosphei', at least as regards the children's language." Without the numeric demands Ragi placed on adults. "He wishes to contact his ship. We consider this a very good idea at this point, nadi-ji." *We,* not *one.* It was the utmost stress, his reputation, his urging. And Jase knew the nuances. "We have cooperation and wish to keep the momentum in developing relations."

It couldn't be an easy decision. It wasn't, for him; and one could only imagine what Sabin would say if Sabin were back on board.

But Sabin wasn't. *"Voice contact,"* Jase said. *"We'll do our best to get you through."*

"Thank you." He meant that. And he wasn't going to explain the rest of it, not until he saw encouraging results. He reached across and turned on Prakuyo's mike. "Prakuyo. Talk. We record—" He made writing motions. "We talk Prakuyo's ship."

Prakuyo leaned forward and did speak, rapidly, a speech laced with gutturals some of which were down at the lower end of human hearing and maybe a few too low to make out. And he paused, waiting, waiting, eyes fixed on the console.

"We're trying," C1 said. *"We have a three-minute window."*

Bren set a timer on the number one clock and called Prakuyo's attention to the ebb of sections. He held up three fingers, and pointed to the minute digit, folded one down.

A person familiar with countdowns, if not their numerical notation, might know what he meant, and get the rhythm of it. Prakuyo watched, and watched the countdown; and as it went negative, seemed to figure that, too.

Then . . . then . . . a static-ridden reply that taxed

the speakers, and Prakuyo's whole face reacted in what was surely the profoundest relief. He replied, rapidly, energetically, and the equipment might or might not handle all those booms and thumps from Prakuyo's throat.

Bren reset the reply clock.

"Prakuyo ship," Prakuyo said, and simultaneous with voice, the oddest trait, came a deep rumbling from somewhere in Prakuyo's throat. "Prakuyo ship come Bren ship."

"Yes," Bren said, there not being damn-all else to say, given the dowager's arrangements. "Associate."

That word . . . Prakuyo found troublesomely worrisome. He glanced at Bren, sucked at his lips as if he was restraining some word or just trying to think of one.

And that, in its way, was a comfortingly straightforward honesty . . . indicative, perhaps, that there were thorny problems, and that Prakuyo wasn't in a position to make guarantees for his own side.

"Associate?" Bren asked, and Prakuyo's frown deepened, and that dammed-up thought just couldn't find a way out.

So if things went badly—on the surface—he could just keep saying, "associate" and expect Prakuyo to know what the sticking-point of negotiations had become. *If* that word had come across with something like its original meaning in the first place.

These were the truly lovely moments in making a linguistic bridge in negotiations, and never so much was at stake, not even in the first days between atevi and humans, who had at least had experience of each other and settled a little common vocabulary before they managed to get completely at loggerheads on the *real* meanings.

Here was where ship and station, who had no experience of any outsiders but each other, had no useful referent that wasn't buried deep in the Archive, unlearned and unstudied in centuries . . . except for Jase's knowledge.

And this was where the paidhi-aiji earned his keep.

The answer came back. Prakuyo listened to all of it, then answered, ticking off points to himself on his fingers, and with a great deal of attendant booming and rumbling, before he reached over and thumped Bren on the back. Hard. Bren caught himself against the counter-edge, tears in his eyes, and hoped the shoulderblade wasn't cracked.

Prakuyo, however, was happy.

"Go Prakuyo ship," Prakuyo said, "go Prakuyo ship."

"Ship come?"

"Come!" Prakuyo said happily, and Bren warily turned toward him, to make another back-slap inconvenient.

"Good," Bren said, feeling less than confident. And saying to himself that if he was going to be going anywhere, he wanted a few words of the language under his belt.

And, God, if Sabin got aboard before Prakuyo's ship got here—as that sight of an incoming alien craft was almost guaranteed to prompt her to do—he was going to have to explain the dowager's decision, and his, and somehow keep bargains they hadn't Sabin's— or Jase's—clearance to make.

He *needed* words. He *needed* some picture of what he was working with, or going into.

"Asicho. Get me C1."

"Yes," she said, and punched buttons. "C1, nandi."

"Captain Graham," he said, sure of his contact.

"I'm on," Jase said, not in Ragi. *"How did that go?"*

"Very well." In Ragi. "The ship will continue to move in, but shooting is less likely."

"It expects him to transfer to it, will it? The stationers are very nervous. One is by no means sure we have removed all resistance, besides it will terrify the passengers. One is not complaining, understand . . . but can one possibly hold that off?"

"We are not yet fluent enough to undertake that topic," Bren said. "One regrets, nadi-ji. He wishes me and the dowager *and* the heir to visit the ship, perhaps to demonstrate us to his fellows; and the dowager has agreed."

"God, Bren." That last was not in Ragi.

"We do intend to return, and consider it no worse risk than parachuting onto a planet." That for Jase, who had done precisely that, so Jase could hardly complain of wild risks. "Our guest seems very reasonable and well-disposed, all considered. Understand, these matters were cordially agreed while I was absent, and our guest's good will and confidence may reasonably be dependent on these representations. It might be a grave mistake to backtrack."

"Is our guest promising to let us out of here?"

"Not entirely clear. Either we have some difficulty communicating that point, or Prakuyo lacks authority or disposition to promise it. I do certainly intend to make that issue a primary point aboard his ship."

"Bren." Jase seemed at a loss.

"Prevent the aiji-senior from forbidding this move. That would be a very great help."

"Got that straight," Jase said. And in Ragi: *"One understands, and one most fervently wishes you success, nandi-ji."*

"A mutual wish. Baji-naji, Jase-nandi." He shut down the contact, and carefully patted Prakuyo on the shoulder, since Prakuyo had touched him with such familiarity. "Come. Rest, Prakuyo-ji. We go rest."

Prakuyo might not have understood the essential word, but he got up and came along, a broad, rolling stride beside him, all the way back to his borrowed quarters.

"Sleep," Bren said then, making the pantomime. "Rest."

"Yes," Prakuyo said with a deep rumble. "Yes." Prakuyo might be exhausted—*he* was exhausted; but precious little time they might have before critical things happened: that the alien craft got close, demanding to come in; or that Sabin decided to come aboard and take command. Both things were possible, concurrently, other people had made agreements without asking, and he was running out of energy and out of ideas simultaneously.

Most of all he'd had to go running off settling that problem and not seeing to personal concerns; and his first question to Asicho, going back to the security post, was Banichi's whereabouts.

"In the clinic, with Jago, nandi. He has followed all of this."

Banichi would; so would Jago. Could he doubt, as long as they were conscious? "I shall see them," he said. "Thank you, Asa-ji."

Off to the clinic, closer to their front door, a little room, seeming smaller still with their casualties and the dowager's physician and a younger aide.

Banichi had gotten a bandage, at least. Bren inhaled to give himself room next a cabinet and Banichi's chair, Jago standing on the other side.

"You know what the dowager has agreed," Bren said straight off.

"Of course," Jago said, and Banichi threw in, "We will be there, Bren-ji."

"I bear a certain guilt, only asking it of you."

"Did I hear asking?" Banichi said with a look at Jago.

"No," Jago said, "one never heard asking."

He laid a hand on Jago's shoulder, Banichi's being likely extremely sore. "Our guest seems civil, at least, nadiin-ji. My greatest worry is Sabin-aiji, if she involves herself in decisions already taken."

"Sabin-aiji seems busy at the moment," Banichi observed.

"May she stay that way long enough." A large breath. He didn't want to leave them. But they were in competent hands, there was nothing useful he could do here, and he had to refocus his attention on his own skills. Most of all he had to make decisions, to think about the core vocabulary they had to have, and what he was going to say, and how he was going to negotiate a peace with a vocabulary of some fifty or so words.

A gentle pat. One for Banichi, a piece of temerity, but Banichi was obliged, occasionally, to put up with human notions. "One needs a little time to think. *Rest*, nadiin-ji. Take painkillers without any consideration of the matter ahead: we wish to project ease and pleasantness."

Short laugh from Banichi. "Pleasantness."

"Think of going home, nadiin-ji," Bren said. "Think of us all going home." A second pat. "Thank you."

He escaped before he could embarrass himself further, shook off the scene in the clinic and the memory of that glowing strand of desperate refugees, the recollection that Gin and Sabin were desperately engaged in a mission that was going to complicate his own, in timing—none of these things could be top priority in his head now.

They needed *go away* and *destroy the station*. They

needed *take the inhabitants* and *excuse us for the inconvenience.*

They possibly needed *please don't come calling at our planet,* but he didn't see how he was going to get at that one if it wasn't a mutual desire for disentanglement.

And he might need stickier words, which could be a provocation to try to pull out of their guest. He might need a pad of paper and a pencil, to do diagrams.

A pocket full of sugar candies. That had been the most useful trade goods—forget trying to pretend all this number of humans and atevi didn't have a planet somewhere, forget trying to conceal where it was. If that alien craft hadn't been sitting here waiting for them they might have lied about that issue—but given a direction and adequate optics, no question they could find the earth of the atevi. Prakuyo's folk might ask about the origin of humans, if they correctly perceived they weren't quite the same biologically, and *that* could be difficult. *No, believe us, we actually misplaced our home planet.*

Trust was such a precious commodity.

He took a little chance, from his own quarters, to consult Gin's staff, wondering how things were going, not wishing to bother Jase with questions; and Gin's staff reported that Gin was tired, that she and Sabin were swearing at each other, and that another of Gin's team was suited and out there.

Excellent. Beyond excellent. He sat down on his bed and fell backwards, eyes shut, seeing Gin, suited, in that lonely camera view. Sabin, in that doorway.

That ship moving in on them, blip on a screen, more ominous than anything Braddock could still throw at them.

What more did he want to say?

Come, go, give, take, you, we, they. Woman, man, child.

Fight, not fight. Shoot. Not shoot.

Food, water.

To, from, out of, on, off, over, under, around, through. Pesky directional words that in some languages weren't words at all.

Not. Ragi was dubious about negatives, wrapped them carefully in courtesies and precise formulae.

Always, never, soon, if. Truly the soft tissue of thought. Time. Time and degree of reality. *May and could,* those words of conjecture. No hope at all of getting that far into the language. They had to stick to concrete, demonstrable items and actions.

And which language? Prakuyo had picked up elementary Ragi hand over fist, in a matter of hours, and six years among humans hadn't made him fluent—that he admitted, that he wanted to admit.

It argued that Ragi was a better bridge for Prakuyo's people. And it stated the truth: that humans weren't the highest power in these regions, that if one wanted to trade—another useful word—or talk—the best language for it was likely going to be Ragi, and the authority that governed it all wasn't on the station, nor even on the ship: it was in Shejidan, and the dowager was its representative—*he* was its representative. He hadn't abdicated his responsibilities. He'd acted on the ship's behalf because the senior captain had stripped all its security away—leaving, perhaps deliberately, atevi as the ship's defense.

Atevi, like nature, abhorred a vacuum. They moved in. He had. He didn't want to argue the point with Sabin, who probably thought she was running things—certainly he didn't want to argue it in front of the neighbors.

So, well. *Leader, authority, government, people, na-*

tion. Those pesky abstract structures that everyone called simple, that provoked so many wars.

Not to mention those pillars of atevi and human civilization *please, thank you,* and *have a nice day.* By the way Prakuyo took to the dowager's society, *that* element was present in yet another species.

The ship whined and flexed elements of its gut it hadn't used this energetically in all his time aboard. It had traveled empty. Now it drank down the survivors of this place, this situation, those desperate families and individuals that wanted most of all to live, who had very little concept where they were going or whether it was going to be better or not—but trusting even the appearance of aliens among them, in what amounted to a rush for the lifeboat. That augured well for their ability to fit in where they were going.

Didn't cure the fact that Braddock was still loose, but the outflux gave Braddock less and less to work with, and Braddock now had very little control over anything mechanical. The wisest among his aides had to be gathering the family silver and running for the exit.

He let his eyes shut. Didn't trust himself and kept a steady count in his head, which if it began to falter, he had to open them at once and stay awake.

One minute, two, three.

Com went off and he yelped as if he'd been shot, grabbed it out of his pocket and thumbed it on, his heart creeping down from a frantic beat. *Had* he slept?

"Bren?" It was Jase. Agitated. *"Bren, do you read?"*

God, what time was it? An hour. *Damn!*

"Listening, listening, Jasi-ji. Go ahead."

"There's fuel. There is fuel, Bren, do you hear?"

His heart leapt up again.

"And that ship's still moving in, and we're still

pinned here with refugees coming aboard. Senior captain wants me to put out a security contingent and bar the cold zones to the refugees so we can move the ship in."

To keep people out of the cold areas and reorient the whole procedure to a stable, locked-down docking configuration. A lot safer for the passengers.

"Which doesn't let us mate up with the alien ship," Jase said further. *"And which is going to create questions on their side if we shift position . . . and is going to bring Sabin back aboard to do it herself if I don't take her request. She's not informed what we're doing. I'm going to have to tell her."*

"Better now than after she's come back. I don't like not having a secure com-line. Braddock's still out there."

"I can send a courier. I can tell her I'm sending one to explain a situation."

That would take time.

"What progress down there?" Jase asked.

"An hour's unintended rest. But our guest had to be frayed, too. I'm going back at it now. We'll be ready, Jase."

"Sleep is progress," Jase said charitably. *"In short supply up here, I'll tell you. But our ETA for that ship is about three hours and docking shortly after. If you're going to put any presentation together, just give us raw sketches and C2 can render them in the same form we've used all along with them."*

"Good idea."

"Got to go."

"Do it. Thanks. I'm back at work."

Feet on the floor. Body upright. Quick pass of a wet cloth to bring the wits back awake.

Sleep was progress, and he hoped Banichi and Jago were making that kind.

He had to go wake Prakuyo up, and hope he could establish a safe mode of communication that had taken his predecessors in Shejidan centuries of careful work.

Three hours. Three very short hours.

He needed more than skill. He needed someone very bright on the other end of the telescope; and he hoped to God that Prakuyo, who'd survived six years of stubborn non-communication, was able to meet him at least halfway.

20

Prakuyo had been sleeping, so Narani said—small wonder, sleeping, Bren thought, having been catch as catch could with bed for what seemed a very long time, now.

It was court dress, no question, with the ship drawing close.

"Advise the dowager's staff," he said to Narani, "that the foreign ship is three hours away. One might add on a little time to establish a link of some sort, nadi-ji, one has no idea. But by no means wake Banichi or Jago. Jeladi can do that duty in the interim."

"Certainly, nandi," Narani said—with Bindanda, helping with the cuffs.

He would not have chosen formal dress at the moment, except that time came in such unpredictable parcels, and one could hardly go visiting in one's bathrobe.

Speaking of which— "One hesitates even to mention it, but what progress with clothes for our guest to wear?"

"Jeladi is assisting him, nandi," Bindanda said. "Our guest indicated a preference for a blue and mauve brocade—we had three materials in sufficient supply. The green seemed an alternate choice. The gray and black he did emphatically reject for the coat. For the trousers, we used a medium weight blue wool.

With a cream silk shirt that seems, by Jeladi's report, to please him."

Three choices. Trust his staff to have had the resources, and the sensitivity to offer a choice and report the outcome.

"Excellent," he said. His staff finished their hasty preparation and he stood ready, immaculate as they could make him.

Not, immediately, for a foray onto the ship. He had a critical job to do before that, and hoped meanwhile that Jase kept Sabin at arm's length.

"Jeladi reports our guest ready, nandi," Narani said, one of those snippets of staff intelligence that let coincidences happen so smoothly.

"Excellent, Rani-ji."

He secured a notebook and pen from the bedside and strolled out into the corridor. Indeed, Jeladi was just bringing their guest out in—Bindanda should be proud—a very elegant coat, with abundant lace on the shirt. For the feet—unatevi and broad—in that essential detail, Bindanda had worked a wonder, an ankle-high boot with lacings that even looked comfortable. Nothing like good footwear to convince a man he was in good hands.

And Prakuyo, seeing him in his court splendor, looked, well—judging any expression on that broad face was difficult—excited, at least. Prakuyo made a nice little bow. He reciprocated with good grace.

"Come," he said, "nadi-ji. Come sit."

Prakuyo seemed amenable, though a little disappointed. Ah, Bren thought: Prakuyo had hoped they were going straight to the ship. And still the working of hydraulics went on, the lift system racing to deliver cars to the airlock and passengers to four-deck, just over their heads . . . crew had to be scrambling, too, on last-moment needs and adjustments.

All of which might persuade an anxious guest that those sounds might include a docking in progress.

They went to the dining hall, sat down at a corner of the large table, and he immediately sketched out themselves, the station, an approaching ship with a directional arrow.

"Prakuyo's ship is coming," he said in Ragi. Measured with his fingers a very small distance. "Close."

"Close." Prakuyo was attentive and cooperative, though rubbing his face in the way of a man with too little sleep. "Close." Measure of two thick fingers, fingers with nails so broad and thick they wrapped half the end of the digit—nails that, when they first dealt with him, had been broken and rough. Now they were manicured, filed short. "Good. Good."

Bren started naming bits of his sketch. And then asked, "Prakuyo talk."

It got only puzzlement. His request wasn't expected, he thought. Six years, and maybe nobody had ever asked Prakuyo to use his own language.

"Table," Bren said. Then said the same in Ragi, and indicated Prakuyo. He did the same for chair, then: "Prakuyo talk."

"Akankh." Prakuyo muttered. Then pointed at the table. "Noph." The language had a difficult popping consonant.

Bren tried it. Prakuyo repeated it three times. There might be a fine distinction on the popping sound—a language with several similar consonants, it might be; and Bren made his utmost effort. "Noph."

Prakuyo gave him, in short order, pen, paper or notebook, floor, ceiling—demonstrable words. Ship. Station, available in the picture.

"Sit," Bren said, and Prakuyo gave him that word. Words they had established, they could call up. Sit and stand. Walk. Give and take. They had fourteen words. With three hundred—a body could get through his entire day, fluently.

Fourteen, however, didn't all apply to what they had to discuss. He had his mental list of vocabulary he wanted. Station, stationer, go. And a frightening decision to take on oneself—but he conceived of very little chance Prakuyo's folk wouldn't cross paths again with atevi, and best try to define that inevitable meeting, set a purpose, try to establish a protocol . . .

Trade. *Trade* was a concept he illustrated by a human and an atevi figure facing a Prakuyo-like figure, with directional signs and representative goods changing hands. Beads on a string. A shirt. A pitcher. A plate of food. He exhausted his artistic skill with those items; and he wasn't sure he had gotten the right words. There were horridly complicated alteratives: tribute, marriage-gifts. God knew whether Prakuyo had understood that human-atevi concept and given him the right word back.

But he kept trying, concentratedly. In all the universe there was only this. In all the wide universe, there was only this one necessity—to engage Prakuyo's equally exhausted wits and to get some sort of communication in three hours before that ship arrived. It didn't matter what Ginny and Sabin were doing; it didn't matter what exchanges Jase was making with Sabin via courier and whether the whole situation was about to blow up. If that happened, the new situation was going to need vocabulary, understanding, negotiation; and this was the safest, fastest way to get it. Down here, things took as long as they took, and the good will of this tired, perhaps questionably sane stranger was all-important.

His notebook disassociated into sheets of paper. He made diagrams of spatial relationships: to, from, toward, away from, off, over, under. He formed hypotheses and rudimentary sentences in this new language in which verb-forms seemed simple and directional elements seemed ungodly complex. Prakuyo, with his newly-refined fingers and a pen delicately held, drew stick figures of his own—not skinny, one-line beings, but beings of substance, rounded beings, beings with U's for legs and arms and heft to the outlines . . . was it surprising?

"Human," Bren said of his own skinny short ones. "Atevi," of the skinny tall ones. He tapped one of Prakuyo's. Twice.

"Kyo," Prakuyo called them. They had not ironed out singular, dual, or plural. His species seemed to be that. Or it was simply the word for man, intelligent being, or us.

Kyo. So was Prakuyo, then, a personal name, or a rank, or a species distinction? *Was* there a concept of individuality? One thought so, since Prakuyo identified him and the dowager by name quite accurately.

Bindanda brought a tray and provided fruit juice. They gained the words for cold and hot. Ice and water; juice, or fluid.

"Banichi and Jago are awake, nandi," Bindanda informed him, with the tray. "The dowager likewise."

He was not surprised, then, when Banichi and Jago turned up in the dining hall, their arrival noted, but not interrupting the flow. They listened—sitting at the end of the table, though their habit was to stand. They knew what he was attempting. They knew—the national experience of atevi and Mospheirans—how desperately risky it was, this speaking to strangers. They remained unobtrusive.

Bren drew pictures, trying to make structure, and pushed for new words, pushed while Prakuyo was still willing. He had by now more than a hundred new words jostling around in his head. A hundred words could be an hour's conversation. Unfortunately one had to know the *useful* words, the ones attached to their personal situation. They hadn't yet communicated trust, or don't blow up our ship, please-thank-you, or, you can have the station; we don't want it any more.

Negatives, God, the negatives, the not's and no's and neither's and nor's and other rejections. They were an unexpected headache, with distinctions that just didn't make sense—a sort of subjunctive of negativity, related—he decided—to degree of reality. There was not, really not, and no way in hell possible; but there was also future-not, and past-not. And—one began to get the nightmarish picture—there were similar distinctions on various other modifiers.

God help him. More to the point, God help the people he represented. He began, for the first time, to believe he'd undertaken the humanly impossible.

He couldn't figure the past tense. He suspected a similar difficulty. And began to suspect Prakuyo's language, besides having an array of nots, didn't use I, was shaky on you, and worse, took truly emotional exception about he and they.

Which wasn't wholly a linguistic worry. It was, granted Prakuyo was sane, a window into a mentality that really wasn't quite human *or* atevi, that had all along had trouble with that he-they concept, and wasn't happy with the you-word, either.

That was where they'd taken their last break. And his brain was fogging. He had a hundred and one methods for getting vocabulary out of an interview and he didn't know how to get past the pronoun problem. It seemed one of those right-wrong things, one of those trained-from-birth things, downright invisible to the owner of the reactions, but yes, Prakuyo got upset about pronouns, and, complicating matters, in adult Ragi, their preferred language of communication, atevi continually shifted the number of persons in *you* or *me.*

And somewhere in the hard-wiring of Prakuyo's own massive body, this damnable elusive quantity was, clearly, so simple—if one were Prakuyo. If one's brain had the sights and sounds and smells and emotional context of being Prakuyo. Which a human hadn't, and wasn't, by a long shot.

"We." Prakuyo said that last in ship-speak. And pointed at him, and Banichi and Jago.

Wrong. That should be a *you,* and he opened his mouth to say so.

And shut it. Prakuyo looked—dared one think—quite earnest about that mistake.

Bren followed a gut instinct. Pointed to himself and Banichi and Jago. "We." To himself and Prakuyo and Banichi and Jago. "We."

Prakuyo got up quickly, making that alarmed booming sound. Banichi and Jago were on their feet just as fast.

But Prakuyo subsided back into his chair as if the air had been let out of him, and thrummed and boomed and clenched his hands together in front of his mouth—not pleased. Or at least—not feeling particularly stable at the moment.

And at a loss for words.

"Not we?" Bren pushed the point.

He won a dark-eyed, distraught look.

Banichi and Jago sat back down, stoic and impeccable.

"We." That word again, indicating him, Banichi and Jago, but not including Prakuyo.

Don't include me. Don't assimilate me. Don't absorb me.

We—some quality of we—was as disturbing to Pra-

kuyo as it was ordinary and all but invisible to humans
and atevi. But not a take-for-granted among atevi; and
not, even in his lifetime, an easy given between humans and atevi. A fogged brain began to gather, beyond the obvious answer of a xenophobia Prakuyo
never had demonstrated, that he simply had no wish
to be included, and did not give his consent to be
included. That somehow, with him and with his kind,
we was a fenced-off, difficult word that might imply
anything from visceral distaste to outright hatred of
outsiders—no evidence in Prakuyo for that; though
that hole in the station might attest differently.

What was behind that reaction? Prakuyo's wrist was
as large as a human upper arm. Strength, immense
strength: this wasn't a species that, in its evolution,
easily hid or ran; it might, perhaps, take direct solutions; but with complementary delicacy, these hands
had built spaceships. Prakuyo's kind must have made
pots, learned agriculture, domesticated animals, made
villages, made towns, made cities, made whatever political structures let Prakuyo's kind cooperate and
launch itself into space.

But Prakuyo's people had trouble including other
species with itself.

Or Prakuyo had trouble being included by others,
or by them, specifically.

Politics? Social structure? Something that disgusted
or frightened?

Prakuyo, however, was willing to sublimate that
feeling enough to talk, to learn, even to express
enjoyment.

And suddenly something reverberated through the
hull, a deep, distant shock. Banichi and Jago both got
up, and Banichi left them.

A shot? Bren wondered with a chill. Hostilities with

the station, or had that ship out there moved in and simply decided to blow its own way into the hull?

Was all time up?

Prakuyo was incapable of looking worried, in human terms, but he looked at the door, looked about him, the same.

"Hear," Bren acknowledged the event. He had not yet gotten words for *know* and *not know,* was unsure of those pesky soft-tissue conditionals *if* and *then.* His attempt to extract them with a flow chart had produced uncertain results—which, along with the absence of pronouns, could mean bad news. A set of conditionals that didn't jibe with Mosphei', which was relatively simple, nor Ragi, which wasn't simple at all. *If* that was an explosion, nadiin, *then* we have a problem . . .

He was losing his focus, getting wobbly.

"Nandi," Jago said, from the doorway, and he looked at her. "Jase reports that the alien craft has arrived and established a connection."

Adrenalin ran like static through nerves already on overload.

Then the habits of the aiji's court came to the rescue, providing stability for a small bow, an utter microfocus on the Prakuyo matter. "Prakuyo ship, Prakuyo-ji. It has come. Go up."

Prakuyo absorbed that information and solemnly rose. Bren started for the door, then remembered the notes, frantically gathered them up and gave them to Jago as they reached the door. "These must get to Jase. To C2."

"Yes," Jago said.

As their party ran up against the resident seven-year-old, rigged out in lace and red and black brocade, and behind Cajeiri his great-grandmother, in much the same, with gold; and behind the dowager, Cenedi and reinforcements.

The dowager didn't move that fast. Someone had been in close touch with Jase while he had been locked in the throes of new vocabulary.

"This has gone on long enough," Ilisidi said, and banged her cane against the deck. "We have our invitation, one supposes, since the ship has complied with Jase-aiji's instruction. Prakuyo-ji, we shall see this ship of yours and settle this business."

Prakuyo bowed, deeply, even gracefully. The change in dress had provoked no comment—of *course* the staff had come up with something suitable: the dowager expected such miracles, and was prepared to lead the way.

"My best car," Cajeiri said, holding it safely in his arms. A bow. Very best behavior, as well.

Banichi came out of the security station and quietly waited for them.

A second stamp of the dowager's cane, a motion down the corridor toward the door. "Well," she said. "Shall we dither here, or have this business on the road?"

"Nandi," Bren murmured, and drew a deep breath, and fell in with her, and with Prakuyo, Cajeiri closing up ranks and staying rather closer to his great-grandmother—not a swift progress: not in the dowager's company, but steady. They gathered up Banichi by the security station, and how the papers got passed, or what arrangements flew in a handful of words between Jago and Asicho, he had no idea, but he trusted the ship would ultimately have diagrams if he needed them.

The guards at the farthest doors opened them, and they walked to the lift and requested a car. Bren drew out his pocket com and requested through to Jase during the wait.

"Jase," he said, "I understand we've got a connection to the ship. We're on our way. Looking reasonably good. Got some graphics coming up to you."

"We'll handle it," Jase said. *"Bren. Bren, take very good care. I wish I was backing you."*

"You are," Bren said. "No question. Our car's coming. Which lock?"

"Number 3. That's 243 on the pad. We're watching you, far as we can. Good luck."

"Good luck to all of us. Back in a few hours. Or not. If not, don't do anything. Let me work it out. I'll do it."

"I trust you," Jase said; and the lift door opened. *"A few hours."*

The last in Ragi. End of the conversation. He thumbed the unit off as he escorted the dowager and Prakuyo through the doors. Cajeiri next. Their bodyguard. He cast a look at Banichi, looking for signs of wear, and found none evident.

He couldn't afford to divert his attention. Made up his mind not to. He wondered if he should have brought a heavy coat. Then recalled that Prakuyo was quite comfortable in five-deck temperatures.

Prakuyo, at the moment, looked from the doors to them and back again, agitated, anxious—dared one say, joyous? One certainly hoped so.

Long, long ride.

"How far up—" Cajeiri began to ask, and the dowager's cane hit the decking. Young arms clenched the car close; young head bowed. "One forgot, mani-ma."

"Then one's attention was not on one's instructions. This will be a strange place, and no questions. Think matters through, young sir."

One did *not* answer the boy's question, no matter how tempted, in the face of the dowager's reprimand.

One simply took that advice for oneself. A strange place, and no questions, indeed. No ability to ask. No words.

But hope. There was that.

The car slowed. The illusion of gravity slowly left them. Bren found his heart pounding and his hands sweating, a fact he chose not to make evident. Cajeiri, who had seen zero-g, restrained himself admirably.

Bren doggedly smiled at Prakuyo drifting next to him, at Banichi and Jago who, one noted, wore no visible armament, no more than the dowager's guard—a peace delegation, Ragi-style; but he wasn't sure they'd pass a security scan. Which was Ragi-style, too.

Doors opened. A handful of *Phoenix* crewmen met them, drifting near the doors. They had sidearms, but nothing ostentatious. They were there to operate the locks for them; and to sound an alarm, one suspected, if anything went massively wrong.

"Good luck, sir. Ma'am. Sir." The last, dubiously, toward Prakuyo. With a bow. Ship's crew had learned such manners with the atevi.

"Good," Prakuyo rumbled, as they drifted into the chamber, breaths frosting into little clouds.

Machinery worked and the doors behind them hissed and sealed, ominous sound. No panic, Bren said to himself, thinking strangely of the hiss of the surf on the North Shore. Sunset. Sea wind.

Pumps worked only a moment; and the doors unsealed facing them.

The air that met them made an ice film on every surface, stung the fingers. Prakuyo bounded along, catching handgrips, and the dowager simply allowed Cenedi to draw her along, while Cajeiri was quite content to help himself. Bren managed, teeth chattering, wishing there were a conveyor line.

Long, long progress; and one had the overwhelming feeling of being watched throughout, watched, analyzed for weakness, and the human in the party was determined not to show how very fast he chilled through.

They were arriving, finally, at an end, a chamber with a metal grid, and Prakuyo entered it cheerfully, beckoned them in and showed them to hold on.

Good idea. Doors banged shut, the whole affair began to move and spun about violently, under unpleasantly heavy acceleration to give them a floor, after which the air that came wafting from the vents came thick as a swamp, still freezing where it hit metal and condensed.

Rough braking. Cenedi supported the dowager, Cajeiri had to catch himself, and Bren just held on.

They weighed too much. The air was thick as a swamp at midnight. Doors whined and banged open on a dim, dank place, dark blue-green floor, dark greenish blue walls intermittent with deeper shadow—a succession of edge-on panels, the light so dim it fooled the eye.

A deep rumbling came from all around, and what might be words. Prakuyo bowed deeply, walked forward a step, and out of the shadows a distance removed appeared a solitary, cloaked figure, with Prakuyo's face, and Prakuyo's bulk.

"Stop here," Ilisidi advised, and the paidhi thoroughly agreed: no one should go further, but Prakuyo, who walked a few paces on, bowed again.

Said a handful of words, it might be, underlain with thrumming and booming.

Stark silence from the other side. And as silently—more cloaked individuals from behind the standing panels, and more voices, more booming and rumbling until the floor seemed to vibrate.

Not good, Bren thought, standing very still, not good if Prakuyo left them. It was not a comfortable place, even to stand. He felt as if he'd gained fifty pounds. The dowager's joints would by no means take this kindly.

But Prakuyo extended an arm toward them—beckoning, one thought. "Dowager-ji," Bren said quietly, and moved forward a little. And bowed, as Prakuyo had. One trusted the dowager gave a slight courtesy. Their bodyguards, by custom, would not, until the situation was certain.

"Introduce us," the dowager said, "paidhi-aiji."

"Indeed," Bren said. He walked forward a step, and bowed, trying to assemble recently gained words. "Bren," he said, laying a hand on his chest. "From human and atevi ship. Good stand here."

One hoped not to have made a vocabulary mistake. An immediate murmur went through the gathering, a visible shifting of stance.

"Ilisidi, ateva, comes, says good on Prakuyo ship."

Ilisidi walked forward a pace, bringing Cajeiri with her, offering a little nod. Cajeiri, wide-eyed, made a little bow of his own, car clutched firmly against his ribs, and wisely kept very quiet.

Prakuyo, however, had a deal to say. He waved an arm and talked—one could pick out words—about the station, about going to the ship, about them, by name and individually: he talked passionately, thrumming softly under his breath, and walked from this side to the other, finally demonstrating his own person.

"Bren," Prakuyo said then. "Come. Come talk. Say."

Bren drew a breath, walked to Prakuyo's side, and gave another bow to the one who had appeared first, the one Prakuyo had addressed. "Bren Cameron," he said, a hand on himself. "Good Prakuyo on Prakuyo ship." Never using that chancy *we*. Never having found Prakuyo's word for the same. "Bren, Ilisidi take humans from station to ship. Ship goes far, far. No fight."

That other person spoke, not two words intelligible, and not thoroughly warm and welcoming, either.

Prakuyo clapped a heavy hand on Bren's shoulder, a comfort, considering the ominous murmur around about; and Prakuyo talked rapidly—shocking his hearers, to judge by the reaction.

"Calm," Bren said in Ragi. "One asks helpful calm."

"Calm," Prakuyo agreed—knowing that word, it turned out. And launched on an oration in his own language, his one hand holding Bren steady, his word-choice something about station and Madison, quite angrily—then something about Ilisidi, and Bren, about Bindanda—perhaps about teacakes, for all Bren could tell, and a torrent besides that.

There was an argument, a clear argument going on.

And one had to think that for well over six years neither humans nor Prakuyo's species had made sense to each other, and that the reason they were all standing here in this fix might well have had to do with a now-deceased captain poking about in solar neighborhoods that weren't his—it wasn't just Prakuyo's grievance; it was likely a number of Prakuyo's people with complaints about the goings-on.

Prakuyo, however, let him go, and engaged in noisy argument with several others. Bren tried to decide whether it was prudent to get out of the way; but then Ilisidi moved, slowly, considerately, with Cajeiri, and Banichi and Jago found opportunity to move up into his vicinity: but a person used to the Assassins' Guild noted Cenedi had not moved with the group—Cenedi had stayed back there with his partner, nearer the door, and most certainly was armed.

"Not come fight," Bren interjected into Prakuyo's argument, seeing tension rising on this side and that, and at a light tap of the dowager's cane, wanting his attention, interposed a translation. "Dowager-ma, I am attempting to assert our benevolent intentions. They are discussing what happened here. Prakuyo-nadi seems to be taking a favorable position. But we have no idea what Ramirez-aiji may have done to provoke this: I am suspicious he, rather than the station, triggered hostilities."

"Pish." A wave of the hand. "One cares very little what they and humans did." Bang went the cane. "Now *we* are annoyed, and we wish a sensible cessation."

There was a moment's startled silence. Prakuyo said something involving Ilisidi, and Cajeiri, and something Bren couldn't remotely follow—a rapidfire something that brought a closer general attention on Ilisidi and the boy.

Then came what might be questions from the senior personage, involving Ilisidi and the boy. And him. And Banichi and Jago. They were short of vocabulary and on very, very dangerous ground, and the argument concerning them was getting altogether past them. Not good.

"Nand' Prakuyo." Respectfully, since Prakuyo was clearly a person able to give and take with the leadership of this vessel. "Say to this person that humans and atevi go away. Not want to fight. Want to go soon."

"We," Prakuyo said, and said a word of his own language, indicating himself and all the others. Then that same word including Bren and Ilisidi and all the rest. And something more complicated, more emphatic, that provoked strong reaction, dismay.

Damn, Bren thought, wondering what that past argument about *we* and *they* might have produced here. Prakuyo's folk didn't like that word. Passionately didn't want to be lumped together with non-whatever-they-were. Prakuyo hadn't been for it, either.

But Prakuyo argued with the idea now. Argued, with occasional booms from deep in his chest that sounded more deeply angry than mournful. And finally gave a wave of his hand, ending argument, producing some instruction to the onlookers.

"Drink," Prakuyo said, "come drink."

Was that the resolution? An offering so deep in the roots of civilized basics it resonated across species lines?

"Nandi," he said to Ilisidi, "we are possibly offered refreshment, which in my best judgment would not be wise to refuse."

"About time," Ilisidi said, hands braced on her cane. "Great-grandson?"

"Mani-ma."

"We shall see the most correct, the most elegant behavior. Shall we not?"

"Yes, mani-ma."

"Come," Prakuyo said to them, "come."

"Cenedi," Ilisidi said, and their rear guard quietly added themselves back to the party as they walked slowly with Prakuyo, between two of the edge-on panels, into deep shadow that gave way to a broad corridor, with adjacent panels sharply slanted, obscuring whatever lay inside.

Two such moved, affording access to a room of cushioned benches of atevi scale; and Prakuyo himself came and offered his hand to Ilisidi, whose face was drawn with the effort of moving in this place.

It wasn't court protocol. It was, however, courtesy, and sensible in this place of dim light, uncertain footing, and exhausting weight: Ilisidi allowed herself to be seated, patted the place beside her for Cajeiri, and on her other side, for Bren.

Prakuyo also sat down, with that other individual, who proved, in better light, to be an older, heavier type, with numerous folds of prosperous fat.

Younger persons brought a tray with a medium-sized pitcher and a set of cups—one would expect tea, and a human experienced in atevi notions of tea worried about alkaloids; but what the young persons poured for them proved to be water, pure, clean water.

"Very good," Ilisidi remarked, which Prakuyo translated; and himself poured more for her and for the rest of them.

"Good," Prakuyo said. "Good come here." He said something more to the older person, and by now others had come in to observe, and to listen to Prakuyo's account, which ranged much farther than Bren could follow.

It took the tone, however, of a storyteller getting the most out of the situation, and came down to mention of their names again, and expansive gestures that looked unpleasantly like explosions.

"Ilisidi," Prakuyo said then. "Say."

"We have come," Ilisidi said, paying no attention to this gross breach of courtly protocols, "we have come to settle matters, to recover these ill-placed humans and take them away, where they will cause you no further trouble. The ship-aiji who caused these difficulties is dead. The station-aiji who treated you badly is deposed and will never have power again, and the ship-aiji who rescued you is now in charge of the ship and the station. We take no responsibility for the doings of these foreign humans but we are glad to have returned you to your ship."

Prakuyo launched into God-knew-how-accurate a translation, or explanation, or simply an elaboration of his prior arguments. At which point he asked for something, and one of the lesser persons ran off, presumably on that errand.

Prakuyo kept talking, overwhelming all argument, dominating the gathering. Clearly, Bren thought, this was *not* a common person, though what the hierarchy was on this ship was not readily clear. Six years they'd sat watching, observing—by all evidence of the damage done to the station, capable of simply taking it out, and of having done so before Prakuyo ever came close enough to get himself in trouble. But they'd taken a twofold approach: first to send in a living observer, then to sit and wait—long on a human timescale—six years.

For what? For Prakuyo to teach the humans to talk to them? For the ship that had left to come back? They hadn't hit it, either, but they might well have tracked it.

A cautious folk. Capable of doing the damage they'd done—but they'd taken a long time to respond to Ramirez's intrusion: they'd come in on the station rather than the mobile ship; they'd gotten provoked into a response, and then sat and watched the result. This wasn't, one could think, a panicked, edge-of-capability sort of action, rather an action of someone as curious as hostile, wanting to know exactly how wide and fast the river was before they tried to swim in it.

The errand-runner came back with a tablet of opaque plastic and a marker, which Prakuyo took, and offered to Bren.

Communicate. Do the pictures. He obliged, and saw

to his amazement that his very first mark appeared on a panel at the end of the room. He had an audience. He could start at the beginning. He could make them understand how the whole business had happened. Or he could try. Or he could just get to the point.

He drew a planet and a sun. "Earth," he said. "Sun." He drew a ship going out. "Ship. Human ship." He shaded a dark spot along its route, drew many arrows going out, drew spirals and circles for the lost ship's route. A dotted line. To a star. Solid line to another star. "Atevi earth. Human ship."

Prakuyo elected to interpret—one only hoped he got it right; but Prakuyo had been locked into this limited vocabulary, part of the attempt to communicate.

"Human station. Atevi world. Human ship goes away. Humans go from station to atevi world."

More translation.

"Humans, atevi on earth. Human, atevi, we. Ship they. Ship goes here, here, here. Ship makes station here. Ship goes here and here." A complicated course, always centering on the second station. "Prakuyo ship comes to the human station, fight. Ship comes to station, comes to atevi world. Atevi and human, we come up to station, say to ship, you take humans from station, bring here to atevi and humans. Atevi and human we want no fight Prakuyo ship. Atevi and humans take Prakuyo on ship, take to Prakuyo ship. No fight."

Again, a translation, vehement and excited. Prakuyo got up and demonstrated his atevi clothing, to the good, one thought: Prakuyo was not at all unhappy with his treatment on the ship.

It seemed an opportune moment, given the precedent of the water offering. Bren took his packet of fruit candies from his pocket and offered them to Prakuyo, who cheerfully took them, ripped the packet with a sharp tooth, and offered them about.

These were appreciated.

"Prakuyo-ji." A young atevi voice, uncharacteristically muted. Cajeiri got up very carefully, and handed Prakuyo his car. "I brought it for you."

Prakuyo took the offering, and took Cajeiri in a strong embrace, and talked with a great deal of booming and humming, even tugging Cajeiri's pigtail, unthinkable familiarity, but Cajeiri was wise and held his peace.

Questions started. A lot of questions. And lengthy answers. Fruits appeared, on platters. It began to be a festivity, and if they could exit unpoisoned, Bren said to himself, they might secure the peace.

One tasted such things very gingerly. Only a taste. But that much surely was mandatory. There was a general easing of tension. More offering of water. Of little bits of bread and oil, which human taste found encouragingly safe-tasting.

"Good," Prakuyo said with enthusiasm. "Good." A powerful pat on the shoulder. "Bren take humans from station. Get all humans. Kyo take station."

"Yes," Bren said. Best they could get. They'd blown the archive. "Kyo good."

"Human-atevi good." Another blow to the shoulder. "Ilisidi go take Cajeiri. Go ship. Prakuyo come, go, come, go, more talk."

Permission to go. Prakuyo would go with them and come and go at will. One could by no means ask better.

"One is grateful." A bow. Perspiration glistened on Ilisidi's brow. They had to get Ilisidi out of this heavy place. "Aiji-ma, we shall go back to the ship and continue negotiations."

"Indeed," Ilisidi said, and—Bren's heart labored for

her—rose, leaning on her cane. Cenedi moved to assist, but bang! went the cane on the floor, startling every person present except those who knew her. "We shall do very well for ourselves," she said, and gave a polite, leisurely nod to Prakuyo. "We shall go to our ship. We shall have a decent rest. Then we shall be pleased to meet your delegation."

"The dowager says good, talk soon," Bren translated the intent into Prakuyo's language, and bowed as the dowager turned, walking slowly. Cajeiri assisted her, providing his young arm under the guise of being shepherded along. Cenedi went close to her.

Prakuyo bowed during this retreat. Wonder of wonders, the rest bowed—perhaps *grandmother* translated very well, and found special resonance among the kyo.

Ilisidi seemed quite pleased with herself, standing square on her feet at the back of the airlock-combined-with-lift, as the rest of their party hastened aboard.

The door shut. The car started through its gyrations, and Ilisidi, off balance, had to accept Cenedi's arm. And her great-grandson's, on the other side.

"They seem perfectly civilized," she said. "One can hardly see why we have had these difficulties."

"Braddock-aiji," Cajeiri said, having a bone-deep atevi understanding of how the intrigues lay.

The lift spun through its path and delivered them to the tube; and here, without gravity, Ilisidi let herself be moved gently along. Bren followed, glancing to be sure Banichi was all right: Jago was close by him, Cenedi's men close behind.

They had done it. Bren allowed himself the dizzying thought. Prakuyo and he would talk, they would take their notebooks and their little dictionaries and make some sort of agreement.

They reached the frosted airlock, and locked

through to the astonishing sight of an ordinary human face—several of them. Jase was one.

"Nandi." Immediately Jase bowed to the dowager, who found it an opportune moment to sit down on the let-down seat at the guard post, her cane braced before her, her hands as pale as ever Bren had seen, and frost a gray sheen on her pepper-shot hair.

Cajeiri got down on his knee beside her and rubbed her arm. "It was very brave, mani-ma."

"The dowager has gotten us an agreement," Bren said quietly, to Jase, in Ragi. "Undefined, as yet, but expressions of willingness to talk."

"Your job," Jase said, laying a hand on his recently bruised shoulder. "You'll do it. We're still boarding passengers. We can do that and talk; and then we get to the fuel. Excellent job, nadi."

"Hardly my doing." He found himself wobbly in the knees and envied the dowager the seat, but would by no means dislodge her, or suggest they send for transport. "One believes the dowager will do very well with a little rest and warmth, Jase-ji. A little hot tea might come quite welcome."

"A little less of talk," Ilisidi said, and gained her feet, frightening them all. "The lift will get us home well enough. Jase-aiji, attend us down."

Jase doubtless had a thousand things on his mind. But he had a key that preempted all other codes, and got them a lift car, despite the traffic that continually whined and thumped its way through the ship's length.

The dowager walked in under her own power. Bren walked in, attended by the rest, all of them in one packet.

"Prakuyo will come back aboard to talk," Bren said.

"Prakuyo." Jase tried the name out.

"We think that's his name. It could be his species." So little they knew, at this point, about each other.

Several things pleased the kyo about their expedition: the presence of an elder was one. Several things the kyo found shocking: the inclusion of themselves in the word *we* certainly seemed a matter of high debate.

But Prakuyo seemed about to make the jump.

21

Not much to report, brother, except ignore the last will and testament, which now seems embarrassing. We've loaded precisely 4043 persons and put their luggage through stringent checks for contraband, though what contraband one could find in this desolate station, I can't imagine. Fruit sugar has produced a few stomach complaints, but the addiction is spreading. Likewise the taste for green plants. A few of the old people insist it gives them stomach ache, and they want their yeasts, but that's only to be expected, I suppose.

I've met numerous times with Prakuyo and his association, there and here, during the last two days, and we're more establishing vocabulary than conducting truly meaningful negotiations, but it's pretty clear they're to take over the station, which is not that far from places they consider theirs—more about that when I get back, when we can discuss this on a suitable beach.

Banichi took a little damage, which is mending nicely. Jago is coddling him shamelessly.

More later.

Aiji-ma, we are about to fuel the ship, and there will be no further difficulty. Gin-aiji has vouched for the machinery as of this morning.

A small note: Prakuyo-aiji indicates the observing

ship was regularly receiving supply and exchanging information with others during the last six years, and that Ramirez-aiji had indeed encroached on places the kyo prefer to keep untraveled. The kyo attempt at approach apparently frightened Braddock, which ended in the kyo envoy being held these last six years. The kyo are very glad to know that responsible persons have shown up to rein in such adventures, so that kyo and atevi and humans may establish the nature and extent of their associations in reasonable security.

It should be noted that the kyo ship is very heavily armed, or at least was capable of extraordinary damage. I directly asked Prakuyo if he had knowledge of any other peoples beyond atevi and humans, and he seemed to say that such persons were not welcome in kyo territory. The kyo may be a barrier to such foreigners arriving in atevi regions, or they may have enmities of their own, a possibility which may indicate more caution in our relations with them. They do seem reasonable once approached at close range, but one cannot give credit enough to the aiji-dowager's wise influence as an elder, which position they do greatly respect, and the fact that she could speak to them in a language recognizably not the language of humans who had offended against the kyo.

They form powerful associations among themselves based on kinships, as best one can guess. They are completely puzzled by the association of atevi and humans: this state of affairs requires an intellectual, perhaps profoundly emotional leap for them to accept as applicable to them, as difficult at least as humans and atevi discussing personal ties on a rational level. But they have moved from passionate rejection to curiosity, at least in the person of several of them. They have never traded outside their own association, except, one gathers, as a preliminary to absorbing that neighbor,

*but do conceive that trade relations with another power-
ful and alien association is a topic for discussion. Since
there seems to be a historical precedent of trade leading
to absorption of neighbors, there may be indications
for caution here. Relations will need to be stabilized
and well-defined. We are attempting to build the foun-
dations for a lexicon, and may appoint Reunion as a
more or less neutral venue in which further discussions
can take place. Prakuyo seems very anxious to have
this established. If I correctly understand him, the kyo
believe that persons once met stay associated—that the
universe will not be whole unless what has met remains
in association. This may be a religious or a philosophi-
cal belief. It is one that may be troublesome in interspecies relations, and may account for the kyo's
persistence. From the time Ramirez began intrusions
into kyo territory, trouble was likely.*

*Ship's crew had intended to place Ramirez's remains
into the station as they destroyed it, for respectful and
fitting cremation; since the station will go into kyo
hands, they have determined instead to give him to the
local sun as we depart this place.*

*For the rest, Sabin-aiji has returned to the ship.
Sabin-aiji has received communication from Braddock-
aiji, who seeks assurances of safe passage, which she
has granted. We shall be very sure he is suitably housed
and protected from those he has offended. We shall
reposition the ship for fueling, preparatory to departure
from this place.*

*Therefore, aiji-ma, I have a great deal of work to do
in a very short time. We have contacted a dangerous
and different set of foreigners who may present far less
danger if our communications can be more accurate . . .*

He hadn't meant to fall asleep on the desk. He had
a meeting to get to. Not with Prakuyo, thank God,

but Jase was coming down to supper. With the dowager. With *Sabin,* God save them.

Staff was in hardly better condition. He had sat about in his bathrobe this morning, Narani arriving late and absolutely scandalized that he had sat in the chill making notes, but that was very well—he was doing what he had studied all his life to do, and so absorbed in it he had little cognizance outside that job, when he was in it.

Lord of the province of the heavens, not by choice. Paidhi-aiji—that, quite happily so, with a half a ream of notes and sketches and a voyage that seemed all too short ahead of him.

"Nandi." Jeladi had come in, hoping to help him dress for dinner. He stood up, and stood thinking about nouns and whether kyo linguistics exactly had tense—now and then were remarkably confusable, or they were simplifying for the foreigners, or using a trade tongue: contact with outsiders seemed to have a formula, among them, and since they tended to swallow what they met, thinking it the proper way to do things, there was a little danger in letting kyo fall into formula at all.

Penetrate beyond the trade tongue, if that was what it was. It might take him coming back to Reunion. He rather well hoped to train a handful of sensible sorts to do that, a human-atevi association that could collect data—damn, he wanted his beachfront and his comforts, not to be sitting out here in a steel vault.

He arranged the cuffs, straightened his coat. Bowed his head so that Jeladi could see to the white ribbon. White, for the paidhiin.

Jeladi gave him a mirror, and he approved. Down several kilos, he was. He could live with that change. He hoped to maintain it.

"Very good, Ladi-ji." A little sound warned him of

a presence in the doorway—he was not surprised to see Banichi and Jago waiting for him.

"Nadiin-ji."

"Nandi," Banichi said, and they escorted him down the corridor toward the dining hall.

Mission all but accomplished.

A pleasant evening. The dowager's table, and Sabin. And Jase, whom the crew took for a bona fide captain these days.

So did Sabin. That was the real change.

Separation of nations that have once met is dangerous: that seems the most accurate expression of kyo views of politics. What has met will meet again. What cannot stay in contact is a constant danger of miscalculation.

Curious notion. Possibly even demonstrable, in history. One wonders whether this is a refined philosophy, out of successful experience.

One is very certain we need to go slow with this.

In that notion, we've said a kyo goodbye to Prakuyo, who avows he will see us again. This somewhere between threat and promise.

The siren went. Warning.

Time to shut down and take hold.

"Takehold, takehold, takehold."

The illusion of gravity left them. The ship was sorting itself out. It had its gut full of stationers who had never been through this. They announced every small move.

Curious, Bren thought, that he'd gotten to view this as easy.

All things being relative—it was.

He shut his eyes. They were supposed to have a little transitional time before they underwent another acceleration. The weightless episode was a test—

convincing stationers that they really had to stow items. So Jase had forewarned him.

He slept a little, drifting with a little safety tether to the head of the bed.

Waked as the warning siren went off. Gravity returned.

Jago wasn't back. She'd gone off on some call from Banichi, and wasn't back yet.

"This is the real one, ladies and gentlemen. We're about to fold space. Kindly stay put until the all-clear."

Maybe she wasn't coming. Maybe something had been going on. Maybe a crisis on staff, someone needing help . . .

He heard running steps in the hall. Sat up. As the siren went off, sharp warning bursts.

Jago came through the door, crossed the floor and landed on the bed in the space he made.

"Nadi-ji?" He was concerned.

A giddy feeling ensued. The ship began to ease its way out of the ordinary universe.

"One apologizes," Jago said, breathless—for her, quite unusual.

"Trouble?" Difficulty breathing, himself, for the moment.

"Nand' Cajeiri had a pocketful of dice."

"Dice?" A common toy. They came in sets of eight. *His* staff had been called in. Cenedi must have been having fits. "Was he *throwing* them?"

"He called it an experiment," Jago said. "To know, one understands, whether the numbers come up the same in freefall as on earth."

He was appalled. The things became missiles under acceleration.

And intrigued. He had to ask.

"Do they?"

Jago laughed. That wonderful sound. And was still

out of breath, as the universe ebbed and flowed around them. "A flaw in the notion, failure to ascertain true rest. Two were lost. Cenedi was entirely out of sorts."

"You did find them."

"Of course."

Of course they had found them, or Jago would not have left.

"Excellent," he said, thinking of dice in freefall. Jago was warm beside him.

Safe. Secure. All dice accounted for. Baji-naji.

They were going home.

CJ Cherryh
EXPLORER

"Serious space opera at its very best by one of the leading SF writers in the field today." —*Publishers Weekly*

The *Foreigner* novels introduced readers to the epic story of a lost human colony struggling to survive on the hostile world of the alien atevi. In this final installment to the second sequence of the series, diplomat Bren Cameron, trapped in a distant star system, faces a potentially bellicose alien ship, and must try to prevent interspecies war, when the secretive Pilot's Guild won't even cooperate with their own ship.

Be sure to read the first five books in this action-packed series:

FOREIGNER	0-88677-637-6
INVADER	0-88677-687-2
INHERITOR	0-88677-728-3
PRECURSOR	0-88677-910-3
DEFENDER	0-7564-0020-1

0-7564-0086-4

To Order Call: 1-800-788-6262

CJ Cherryh
Classic Series in New Omnibus Editions

THE DREAMING TREE
Contains the complete duology *The Dreamstone* and *The Tree of Swords and Jewels*.   0-88677-782-8

THE FADED SUN TRILOGY
Contains the complete novels *Kesrith*, *Shon'jir*, and *Kutath*.   0-88677-836-0

THE MORGAINE SAGA
Contains the complete novels *Gate of Ivrel*, *Well of Shiuan*, and *Fires of Azeroth*.   0-88677-877-8

THE CHANUR SAGA
Contains the complete novels *The Pride of Chanur*, *Chanur's Venture* and *The Kif Strike Back*.
          0-88677-930-8

ALTERNATE REALITIES
Contains the complete novels *Port Eterntiy*, *Voyager in Night*, and *Wave Without a Shore*   0-88677-946-4

AT THE EDGE OF SPACE
Contains the complete novels *Brothers of Earth* and *Hunter of Worlds*.   0-7564-0160-7

To Order Call: 1-800-788-6262

Julie E. Czerneda

Web Shifters

"A great adventure following an engaging character across a divertingly varied series of worlds."—*Locus*

Esen is a shapeshifter, one of the last of an ancient race. Only one Human knows her true nature—but those who suspect are determined to destroy her!

BEHOLDER'S EYE
0-88677-818-2
CHANGING VISION
0-88677-815-8
HIDDEN IN SIGHT
0-7564-0139-9

Also by Julie E. Czerneda:
IN THE COMPANY OF OTHERS
0-88677-999-7
"An exhilarating science fiction thriller"
—*Romantic Times*

To Order Call: 1-800-788-6262

Tanya Huff

The Confederation Novels

VALOR'S CHOICE
0-88677-896-4

When a diplomatic mission becomes a battle for survival, the price of failure will be far worse than death...

THE BETTER PART OF VALOR
0-7564-0062-7

Could Torin Kerr keep disaster from striking while escorting a scientific expedition to an enormous spacecraft of unknown origin?

To Order Call: 1-800-788-6262

DAW 19